"What the he...

Vivi jerke... ...wiped the wet hair off... ...And don't grab me like that."

"I've swept the room and there is no hidden camera, no microphone, no nothing. We're alone."

"Then why'd you pull me into the shower?"

He dropped his gaze to her soaking body, lingering where the thin yellow fabric molded to her breasts. "I wanted to see you wet."

She swallowed, all her lovely control washed away. "You wanted me off guard."

He lifted a ripped, muscular shoulder. "Then we're even. What the hell is going on?"

"I had to keep you quiet, Lang. I had to shut you up and stop the questions."

"So you basically seduced me into silence?"

"Hey, it worked. That's all I care about."

Something flickered over his face. His eyes, golden green again instead of dark with lust, narrowed like an angry lion's...

———————————

"A bold new series...[a] taut, complex, and intelligent page-turner...Readers will thrill to this dynamic tale and its nonstop action, sweet and sexy romance, lively characters, and celebration of family and forgiveness."

—*Publishers Weekly* on *Edge of Sight*

EDGE OF SIGHT

ROXANNE
ST. CLAIRE

FACE OF
DANGER

FOREVER

NEW YORK   BOSTON

This book is a work of fiction. Names, characters, places, and incidents are the product of the author's imagination or are used fictitiously. Any resemblance to actual events, locales, or persons, living or dead, is coincidental.

Copyright © 2011 by Roxanne St. Claire
Excerpt from *Shiver of Fear* copyright © 2010 by Roxanne St. Claire
Excerpt from *Edge of Sight* copyright © 2010 by Roxanne St. Claire
All rights reserved. Except as permitted under the U.S. Copyright Act of 1976, no part of this publication may be reproduced, distributed, or transmitted in any form or by any means, or stored in a database or retrieval system, without the prior written permission of the publisher.

Book design by Giorgetta Bell McRee

Forever
Hachette Book Group
237 Park Avenue
New York, NY 10017
Visit our website at www.HachetteBookGroup.com.

Forever is an imprint of Grand Central Publishing. The Forever name and logo is a trademark of Hachette Book Group, Inc.

The Publisher is not responsible for websites (or their content) that are not owned by the publisher.

Printed in the United States of America

First Printing: May 2011

10 9 8 7 6 5 4 3 2 1

For the survivors.
You know who you are.

ACKNOWLEDGMENTS

Every book is a joint effort and, once again, I've had an embarrassment of riches when it comes to people willing to help. In particular, there are a few standouts who deserve praise on the page:

Barbie Furtado, beta reader and dear friend, who deserves far more credit than this simple acknowledgment. She read the manuscript as many times as I wrote it (we lost count), sacrificed hours of sleep so that I could wake to a lengthy critique, and gave of herself on a personal level to be sure I had some very important facts straight. She even made it six thousand miles from Fortaleza to Florida to hand deliver her love and support. Thank you, CD.

EMT John Johnson of the Atlanta area, for emergency medical support (on the facts, not the author), the lovely ladies of Windwalker Real Estate in Nantucket, Mass., who provided in-depth information about their glorious island, publicist Sharon Newcomb of Ocean Spray who offered assistance on the cranberry bogs, former FBI agent James Vatter, who is just an all-around priceless law enforcement resource, and Rossella Re, my Italian language specialist. Any errors are mine, not theirs.

My right hand and left, Kristen Painter and Louisa Edwards, who read snippets, brainstorm plot twists, open wine bottles, and generally perform the BFF task with style and substance. The über-talented ladies of Murder She Writes, as well, provide daily support, advice, ideas, and a safe place to rant, making it impossible to do my job without them. A special shout-out to Allison Brennan, always the voice of reason in a sea of crazy, and Kresley Cole, who just plain rocks.

My publishing team: Executive Editor Amy Pierpont, Editorial Assistant Lauren Plude, and the legions of brilliant professionals at Grand Central/Forever who guided this manuscript from concept to completion. And Robin Rue, literary agent without equal, who does everything she's supposed to do (and more) with grace, humor, and patience.

And, as always, my loving husband, Rich, creator of Uncle Nino's Comforting Cacciatore, and my dream-come-true kids, Dante and Mia, who teach me more about life than I could ever teach them. I fluff you all.

FACE OF
DANGER

ACTRESS ISOBEL DESOTO FOUND DEAD IN HER HOME

Second Oscar Winner's Death Fuels Conspiracy: Coincidence, Curse, or Red Carpet Killer?

Los Angeles, California, April 18

*T*he body of Oscar-winning actress Isobel DeSoto, 36, was found in her Malibu Canyon home early this morning by her housekeeper. Sources close to the investigation say numerous prescription medications were found at the scene.

The actress was last seen leaving the Hollywood Hills home of director Angus Gaites, where she attended a dinner party given in honor of her recent Academy Award for Best Actress for her role as a young widow in the film The Devil's Compass, *directed by Gaites. Ms. DeSoto's death is fueling a groundswell of Internet and media speculation regarding the untimely deaths of two consecutive winners of the Best Actress Oscar. One year ago, just weeks after winning the Academy Award for her leading role as Madame de Pompadour in the blockbuster film* Hall of Mirrors, *actress Adrienne Dwight lost control of her car and careened over a Los Angeles hillside to what has been officially called an accidental death.*

Assistant Director Joseph Gagliardi, head of the Criminal Programs Division of the FBI's Los Angeles Field Office, has confirmed that the investigation is being turned over to the FBI, indicating that authorities think these deaths could be the act of a serial killer.

When asked about the reaction of the Academy of Motion Picture Arts and Sciences, President Gilbert Gordon confirmed that nothing about the Oscar tradition would change. However, a source within the Academy added that "if there's a Red Carpet Killer, then next year's nominees may very well be hoping to lose."

CHAPTER 1

The Bunker Hill Bridge cast a long shadow over the sea of slate gray concrete bowls and ramps, the whine of traffic competing with the constant whirl of BMX and skate wheels on concrete. It was music to Vivi Angelino's ears.

Trotting down the hill from one of the viewing areas, she scooped up a discarded napkin that had blown from the refreshment stand and popped it into the trash. Charles River Skate Park was her baby, and even the smallest piece of trash marred its perfection.

Switching her board from one hand to the other, she paused at the bottom of the half-pipe to watch as some kid attempted a five-forty McTwist. A thrum of empathetic exhilaration pulsed through her as the skater sailed into the air and spun gracefully into the move.

Vivi had yet to land the five-forty, but when she did it would be here, at the Boston park she'd spent every spare minute raising money and corralling support to build.

The McTwister wiped out right in front of her with a slam and a loud "Sonofabitch!"

Vivi walked over to help the kid up, offering knuckles to the failed skater. "You'll get it."

"Damn right I will," he said, popping up even though his butt had to burn. "The McTwist is better than sex."

"I wouldn't know," she said, half to herself as she checked out the top of the ramp. "Haven't tried it yet."

The cement reflected silver white in the rare winter sunshine, a gift on a Sunday in February, when the weather gods usually tortured Boston with snow.

The pipe was crowded, so she decided to cruise the park some more and give herself mental back pats for the all the hard volunteer work she'd done. All the years of trips to City Hall, all the presentations to council members, all the free time she'd sacrificed had been worth it to give the skaters of Boston a home for their passion. These kids, city rats most of them, had no idea how to rally politicians and city leaders to get what they wanted. But Vivi was older—though no less passionate about her pastime—and remembered how frustrating it could be to be a teenager with no voice.

So she'd been their voice, and this glorious jigsaw of concrete and grass was the result. She eyed the strategically placed viewing areas where parents and partners, newbs and wannabes looked out over the courses and—*shit*. Her heart dropped like a longboard on the eight-foot ramp.

"What the hell is *he* doing here?"

Assistant Special Agent in Charge Colton Lang stood with strong hands gripping the rail, broad shoulders tensed in determination, his relentless gaze sweeping over the ramps like a deadly sniper intent on finding his next victim.

Lang was the very last person she'd ever expect to see at Charles River Skate Park.

He'd only make fun of it. Tease her for being a little old for a skateboard.

Not that his opinion mattered. He was a client of her security and investigation firm, and this was a nonworking Sunday morning. Who cared if he saw her hanging at the park she had built?

She did. She cared too freaking much about everything that concerned Colt Lang. And that was her problem. Her dirty little secret problem.

So what the hell was this uptight white-bread FBI agent doing on her sacrosanct skate park grounds, wrecking her perfectly awesome Sunday morning? How could he have found her here?

And now he would see her with three inches of hair standing on end from her last trip down the vert pipe, her face damp with sweat, her clothes hanging off her like she'd grabbed them from her bedroom floor and stepped in without even glancing in the mirror. Because, well, she had.

But it doesn't matter, right, Viviana? He's just a client. Right.

She stole another look, and saw him take his phone out of his pocket.

Maybe he wouldn't recognize her—he'd have to have a really excellent eye to pick her up in this sea of skaters, every single one wearing the same uniform of baggy top and cargo pants, sunglasses, and helmet.

Inside the pocket of her cargo pants, her phone rang. Damn. He was *calling* her.

She turned, trying to use her board to shield herself as she slipped the phone out, hoping he wasn't scanning the crowd to spot anyone answering a cell phone at that moment. It would be so like him to use that sneaky tactic to find her.

"Yeah?" The word sounded as on edge as he made her feel.

"Yeah?" His baritone tickled her ear. "That's how you answer the phone?"

"Oh, so *sorry*, Assistant Special Agent in Charge of Proper Phone Etiquette and Manners. Let's have a do-over." She cleared her throat. "Good morning, Mr. Lang. Viviana Angelino at your service—despite the fact that it is Sunday morning and I am not anywhere near the Guardian Angelinos office. How can I help you?"

He laughed, a mix of a grunt and a low catch in his throat, hating, absolutely *hating*, that the sound sent a little jolt right down to her toes.

"Turn around," he ordered.

Goddamn him. "What are you talking about?"

"I think I see you, but I need you to turn around."

"You see me? I'm in church right now, so I seriously doubt that you see me."

"Church? Right. You're worshipping at the altar of Airwalk."

How'd he know that brand? And what made her think she could lie to him?

"Turn around, Vivi." He said her name just the way she liked it: Vee-vee. He drew out those twin syllables and made those long e's sound... sexy.

Still, she refused to move. "Just tell me what you want, Lang." She'd long ago dispensed with his unwieldy title, since she got it wrong most of the time anyway. He'd told her it was proper to call an ASAC "Mr. Lang" but she'd dropped the "Mr." after their first case together. And he didn't seem to care.

"I want you to turn around."

"Do you have a job for the Guardian Angelinos?" she asked.

"No."

The single syllable, invasive, and, oh Lord, *sexy*, punched her gut. "Do you need a report on the assignment that Zach is currently working on?"

"No."

"Do you have a big fat check to give me for all the consulting work we do on behalf of the Federal Bureau of Investigation?"

"No."

"Then go away and I'll see you at our scheduled meeting Monday at eleven o'clock."

A hand landed on her shoulder, making her jump.

"No." He tightened his grip and eased her around. "Turn around."

She felt the heat of his body behind her, his presence so strong it made her go weak behind the knee pads.

"Damn you, Lang." She pivoted, her gaze landing on the Izod logo on his chest, his jacket hanging open to confirm what she already suspected. He was a nerd who wore collared pullovers. And they fit like a dream.

With one finger, he gently tapped the brim of her helmet. "This is very cute, Angelino."

"I told you I hate to be called—"

"Cute. I know."

The air cooled her sweaty head when he took the helmet off. Great. Helmet hair.

His smile deepened and his hazel eyes glinted gold and green. "What else could you call this, other than cute?"

Mortifying?

She stepped back and glared at him. What the hell did she care what Lang thought of her? "This is my Sunday special. I'm off the clock right now, Lang, so what do you want?"

"A good security specialist and investigator is never off the clock," he said, all condescension and good reason. "I thought you were a little business-owning tigress, working tirelessly to build your new organization into a force in the security industry."

"Remind me never to confide anything in you again." Anything. Especially her fantasies.

She eased the longboard between them, desperate to put any kind of barrier between them.

Lang seemed to be getting way too much enjoyment from her disheveled state. Of course he was amused. He'd cruised into her world like a package of perfection—not a chestnut hair out of place, his stupid preppy shirt pressed like it just came off the rack at Bloomingdale's and fitting so snug over his expansive shoulders. She'd bet her life he was carrying a Glock under that jacket, too.

"What are you looking at?" he demanded.

"You shaved, Lang? On a *Sunday*? What's wrong with you?"

He brushed his whiskerless face. "It's the former Boy Scout in me."

She rolled her eyes. It was the nerd in him. And, God, that nerd did unholy things to her insides.

"Want something to drink?" he asked, putting a casual hand on her shoulder like he owned her. She'd tied her sweatshirt around her waist after her last run, so no doubt her skin felt damp through the cotton T-shirt he touched. Oh, fabulous. Now he was *sticking* to her. "There's a refreshment stand over there."

"I know." She dropped the board and hopped on, zipping a few feet ahead of him. "I built it."

Before he could answer, she kicked to the ground and took off ahead of him, rounded a concrete hill, swerved up the side, twisted the board into a perfect one-eighty, then landed hard.

"You built it?" he asked, reaching her just as she toed the board and gave him a cocky look.

"I supervised the fund-raising team that scared up the dollars to build it," she explained. "Charles River Skate Park is the result of the hard work of a major community volunteer organization. One that I happen to be extremely involved with."

"Really." He scrutinized her for a moment, like an art dealer who kind of saw something worthwhile—but then he looked away. Like he'd rather pass.

She hated that his disinterest torqued her.

Disinterest is good, Vivi. He's a client. Client. Cli-ent. How often did she need to remind herself of that?

He slipped her helmet back on her head. "Don't skate without this."

She took it back off again. "I'm walking, not skating. What do you want from me today, Lang?"

"I just came to tell you I have to cancel our meeting tomorrow. I had a change in my schedule. I can come over to your offices on Wednesday if you have time."

Like he couldn't have called to tell her that. Or sent a text, since they seemed to be exchanging plenty of them on a regular basis. Couldn't he just leave a message with Chessie? Why did control-freak Lang always need to do business in person?

Was it because he didn't trust the efficient delivery of an e-mail message, or because he wanted to see her? She squashed the thought, and considered how much to tell him when she replied.

"You'll have to meet with my brother on Wednesday. I'll be out of town."

He gave her an interested look. "Work or fun?"

"Work *is* fun. Maybe not for hardened FBI agents, but we budding security-business owners have a blast."

"I'm serious."

That made her laugh. "You were born serious, Lang."

He almost smiled. But not quite. "Where are you going?"

"Need-to-know basis. And sorry, but you don't." He'd just scoff at the whole idea anyway. "You're not our only client, you know."

"I'm the only one here."

Just the way he said it sent warmth rolling through every female corner of her body.

"You can meet with Zach," she said. "My brother is up to speed on all our open cases. You'll never miss me."

His brow twitched upward, ever so imperceptibly. Like...like maybe he *would* miss her. "I was hoping you'd give a full report on the Berkower case I handed over to the Guardian Angelinos last month. That case is in your bailiwick."

"Bailiwick?" She choked a derisive laugh. "Where do you get these words? Everything's in my *bailiwick*, but I'm going to be in L.A., so—"

"You've got clients in L.A. now?" He sounded surprised, and way too interested. "I didn't realize your little company was going national."

Your little company. She should be used to slight putdowns from Lang by now. They were a fact of life, no different from the teasing she took from the cousins she and Zach were raised with. She knew it was just his way of maintaining control. Still, they irked her.

"If you knew why I was going, you wouldn't be so liberal with your thinly veiled insults."

"Then tell me."

Some skaters whizzed by, swerving to miss Lang, who strode down the path like he'd built the place instead of Vivi and her band of volunteers.

"Can't," she said simply. "It's client confidential." Or it would be. As soon as she got the job.

"So you do have a California client? That's interesting."

She almost lied, but her mother's well-painted image of St. Peter at the pearly gates counting up her lifetime tally stopped her, as it always did. "To be honest, it's just a pitch for new business, but I think we have a shot." A very long shot. But that was her favorite kind. "Why is that interesting?"

"Because..." He hesitated, sliding a glance at her. "I may be moving out there."

Her heart dropped so hard and fast she felt it hit bottom. "Really?"

He shrugged, feigning a casualness that something told her he didn't feel. "Possibly. There's an opening for an SAC position out there that I've been interviewing for."

"Whoa, Lang." She gave him a playful punch in the arm, using the opportunity to let her knuckles enjoy the hard bump of his bicep. "Big promotion to Special Agent in Charge, losing that pesky 'assistant' handle." A promotion that would put him three thousand miles away. "You'd be running the whole office?"

"God, no. Only the Criminal Programs Division, which is pretty big. There are multiple SACs in an office that size, so it'd still be a move out—er, up."

And out. "You're from L.A., aren't you? Your family's there?"

"Just my dad, and he's getting on. I'm the only kid around to help, since my brother lives in Europe and is a complete waste of a human."

She snorted softly. "Nice."

"Maybe not, but it's true."

He guided her toward the snack shack. "Tell me about the L.A. job."

"No, thanks. I try to avoid your ridicule whenever possible."

"I won't ridicule you." He walked up to the window. "Want a Coke?"

"Cherry slurpy."

He rolled his eyes. "And you make fun of me."

"See? Ridicule because I want a slurpy."

"Vivi, you're thirty-one years old."

"Right. So make it a vodka slurpy and meet me at that table." She walked to an empty round table with matching cement benches and sat down. There, she positioned herself to watch Lang buy their drinks.

And think about him moving to Los Angeles.

Lang leaving was a good thing, she told herself, but she couldn't deny the pressure on her heart. She would be able to work with another ASAC, someone who didn't wreck her balance and make her freaking heart stutter every time his ID showed up on her phone. Like the man said, she was thirty-one years old and way past the time of teenage crushes.

But look at him. Even his doofus Izod shirt looked... hot. And as much as she loathed a pair of khaki Dockers, his covered a world-class backside and had just enough of a bulge in the front to send her imagination into overdrive and make her little vibrator seem inadequate.

Sunlight pouring over him, he was all goodness and strength. The gold flecks in his eyes and hair looked like God had dipped him in bronze when he was born. The sun highlighted the sharp angle of his cheekbone and jaw and the fullness of a mouth that rarely smiled, but when it did, stupid things happened in her lower half.

She blew out a shaky breath. So, yeah. L.A. Good move for everyone.

He strolled over with the drinks, his eyes locking on her as if he knew what she was thinking. Thank God that was impossible, because Lord knows if he had even an inkling of the direction her thoughts took when she looked at him he'd laugh himself silly. She was a colleague, a consultant, a friend at best. Nothing more to him. Nothing would be more humiliating than him knowing just how many times she'd fantasized about tearing off that golf shirt. With her teeth.

"Interesting hairstyle," he said, placing the drinks on the table. "Even for you."

Yeah. They were most definitely not on the same wavelength.

"Is this your way of sweet-talking information about my new client out of me? So effective." She took the slurpy and tore the paper off the top of the straw, turning it around to blow the wrapper in his face.

He snapped it midair with one lightning-fast hand. "You know you want to tell me." He leaned over the table. "Just give in to it, Vivi."

Her nether regions took another thrill ride.

"Give me one good reason why I should tell you anything."

"Because," he said, lowering his voice to that I-call-the-shots tone she found maddening and sexy and, every once in a while, a little scary, "I want to know."

And just like that, she capitulated. No man had ever had that effect on her. Ever.

When Vivi Angelino closed her mouth over a wide straw and sucked hard enough to hollow her delicate cheeks, Colton Lang almost got a boner.

Almost.

The state of damn-near-hard was status quo around this woman, so in the few months he'd been sending consulting jobs to her firm, Colt had learned a couple of tricks to ensure that "almost" didn't become "obvious."

Like focusing on her outlandish black hair, made even more so today by the helmet and what appeared to be yesterday's hair gel. Or he'd let his gaze settle on the diamond dot in the side of her nose, concentrating on how much that puncture had to hurt instead of how it would feel to run his tongue over the stone.

Or he'd simply remind himself that this skateboard-riding, sneaker-wearing, guitar-playing tomboy happened to have some of the best investigative instincts around, and if he wanted to keep the Guardian Angelinos in his back pocket for certain jobs, acting on a mindless surge of blood to his dick would be not only unprofessional, but also foolish.

That was usually enough to quell the erection. Sometimes. Today, finding her in this skate park with a little sheen of perspiration making her pixie-like features glisten and her coffee-brown eyes spark with unexpected interest, the boner might win this battle.

But look at that outfit, Colt. A long-sleeved cotton T-shirt that dangled off her narrow frame and faded green cargo pants frayed at the cuffs. He could never be attracted to a woman who cared so little about her appearance that she rolled around Boston dressed like she'd shopped at Goodwill.

He preferred a woman who looked like a woman, who wore a little makeup, had hair falling to her shoulders, and maybe strolled—not rolled—through a park in a pretty sundress. He'd bet his bottom dollar she didn't own a dress.

"All right, I'll tell you," she said after swallowing. "But I swear to God, Lang, don't try to talk me out of it, because I want this job."

"What job?"

"You've heard about the Red Carpet Killer, of course."

He held his Coke, frozen midway to his mouth. "You don't buy that malarkey, do you?"

She smiled. "Lang, malarkey hasn't been sold for forty years. Can you get with this century? And do you really think two Oscar-winning actresses being killed in two consecutive years, weeks after winning, isn't more than simple coincidence?"

"One was an overdose, one was an accident. No

matching MO, no serial killer. But I do know there's an FBI task force out of L.A. with an eye on the possibility of a copycat killer."

"Exactly." She pointed at him. "I don't happen to think there's a serial killer, but I do know there are five women in Hollywood who are scared spitless right now. They are ramping up security like you wouldn't believe."

"You think they're going to hire your firm for protection?" He tried not to scoff, he really did. But it was ludicrous. "A brand-new firm made up of an extended family of renegade Angelinos and Rossi cousins?"

No surprise, her espresso eyes narrowed in disgust. "We are not renegades, for God's sake. I'm a former investigative journalist, in case you forgot, so getting a PI license was a natural move. Zach is a former Army Ranger. And, yeah, our core employee base happens to be a few cousins my brother and I were raised with—"

"Don't forget Uncle Nino, providing pasta and daily encouragement."

"Don't knock my Nino," she shot back. "And, for your information, we're interviewing protection and security specialists, including some highly qualified bodyguards. The Guardian Angelinos are experiencing a growth spurt."

He angled his head in acknowledgment. "I know that, Vivi, especially since I keep throwing FBI consulting jobs at you. I just think the actresses who are worried about being victims of a curse or a killer will hire the biggest and best in the protection industry."

"Maybe." She took another drink, her eyes dancing with some untold secret. "What do you think of Cara Ferrari?"

"I think I wouldn't kick her out of bed for eating crackers."

She looked skyward with a loud tsk. "I meant of her chances to win."

"I don't follow Hollywood too closely, but I did see that remake of *Now, Voyager*. My opinion? She was too melodramatic."

"Fortunately, your opinion doesn't matter. She's got a chance." She gave him a slow smile, revealing that tiny chip on her front tooth. God, he'd thought about licking that, too. "So I think I have a chance, too."

He just shook his head, not following, but maybe because his body was betraying him again.

"Look at me," she demanded, leaning back to prop her hands on her hips and cock her head to one side.

"I'm looking." That was the problem. She was so damn cute he forgot what they were talking about.

"*Look*, Lang."

At what? The way her position pulled the T-shirt just tight enough to outline her breasts? They weren't big but perky and sweet, just as spunky as she was and, well, even on Vivi some things were feminine. Was that what she wanted him to look at? Because if he eyed them any longer, his hard-on was poised to make a reappearance.

"Don't you see the resemblance?" She turned her face to give him a profile, lifting her chin, closing her eyes, and dropping her head back in a classic movie-star pose. His gaze drifted over her throat which was—just another fucking thing he wanted to lick.

Jesus, Colt. Get a grip.

She spun her face around and for one insane second he thought she'd read his mind.

"I look exactly like Cara Ferrari," she insisted.

He let out a soft hoot of laughter. "Are you as stoned as half these other skaters?"

She scowled at him. "Real skaters don't get high—posers do. And look at this face," she demanded, pointing to her cheeks with two index fingers. "Is this not Cara Ferrari's twin sister?"

He chuckled again. "Speaking of posers."

"Lang, *damn* it." Frustration heightened her color, making her even cuter. "Everyone says I look like her. I mean if my hair were longer and I—you know, had some makeup on."

"Like a truckload."

"I get stopped and asked if I'm Cara Ferrari all the time," she insisted.

"And you believe what drunks say to you in bars?"

"Jeez, you're as bad as my cousins. Quit teasing me and take this seriously."

He worked his face into the most humorless expression he had, and he had many. "Cara Ferrari is a movie star, Vivi."

"So?"

How deep was she going to let him dig himself? "I mean, she's a gorgeous icon...."

Deep.

"Not that you're not attractive in your own way." This was getting worse, but on he went. "It's just that she's all glitz and glamour and gloss and you're..." Not.

"I can glam up."

Now that, he'd like to see. "All right," he relented, not wanting to hurt her. He squinted at her, and made a camera viewing box with his fingers. "Yeah, I can see the similarity. You both have dark hair and dark eyes."

She swiped his hands down. "Never mind, Lang. I should have known you couldn't think outside the box. You're all linear, trapped by your rules and the way things are *supposed* to be done. I shouldn't ever dream that you might approach something creatively. That would just be asking too much from your structured, formulaic, uninspired brain."

All right, he deserved that after the insults he'd just heaped on her, but something was really off in this conversation, even for them. "What the hell are you getting at, Vivi?"

"A body double."

This time he just stared at her for a minute. "You're not serious."

She thumped her fist on the table. "I knew I shouldn't have told you."

"Told me what?"

"C'mon, Lang, it's the oldest form of security in the world. Put a fake—a *professional* fake—in her shoes until the killer is caught. If there even is a killer, which I don't happen to think there is. But, still, we bait with a decoy and—"

"Stop it," he said, his voice low and harsh, not having to pretend seriousness at all now. "All kidding aside, you'd need an extreme makeover to pass as Cara Ferrari."

"Not from a distance."

"A job like that should go to a trained professional, not an outside consultant. And good luck getting to Cara Ferrari. It's easier to get an appointment with the President."

A flicker of arrogance crossed her face. "Maybe I already have."

"What? How?"

She shrugged. "What do they say—everyone is six degrees of separation from someone."

"You are not six degrees of anything from Cara Ferrari." Was she?

She picked up her drink and then set it down again. "Forget it, Lang. You're right, she did suck in *Now, Voyager*. She should stick to the trashy stuff that made her real money."

"Absolutely," he agreed, ignoring her sarcasm. "Like one of her really early B movies, the one where she played the undercover cop working as a stripper? I liked that."

"Of course you did. What man doesn't love the raw acting talent it takes for a woman to use her mouth to unzip thigh-high boots during a lap dance?"

"You have to admit that was a memorable scene."

"Yeah, that took mad acting skills."

"And coordination," he agreed. "Just think how many college boys she made happy."

"Were you one of them, Lang?"

"Please. I was in the FBI Academy when that movie came out." Still, he fought a smile. "But it was a pretty sexy lap dance. Although, I guess that's redundant."

"Yeah, whatever. Can we just forget we had this conversation? It's moot anyway. They say Kimberly Horne has the Oscar in the bag."

He relaxed a little. "Vivi, you can't seriously think you could convince Cara Ferrari to let you *be* her for however long it takes for this Red Carpet Killer brouhaha to die down. I think you should forget this idea completely."

"Brouhaha." She rolled her eyes and grabbed her drink. "I don't care what you think."

He didn't respond and she sucked the straw again,

looking up at him with her wide eyes—kind of exactly like she'd look up from a blow job.

Goddamn his dancing dick.

"Just forget it," he said, as much to his disobedient organ as to his unintentionally sexy consultant. "It's a cute idea, but—"

"Fuck you, Lang."

"Sorry, I know you hate anything cute."

"You just don't get it, do you?"

Evidently not. "Get what?"

"What I'm trying to do with this business my brother and I started."

"How can you say that?" He pushed his drink aside to move closer to Vivi. "I believe in your business. Hell, if I'm not careful, my boss is going to start questioning just why I've given you—what, four or five assignments in as many months? We're supposed to spread the outsourcing wealth, not focus on one firm."

She just shook her head. "This isn't about you and your office. This is about *me* and *my* office."

"Seriously, Vivi. You only started this business last fall. What do you expect?"

"Greatness," she replied without pause. "There are companies doing what mine does and making millions. They've got multiple offices and hundreds of investigators and bodyguards and security specialists on their payroll."

"And that's what you want?" Somehow, the dream of big business just didn't fit this skater chick. The raw ambition, like so many things about Vivi, surprised him.

"I always want to be the best," she told him. "I don't like to do things half-assed."

"I respect that, but"—he placed both his hands over hers, damning the electrical charge he got every time his skin made contact with hers—"you're not starting with Cara and your body-double idea."

She snapped her hands away. "You can't tell me what to do, Lang. No one can."

Obviously.

"Give me one good reason why not, *other* than the fact that I don't look like a movie star, as you've pointed out with great relish and candor."

"What if there really is a Red Carpet Killer? Or a copycat? It's dangerous."

"My job is dangerous," she replied. "Your job is dangerous. That's the life we've chosen. If we get the assignment, Zach has three excellent bodyguards who can come stay with me twenty-four/seven."

Three guys with her twenty-four/seven? Unfamiliar and ugly jealousy rolled through him. "Doesn't matter. With all the nutcases out there, it's too risky."

She pushed back with a disgusted breath. "You are so...careful."

"You say that like it's a detriment. I'm an FBI agent, Vivi. Cautious is my middle name. And if you're going to make it in the security consulting business, you'd do well to adopt the same one."

"Well, my middle name is Belladonna," she informed him.

"A poison."

"'Beautiful woman' in Italian," she corrected him, then raised a palm to stop his response. "Don't. You've insulted me enough for one day. My point is, *cautious* doesn't always work in business, Lang."

"It does in the security business." Three bodyguards? Shit, he hated that.

"Nobody gets ahead playing it safe. It's like that half-pipe over there." She tipped her head to the concrete slopes where skaters flew and flipped. And fell on their asses. "You gotta go big or go down."

"Yeah, well, I've gone big and gone down hard." No, he hadn't gone down. The one and only woman he'd ever loved had gone down. All the way down. Six-feet-under down.

"What happened?" she asked.

He shook his head. "Just don't take crazy risks, Vivi."

"Can't help it—that's how I roll." She got up, kicked her board out from under the table, and hopped on it. "I'm going to be late for the Rossi family Sunday dinner if I don't leave now. See ya, Assistant Special Agent in Charge Colton *Cautious* Lang."

"Bye, Private Investigator Viviana *Poison* Angelino."

She untied a ratty sweatshirt and pulled it over her head, then tugged on her helmet. "Thanks for the slurpy and the advice."

She zipped off, giving him a perfect shot of her ass as she kicked into high speed.

There went his cock again.

To make the blood flow north to his brain, he forced himself to think about her stupid, foolish, crazy idea. Okay, it wasn't entirely stupid, but the last time he took a risk like that, he'd lost everything.

Never again.

CHAPTER 2

Lang had gotten one thing right: Vivi wasn't six degrees from Cara Ferrari. She was three. Her cousin Nicki had gone to shrink graduate school with a guy who was the brother of Cara's stylist, Bridget McKeever, who'd agreed to help arrange a meeting because the brother convinced the stylist that Cara should at least talk to Vivi.

So maybe that was four degrees from Cara, but it really didn't matter. Because three days after the little run-in with Lang at the park, Vivi drove under the world-famous arches of the Paramount Studios lot, flashed her license to a security guard, and headed for the set of *Jehovah's Witness*, the legal thriller Cara was wrapping this week.

The end-of-filming schedule was perfect, no doubt forced by the star herself, giving her the ability to disappear for a few weeks following the Academy Awards this coming weekend. Although all five of the nominated actresses had made public statements that they were not the least bit concerned about the folklore of a Red Carpet Killer or

Curse, they'd all somehow managed to clear their calendars for the next six weeks.

All five women had a life-or-death reason to not want that statuette on their mantel.

Of course they wanted it, Vivi mused as she parked and followed the directions Bridget had given her to the set. Who wouldn't want to achieve that pinnacle of success? But they also wanted to be safe, and live to enjoy it, which was why Vivi's idea was such a good one.

If Cara liked the body-double strategy, it could set up the Guardian Angelinos as one of the most sought-after security firms in the country. And, dream of dreams, if there really was a Red Carpet Killer and Vivi lured and caught him—bingo! They'd be made.

Besides, Vivi's investigator's instinct told her there was no real threat, making the assignment easy money and a brilliant career move.

Screw Lang and his pessimism. This was a risk, but as Uncle Nino would say, you can't get the good fruit if you don't go out on a limb. And he'd be right.

Worse things had happened to Vivi, and she'd weathered them. Pretty much.

She ran a hand over her smooth hair, purposely combed and gelled down into a tame style that went along with her simple skirt and jacket, both borrowed from her best friend Sam, the woman who someday soon would be marrying her brother, Zach.

Vivi scanned the lot, passing the commissary and turning a corner that opened up to several large white buildings, each marked with studio numbers. People milled about, a few on foot, some on golf carts, the pavement warm from the California sun under the soles of Vivi's brand-new and horrifically uncomfortable high-heeled shoes. She spotted her makeup artist contact striding toward her, all long skinny legs in pencil jeans and flying platinum hair.

Bridget looked more like a movie star than some of the real stars, but, then, so did damn near every woman in Los Angeles.

Lang would love it here in the land of milk and honeys.

"Hey," Bridget called as she approached, not slowed by even higher heels. "Sorry, I was stuck on the set."

When they reached each other, Bridget gave Vivi air-kisses on both cheeks, then leaned back, assessing Vivi.

"Good look for you," she said, all professional and serious. "But we're going with Plan A. We really have to blow Cara away."

"I'm ready," Vivi assured her.

"So am I. She's doing a scene that will definitely go ten takes, on an inside set, so we have an hour. Let's go clear her trailer and get it done."

"Have you told her anything?" Vivi asked.

"Just that I have a solution and asked her to consider it, no matter how off the wall. Beyond that, I think it's better if she sees you exactly as we planned: in full Cara costume."

The "trailer" was hardly a doublewide. Set off from the rest of a row of motor homes along the side of a long parking lot, Cara's "dressing room" stood two stories high and at least seventy feet long. A husky guard lingered outside the entrance but said nothing as Bridget and Vivi breezed by him.

Sloppy, Vivi thought. If he worked for the Guardian Angelinos, he'd have asked for ID.

Inside the trailer, it was as bright as sunshine with shades of yellow on every wall, floor, and seat. Classical music played from invisible speakers, the notes competing with the high-pitched yelp of a dog. A copper-colored dachshund leaped off a leather sofa and launched at Vivi's feet, barking, panting, and circling her with suspicious dark eyes and the strangest hint of a limp.

"Stella!" Bridget said, trying to appease the little dog. "Hush."

Vivi reached down to give the dog a cursory hello and got a low, throaty growl in response.

"Don't mind Stella," Bridget said. "She basically hates anyone who isn't Cara. But she doesn't bite."

"It's all right." She looked around, taking in the living area that had been divided between a luxurious sitting room and kitchen on one side and a makeup station on the other. Half of the marble countertop was used to display Styrofoam heads covered with black wigs of various lengths and styles.

Another woman walked in from a back room, shutting her phone with an officious snap as she zeroed in on Vivi.

"Who are you?" she demanded. "There wasn't an appointment on Ms. Ferrari's book."

"She's with me," Bridget said. "Vivi, this is Marissa Hunter, one of Cara's personal assistants."

"Not *one* of them." Marissa threw a contemptible look at Bridget, but then rearranged her rather plain features into a fake smile. A small space between less-than-pearly teeth didn't make her any prettier, but it did detract from an unattractive frown line between her dark brows. "I'm *the* assistant."

Bridget just gave Vivi a little nudge toward a small stairway. "We'll be upstairs in wardrobe. When I come down, Marissa, you'll be gone. That's not a suggestion."

Vivi followed her up spiral stairs to a second floor. There the walls were lined with handrails full of hanging outfits all displayed face out, with shoes, bags, and jewelry next to each on individual tables. A platform rose from the center of the room, directly between two three-way mirrors.

Stella tip-tapped on long nails right into the room, still eyeing Vivi with distrust.

"Get up on the dressing stage," Bridget said, gesturing to the platform. "Let me pick something that is totally Cara. Then we'll do hair and makeup downstairs when Marissa's gone. She can be a real pain, but not as bad as Joellen, who's usually sprawled out on the sofa, half toasted."

"Joellen Mugg is Cara's sister, right?" Vivi had spent days reading everything she could get her hands on about Cara Ferrari.

"Correct." She considered, then passed on a whole series of lawyerly-looking outfits that were probably costumes from the current film. "There are a few of us who form a human wall around Cara. And, of course, Stella Dallas, the four-legged toddler."

At the sound of her name, the little dog circled the platform, nothing but dislike in her glassy brown eyes.

"I guessed wrong, then," Vivi said. "I figured Stella from *A Streetcar Named Desire.*"

"Wrong movie, but the right idea. And that pooch'll be our litmus test. If we can fool Stella Dallas, then we can fool anyone."

Vivi gave the dog a tight smile. "Can we fool you, little hot dog?"

The dachshund growled low, settling down to watch for one false move. There'd be no fooling Stella.

"I've seen that dog with Cara in pictures," Vivi said to Bridget, stepping up to the raised platform. "They're pretty attached."

"At the hip," Bridget said, flipping through some dresses and checking out Vivi as if she were imagining her in each. "We're going to have to go with yellow. That's Cara's signature color."

Of course it was. The one color—okay, two, counting pink—that would never be found in Viviana Angelino's closet. She eyed a row of shoes with heels higher than the Prudential Building, including three pairs of thigh-high boots.

"Does she still wear those boots?"

Bridget laughed softly. "As often as possible. *Exposed* might have bombed at the box office, but it made a star out of Cara Ferrari."

And gave millions of young men—and FBI agents—a thrill they would obviously never forget.

Bridget pulled down a lemon-colored one-shouldered knit thing. Too short to be a dress, too long to be a shirt. "This'll work."

Work as what? A handkerchief?

Forty-five minutes later, after the total invasion of personal space called "hair and makeup," Vivi stepped into the dress and slid into the boots halfway up her thigh. And still they didn't reach the hem of the little bit of yellow fabric.

She turned to the mirror and sucked in a soft breath.

"I know, right?" Bridget said. "You totally look like her. It's kind of creepy. In a good way."

She did look like Cara, but that wasn't why she gasped. The strangest sensation rolled through her, a quick kick of sex and power. Two things she rarely equated with her own reflection.

And she *liked* it. Whoa. Wasn't expecting *that*.

Was that why women dressed like this? Because it made them feel sexy and strong? She'd always thought it was just a plea for attention, a red flag in front of a bull.

Or, in this case, a yellow flag. For caution.

She put her hands on her hips and shook the long-haired wig over her shoulders.

Take that, Colton Cautious Lang.

She'd be sure to give him a picture when this was all over. Let him fantasize about that instead of Cara's sleazy stripper movie. The thought gave her a downright unnatural thrill.

Bridget reached into her pocket for a buzzing cell phone to check the incoming text. "She's on her way. Stay here. Don't move a muscle until I open the door."

"As if I could. I'm so pinned, glued, painted, and stuck I'm immobilized."

Bridget grinned as she gave Vivi a quick once-over, her keen, critical eye looking for flaws. "I'm not sure even *I* could tell you're not Cara." She studied her face and tilted her head. "Up close, yeah, your nose is different and your teeth need some work."

Vivi smiled. "Thanks."

"Just don't get too close to anyone and you'll be a perfect match. We've never even had a body or stunt double who looked so much like her."

She left and Vivi took one more look in the mirror, giving some sass with her shoulder and testing her stability in the heels. Only a moment passed before she heard footsteps on the stairs up to the dressing room.

Stella jumped up and waddled to the door.

"What is this surprise, Bridget?" a voice said as the door opened. The dog barked excitedly, standing on her hind legs to greet a woman who looked eerily like the one Vivi had been admiring in the mirror.

Dressed in a dark business suit for her role as a prosecuting attorney, Cara Ferrari blinked once and let her jaw drop as she scooped up the dog without taking her eyes off Vivi.

"Jesus Christ on a hot dog bun." Her voice was lower, smoother, softer than Vivi's. "That is fucking amazing."

"My name is Viviana Angelino," Vivi said, extending her hand. "I own a protection and private investigation firm in Boston. I have a proposal for you, Ms. Ferrari. I'd like to be your—"

"Body double," she whispered, leaning against the doorjamb as if she needed support, ignoring the offered hand. "Yes, oh God in heaven, *yes*. Bridget, is this your idea?"

"Her idea," Bridget offered. "I just helped her get to you, Cara."

Cara just stared. "I take it you want to 'be' me if I win on Sunday night?"

"That would be the plan, if you'd be willing to work with me."

"Oh, I'm willing."

Vivi lifted a brow. "Don't you even want to know the cost?"

Cara closed her eyes, the lids as heavily made up as Vivi's, her mouth downturned. "The cost is astronomical if I *don't* do something like this," she said.

Vivi mentally doubled her fee and resisted the urge to pump her still unshaken fist in the air.

"Get back up and turn around," she ordered, twirling her finger. Vivi returned to the platform and rotated as directed.

"Wow," Cara said.

"With me as your double, Ms. Ferrari, you would be completely safe."

Cara considered that, eyes on Vivi while she kissed the dog's head. "But what's in it for you? Why would you want to be me if someone wants me dead?"

"I run a professional security firm called the Guardian Angelinos," Vivi answered. "And like I said, you haven't asked my fee."

Cara tilted her head and gave a wistful smile, a well-known expression the camera loved. "There's always more to it than money. As an artist, a character's motivation is of paramount importance to me."

"I believe that this assignment could allow our business to greatly expand."

"A *private* security business?" Cara asked quickly. "Not associated with any law enforcement agency?"

Was that a trick question? "We're completely private," she said. "It's a family business, as you might tell from the name." Encouraged by Cara's nod, Vivi continued, "I want it to succeed, so that my family can continue to work together and grow the business. Family's important to me."

Cara smiled. "I understand that. Clever name, too, the Guardian Angelinos."

"And we're qualified," Vivi added, knowing this was a job interview despite the bizarre circumstances of being on a platform in a banana-colored napkin for a dress. "Although my brother, cousins, and I only started the business about six months ago, we've already amassed some excellent references." Would Lang give her a reference?

"You've invested quite a bit in this company, I imagine."

"Of course." Vivi turned to maintain eye contact as Cara slowly walked around the raised platform, petting the dog, scrutinizing Vivi.

"Well, let's start with the bad news, then," Cara said.

Damn. "Hit me."

"If you screw up, your business will fold."

For the first time, Vivi wobbled slightly on her high heels. "I have no intention of making a mistake."

"I have very strict stipulations," she said, her enunciation letter perfect. "If you follow them, we're fine. If you don't, I'll suck the life out of you, your business, your family, and everything else I can get my hands on."

Whoa, seriously? Yes, seriously. This lady was *so* not kidding.

"Are you familiar with a nondisclosure agreement, Ms. Angelino?"

"Of course."

"Anyone who works for me, around me, with me, or near me is expected to sign one," she said, continuing her predatory circle around Vivi. "In this case, under these very unusual circumstances, the penalty for breaking that nondisclosure will be a flat ten million dollars. And I will get it from you or your business if I have to put a lien on everything you own or ever will own, or anything your family owns or ever will own. Is that clear?"

"Crystal." Her brother would *love* that.

"Is it?" Cara volleyed back. "Because there is a bright side to working for me, and that would be that if you do succeed in making the world believe you are me and if the truth is not leaked out to any media, law enforcement, or otherwise nosy party for the duration of one month following the Academy Awards, assuming I win, then..."

Vivi felt her hands fist in anticipation, the seconds dragging out as Cara no doubt timed the delivery of her next line for maximum impact.

"Then I will pay you one million dollars."

Vivi almost fell off the heels. *One million dollars?* And she'd been ready to ask for a hundred grand. "That would be"—*life changing*—"excellent."

"Do we have a deal, then? On *my* terms?"

Did they ever. Vivi stepped down, without so much as a wobble in the boots. Her gaze was direct as she reached out her hand one more time. "We do. And I give you my word that every aspect of this assignment will be treated with the utmost confidentiality."

"I don't need your word," Cara said. "I'll take ten million dollars and ruin you if you fail. Both our lives are at risk here, Miss Angelino."

"I'm not afraid of risks," Vivi said honestly. "I live for them."

"Good." Cara shook her hand. "I hope you don't die for them, too."

• • •

Colt had to stop coming to the Newton Commonwealth Golf Course on Sundays, even if it hadn't snowed in six weeks and the fairways weren't frozen. Last week's trip to the skate park had been a nice diversion, but every time he came back here, he slipped into a place he didn't want to be.

He remembered happier rounds of golf, with a lot of laughter, a lot of love. A woman who played with heart— and a life snuffed out before it really had a chance to be lived.

Why didn't he insist on a different course?

Because his three golfing buddies loved this course and had no idea what was going on in his head. Just like at the office, they assumed he was just an unemotional hard-ass on his way up and out. Especially out.

His cell phone buzzed as they loaded their clubs into the cart.

"Shit, Colt, if that's work we're going to go get a sub before we tee off," one of his friends said.

"Could be a break in the Charlestown robberies," he said, pulling out the phone. "Let me just get someone out..." His voice trailed off as he read the ID.

Federal Bureau of Investigation Los Angeles. *Yes.*

"Sorry, guys. Start the first hole without me." Without listening to their complaints, he strode away. Finally, the offer call.

"Mr. Lang, please hold for Assistant Director Joseph Gagliardi," a woman commanded. This was the call he'd been waiting for.

In a matter of weeks he could golf on some memory-free course in L.A.

"Are you in a private location, Mr. Lang?" Gagliardi asked without preamble.

Would he need to be secluded to accept the offer? "I can be, Mr. Gagliardi," he assured his potential new boss. They were on a first-name basis by now, but if Joe was going formal, Colt would follow his lead.

He cut through the clubhouse to the parking lot, his steps determined, his need to hear the words that he'd been promoted to SAC in L.A. burning.

Of course, the promotion to SAC was secondary, but he'd never let Gagliardi know that. He'd never let anyone know that.

"All right, sir," he said as he reached a deserted area of the lot, not far from where he'd parked. "How can I help you?"

"We're on a conference call, Mr. Lang," he said, which explained the "Mr. Lang." "Let me introduce to you Special Agent Thomas Tuttle."

The first twinge of worry started. Why would there be two guys calling about a job offer?

"Hello, Special Agent Tuttle," he said automatically, keeping the question out of his voice.

"Tom's currently heading a task force investigating the deaths of two actresses and the possibility of a serial killer targeting Oscar-winning movie stars."

Something inside him slipped, disappointment wending down to his gut. The hope that this was a call regarding a promotion to the L.A. office faded, replaced by the memory of his conversation with Vivi about the so-called Red Carpet Killer.

Why were they calling him? Had something happened to Vivi? A knot formed in his gut as he answered. "I'm vaguely familiar with the task force, sir," he said.

"Well, you're about to get a hell of a lot more familiar with it, since tonight's winner is going to land in your jurisdiction on Tuesday morning."

He frowned into the phone. "Tonight's winner?" The Oscars would be awarded later that evening—even a casual observer like Colt knew that. The knot grew tighter. If Gagliardi knew the winner already, there was a damn good reason why. "There's evidence to suggest the first two deaths were linked?" he asked.

"There is," he said. "I'll let Tom tell you the details before we brief you on the responsibilities regarding this case."

It was a case now, not speculation, not a task force. And, damn, he hadn't heard a word from Vivi other than superficial texts all week.

"My forensic specialists have uncovered a connection between two pieces of evidence that the LAPD investigators missed when they analyzed the crime scenes," Agent Tuttle said, the slightest tone of wry condescension in his voice. Of course the LAPD screwed up. Of course the FBI fixed it. "Human hair not belonging to either victim was found at both crime scenes. Most likely from a wig or hair extensions."

Interesting, except for the fact that every actress in Hollywood wore fake hair. Still, Colt listened as Tuttle continued.

"A long brown hair was found in Adrienne Dwight's wrecked car, not matching her DNA or the DNA of any friends, staffers, or co-workers who had reportedly been in her car. Final analysis showed that the hair had come from a wig or extensions, which, considering her occupation, isn't a surprise. One year later, another human hair from a wig, a different color, was also found near the body of Isobel DeSoto."

"The consensus by the LAPD was that both these women constantly changed wigs and had hair extensions," Gagliardi chimed in. "And they were around people who did the same. And after reading the evidence, I can see why hairs that didn't match the victim didn't generate more attention in the LAPD. But our lab guys discovered two very interesting things."

"*Very* interesting," Tom noted. "Both human hairs, which, by the way, are commonly used for wigs and extensions, had been affixed using a protein called keratin. First, super-expensive star-quality extensions don't use keratin; there are better glues. Second, Isobel DeSoto was allergic to keratin, so the wig or extension the hair came from definitely wasn't hers."

He followed what they were establishing: The same type of hair extension, if not the same person, might have been present at both scenes. "Still not a stretch in Hollywood, the land of hair extensions," Colt said. "Could be from anyone who'd visited one of the victims or ridden in the car of the other or worked at a car wash, for that matter."

"True, but these two hairs were coated in an unusual phenol formaldehyde glue that is used only on wigs from India."

Big country. Big wig industry, too. "The only way it matters is if you can prove the two hairs at two different crime scenes may have come from the same person wearing the same wig," Lang said.

"Or two different wigs both purchased from the same, rather obscure, Indian manufacturer," Gagliardi replied. "We don't have this confirmed yet, but we believe it's possible that both wigs were made by the same company, one of the few still using this glue with a certain dye combination. We're analyzing the dye, which might tell us a lot, including the manufacturer. If we get that, we're sending someone to India for access to the sales files."

"Until then?" he asked.

"We have a Best Actress winner to protect," Tuttle said.

Vivi's face flashed in his head, not an unusual occurrence. Except that this time she was posing as a movie star.

"The accounting firm tallying the Oscar votes released the winner's name to the task force. So we know who is going to win, and where she's going to be for the next month. It appears she's headed to her place on Nantucket Island, and we want an agent with her twenty-four/seven, on alert for anything out of the ordinary."

What was ordinary where a movie star was concerned? At least he hoped it was a movie star, and not—

No, she couldn't. She wouldn't. Oh, hell, she might.

Wait, he didn't know the name of the winner yet. They could be talking about Kimberly Horne or Colleen True or—he couldn't remember any other names except Cara Ferrari. If someone else won, Vivi's involvement would be a moot point.

"Who's the lucky girl?" Praying to hear any name other than—

"Cara Ferrari."

Damn. A bad, bad feeling crawled up his spine. "Really?"

"Yeah," Tom said. "But she doesn't know, so all five of them had to give us an itinerary of where they were planning to spend the next several weeks. She's going to be in your backyard."

Well, in Nantucket, off the coast of Cape Cod. Not exactly downtown Boston, but still within his jurisdiction. "So the actresses believe the serial-killer theory?" he asked.

"Who knows what they believe. Four of them were cooperative when told about the new evidence," Tom told him. "Unfortunately, the least cooperative is Ferrari, who insists she has private security that far exceeds the capabilities of the FBI and doesn't want any agents on site."

It couldn't be the Guardian Angelinos. Surely an actress like Cara Ferrari would demand the largest, most well-established private security firm in the world. Why would she go with a scrappy skater who had no experience and a harebrained idea to be a decoy based on a vague resemblance?

He wanted to relax, and would have if he didn't know Vivi Angelino, human tornado.

"Colt, I want the best there is in the Boston office on this," Gagliardi said. "And, frankly, after our conversations and my review of your files and records, I think that's you."

"Thank you, sir." He wanted Gagliardi to think he was the best, but not because he wanted a job babysitting a movie star—or her body double.

"And, to be perfectly honest, this is a high-profile situation, with a lot of media breathing down our neck. If something happens to her and the FBI isn't at least visible on site, we'll get hammered in the press. I'd like to consider it a final test, if you know what I mean. A job in L.A.

means enormous work in the media spotlight. I'd like to see how you handle this."

Son of a bitch. This was part of his job interview. "I understand, sir." But that knot in his gut was growing into a bowling ball of worry. The job could get extremely complicated if... "What security firm is Ms. Ferrari using?"

"She won't say," Tuttle said. "Called it a potential leak for us to know. Claimed her nondisclosures are airtight and she doesn't have to tell us anything. I hate to tell you, she's a classic diva bitch."

When, exactly, was the last time he heard from Vivi?

"You can handle that, Colt," Gagliardi said with a subtle laugh. "It'll be a good opportunity for you to learn the mind-set of the women in L.A. You'll need that information when you get out here. Assuming, of course, you get the job."

Dangle a carrot much? "I understand," he repeated. "Let me clear my calendar and straighten up my case files and arrange to get to Nantucket."

"Oh, we'll get you to Nantucket," Gagliardi assured him. "That's part of the whole operation. Your travel arrangements will be e-mailed shortly."

"Thank you, sir. And thank you for the vote of confidence." However qualified it might be.

"I'm happy you're there to handle this," Gagliardi said. "And grateful for the chance to see you in action."

In other words, Screw up and you lose the promotion.

"Although once you're an SAC, you can happily kiss the field good-bye," Gagliardi added.

"I know that." He didn't really want to kiss the field good-bye; he wanted to kiss Boston good-bye. And now he had one last test before he could do that. One that damn well better not involve Vivi Angelino. "Thank you, sir."

As soon as he signed off, he scrolled through his phone to find the thread of texts from Vivi. The last one was on Thursday, and then it was just to answer a quick question, her response vague—and distant.

If she got the job with Ferrari, wouldn't she have told him, even just to gloat?

He touched her name and typed: *Where are you? Need to talk to you.* He obviously couldn't tell her that Cara Ferrari would win tonight, but he had to know where she was.

While he waited for a response he looked out over the rolling hills at the Sunday golfers, expecting some sort of memory jab of Jennifer in khaki golf pants and a pink button-down.

But all he could visualize right then was Vivi, with her funky hair and vibrant features, her body-skimming unisex tops and her weird checkered sneakers. Skateboarding, not golfing.

It would take some expertise to turn her into a movie star.

He could hear her voice. "C'mon, Lang, it's the oldest form of security in the world. . . . Bait the killer with a decoy. . . ."

The vibration of his cell phone jerked him out of the thought he didn't want to have anyway.

Did you need me for something, Agent Colton Cautious Lang? ☺

Yeah, hell if he'd ever admit it to her. But right now, he needed her to tell him exactly where she was, without giving away the confidential information he had. No easy task with her investigator's nose for anything suspicious.

Just want to be sure you're not doing anything you shouldn't be doing, he wrote. He avoided adding *anything like trading places with Cara Ferrari*.

Waiting for her response, he strolled in the direction of the golf course, but only to tell his golfing buddies that an emergency case had come up and he'd have to take a rain check on the game.

They weren't happy. But not as unhappy as he was every time he checked his phone for an answer or sent another *What are you doing?* text to Vivi.

Finally, the phone vibrated.

Just doing what I always do on a Sunday, Lang. What are you doing?

What did she always do on a Sunday? Skateboarded in a park and went out to Sudbury to her family's house for dinner.

Golfing, he wrote.

Oooh. Super fun!

He laughed, imagining the tease in her tone, the light in her eyes. What if she took some crazy risk and someone snuffed that light out? An old familiar band tightened a little around his chest. Stuff like that happened. To women with less of a wild streak than Vivi.

Still, it was too early to tell her anything and if he pushed, she'd guess. She was so smart. And capable. And cute, damn it.

He wrote: *You watching the Oscars tonight?*

Her response was lightning fast. *Of course!*

Did you sell that cockamamie idea to the new client? He hit Send with a little too much force, like he could make her answer. With a resounding "No."

Cockamamie! ☺

What the hell did that mean? Before he asked, she wrote again.

Gotta run, Lang. Nice to know you miss me. See you soon.

Maybe, he typed, then deleted the word. He had a better plan.

CHAPTER 3

I have to tell you something, Vivi." Cara Ferrari leaned across the open space of the limousine, the fiber-optic light casting a blue glow on her pale skin.

"What is it?"

"I'm scared." Her voice cracked with admission as she closed eyes unadorned by anything but purple circles of sleeplessness, magnified because her long hair was pulled back in a sloppy ponytail.

She'd been silent since they'd climbed into the limo together in the garage of Cara's Brentwood home. A second limo followed, carrying the rest of the entourage. That included Bridget, the stylist who'd taken such great pains to turn Vivi into a carbon copy of Cara Ferrari; Marissa, the assistant; and a publicist named Leon who followed Cara everywhere. A third vehicle was full of bodyguards.

Only Joellen Mugg joined Vivi and Cara in the limousine, the quintessential hanger-on sister who, as Bridget had warned, seemed to spend the days and nights in a constant state of pretty much toasted. She appeared to be languishing there now, curled into a corner with earbuds in place, an iPod in her hand, eyes closed. She still used the less glamorous last name the two of them had been born with, and she still called Cara by her birth name, Karen.

They looked nothing alike, but Joellen used every opportunity to say the words "my sister" when talking about Cara. But mostly she hid behind a bottle and an iPod, and Vivi had tried to avoid her as much as possible.

"Don't be scared," Vivi replied to Cara's admission. "We have a plan, and it's a good one. You're safe."

Cara looked doubtful, more vulnerable than Vivi had seen her in the past week. "What about you?"

"I'm a professional," Vivi said. "We'll be sealed up in Nantucket, making just enough appearances for the paps to believe it's you."

"What if the . . . killer shows up?"

She sincerely doubted one would, but for a million smackeroos, she wanted Cara to believe she was getting her money's worth. "We'll catch him," Vivi assured her with a smile.

"About our plan . . ." Cara said, one hand on Stella, who flattened her length against Cara's thigh and rested her snout on her lap. Her other hand still held the gold statuette. It had to be hot from almost twenty-four hours of nonstop handling. Cara had yet to put that sucker down since it had been handed to her onstage.

"What about the plan?" Vivi asked.

"I'm changing it."

Vivi remained still, despite the full-body discomfort caused by the extensions pricking at her hair, the false eyelashes pinching her lids, the stilettos squashing her toes, and, now, the sixth sense that she wasn't going to like this change in plans.

The plan called for Vivi's trial run as Cara to be the most difficult test of all: getting through the gauntlet of paparazzi and fans, encircled by bodyguards and the pack of people in the other car. Cara would blend in as just another in the group, while all eyes would be on Vivi, still dressed in the last outfit Cara had worn for interviews, including a hat worn in the movie, complete with netting covering her face. And, of course, she'd be waving the Oscar for all the world to see.

Then they'd all fly to Nantucket together on a Gulfstream G650, a brand-new private jet Cara had rented for an entire month. After landing on the island, Cara would take some of her entourage to a safe house that the Guardian Angelinos had already found and rented, while others would stay with Vivi to ensure the trick worked.

"There's nothing wrong with our plan," Vivi said. "You're just nervous."

Cara looked out the window as they pulled into the traffic of the Burbank airport. "Damn right I am. One of the people in that pack of paps could be him. Bullets could fly."

"You'll be well protected in the middle of the circle, and it's not far from the VIP limo parking to the private planes. I've checked all this already, here and in Nantucket." Vivi leaned forward and Stella snarled. "Trust me, Cara. We can do this."

Cara shook her head, her eyes filling. "I'm scared."

"You've been out all day doing interviews. That didn't scare you."

"All in protected environments." She nestled next to the dog. "I'm not getting out of this limo."

Vivi leaned back, practically tasting the other woman's fear. She knew fear, knew the desire to hide from a threat. "Fine. We'll stay in L.A. This same plan can work from your house in Brentwood. There's no reason for you to fly to Nantucket. You can change your mind and go home right now."

"No, I can't. But I'm not going to Nantucket."

"Then we'll—"

"You are."

"Where will you be?"

"I'm not going to say."

"I need to know where you are."

"Why?" Cara shot back. "You actually don't need to know. It's safer that way."

Safer for Cara? Maybe, maybe not. Vivi should know where her client is at all times. "Look, you have to trust me. I need to know where you are."

"You'll have Marissa's number." She held out the Oscar to Vivi. "When you get to Nantucket, give this to Mercedes. She's my housekeeper. She knows you're coming in my place."

Vivi took the Oscar; she didn't like this plan. Cara was supposed to be close by, not at some undisclosed location. "The Guardian Angelinos have arranged a completely safe place for you to stay," Vivi said.

"Of course you have to take Stella."

She hadn't even heard Vivi. Instead, Cara's focus was on the dog as she closed her hand around Stella's belly, lifting the tiny body and kissing her head. "Be careful not to let her run too much. She was the runt of the litter, born with a funky foot. Weren't you, baby?" She cradled the dog's left front paw. "But you're perfect to me. You be a good girl, little one. I'll get you back soon."

As she handed the squirming dog over, Cara's eyes filled. Vivi tried to take Stella, but she squiggled away.

"Listen, Cara, I don't think this is a smart plan. I should know where you—"

"No!" Stella jumped at Cara's sharp reprimand, but it wasn't directed at the dog. "You listen to me"—Cara pointed a white-tipped talon at Vivi—"I'm not getting on that plane. And neither are any of the people who work for me. Except you, obviously." She leaned across the space and put two hands on Vivi's knees, getting very much in Vivi's face. "But that doesn't mean I'm not watching you."

An unexpected chill danced up Vivi's spine. "Excuse me?"

"Or listening to every word you say."

Vivi leaned away, eyes wide. "You'll be spying on me?"

"Did you forget the nondisclosure you signed?"

"Of course not, but—"

"Well, how else would I know you haven't told anyone?"

"You could trust me. With your life."

"I am trusting you with my life, but there will be law enforcement people and—others."

Vivi frowned. "I'm not going to lie to the police or FBI about who I am."

Cara's teary eyes grew narrow and harsh. "You will tell no one or I will consider it a breach of the nondisclosure."

"Even the police? The FBI?" Vivi choked softly. "They're on our side, Cara."

"No one is on our side, Vivi," she said darkly. "I know

from experience that the police create the worst media leaks. The *worst*. They refuse to sign nondisclosures."

She blew out a sigh. "The pilots?"

"No one," Cara said. "There's a private bedroom cabin in the back of the plane. You go straight there, and don't come out. Believe me, no one asks questions when I want to be alone."

"And in Nantucket?" Vivi asked.

"I told you my housekeeper, Mercedes, will be there to meet you," Cara said. "She knows I'm sending a decoy. You can't tell anyone else you aren't me, and that is final. And believe me, I will know."

She'd be under constant observation. "I wish you trusted me."

"It's not you I don't trust. It's them. The FBI, everyone."

"Have you talked to the FBI?"

"Briefly," she said. "After I won the Oscar."

"And?"

"They'll be around, but you'll fool them."

Not all of them. "What did they say?"

"Just that they wanted to send someone to protect me, but I told them I already had private security."

The FBI might lurk, but they wouldn't force their way onto the property. If they did, could she fool them? Only if whatever agents arrived didn't know her. Would FBI agents on Nantucket work with the Boston office?

With the ASAC of the Boston office? "Cara, I have contacts in the FBI—"

"No one can know!"

Joellen opened her eyes at the sound of Cara's raised voice, yanking an earbud out. "What the fuck is going on?" she asked.

"Vivi needs some acting lessons," Cara said coolly. "She's wondering what to do if the FBI recognizes her as an impostor."

Joellen's blue eyes, small and close together, absolutely nothing like her sister's, widened as she leaned forward. "You convince them they're wrong."

Had Joellen had been following the conversation all along? "What if I can't convince them? What if one of the agents knows me?"

"Avoid that agent," Cara said.

"Or be ready to part with ten million dollars." Joellen's smile was smug.

"One good look at me and—"

Cara reached over and pulled netting down over Vivi's face. "Don't let them get a good look at you," she said harshly. "And if they do, then your job is to do *whatever it takes* to convince *everyone* you are me. Whatever. Be creative, but get the job done. Clear?"

Joellen dropped back on the seat and replaced her earbud as the car came to a stop.

"It's showtime," Cara said. "Go walk across that tarmac the way Bridget taught you, look like an exhausted and very self-involved Oscar-winning actress, throw a few waves of the statuette, blow them some kisses, hang on to Stella, get your ass on that plane, and keep your mouth shut. Please?" She went soft again, as if some inner director had just reminded her she was supposed to be scared. "For me?"

No wonder she'd won an Oscar.

The noise of the crowd had already penetrated the limo. "How can I reach you in an emergency?" she asked.

"Just call Marissa. And, remember, I'll be watching.

I chartered that plane days ago, and Leon has specially prepared it." She underscored the not-so-subtle message with a tight smile. "So be convincing."

Surely she could convince the pilots, then hide in that back cabin for the duration of the night flight. Once she got to Nantucket, she'd figure out what to do about the FBI.

"Fine," Vivi said. "I have no issue with being monitored. It's not being trusted I don't like."

Cara reached out a hand. "In my business, you can't trust anyone."

The car slowed and they peered out the darkened windows. The crowd was cordoned off, about forty feet from the plane, but the limo couldn't get any closer than it was to the plane, leaving a long walk of fame for Vivi.

Cara let out a slow whistle. "The most I've ever seen." She turned back to Vivi, giving her a critical up-and-down. "I know it's a little over the top, but the *Now, Voyager* costume was pretty smart on Bridget's part. It's so distinctively me and, honestly, you cannot see your face through that net." Once more she reached over and adjusted the screen of material over Vivi's face. "You realize this was the actual hat Bette Davis wore in the original movie?"

Could she have cared less? Unlikely. All she cared about now was doing this job, and doing it right.

"Cool," she said, her focus outside as the bodyguards reached the limo. Someone got her luggage from the trunk. But nothing was cool. Not her skin, not her nerves, not her client.

One of the guards tapped four times on the window.

"That's the signal," Cara said, her expression softening. "Break a leg and keep your phone handy. We'll text you."

The door opened to a blast of noise, along with enough camera flashes to bathe the tarmac in near daylight.

Vivi's pulse thudded as she took a deep breath and pulled the heavy designer bag they'd given her up on her shoulder. The skirt she wore was slit thigh high, but tight enough to make getting out of the limo a challenge.

"Let 'em see the tattoo," Cara whispered.

Vivi nodded, placing her left leg out of the limo door, letting the slit skirt ride high to reveal the temporary tattoo that every photographer in Hollywood wanted to snap: the Ferrari logo in deep purple, high and on the inside of "Cara's" thigh, leaving no doubt that this woman was Cara Ferrari.

"Wave!" Cara ordered from the limo. "And for God's sake, don't forget Stella!"

Vivi turned into the limo cab again, reaching out for the dog, who yelped mightily but let Vivi take her.

"Vivi, look at me," Cara demanded, forcing Vivi to dip low and stick her head back through the door.

Cara put her fingers to her mouth, zipped her lips, and twisted an imaginary key.

"Got it," Vivi said.

"Remember." She stabbed her finger in the air, inches from Vivi's face. "I've got eyes and ears."

Vivi gave her a tight smile and backed out. The bodyguards flanked her as she started her march, squirmy pet under one arm, sweat-dampened statuette under the other. Stella was heavy, but the Oscar was surprisingly light, making Vivi wonder fleetingly if the impostor had gotten an impostor. Fitting.

From behind the chain-link fence the crowd screamed for Cara.

She waved and made a show of cuddling the dog, keeping her face in Stella's short-cropped fur. She walked as quickly as she could, considering she had on four-inch heels and a tight skirt. The noise of the screams and hundreds of cameras snapping was barely drowned out by the engines of a sizable private plane waiting with the stairs open.

The pilot stepped forward and smiled, the first person Vivi would talk to as "Cara." She climbed the steps, paused to give one more wave to the cameras, then slipped inside, daring direct eye contact from behind the protective netting.

"Welcome aboard and congratulations, Ms. Ferrari."

"Thank you."

"I'm Captain Wahl. My copilot is Captain Klossberg, and we are delighted to have you on our flight this evening."

She nodded, easing the dog to the ground. The instant she was out of her hands, Stella bolted toward the door, and Vivi spun for her with a little shriek. But damn if the little beast didn't shoot right back down the steps and tear ass across the tarmac like freaking Toto escaping the Wicked Witch.

"Get her!" she hollered to one of the bodyguards headed back to the limo, just as an uproar of laughter from the crowd made the poor little dog run faster. "Oh my God, she's going to kill me," Vivi whispered into her hand, still covering her mouth in disbelief as the dog ran right to the limo, the birth defect obvious in a clumsy stumble of a gait that slowed her down.

The crowd exploded with a scream of "Stelllllllaaaaa!" sounding like two hundred bad imitations of Marlon Brando, and Vivi didn't know whether to laugh or cry or scream with them.

"Maybe she hates to fly," the pilot suggested, eyes crinkling with laughter.

Vivi bent down in time to see the dog reach the limo and jump toward the door, finally caught by one of the bodyguards. This elicited another roar from the onlookers and another six billion flashes. Stella's attempted escape would be on every blog in the world before their plane landed in Nantucket.

Vivi's cell vibrated. That would be Cara, no doubt. Pointing her little finger from four hundred feet away. She pulled out the phone, expecting a text of chastisement, or maybe something simple like *You're fired*. But the screen was blank except for Lang's phone number. He'd texted nothing?

Vivi scrolled down to see if she just missed his message, but there was nothing. Why would he text nothing?

She stepped away from the door, turning to the main cabin. Her gaze settled on a man reclining in a leather seat, his legs up and ankles crossed, a phone blocking his face.

Who the hell was...

No—oh, God, no. This was not possible. *This was not happening.*

He inched the phone to the right, just enough to reveal half his face. Enough to confirm her worst nightmare. "How many times are you going to fall for the same trick?" he asked.

What the holy hell was he doing here?

She stared through the netting, the thin black gauze of her hat's veil not doing enough to temper the heat of his gaze as it took a slow, easy trip over her, from shiny black extensions all the way down to the peekaboo toes and ankle-strap shoes. Back up to her face, he lifted one brow and barely nodded in appreciation. "This is a good look for you, Vi—"

"Who are you?" *Please, Lang, don't say my name.*

For a moment, he was fooled. She could see the flicker of doubt in his eyes, then his mouth set in one of his most humorless expressions. "FBI. Who are *you*?"

Her knees weakened at the thought of hidden cameras and secret microphones, the conversation being played into the back of that limo right this minute. She'd be fired before takeoff.

"I'm the one who calls the shots on this plane." She channeled every nuance of Cara's inflection and personality into the words, even lowering her voice to the actress's more throaty register. "So let's get something straight. I don't want to talk to anyone until we land and I'm home in Nantucket. I'll be in the back cabin for the duration of the flight and I do not want to be disturbed for *any* reason."

His jaw unhinged just enough to know she'd nailed the sultry voice and diva attitude. Maybe he was unsure who she was. More likely, he saw through the disguise and was humoring her.

So before he could whip off her hat and confirm whatever suspicions he might have, she waltzed right past him, opened the back door to the bedroom cabin, and slammed it closed, locking the door with trembling fingers. Then she fell against it.

Now what? She had to do something, and fast. Lang

would be pounding on the door any second, calling her by her real name, demanding she come out and reveal her true self. Every word would be transmitted to Cara, who'd have the Guardian Angelinos out of business before this flight landed in Massachusetts.

She *couldn't* let him say her name. But how could she stop him? She could text him. Would a camera see her send a text and see him read it?

Do whatever it takes to convince anyone you are me. Cara's voice rang in her ears. What would it take?

Be creative.

A soft tap, much too gentle to be Lang, made her back away from the door. "What is it?" she demanded, matching Cara's superstar arrogance.

"Uh, Ms. Ferrari?" It was Lang. Calling her Ms. Ferrari?

She swallowed hard. "What?"

"I have something I think you want."

"Unless it's privacy, I don't want a thing."

A small whining sound squeaked through the door. "Your dog is crying, Ms. Ferrari. I think she wants you."

Doubtful she wanted Vivi, but Cara would never ignore her dog. Slowly, she turned the latch, then inched the door open. Lang stood just on the other side with a tiny dog curled against his chest.

Stella let out a low, hateful growl at Vivi.

"Or maybe she doesn't want you," Lang said, fighting a smile. "Why don't I just bring her in?" Before she could stop him, he muscled the door open and got inside, instantly closing the door behind him.

She shook her head, hoping the plea in her eyes would keep him from opening his mouth. He wasn't fooled by the disguise, that much she could tell by the amusement and amazement in his eyes. But he couldn't say a word. He *couldn't* say her name. She had to pray there were only listening devices, not cameras, embedded in the plane.

Be creative.

He took a breath, ready to launch into a speech. "Listen to me, V—"

She put both hands on the collar of her shirt and ripped it open, popping the buttons and tearing the fabric, revealing a wisp of lace that Cara called a bra.

That shut him up.

"I told you I want privacy."

"I see..." *Breasts.* "That."

"So if your job requires you to stare at me, then fine. Have a seat, I'm going to change out of this ridiculous costume. My stylist is absolutely over the top sometimes, dressing me from the movie."

Colt couldn't move, so he remained rooted to the floor, the dog folded in his arms like she never wanted to leave. He knew the feeling. Nothing could get him to move as he drank in the sight of Vivi Angelino doing something she'd only done in his imagination. Strip.

It was Vivi, wasn't it? He'd bet everything he had that behind that black net, underneath two feet of fake hair, and just inside that lacy piece of nothing was a woman he *thought* he knew very well. So what the hell was she up to? This was the last thing he'd ever expect from her.

The jacket fell, followed by the torn blouse, revealing curves and cleavage he didn't think Vivi had. A thread of doubt wrapped around his always certain brain.

He tore his gaze from the beautiful body to peer hard through the netting. Under it, he could see midnight eyes that should be Vivi's, could be Vivi's, but they were heavily disguised by black eyeliner and a broom's worth of thick lashes and a smear of shadow that shimmered when she looked down. Her lips, glossier and fuller than he'd ever noticed, tipped in a whisper of a smile as she gave all that hair—all that glorious, sexy, amazing, long hair—a purposeful shimmy behind her shoulders so it couldn't block an inch of her nearly naked torso.

"What are you doing?" he asked, his throat surprisingly dry.

"I told you." As she reached behind her, in a move that jutted out her breasts even more, a zipper scraped and the skirt loosened. She waited a beat, almost as if she wanted the dramatic effect, then slowly maneuvered the material over her hips, inching it down to reveal a taut, flat belly, an adorable inny navel, and the skinniest scrap of more white lace between her legs. "I'm changing."

The skirt hit the floor, and his pulse tripled. Her legs were forever long, muscular, sleek, and—holy shit—she had a tattoo on her inner thigh, three-quarters of the way up, a palm's-width from the patch of white lace.

Wordlessly, she pivoted, and as if the front weren't stupefying enough, she offered a shot of her ass: tight, high, round, and bare but for a thong strap that nestled between her cheeks and rested just under the dimples of her lower back.

Vivi?

He opened his mouth to speak, but nothing came out. Of course. All blood necessary for brain function had cascaded south, already gathering in one about-to-be-obvious place.

A suitcase had been delivered while he'd waited on the

plane, and it lay on the bed. She leaned over to open it, propping her ass a little higher, spreading her legs a little wider, killing his ability to think a little more.

She unzipped the bag and pulled out something yellow, which she threw on the floor. Then she dug around and dragged out one long, shiny black boot, then the other.

She wouldn't put those on. She wouldn't.

Would she?

Still unable to talk or breathe, he slowly set the dog down, letting her scamper away toward the en suite bathroom. Colt leaned back against the door, crossed his arms, and did the only thing a red-blooded human male could do. He watched.

She stepped away from the bed, her back still to him, as shockingly at ease with her body as any woman he'd ever seen. She lifted one knee and pointed her toe, slowly sliding it into the boot. She eased it up to her thigh, then folded practically in half, the hat staying pinned in place. With her knees locked, ass up, tits visible from between her legs, nearly falling out of the bra as she held the position, she speared him with a look of pure sex from between her legs.

Could Vivi even think of something like that? Doubt shadowed his mind.

She slowly zipped up the boot, standing as she finished.

"Everybody loves these on me," she said, her voice kind of like Vivi's, but kind of not. "Reminds them of— you know—that movie."

He nodded. Maybe. He thought about nodding. "Yeah."

She started on the other boot. "You like your job, FBI Man?"

"Most of the time." Right now he loved it.

"You look like you'd be good at it." Still the little throaty sound of Vivi, but her diction was perfect, the trace of a Boston accent was gone, and—

Jesus Christ, it *was* Vivi, wasn't it?

For the first time since the woman had gotten on the plane he seriously wondered if maybe he was wrong. Maybe this really was Cara Ferrari. Maybe Vivi, was right about the resemblance.

She bent over again, pole-dancer style, her hair draping on the floor, but the hat must have been pinned in place.

But what about that hair? If that was a wig wouldn't it come off? Was Vivi Angelino even able to move like that? Look like sin in leather and lace? Vivi, who favored cargo pants and shapeless T-shirts?

When she finished the zipping, she turned to him, hand on one hip, head tilted flirtatiously. "If you want, I'll skip the dress, but it does kind of complete the outfit."

A speaker crackled and she visibly startled, glancing side to side for the source of the sound.

"Ms. Ferrari, this is Captain Wahl. We're just about ready to taxi out of here, so if you and Assistant Special Agent in Charge Lang would be kind enough to buckle up back there, we'll get you on your way to Nantucket promptly. Looks like smooth flying ahead."

It certainly looked smooth in the back cabin.

She smiled. "That's quite a title you've got. What should I call you?"

Of course, Vivi would joke about the title. So was this Vivi? "Call me crazy for letting this go on so long."

With a sex-kitten laugh, she strutted like liquid sin to the two leather recliners on the other side of the small cabin, side by side, there for the sole purpose of buckling up during takeoff and landing.

He followed, of course. Because keeping an eye on her was his job. And figuring out what the hell she was up to was also his job. Was this Vivi Angelino's version of going undercover? Then someone was in big trouble. Like him.

She slipped into one of the chairs, stretching out like a cat. A cat in white wisps of lingerie and thigh-high black boots. The netting stayed securely over her face, but this close, he could scrutinize her features. That was Vivi. It had to be.

Right?

Uncertainty gnawed as he sat next to her and automatically pulled on his seat belt, aware that a bit of a tent had already grown in the crotch of his khakis.

She skipped the seat belt, but leaned close to him, stared at that rise, and slipped one glossy lip under a tooth, biting the blood right out of it. "I'm sorry. Am I making you uncomfortable, Mr. FBI Agent?"

"I'm very comfortable," he said, not pulling away. "Ms. Ferrari."

At the use of her name she dropped back, seemingly satisfied as the whine of the engines filled the cabin.

"How long are you going to play this game?" he asked.

She bristled. "This is not a game."

"Then what do you call it, Vi—"

"Please." She closed her hand over his arm, squeezing hard as she turned to him, the net veil a thin barricade between their faces, her dark eyes pleading.

"Yes?"

Very slowly, she slid her hand from his arm to his thigh, spreading white-tipped, diamond-covered fingers. Not the hands of Vivi Angelino, who never wore nail polish and kept her only diamond poked in the side of her nose.

"Could you buckle my seat belt for me? You know, just to make sure it's...secure."

He said nothing, aware of how close her hand was to his growing erection. "If you'd like," he said.

"I think we'd both like," she said suggestively.

He dragged the belt over her bare belly, his forearm brushing the bottom of her breasts as his fingers dug for the end of the seat belt. Click. "Got it," he said.

"Mmmm." She rocked just a little in the seat, the plane's acceleration pushing his arm against the swell of her breasts. "You certainly do."

As he drew away, her fingers tightened on his thigh, the pressure and heat shooting more life into his already stiff cock. "Takeoff scares me a little," she whispered.

"*You* scare me a little."

She laughed. "Thank you."

Centimeters from her face, he could feel the warmth of her breath and inhale a flowery, feminine smell that was so not Vivi.

His fingers itched to lift that veil and study the angles of her face he knew so well. Without giving into the urge, he looked hard through the net. Where was the nose piercing? Not so much as a pore was visible on her creamy skin, let alone a pierced hole for jewelry. Could she hide that? He'd never seen it out before.

The G-force of takeoff pushed him back to his seat, the

Rolls-Royce engines on a plane so new it still smelled like the Gulfstream factory escalating to a nice, loud scream.

"Are you really scared?" he asked.

"Are you?" She smiled, enough for him to see she had perfect teeth—with no teeny-tiny chip on one in the front.

Christ alive, it wasn't Vivi.

The landing gear rose up and the nose shot through the clouds like the knife through his gut at the realization.

He reached for the net but she backed off, finally releasing her grip on his leg.

"Uh-uh," she warned. "No touching."

He snorted softly. "That doesn't seem to go both ways."

"Are you complaining?" She laughed, low and sweet. "Just forgive me if I'm a little silly tonight. I haven't slept for two days, and I won an Oscar last night. I'm feeling— wild."

Her voice, her eyes, her essence was Vivi. But every- thing else was something else altogether. Something raw and sexy.

Still, damn it all. He wasn't sure.

"I know Cara Ferrari won an Oscar. And you"—he pointed at her—"might win another for this. So, let's cut the crap and—"

She put one hand over his mouth and unlatched her seat belt with the other, rolling closer, pressing those barely covered breasts against his biceps.

"You call this crap?" she whispered, the warmth of her breath tickling his ear.

"I call it game over, Vi—"

She snapped up the armrest and flipped one boot-clad leg over his thighs. "This is so not a game." She slid her leg right over his erection.

"I don't know what you're trying to prove." He ground out the words as his dick stiffened against the pressure.

"I'm trying to prove"—the Ferrari tattoo rode right over his erection—"who I am."

"I know who you are." Didn't he?

"Only one woman in the world is known for..." She climbed right on top of him, wedging her knees on either side of his legs and arching her back just enough to put her breasts inches from his mouth. "The most memorable lap dance in film history."

He almost laughed, but his blood had done another brain drain and his cock hummed like an electric buzzsaw.

"It wasn't that long ago, one of my earliest films." She kneeled high enough that her lace crotch didn't quite touch his growing tent. "So I remember all the moves." It took some powerful thigh muscles to hold the position, but she didn't flinch.

Could Vivi do that? All that skateboarding made her strong, but this was crazy. Everything about this was crazy. He had to know who was doing this to him. Reaching up to the hat, she dodged again, leaving him with nothing but a handful of her hair, thick, smooth and definitely real, or firmly attached.

But some fake hair felt real. The wisp of a thought took hold of what was left of his working brain cells. Fake hair. Fake hair was why he was here. But before he could process that thought, she flipped her hair out of his touch, flinging the locks over her shoulder like a weapon she was completely familiar with.

"You know the rules, honey. No hands. Just eyes. Just... watch. Just feel. Just lose control."

He tried to shake his head.

"Never lose control, do you?"

"Rarely."

"Let's make this one of those rare times, then." She breathed the last word, rolling her hips achingly close, then away.

"What the hell are you doing?" His voice was rough with arousal. And frustration. And dismay. And—shit—a complete loss of sanity and control.

"You have to ask? What do they teach you in that FBI academy?"

"Control."

She laughed softly and leaned over him, her breasts against his chest, her mouth to his ear. "You know what I say?"

"I can't imagine."

"Control is overrated."

Now if that wasn't a Vivi-ism, what was? One more time, he peeked under the veil. If this wasn't Vivi, he was in a boatload of trouble. But if it was...

He was in a different boatload of trouble.

She pressed her mouth against his ear. "Just don't say my name. Ever."

What name? Before he could get the question out, she rose again on her knees, her fingers brushing over a button on the armrest. Instantly, music came out of tiny speakers built into the chair behind his ears, filling the small cabin with a pulsing, bass-heavy song. A slow song, a female artist, he had no idea who or what, but Vivi—Cara—*someone*, moved her body in perfect rhythm.

She undulated and dipped, her crotch grazing his erection, her breasts rising and falling with each beat, each breath. His cock hardened to a painful plank of wood that strained his pants and his composure.

She mouthed the words of the song, licking her lips and slipping a finger into her cleavage. Sliding it over her nipple, arousing the peak.

His jaw hurt from how much he wanted to close his mouth over that lace, tear it off with his teeth—and suck. He dragged his attention to her face, hidden in shadow enough to make him question his certainty that this was Vivi and not some pole-dancing, moviemaking, strip-teasing—

She rubbed both breasts and glided her hands down her belly, slipping one into her panties, then out again, her body jumping slightly as they hit turbulence.

Vivi. Like he'd never imagined her before. And he'd done some pretty thorough imagining of her.

Blood surged and slammed and his balls tightened up to needy, swollen walnuts. A drop of semen darkened his khakis. Jesus Christ, she was going to make him come.

"You better..." he rasped. "Not..."

"Better not forget the best part?" she coaxed. "Of course not. Who else could do this but me?" She lifted one booted leg and planted her foot on the armrest. The tattoo, a perfect replica of a Ferrari logo, was inches from his mouth. It looked real. It looked permanent. It looked edible.

Would Vivi get that tattoo just to play a part?

He didn't know. He didn't know anything anymore. Not why he was here, not her name, not his own. He just knew—

She closed her teeth over the zipper of the boots, dragging it a few inches. The move put her crotch against his, and, holy hell, she was wet.

That was all it took.

His dick jerked, needing to rub, needing to roll against her, needing to be deep inside that wet, white lace and shoot the wad that was ready to burst. He gripped the armrests so hard he could feel the skeleton of the seat under the leather pad. If he let go, he'd touch her. He *had* to touch her.

She finished the boot zipper with her fingers, stretching her leg to kick it off, exactly as she had in the movie. It was burned in his memory. He'd shot a few loads to that image in his life, and was about to again.

"Please," he whispered. "I...can't...control..."

Her eyes flashed with victory. "Never thought I'd hear you say that."

Vivi. Only Vivi would say that to him. At the confirmation that this woman was no stranger, but Vivi, he just got harder.

She repeated the whole boot-teeth-kick move on the other leg. There was only one move left in this famous dance.

Would she?

She flattened her palms on his chest, no doubt feeling the insane hammer of his heart. She drew her hands down, over his stomach, lingering on muscles with an appreciative moan.

"No hands," he reminded her. If she touched his dick, even just got within a hair's breath of it, he'd implode.

"No hands for you. Hands for me are fine." She unbuttoned his pants. Unzipped his fly. Spread his boxers and out he came, as massive and hard as he could ever remember, a swollen, throbbing, desperate dick that owned him right now. "But tongue is even better."

He almost broke the armrest, his breath jagged and furious now. Sweat trickled down one temple, rolled down his back, soaked his balls.

She zeroed in on his cock, sliding her body lower, her thighs dragging over his, her breasts scorching his chest, her mouth inches from his jutting hard-on. He couldn't stand it anymore. He seized the hat and pulled it off, taking some hairs with it as she let out a small cry of dismay.

She looked up at him, the netting barrier gone, her face completely familiar, and shockingly beautiful.

Vivi.

Instantly she put her face back down, hiding herself.

The song reached a crescendo. The plane reached cruising altitude. And she reached his shiny wet tip and—"Oh, my God, Viv—"

Licked.

The lights went out in his head.

CHAPTER 4

Vivi knew she'd gone too far. She shouldn't make him come.

The bone-deep scary thing was, she couldn't stop. In fact, when she closed her mouth over Lang's glorious, masculine, pulsing erection, Vivi was so turned on she was shaking harder than he was.

So she sucked, the size and sweetness of his hard-on making her head light. For the first time—for the very first time—she felt the ecstasy of making this man helpless with desire.

For the first time, sex didn't threaten her, it thrilled her. That was why she couldn't stop. That and the fact that she'd secretly fantasized about kissing, touching, devouring Lang with her mouth. She was a starved, starved woman and Colton Cautious Lang was a ten-course gourmet meal.

He climaxed viciously, warm liquid filling her mouth as he grunted and groaned, gripping the armrests, giving in to her completely. He swore, he moaned, he took a few heavenly deities' names in vain, but he didn't say *her* name.

If that didn't prove to prying eyes and hidden microphones that she was willing to do whatever it took to convince anyone that she was Cara Ferrari, then nothing would.

Way in the back of her sex-addled brain, she had to remember that was the reason for this reckless behavior.

She could hear his strained breathing, her pounding pulse, and the cry of the engines just behind them.

She kept her mouth on his hard-on, unable to let go, even after his juices slid down her throat. Part of her didn't want to release him. Part of her didn't want to *face* him.

Why the hell was he here, anyway? Was there a real threat to Cara or was he just the lucky lotto winner of the FBI babysitting job? That was unlikely, considering his level in the Bureau.

She'd find out. And when she did, she'd also explain why she'd chosen sex to silence him. He was an FBI agent, and he should understand doing "whatever it takes" when undercover.

She had to keep him quiet, and that, she continued to rationalize, was the *only reason* she had stripped and sucked him to an orgasm.

The only reason? *Ignore that, St. Peter.*

His hands threaded into her hair. If he felt thoroughly enough, he'd find the extensions. If he looked long enough at her face, he'd see the little piece of porcelain that fixed her chipped tooth and the makeup that covered her nose piercing and the padding at the bottom of the bra that took her into C-cup land.

All the trappings that made this act, well, an act. None of this was real.

Except the salty sweet taste of his release, the sound of his strangled breaths, the smell of sweat and leather and Lang, and, holy hell, the hot knot of need between her legs. All that was very real.

Slowly, she lifted her head, used her extra-long acrylic tips to wipe gently under her lips, the move clearly killing him as he grunted and dropped his head back helplessly.

He still couldn't talk, fighting to calm his breathing and his heart, a sheen of sweat all over his face. She pulled herself up and put her mouth near his ear, hoping anyone watching through a camera would imagine this was the secret whispering of pillow talk.

"You owe me now." She breathed the words so only he could hear.

He tried to shake his head.

"Yes, you do. I need a promise. I need your word. Don't say my name for the duration of this flight and we'll call it even. Don't accuse me of being a fake, don't try to trick me, don't do anything until we are somewhere entirely private."

"You mean we're not?" He whispered the question, but the briefest note of horror came through.

"I don't know. And, Lang, everything that ever mattered in the whole world to me or my family is resting on this." She was certain no microphone, no matter how close, could pick up the words she whispered. "Do you understand?"

She finally drew back, trusting him to follow the instructions.

"I don't understand anything right now."

She smiled at the admission, not something she'd hear often from Lang. "Then maybe you should go in the bathroom and clean up. You know, take a shower." When he frowned she returned to his ear. "Make a lot of noise with the water, do a thorough check for hidden cameras or mics, and then maybe we can talk. Maybe."

She didn't wait for his response but slid back to her chair, drawing up her legs and wrapping her arms around them.

He gave her a long, hard look while zipping up his pants but not buttoning them. "Excuse me, then," he said. The little words of polite chivalry tweaked her heart. Then he leaned over, his mouth on top of hers, so close she thought he'd kiss her, but he didn't. "Get your ass in there, woman."

A gentleman who knew how to throw around commands.

As he walked away, little Stella popped out from the other side of the bed, her glassy eyes wide, no doubt scarred for life from all the sex and confusion. Vivi expected Lang to step over the dog, but he picked her up, petting her head once, then setting her on the bed.

A dog lover. A gentleman. A sex machine. Couldn't he do something to make her hate him?

Oh, right, he already had. He was on this plane and jeopardizing her and her family's future. Why? And, oh Lord, how could she make him promise to keep her identity secret—as she'd promised Cara she would?

Shit. She closed her eyes, but all she could see was him.

So she'd finally had her secret fantasy fulfilled and half the time he wasn't even sure it was her. And when he finally knew, without a doubt, he *came*.

What did that say about Lang's feelings for her?

Nothing. It said he was a normal red-blooded male who was getting his cock sucked off by a woman made up like a hooker. A woman who *teased* him.

Her stomach rolled a little, and not because the plane banked.

Was that the real reason she'd thrown caution to the wind and played her little game with the man who made her crazy? Because he was probably the safest man she'd ever met. So this was the first time she could—

No, she couldn't. That barrier couldn't be breached, no matter how much she wanted him. That old pain was always too close to the surface.

"It's Lang," she whispered to herself, forcing her brain to go to its usual litany of don't-even-think-about-its when she got lost in her daydreams about him. He was an FBI geek. Uptight Dudley Do-Right. And, let's not forget, a major client of the Guardian Angelinos.

Usually those admonitions did the trick to crush her crush. Today, her crush was having none of it. And her body was having a throbbing, aching, ardent field day.

She heard the shower start in the small bathroom. She prayed Cara hadn't wired the bathroom. That was something only a truly paranoid person would do. Who was she kidding? That was just the kind of thing Cara would do. But she and Lang had to talk and, like it or not, the bathroom was looking like their best option.

Pushing up from the seat and crossing the small cabin, she grabbed the yellow dress she'd considered wearing before deciding underwear was more expedient for keeping Lang's questions to a minimum.

She slipped the dress over her, looking at Stella, who growled when Vivi's head popped through the top, obviously expecting the rightful owner of the dress.

"Sorry, Stell. It's still just me."

Stella dropped her head on the comforter, her eyes full of distaste as she watched Vivi tap on the bathroom door.

"It's unlocked," Lang said.

She opened the door and froze at the sight of Lang behind glass. Sheesh. She hadn't meant for him to *really* take a shower.

He opened the door, giving her a full view of his magnificently naked and wet body. Her breath caught in her lungs. He was so not playing fair.

"Come on in." He smoked her with a look, untempered with anything resembling a smile. He was serious. He was naked. He was gorgeous.

"My makeup will come off," she said.

He reached out and yanked her in, right under the stream. "Precisely my plan," he said over her gasp of surprise.

She sputtered and tried to dodge the water, but he held her head, letting the water sluice down. She had to close her eyes as the mascara flowed and the false eyelashes became nothing but wet black spiders sliding down her cheek.

"What the hell, Lang?"

"What the hell is right, Angelino."

She jerked out of the water and swiped the wet hair and stray lashes off her face. "Don't say my name. And don't grab me like that."

"I've cleaned the room. There is no hidden camera, no microphone, no nothing. We're alone."

"Then why the shower?"

He dropped his gaze to her soaking body, lingering where the thin yellow fabric molded to her breasts. "I wanted to see you wet."

She swallowed, all her lovely control in the cabin washed away in the shower. "You wanted me off guard."

He raised his muscular shoulder, even more impressive without his usual golf shirt covering it. "Then we're even. What the hell is going on?"

"You tell me," she insisted, still keeping her voice down despite the water noise and his assurances. "What are you doing here?"

He scrutinized her hard and long, pushing the hair back off her face. "It is you," he finally said, no small amount of relief in his voice.

"You weren't sure?" She couldn't help smiling. "I do deserve an Oscar."

"Why did you do that to me?"

"I had to keep you quiet, Lang. I had to stop the questions and demands. Cara has cameras or hidden microphones all over this plane, if you had said anything you would have blown my cover and this job before takeoff."

"So you blew *me* and risked my job instead?"

"I had to think fast and . . . it worked."

Something flickered over his face. Or he had water in his eye; she couldn't tell. But he wasn't happy, that much was clear. "All I care about is doing my job and doing it right," he said.

"Me too. And I'd say by your response, I did it right."

"You bamboozled me."

She couldn't help smiling. "Never heard it called that."

His eyes, golden green again instead of dark with lust like they were ten minutes ago, narrowed like the eyes of an angry lion, any hope of humor gone. "You took a huge risk."

"What, no seat belt during takeoff?"

"Don't joke about this, damn it. Another man could have raped you."

The words slugged her. She opened her mouth to argue, then shut it, and not because water poured into her mouth. Another man could have. "But it wasn't another man— it was you." And that was the real reason she'd chosen sex for silence, wasn't it? Because she trusted him, and she wanted him. "I got the job done," she said softly. "I needed to not blow my cover."

"Well, I needed not to blow my wad, sweetheart, since it's generally frowned upon in the line of duty."

"Sometimes rules need to be broken, Lang."

He put his hands on her shoulders, pressing her against the shower wall, his face inches from her, his bare chest skimming her dripping dress. "Rules exist for a reason. You follow them because when you don't, you die. Is that clear?"

She lifted her chin, determined not to let him intimidate and overpower her. "You would have said my name and I couldn't let that happen."

"Is. That. Clear?" His nostrils flared and she could feel his breath on her face.

"You made your point. But we don't agree and you don't happen to be my client on this assignment."

He clenched his jaw so hard she could hear his teeth grind. "Where *is* your client?"

She shrugged, her mouth slammed shut. His grip tightened on her shoulders.

"Where, Vivi?"

She shook her head.

"Goddamn it!"

"Look, even *if* I knew, I couldn't tell you."

"You don't know?" Fury sparked in his eyes.

"It doesn't matter if I do or don't, I've signed a nondisclosure—an over-the-top nondisclosure, I might add—and I can't reveal anything about my assignment to anyone—not even the FBI."

He stared hard at her, searching her face, thinking.

"Then she probably won't be too happy when you get off this plane in Nantucket cuffed and arrested for obstruction of justice."

She sputtered some shower water. "Why? She hired a body double. That's not breaking the law or obstructing anything."

"The FBI is providing protection for her."

"What happened that put you guys on such high alert? A threat? A copycat?"

"Didn't she tell you?"

Goddamn Cara Ferrari and her secrets. "Tell me what?"

"There's new evidence."

"Of what? The possibility of a real serial killer?" Up to this moment, Vivi hadn't bought the media hype, especially after everything she'd read about the prior deaths. Except for the Oscar win, there was no pattern at all, absolutely no evidence that linked the deaths.

"A possibility, yes." Lang shook water off his face, stepping out of the stream. Vivi had to work not to let her eyes follow the water as it cascaded over the dusting of dark curls on his chest, down his six-pack abs, down to his—

Damn it. She lost the fight and looked.

He wasn't completely hard anymore, but the nest was dark and his manhood was still swollen and although she was no expert, pretty impressive. What would that feel like...

He tipped her chin up to look at him. "You've had enough for one day."

Heat burned her cheeks as she stepped under the spray. "I hate you."

"Yeah, I can see that."

"You know I was acting before."

"Like you said, Oscar worthy."

She gave him a harsh look. "But *you* weren't. You liked it."

"That's an understatement, Vivi, but—"

She put her hand on his mouth. "You cannot call me that. It's Cara. Or"—she dropped her gaze one more time—"nothing at all."

"Are you trying to bribe me with sex? Because that *is* against the law."

She let out a sigh, finally managing to escape his grip. "Please, just tell me why you're here and what evidence the FBI has."

"The FBI task force discovered two hairs that might connect the first two victims. Since Cara is supposed to be headed to Nantucket, which is under the jurisdiction of the Boston office, I was asked to protect her and investigate anyone who comes near her. Especially anyone wearing a wig." He slid his hand into her wet hair. "Anyone."

"These are extensions and I am sure as hell not your perp." She pulled away and let his hand drag through the length of an extension so expertly woven into her own hair that it would take an act of God to pull one out. "Why you?"

He hesitated a second. "The orders came out of L.A."

He made it sound as though that should answer her question. "And—what—they're trying you out for the job you want?"

"In essence, yes."

Oh, that was just great. "So your success in protecting Cara will impact your ability to get this promotion you want so much."

"Yep."

Shit. "Seems we both have a lot at stake." She reached for the door, but he pulled her back.

"Yes, we do. Because if there really is a serial killer, you just put your family's future, your business, *and* your life on the line. Why the hell would you do that, Vivi?"

She stepped away, plucking a false eyelash off her cheek. "I think we covered my attraction to risk and your aversion to it. But, sorry, I'm not doing anything that any good Guardian Angelino wouldn't do. This is my job and I'm going to do it."

Disgust and frustration practically rocked him. "Where is she?"

"Sorry, but I don't know." She tried to escape again, to no avail.

"Do you have a number for her?"

Yeah, ten million dollars if she breathed a word. "No." Which wasn't a lie. She only had a number for her assistant. "Please, Lang. If you give me away, she'll crucify me professionally and personally. I honestly don't know where she is, and that's the way she wants it for her own personal safety, which, as her security professional, is my top priority. I'm going to her house in Nantucket to let the media think that's where she is, and if that brings a killer to the door, then I'll catch him."

He took her wrists in his hands and raised them over her head, bracing her against the slick shower wall, immobilizing her with his power and size. "You are *not* going to be bait for a killer."

She almost buckled under the vulnerability of her position. But she couldn't let him know that. Wouldn't give him the satisfaction. Instead, she looked up at him, digging deep for the power she needed when a man—any man—even thought about pinning her. She couldn't take it.

"Let me go, Lang." She ground out the words, her throat closing more with each passing second.

"You are not—"

"Let me go!" She jerked her hands so hard that he had to let go, his eyes widening at her raised voice. She shook her wrist, despising herself for the outburst and the sense of helplessness. "I don't answer to you and you cannot tell me what to do," she said, steadying her voice. "So don't even try. And do not ever grab me like that again."

"Then I'll blow your cover and force her out."

"Which just makes *her* bait for a killer."

He sucked in a breath to respond, then blew it out, obviously seeing the sense of that argument, so she pushed it. "If you want to protect her, let her stay hidden. Just pretend you don't know I'm Vivi and let's do this together."

He turned away, his hand on the faucet, ready to turn it off, the internal debate raging on his features. "If I protect you, then I put her in danger."

"I don't need protecting."

The look he gave her said he disagreed.

"What I need is your cooperation. We can do this together, Lang. If you cover for me, we can pull this off together."

"I don't want to pull anything off except catch the son of a bitch who's killing movie stars."

"Are you sure there is one? Two hairs isn't exactly ironclad evidence."

He shrugged his shoulders. "We have to work under the belief that it is."

"If that's the case, then all the more reason to keep her location hidden."

He looked straight up into the spray, letting the now icy water pour over his face. Then he got out, grabbed a towel, and left without another word.

She turned off the water, stepped out of the shower, and let out a low moan at the sight of her bedraggled, smeared, soaked self. Bridget had taught her how to apply the makeup and lashes, but, damn, it would take her at least two hours to put Cara back together again.

In the meantime, it was almost midnight on the West Coast and she was toast. After washing her face and towel-drying her hair, she slipped on a robe and returned to the cabin, surprised at how disappointed she was to find it empty.

And he took the dog, proof that he had a powerful protective streak. But who would he protect: her or Cara—or his own pending promotion?

At 6:00 a.m., Vivi finished the process of transforming herself, dressing in a much more reasonable T-shirt and low-rise jeans—still had to wear heels, though, as Cara didn't own a pair of sneakers—and emerged into the sunlight of the main cabin. The copilot leaned against a bulkhead, a cup of coffee in his hand, chatting with Lang, who reclined on one of the large chairs, his own coffee steaming on a table in front of him. In the seat next to him Stella snoozed contentedly. Little traitor.

"Are we landing soon?" she asked, pointing at the boomerang-shaped island off to the left and recognizing it as Nantucket.

The copilot pushed off from his comfortable position

to greet her. "We most certainly are, Ms. Ferrari. Good to see you."

She gave him her best Cara smile, her heart jumping. Lang had actually done as she asked?

"And you," she replied.

"Would you like coffee?" he asked. Lang still didn't so much as turn to look at her.

"Yes, please."

As the copilot set off for the galley area, she took a slow, steadying breath, then walked over to take the seat facing Lang, forcing him to look at her. Would he remember that every word might be monitored? Or follow his well-worn rule book one more time?

"Good morning, Assistant Special Agent in Charge Lang."

He almost smiled, giving her another measure of relief. Her usual butchering of his title was a long-standing inside joke. If Cara heard, she'd have no idea of the verbal wink she'd just given Lang.

"Mr. Lang will do," he said dryly.

She searched his face, seeing nothing but a look of exhaustion in his hazel eyes, a stark contrast to his clean-shaven face. No crisis on earth or in the air would keep Lang from shaving.

"Did you get any sleep?" she asked.

"I worked out a plan." He lifted the cup and drank his coffee, studying her over the rim.

"A plan? That sounds intriguing."

"We'll talk about it when we land. We'll drive to the house in an FBI vehicle."

In other words, a safe car where they could talk openly.

"Thank you," she said softly as she continued to choose

every word for its possible interpretation by her client. "I appreciate you working with me on this."

He just nodded and turned to the window as the copilot brought her coffee on a tray, cream and sugar, and a platter of fruit and croissants. "Would have served you this earlier, Ms. Ferrari, but Mr. Lang suggested we let you rest."

She thanked him and pushed the tray toward Lang. "Help yourself."

But he just rose and headed toward the bathroom, and Stella jumped off her seat to follow him.

Either he wasn't talking to her because he was still furious about last night, or he was intentionally keeping silent while they were under surveillance. How difficult would it be to live under a microscope in Nantucket?

Well, that was what she'd signed up for, Vivi thought as she bit into a juicy strawberry. She just hadn't signed up to do it with Lang.

He returned when they started the descent, buckling up and laughing softly when Stella jumped on his lap.

"Looks like you have a friend," Vivi said.

He petted the dog, his big hand surprisingly masculine in the gentle gesture. "I love dogs."

"Do you?" How did she not know that about Lang? "Do you have one?"

"Can't. I'm gone too much," he replied. "I had the last one trained, and he did okay staying with my—"He looked out the window. "My dog died and I didn't want to break in a new one."

The possibility that every conversation was monitored stopped her from asking anything but the most mundane question. "What kind of dog was it?" she asked. Not the question she wanted to ask.

He did okay staying with my—his what? Girlfriend?

"Golden." He gave her a wry smile. "A guy's dog."

"Unlike Stella," she said with a laugh. "An actress's dog."

"She's a good kid." He petted her again, and Stella looked up at him with adoring eyes. She'd forgotten Cara Ferrari and found a new love. "You're a good kid, right, Stell?"

The exchange was so endearing. And encouraging. Surely a man that sweet with dogs would not let her business and life fold under the weight of a ten-million-dollar debt just because he didn't agree with her methods—would he?

Hard to tell with Dudley D. He clearly chose the conventional path when faced with an option. And Vivi avoided the conventional path by nature.

"I have agents to meet us when we land," he said.

"Agents from the Boston office?" Not good. They'd recognize her from work the Guardian Angelinos had done for the FBI for sure.

"No, these are agents who are in a satellite office out in Cape Cod."

In other words, she was safe.

"They'll escort you past the media. Under the circumstances, we're keeping media out of the terminal in Nantucket. They'll be approximately forty to fifty feet away."

And none of those reporters, or fans, would know she wasn't Cara Ferrari. "Thank you," she said again, sipping her coffee. "Will the agents stay?"

"We'll discuss that later."

Right now, she had to focus on getting to the house as Cara Ferrari.

The landing gear dropped and the airfield came into sight. Almost immediately she could see the penned-in crowd, as heavy as it had been in L.A., despite the early hour. After they landed, the pilot and copilot handled her luggage, said good-bye, and dropped the stairs. She checked her phone—nothing from Cara and crew—then pulled on a baseball cap that had been packed in the bag and slid on sunglasses.

"I'm ready," she said to Lang. "Let's do this."

"You're missing something," he said.

She tapped the hat and sunglasses, did a mental inventory of her bag. "Oh, jeez. I guess I should carry it." She stuffed her hand into the bag and pulled out the Oscar.

"I meant woman's best friend." He lifted Stella from the floor and gave the wiggling dog to Vivi.

"I think she'd rather be with her new best friend."

He shook his head. "That won't fly in your pictures, Ms. Ferrari."

"You can call me Cara," she said, giving him a grateful look, then snuggling the dog, who wanted no part of her. "Hey, pooch, help me out here." She buried her face in Stella's neck. "If this big law-abiding FBI dude can fake it, so can you."

Stella rumbled a growl and Lang, damn him, actually smiled in collusion.

Two men and a woman waited at the bottom of the steps. If their serious expressions and conservative dress didn't give them away as FBI agents, the holstered Glocks on their hips certainly did.

Lang nodded to them, then put a hand on Vivi's back to lead her down the stairs, toward the noise, cheers, questions, and flashbulbs.

The pressure of his hand increased when she hesitated. "One step at a time, Cara," he said into her ear, sending a chill straight down to the toes crammed into pointed shoes. "This is just another Oscar-winning performance for you."

With that, she lifted the hand not holding Stella, waved the Oscar the way she'd seen Cara do, then strode toward the waiting car, aware of the agents shooting glances at her.

Had she passed the test with them? When they reached the car, a simple black limo, the other agents fell away and Lang ushered her into the back, then reached for Stella.

"Let me give the dog and statuette to them," he said, motioning to the other agents. "They'll take care of both."

She looked up, surprised at the suggestion, then Lang pointed to her collar and lifted a brow. A listening device in Stella's collar? Or the Oscar? Could Cara be that clever?

She handed both to him, then slid across the bench, noticing the plastic barrier between the back and driver. The trunk slammed as someone loaded her bag, then Lang returned, and they were cocooned in silence.

"This is one of our cars," he said, settling into the seat with his back to the driver. "Completely bulletproof and soundproofed, and not a single possibility you're being heard by anyone but me." He tapped on the glass behind him with his knuckles. "Not even him. So we can talk."

"So what's your plan?" Vivi asked.

"I have to tell Joseph Gagliardi, the assistant director in Los Angeles, and his task force that Cara sent a body double."

She let out a soft grunt of frustration and disappointment.

"Why? Why do you have to tell anyone? Can't you just pretend you don't know who I am?"

"No." Zero room for argument in that one syllable. "I don't *pretend* with my boss."

"Would-be boss," she corrected.

"On this assignment, I report to him. We'll tell them, explain the nondisclosure situation and—"

"That's not good enough."

"Vivi, this isn't a negotiation," he said, leaning forward to skewer her with a dark, unwavering look. "It's my way or the highway."

"Don't throw your 1950s clichés at me. There's always another way."

He was silent for a second, his seething still in check. "Okay, what do you suggest?"

"I told you—just pretend you don't know me."

"I can't do that, Vivi. We're on record as associates, I use your firm all the time, and I can't and won't play dumb. It'll come back and bite us both in the ass."

"If anyone else were on this case, I could have pulled this off."

He cocked his head in acknowledgment. "True enough. You look like her. You might have fooled someone who doesn't know you. But I'm on this case and that changes everything."

It certainly did. Vivi turned to look out the window at the sunrise over the sea of reporters. "Let me talk to Cara."

"You can talk to her?"

"I can get a message to her. Let me explain that you've found evidence to suggest a connection between the first two deaths, which has brought the FBI in—"

"She knows that."

And didn't tell me. So much for client confidence. "I'll tell her they sent an agent who knows me," she said. Would that fly with Cara Ferrari? She was unpredictable, and Vivi had no way of knowing how she'd respond. Ten million dollars because the FBI sent someone who knew Vivi? That didn't seem fair.

Cara probably didn't give a flying pig about fair.

"You can have until this afternoon," Lang said, sounding like he was giving her a concession on a silver platter.

"Which is what—five o'clock?"

"Twelve-o-one p.m. Eastern time."

She smiled. "Of course, I forgot who I'm dealing with."

"You have six hours, Vivi. We call the FBI at noon."

"Noon-o-one, Mr. By the Book."

"Don't knock what you haven't tried." His phone rang and he took the call, speaking softly about a drug raid in the South End, staying on the phone until the limo slowed at a set of wrought-iron gates in front of a walled-in property, the evergreens thick enough that she could see only the roof and some chimneys from a large home tucked way off the road.

A pack of reporters already waited in the driveway, creating a block at the gate. They were pushed back by men she assumed were more FBI agents. Once on the property, they followed a long and winding drive to an enormous country French–style house. A few hundred feet away, another, smaller, version of the same house was tucked into the wooded lot, connected to the main house by a long, enclosed walkway.

The car rolled over the brick pavers, then drove around the side of the house to a parking garage.

Lang helped Vivi climb out of the car and guided her into the house, pausing in a large utility room.

"Stay here and wait for me. I want to talk to the other agents."

"Are you going to tell them?"

"At noon-o-one," he said, disappearing back into the garage.

He hadn't been gone five seconds when the door to the rest of the house popped open and a woman appeared and stared at Vivi. She looked about sixty years old, with curly once-blonde-now-bland hair pulled back into a severe bun. Her eyes were vivid blue, her skin weathered, her smile—well, there was no smile.

"You're an excellent choice," she finally said.

The housekeeper who knew all.

"Mercedes Graff," the woman confirmed with a tight nod, still scrutinizing Vivi. "Where's the *Hund*?"

"Excuse me?"

"The dog."

"Stella? Oh, they're bringing her."

"One drop of urine in this house and she's outside," Mercedes said. "And she will not sleep in your bed."

Vivi almost laughed. "No worries there." The woman pointed forward. "This way."

"One of the FBI agents is bringing my luggage."

"They'll stay in the guesthouse," she said, as if Vivi's statement meant nothing. "I'll show you to your room."

Not a chance she was going to piss off Lang when they were in the middle of such delicate negotiations. The last thing she wanted to do was lose the few hours she'd bought in the limo.

"I'll wait for him."

Mercedes looked disgusted as she marched past Vivi and opened the door to the garage; it was empty. "He's gone to the guesthouse." She turned and got right in Vivi's face. "This would be a good opportunity for us to talk privately. About Cara."

Maybe *she* could tell Vivi where Cara was, something she wouldn't do with Lang on their heels. And if Vivi got that information, it might make up for not following his orders. "Okay. Let's go."

They walked out into a wide hallway, heading to the right, away from a large kitchen in the other direction.

"This is the main living area," the other woman said, indicating the back of the house, giving Vivi a glimpse of luxury, all decorated in the ubiquitous shades of yellow. "My quarters are downstairs, below the kitchen and utility room. The first floor is for living and lounging, with several guest suites, and upstairs is your exclusive domain. The pool is private and completely inaccessible from the outside, so if you want to be seen from a distance, I suggest the balcony from your upstairs living room or take a drive."

Mercedes was obviously in the know on the whole deal. And no doubt every word she overheard Vivi say would go straight to her boss.

In a vestibule at the top of the stairs, an oil painting of a fog-shrouded landscape dominated one wall across from a set of mahogany double doors. They opened to a dreamy sort of paradise, with a bank of windows looking out toward the ocean. The sprawling living area was decorated in the usual color, but pale in this room, more buttery than lemon.

"There's a small kitchen over there, with an office and

complete gym, and this way is your bedroom." Mercedes took her under an arched threshold, to a plush room with a massive California king bed at the center. Across from it, a fireplace took up most of the wall.

All lovely, but not important to Vivi. "What did you want to tell me about Cara?"

"That is a closet," she said, opening another door that led to a room the size of a small country, completely stocked with clothes and more nightmarish shoes, a chaise longue, and a three-way dressing mirror. "And here is the bathroom."

Dropped down from Mount Olympus by the Goddess of Decadence.

"I could get used to that tub," Vivi said, eyeing the Jacuzzi that took up a third of the room, a floor-to-ceiling, wall-to-wall mirror behind it. A flash of Lang in that tub tortured her for a second.

"There's a steam room and sauna, of course."

Of course. "What did you want to tell me about Cara?"

She just gave her a blank look. "I wanted to show you her rooms."

"That's not…" Vivi shook her head, knowing a brick wall when she saw one. "Do you know where she is?"

"No."

"Mercedes," she said softly. "This whole thing"—she waved a hand at her face to indicate the disguise—"is not about avoiding a curse or folklore or media speculation anymore."

"It never was," the woman said simply.

"There is evidence." She had to be very careful, because even if the walls didn't have eyes and ears, this woman did. Everything she said could go right back to

Cara. "Additional evidence that there could be a connection between the deaths of Isobel DeSoto and Adrienne Dwight."

Still an expressionless stare was the only response.

"That means," Vivi said slowly, "Cara is in genuine danger."

She blinked. "I thought that's why you're here."

"It is, but the authorities . . . will need to know where she is. Soon." Like at one minute after noon today.

"They don't need to know. You're here and you've obviously fooled at least one FBI agent. I have no intention of letting out the truth about who you are."

"I need to talk to her, Mercedes. Please."

"Contact Marissa Hunter. That's the only way to speak with Karen—er, Cara."

She wasn't going to get anywhere badgering this woman. Not yet, anyway. "If you hear from her, will you tell me? Immediately?"

She barely nodded. "Now you just get situated and comfortable and your bags will be up shortly."

She left the room and Vivi headed to use the bathroom, locking the door in case Lang came barreling up to let her have it for leaving the utility room. She paused at the mirror, startled for a split second at her own image, still not used to her new reflection.

Leaning on the counter, she got closer, looking at her face. This disguise was supposed to be from a distance, or under a hat and sunglasses. She couldn't fool Lang, and she probably couldn't fool those other agents if they spent time here.

She just had to hope Cara would understand that new evidence changed everything and the FBI could be trusted. Exhaustion and jet lag pressed down on her and a muscle throbbed at the base of her neck, as it always did when things weren't quite right. Since she was a teenager, since...that night...she'd carried her stress in her neck and she usually listened to that miserable muscle when it screamed at her.

Like it was doing now.

She dropped her head forward to stretch her neck, the weight of all the fake hair making it worse. Closing her eyes, she reached up to rub the throbbing pain, bending farther over the sink, tempted by the faucets just inches away. Was it too soon to take off all the crap off her face and—

The force from behind knocked her right into the mirror as one hand slammed over her mouth and another yanked her head farther into her chest with brute strength.

A scream bubbling up with a flash of revulsion and horror triggered by the crush of a man from behind.

She fought the panic, managing to flip her elbow around and get a dig into the ribs of her attacker. The jab of a gun in her back made her freeze.

"Welcome home, Cara."

CHAPTER 5

How the hell did you find this place?" Cara stepped into the cool morning air, the pungent, distinctive smell of salt air clearing her head from the hours of travel and a few milligrams of Xanax.

Next to her on the wide porch, her sister gave a smug shrug. "This is me you're talking about." She lifted a steaming mug to her mouth, her brown hair getting frizzier by the moment this close to the sea. Dry California air was much kinder to Joellen's kinks. "I'm the original miracle worker."

Or so she liked to think. No doubt Marissa had dug it up and paid a small fortune out of Cara's bank account for it. A hundred yards away, the surf crashed on a wide beach, the dunes blocking the view to the left and right. "It's so private."

"That's the idea, sister mine. You're safe here."

Cara turned to eye Joellen. "This is not Nantucket."

She shook her head, sharpening mud-brown eyes. "And they say you're not bright."

They did? Or she did? "My guess is the Vineyard or Cape Cod, close enough but not on the island crawling with media." And other people.

"You don't want to take the chance of being on Nantucket," Jo said, avoiding the question. "Not even to see Stella."

At the mention of her dog, Cara let out a sad sigh. No one had been able to find a dog that matched her baby, and it would have been weird for "Cara" to be seen without Stella. And if *he* saw, he'd know that woman wasn't Cara.

"I'm going with the Vineyard," she said, based on the color of the sand and the height of the dune grass. She'd been born and raised on Nantucket; these islands off the coast of Cape Cod were in her blood.

"You don't need to know where we are, hon." Joellen took a step closer and put a patronizing hand on Cara's arm. "You'll slip and tell someone. And he'll find out. You know he'll do everything to hunt you down, with his god-awful—hired help. You know he has those minions everywhere, all willing to do anything to—"

"Stop." Cara held up her hand. She hated when Joellen talked about it. "I won't tell anyone anything. I haven't yet, and I won't."

"But now he has an excuse to kill you, Cara, and never risk getting blamed."

Cara gripped the railing as a wave rolled through her with the same power as the surf. Just a little travel nausea mixed with Xanax and Oscar fatigue, she told herself. Not fear.

Didn't he know she'd never risk her career by telling anyone anything? Even those creepy FBI agents who'd come to her house last month, mentioning his name, scrutinizing her for any response? She'd just played dumb. She'd *acted* dumb. Because Joellen was right about one thing: She *was* the smart sister, *and* she could act. And this was the role of her lifetime.

But still he'd want to get rid of her, just in case. Now he could lay her death at the feet of the Red Carpet Killer, a fact so loaded with irony she could laugh, except it just wasn't funny.

There had to be a way out of this; she just hadn't figured it out yet.

"Are you sure no one knows we're here?" Cara asked her sister.

"I'm sure," Joellen said, dropping onto a chaise and propping up her feet like royalty. "First, the free world thinks you're in Nantucket. Second, Leon and Bridget are a few miles away. Marissa and I will be the go-betweens, and God knows Mercedes has everything under control over in Nantucket. You can relax."

"I don't want to relax," Cara said. She wanted to figure a way out of the mess she'd gotten into.

"I know," Joellen said, lifting her foot to pick at her pedicure. "You want to celebrate. Too bad the Red Carpet Curse had to ruin all that fun for you."

Cara glanced at her sister. Had she already had a drink, or maybe she just hadn't slept enough on the flight here? "Yeah, too bad."

"And too bad he has an excuse if you end up dead."

Cara closed her eyes, sick of how Joellen kept harping on it. She *knew*, already. "He'd have to be pretty clever to make it look like an accident or not leave any evidence."

Her sister snorted. "He *is* clever, Cara."

"Then why hasn't he killed me before this?" she shot back.

"Because the FBI wasn't on his ass. You know damn well they've practically got him. He's being smart now, but you are the wild card, sister mine."

She closed her eyes and shook her head. "You know as well as I do that I have no intention of ruining my career with that kind of scandal."

"Then why don't you just give him what he wants and get out of it?"

"Because I don't trust him. He'd still want me dead." A chill crawled down Cara's arms despite the hoodie she'd been wearing since she'd gotten on the small private jet that had brought them...wherever they were. She backed away from the railing and perched on the other chair. "I'm scared, Jo."

"You don't have to be," she said. "We've been through worse. And we were younger, and dumber."

"Hey, where are you two?" Marissa's voice reached the porch, the front door slamming behind her. "We've got a problem."

"We've got a lot of them," Joellen said bitterly.

"What is it, Marissa?"

"Leon just called. He's monitoring all the media. The 'bodyguards' who are supposed to be with fake Cara?" Marissa put her hand on her hips, thoroughly disgusted. "FBI agents, every one of them. One of the reporters identified them."

Joellen looked surprised and a little horrified, but Cara easily covered her reaction. Of course they already knew there was an FBI agent on the plane. That was why she'd come up with the whole escape plan and sent Vivi by herself.

But Marissa knew nothing about why they were really hiding, and Cara intended for it to stay that way. "As long as Vivi doesn't shoot her mouth off about being a body double, it's fine," Cara said. "Frankly, I don't care if the Secret Service is guarding her. If they don't know her she can pull it off. And it looks legit to have protection."

"You were very clear with her, Cara," Joellen said. "Maybe I ought to hop over there and keep an eye on things."

"I'll go for you," Marissa said quickly.

Cara shook her head. "I need you two here. And, call me crazy, but I trust that woman. At least I trust her not to break a nondisclosure that would ruin her life. And she totally fell for the secret listening devices, like I really had the ability to do something so James Bond–ish."

Joellen grinned. "It was brilliant—I gotta give you props."

Marissa came closer. "You look pale," she said. "And you seem upset."

Cara just eyed her, still unsure just how much of herself she could reveal to her awkward, but efficient, assistant.

"What she seems is in need of a cup of coffee." Joellen leaped off the chaise and gave the assistant a nudge. "Do your job and make it, Marissa."

Color rose in Marissa's long face, all the way up to her hairline, then she turned, going back inside.

"Why are you so nasty to her?" Cara asked. "She's just trying to be kind."

"She's got her hawk's beak too deep in your business."

Cara closed her eyes in disgust. As if Joellen had any room to make fun of other people's looks.

"Don't act like you're a fucking saint, Cara. You've called her butt ugly, too."

"I've also called her the best assistant I've ever had, so be nice to her. She knows a lot, too."

"Not everything. Let's send her away."

"No, I need you all with me. You're my support, my foundation." *My protection.*

"*I* am," Joellen corrected. "The rest of them are just hangers-on."

Cara gave her a blank look, holding her thoughts at bay. The rest of them had jobs to do, but Joellen was the *definition* of a hanger-on. "I just want everyone near me, and not the pretend version of me."

"Well, now she's got the FBI near her," Joellen said, heading inside. "So I hope you did the right thing by sending a total stranger into that situation."

"Of course I did," Cara said. "If he tries to kill her, he'll get caught."

"One of his hired guns will, you mean."

She cringed. "Who might not cover for him. The FBI will have something on him, and that's all they want."

"But your name will be dragged into it."

"But the media is obsessed with a Red Carpet Killer and I'll just look very smart for having a decoy take the hit for me."

"I hope you're right."

"I hope so, too."

When she was alone, Cara returned to the railing, looking out at the distinct blue gray of the Atlantic beyond the lower dunes. In the far distance, maybe a mile away, she thought she saw something glint, a split-second flash of light or glass. A camera? A gun scope?

Or her cursed imagination?

Could he have found her already? Or a Red Carpet Killer wannabe? She had that to worry about, too.

She peered again, seeing nothing but the edge of the world, sand, surf, and dune grass. No, she was fine.

Vivi Angelino, on the other hand, was a sitting duck.

"Just give it up, Cara," he breathed into Vivi's ear. "Just give it up, and you'll live."

He had her in a head lock, the solid, effortless grip of a man who knew exactly how to immobilize a victim. The pressure of his silencing hand, the threat of his heavy body, the wave of helpless vulnerability—and a cocktail of an old terror bubbled up, momentarily stealing her ability to think or fight or breathe.

"Tell me where it is and I'm gone, out the same way I got in, and everything is cool."

His voice was accented, a weird mix of an Asian tone with guttural English.

She still didn't move, all her options exploding in her head, too shocked to settle on one, too many questions to risk a fast, but dumb, move. The longer she stayed just like this, the longer she had to get those questions answered.

And for Lang to come up and kick the holy shit out of this guy.

"Come on, Cara. You know you can't win this. The whole game changed when you got that fucking Oscar. You're dead now. So just give it to me."

Give what to him?

"What do you want?" she asked into his hand, praying that he didn't realize it wasn't Cara's voice. Or this could be the last question she ever asked.

"You know what I want."

Cara might; Vivi didn't. With her head locked down, she couldn't see him, but he couldn't see her face.

"How did you get in here?"

He snorted softly. "Roman's alleys."

Roman Sallies?

He squeezed her. "Good thing, too, because the place is crawling with Feds." He dug a knee into the back of her legs. "We think that's a pretty ballsy move on your part."

We?

"You just open the door and let them in, like you are a complete innocent." He twisted her neck a little, jabbing the gun deeper at the same time. "Roman wants the fucking key, Cara."

What key?

She closed her eyes, taking a slow breath, trying so hard to think through her options and not about that gun. If this guy knew Cara well enough, and it sounded like he did, then he'd know she was a body double the minute he got a good look at her face.

But he kept her head locked down, as if he didn't want her to see him, either.

Where the hell was Lang?

Oh, shit, she'd locked the bathroom door! Then how had this guy gotten in? Had he been waiting for her?

Think, Vivi, think. Her gun. Her gun...it was deep in her bag, useless and far away.

"The key," he insisted.

She had to buy enough time for Lang to get up here. But then what? What would this guy do? "Listen, I don't—"

"Don't even try to lie." He jammed the gun. "Five seconds and you're a victim of the Red Carpet Killer."

"You're not a serial killer."

He grunted in her ear. "I fucking could be. Like Roman said, your little chess game changed when you got the gold."

Chess game?

"Now you have four seconds, Cara!"

She squeezed her eyes at the prod of the gun barrel deep into her ribs. She knew all too well the pain of a gunshot in the gut, the horror of that moment of near death. This time she wouldn't be so lucky.

If she screamed for help, she was dead. If she looked up at him, she was dead. If she moved, she was—

"Three!"

Very slowly, she lifted her head, keeping her eyes downcast until her face was directly in the mirror in front of both of them. She waited for his gasp, for the instant he realized she was not who he thought she was.

"Two!"

She met his eyes in the mirror. He didn't flinch, didn't react, not even a blink of surprise. He didn't know she wasn't Cara.

Emboldened by that, she tried to memorize his face, which was thick and puffy, definitely Asian, not more than thirty years old, shaved head, thick neck, and deadly looking.

"One second, Cara." He dragged the gun up her back, the barrel warm on the flesh of her neck, over her ear, against her temple. It was a Glock 19, she noticed, and far too steady and comfortable in his chunky hand. Fear burned her skin and tightened her stomach.

"Don't you see you're in a no-win situation?" His body smashed against hers, pushing her hipbones against the marble counter, making her want to retch. "You don't cooperate, you die. And then he gets what he wants anyway. So give me the fucking key and you can live."

They both jerked at the hard rap on the suite door. "Vivi! It's me."

Lang! She sucked in a breath, braced for death, but her captor scowled.

"Vivi? Who the fuck is that?"

"Like you said, we're crawling with Feds. You pull that trigger and you're toast."

He backed away, the first look of panic in his eyes. "You're not Cara."

"Vivi?" Lang knocked on the bedroom door. Would he walk into the suite? *Come on, Colton Lang. Charge your way in like the alpha stud I know you are.*

The man grabbed Vivi in an instant, pulling her deeper into the bathroom. He stabbed her side with the gun, wrapping a steel arm around her. Maybe he thought she was an FBI agent. Would he kill an FBI agent?

"Keep him out," he ordered in a harsh whisper. "Or you're dead."

She heard the bedroom door open, soft steps on the floor. *Come on, Lang.*

"I should have known you wouldn't stay put." Lang tapped on the bathroom door. "You in there?"

The man clutched her tighter, the smell of sweat and fear emanating from him now.

"Yeah," she answered in her weakest voice. Would Lang notice if she seemed out of character? Or would he think she was just trying to pretend to be Cara? Or, hell, maybe he'd just be a gentleman and give her privacy in the bathroom.

Please don't be a gentleman. Not this time.

"I have your bag," he said. "And I made a decision."

She didn't reply and the man gave her another harsh squeeze, standing behind her to use her as a human shield.

"Talk!" he ordered in a hot breath.

"Oh, okay." She did her best to sound lifeless and disinterested. That had to be a major clue to Lang.

"You want to know what it is?"

What would she normally say and do? She'd kick that door open and say, Hells to the nine I do, Lang. What did *you* decide *I* should do? That's what he expected, right?

"Whatever you want," she said meekly. From behind her, the man intensified his grip, the gun so deep into her it practically cracked her rib. "It doesn't matter to me."

"Tell him to leave you alone," he demanded, again in a voiceless whisper.

"Are you okay?" Lang asked.

Thank God he was perceptive. *Now open the door, big guy, and be a hero.*

But she'd locked the door.

"I'm fine," she said, getting another brutal squeeze and a shake of the gun as if she might have forgotten it was sticking into her kidney. "I just want to be alone now."

"Are you sick?" he asked.

"I'm just...you know..." What? Her mind went blank.

No clever clues, no brilliant secret messages. "I'm… busy."

The man put his lips right on her ear. "Get rid of him."

"Just leave me alone, Lang. I don't care what you decided. It doesn't matter to me."

No answer, just a long silence. Too long. He had to know something was wrong. She would never say that.

"All right," he finally said, his voice as defeated as hers.

No! No, it is not all right, damn it.

"I'll be downstairs. Come down when you're ready and want to talk."

How could he be so dense?

"Okay," she said, sounding as lifeless and lethargic as she knew how. If that wasn't a cry for help, then she didn't know what was. Surely Lang wouldn't think that was normal.

But why would he ever imagine that someone was in the bathroom holding her captive?

"Talk to you later, then," he said, his footsteps definitely going the wrong way.

She wanted to scream but didn't make a sound or movement as the bedroom door slammed shut.

"Who the fuck are you?" the man demanded, spinning her around and pointing the gun in her face.

"FBI," she lied. "Who the fuck are you?"

He backed away, slowly, not dropping the gun. "Where is she?"

"I don't know."

"Bullshit!" His beady eyes were on fire now as he circled her, getting closer to the door. Maybe he'd run. Now that he knew he had the wrong woman, maybe he'd—

The door exploded with a loud gunshot, kicked open from the other side. "Get down, Vivi!" Lang yelled.

Vivi instantly fell to her knees, diving for cover under the vanity.

"FBI! Drop your weapon!"

The man lowered his gun, just enough for the barrel to aim at Vivi on the floor.

"Drop it!" Lang ordered.

The assailant made a grunting sound and pulled the trigger. Vivi rolled deeper under the vanity, just missing a bullet that hit the floor inches away from her. Lang fired before the echo of the first shot died, hitting the man in the chest, but not before the guy got off one more wild shot, cracking the mirror over the Jacuzzi, a million shards raining into the tub and on the floor.

Vivi shrieked at the crash, watching the body drop a few feet from her, blood oozing from the bullet hole in his chest. His gun clunked on the marble floor right before his body followed, and the room suddenly filled with the other FBI agents swarming in behind Lang.

Lang vaulted over the assailant, dropping down to his knees, reaching to Vivi. "Are you hit?"

She just shook her head, adrenaline coursing through her, making her quiver as she let him drag her up. "Lang..." She could barely talk. "He wanted something."

"Yeah, you." He pulled her into him, his face pale, his eyes more concerned than she'd ever seen him before. "Are you sure you're okay?"

"I'm sure." She closed her hands over his arms, squeezing with the wild pump of her heart. She tried to push him away so she could get to the man on the floor and find out what the hell he was talking about. "Is he dead?"

The female agent kneeled by the body, taking a pulse. "As a doornail," she said dryly, then looked at Lang. "Nice save, Mr. Lang."

"But now he can't talk," Vivi said, disappointment cascading with adrenaline in her veins. Now they'd never know what key he wanted and why he was willing to kill for it.

"She's the one who did the nice work," Lang said, easing Vivi up to a stand. "Very smart way to get me in here." His eyes shone with admiration. And not the kind she saw when he was gaping at her in her underwear. A different kind of admiration. The kind that made a girl's knees go weak. But that could just be the adrenaline rush.

Behind him, the two agents scurried, one calling the local police for first response, the woman already taking crime-scene pictures.

"I want to know how the hell he got in here," Lang said. "Where is the security breach?"

"Do you know him, Ms. Ferrari?" the female agent asked, reminding Vivi that her true identity still hadn't been revealed to the other agents. Points for Lang.

"I don't know him," Vivi said, looking up to Lang, her mind whirring. She had to tell him everything the man had said to her.

But he was already leading her around the body and out of the bathroom.

"Didn't," he corrected. "Past tense for that one. This is a crime-scene hot zone—let's get you out of here."

Outside of the bathroom he pulled her into his chest, his pounding heart surprising her as much as his mouth on her ear. "Good job, Vivi Poison Angelino," he whispered, his breath so close and warm it was almost a kiss. "You brought in the Red Carpet Killer on day one."

She leaned back, still in his arms, but far enough away to give him a hard, serious look. "That wasn't the Red Carpet Killer, Lang. And whoever sent him isn't done with me yet."

CHAPTER 6

Come here." Vivi practically dragged Colt across the room, putting an end to his whispers and the unexpected emotion that overtook him.

"We're fanning out and looking for anyone else!" Special Agent Iverson shouted at him, heading out the door.

He started to respond, but Vivi dug her hands into his arm and yanked him aside. "I don't want anyone to hear this," she insisted. "It's important, Lang."

"So is finding out if anyone else broke into this house. What is it?"

She looked over his shoulder again, as another agent brushed by them. "C'mere. In the closet."

Pulling him to a door, she practically threw him into the giant walk-in closet and he was still so deeply grateful that she was alive, he let her.

"Vivi—"

She slammed her hand on his mouth and flung the door shut behind them. "Cara!" She leaned against the door as though she'd physically fight anyone trying to get in. Or out. "You have to call me Cara, damn it!"

He sucked in a breath, staring at the red marks on her neck. "Jesus, what did he do to you?" He reached for her, her throat warm, her pulse as crazy as his underneath.

"I'm okay," she insisted, dipping from his touch.

"A gun and threat is not the usual MO of a serial killer," he said, thinking out loud.

"No shit, Sherlock." She practically ground out the words in impatience. "Did you not hear me, Lang? That was not the Red Carpet Killer."

"Then it was a damn determined copycat, and we got him. Which, I promise you, will deter anyone thinking about trying the same thing."

"I'm not worried about a copycat. That guy said a lot of things to me that had nothing to do with killing actresses who'd won the Oscar."

He abandoned his examination of her neck. "Like what?"

"Like someone named Roman sent him, and told him how to get in here, and that he wanted something Cara has. A key. And...and..." She visibly searched her memory, fighting to get everything out. "He didn't know I wasn't Cara, at least not at first, but he sure as heck knew a lot of other stuff. Like wasn't it 'ballsy' of her to open the place to the Feds, as though she's not 'a complete innocent' in all this." She used air quotes around the words. "Not innocent in all *what*, Lang?"

He shook his head, already thinking through the mountain of procedures ahead. "I don't know. But we have to figure out where the breach of security is on the grounds and in the house and make sure this compound is secure. Nantucket cops and Massachusetts State Police will be here soon, the ME has to pronounce, and we've got to get an ID on that guy. I'll contact the FBI and Internal Affairs will need to send someone to prove this was justifiable."

She waved her hand. "And how could it not be justifiable? He was about to kill me and you if he could have managed it. Cara is involved in something serious here."

He put his hands on her shoulders, trying to subdue her impatience physically, which was no small feat at the moment. Still, he had to make her see the importance of how this was managed by the FBI. "A man is dead, Vivi. That is more important than the fact that you're pretending to be a movie star."

"Oh my God!" She blew the words up to the sky. "Are you not listening to me?"

"Are you not listening to me? An armed man broke into the bathroom to attack you. The only way to handle that is—"

"He broke into Cara Ferrari's bathroom," she corrected, managing to escape his grip. "And I still don't want anyone to know I'm not Cara Ferrari."

He nearly choked. "Vivi, that game is over."

Her dark eyes flashed like his words had electrocuted her. "It isn't a game and now it's more important than ever. He was working for someone, which means Cara's still at risk and I'm still needed here."

"Sorry about your assignment, Vivi, but everything's changed in the last ten minutes."

"Come on, Lang," she said, giving his shoulder a frustrated push. "Think like the by-the-book FBI guy we both know you are and let me tell you everything he said to me. Because"—she closed her eyes, taking a deep, slow breath before she finished—"if you tell the Nantucket Freaking Police Department and the Massachusetts State Police and the DA and the ME and the rest of New England law enforcement who I am, this will be all over the news in minutes and—"

"Is that what you're worried about?" He flicked his hand, swiping at her worries. "You can forget the nondisclosure, Vivi. It's moot now. She can't hold you to it; nothing would stand up in court. No way you can hide your role as a body double now that a man's been killed in her house. And, frankly, you could have just as easily been the one lying on that bathroom floor."

"But I'm not *because* I kept up the act. He didn't kill me, but he gave me some very important information."

The very thought of what had almost transpired in that bathroom punched him. "I will admit you did the right thing. Risky as hell, but you sent me the message and, I'll also admit, it probably saved your life. Good work, but I'm afraid the charade is up. I refuse to keep this from the FBI. Especially if what you're saying is true."

"Of course it's true!"

"I'm sure you think you know what you heard, but in a situation like that, you can't be sure you have the facts or names right. He might have said 'Roman' or something that sounded like it. He had you at gunpoint, right?"

"From behind."

"You could have easily misunderstood."

"But I didn't, and as soon as he learns his hit man got killed, he'll send another."

"Not if it's out that you're a decoy."

"Exactly, because if he knows I'm a decoy, he'll start trying to find the real Cara! Putting Cara in more danger because this guy knows an awful lot about her. And he wants something she has. If we go public with the decoy, then she'll just go deeper into hiding and be in more danger." When he didn't respond, she pointed at him. "You have to agree that makes sense."

Nothing made sense, not his visceral reaction to Vivi being in danger and not her ability to derail him from what he should be doing.

"Some," he conceded. "We do need to find her, but I have more immediate concerns." He turned to the door and she grabbed him again.

"Don't tell anyone yet, Lang."

"I can't make any promises."

"I'll make you a deal," she said quickly, a little desperate.

"I just made a deal," he said roughly. "I gave you until twelve-o-one p.m., and in the space of less than fifteen minutes, you were almost dead."

"But I'm not," she said. "I'm fine, Lang, really. Listen to my deal."

A memory flashed. *Let me make you a deal, Colt.* And he'd agreed. He'd agreed to take a risk that cost him everything. "No fucking deals, Vivi. No bending the rules, no trying to outsmart the system. Let's go."

"Where?"

"Straight to the FBI with your information—all of it, including who you are—and then let's figure out who this guy was, how he got in here, and why. We'll need you to share everything he said, of course. That's the only deal I'm making with you."

"Fine," she agreed. "If we do it without revealing that I'm not Cara Ferrari."

"That's kind of an important element of the investigation, don't you think?"

"Why? I mean, at least as far as the Nantucket police are concerned?" She leaned against the door, her arms crossed. "Will you just listen to my proposal?"

"No."

"Just *listen*."

"You have thirty seconds."

"You and your time lines."

He looked at his watch. "Now you have twenty-eight."

She shoved his arm down to make his eyes meet hers. "We tell your boss and your task-force guy the truth."

"And Internal Affairs."

"And Internal Affairs. But that's it. No one else. And"— she gave him a flat palm to stave off his objections—"we tell them everything I just heard and do not reveal my identity to the local police until—*until*..."

He took a step toward the door, so she put her hand right on his chest. "We learn the identity of the assailant and...*and*..."

"Fifteen seconds. And, frankly, that's quite enough demands for one deal."

She balled his shirt up in her fist to make her point. "And you give me the entire day to get ahold of Cara and try to get a location out of her. She's in as much danger as I am. If she gets wind of this and knows I told everyone— forget the nondisclosure—she'll *never* say where she is."

He knew she was right, and his arguments faded in the face of her firm resolve. "All I'm asking for is a little bit more time so I can get to her first without tipping her off that I've blown the deal. And in the meantime, we'll tell your L.A. office everything. Deal?"

He opened his mouth to argue, then shut it. The way she looked up at him, the fire in her eyes, the strength in her fist, the determination that thrummed through her blood—how could he argue with that?

How could he do anything but kiss her? Because that was all he wanted to do, which was fucking idiotic right then. Ever. But he was so relieved she wasn't dead.

"I'm not sure we can get Gagliardi and Tuttle on the phone right now; it's about five in the morning in L.A."

"You Feds get up at dawn." She finally let go of his shirt but kept her hand on his chest, which was still hammering. "You always beat this fast, Lang?"

"When I'm about to be run over by a ninety-nine-pound human bulldozer in a wig."

"Hundred and twelve and they're extensions."

He reached for her hair, curling his fingers around a thick, straight lock. "We need to get some of this to the lab," he said roughly. "See if it matches the others."

She rolled her head, letting some of the hair slide through his fingers like a cat enjoying a slow, easy stroke. "First time a guy ever ran his fingers through my hair and said that."

"You don't have hair." He gave the strands a light tug. "But maybe after this, you'll grow it."

She slinked out of his touch, a flash of disappointment on her face. "Hey, if I'd known all it took was long hair and high heels to get my way with you, I might have tried that a long time ago."

"You didn't get your way with me," he said. "I'm just agreeing to let the word out in a controlled and strategic way so that the media doesn't ruin the investigation."

The corners of her mouth lifted, revealing the shadow of dimples and her newly perfect front teeth. Funny thing, he kind of missed the chipped one. "Whatever bullcrap you need to rationalize this works for me, Lang. Thank you. Where are we making this call?"

"I saw an office or library downstairs. I'll handle these people, and talk to the first responding officer from the Nantucket police, then delay your interview until we've made our call. Detectives will be here soon, and I also want to interrogate the housekeeper—"

"Me too."

He gave her a quizzical look. "I thought you were in hiding."

"I'm an *investigator*, Lang."

"You're a recently attacked movie star, *Ferrari*."

"Not as far as Mercedes the housekeeper is concerned. She's in the know." She snapped her fingers and pointed to him as a thought occurred. "She was awfully damn anxious to get me up here, by the way. We definitely need to talk to her. And she might be in touch with Cara. We should have the lines out of the house tapped, in case we need to find Cara and she won't tell us where she is."

Good God, what next? "We'd never get a court order for that."

Vivi rolled her eyes. "Guardian Angelinos don't need no stinkin' court order."

"We are not going to tap her phone," he said, pinning her with a look he'd already learned didn't stop her when she wanted something.

"Okay, okay," she agreed. "I can't push every one of your buttons, can I?"

"But something tells me you'll try." He couldn't resist

one more brush of his knuckles over her reddened neck. The touch made her draw in a soft breath and took the spark out of her eyes, replacing it with something softer.

"Thanks, Lang. I appreciate your working with me on this."

"I'm not working *with* you on anything. I'm in charge of this investigation, and right now, you're a victim and witness."

She smiled deeper. "Whatever you say."

"Why does it scare me when you acquiesce so easily?"

"I don't acquiesce so easily," she said, closing her heavy lashes as he grazed the welt on her flesh. "Why are you doing that, Lang?" For the first time since someone had tried to kill her, Vivi's voice sounded nervous.

"I just want to be sure you're okay."

"I'm fine, as long as you keep—"

He kissed her. There was no way to stop himself, so he didn't try, leaning close to put his mouth on her lips. They were soft, dizzyingly soft, and parted in surprise, her words trapped.

He was tempted to slide his tongue over those pretty, pearly teeth, but fought the urge, pulling back.

"As long as I keep what?" he asked huskily.

"Your promise," she whispered, her eyes still closed, her hand flat on his chest as though she needed to use him for balance.

"We'll talk to Gagliardi before anybody knows anything."

She didn't reply, finally opening her eyes to look up at him. "Why did you do that?"

He had no fucking idea. Except that he had to. "So you know I'm serious."

"You're always serious, Lang."

He just looked at her, then reached behind her to the knob, opening the door to come face-to-face with Special Agent Iverson. "Ms. Ferrari is going to be sequestered downstairs," he said to the woman, ignoring her look of surprise and curiosity as they emerged from the closet. "Absolutely no one is to disturb her. I'll be with her during any and all questioning."

"Mr. Lang, she'll have to talk to the police and IA alone, under the circumstances," the agent said.

"We'll handle that later." He turned to Vivi, who still looked a little shell-shocked, her fingers on the lips he'd just kissed. "Come with me."

For once, she didn't argue.

What surprised Vivi most during the first few minutes of the conference call with Assistant Director Joseph Gagliardi and his right-hand agent, Thomas Tuttle, wasn't the fact that they weren't really fazed by the fact that Cara had hired a decoy or that Lang had waited a few hours and one attack to break that news to them. It was the way they responded when she told her story and mentioned the name Roman.

From that moment on, they flung questions at her. What else did the attacker say? Did he mention another name besides Roman? Was she certain he was looking for a key? Had he indicated how he'd gotten into the house?

"Did he only say the name Roman—no other?" Gagliardi asked for what had to be the fourth time.

Vivi nodded vigorously. "He said Roman told him everything, including how to get into the house."

"And he asked about a key? Did he say what it was a key to?"

"No," Vivi said. "But he seemed certain Cara had it, said the game changed when she won the Oscar. I have no idea why."

On the other end, a long silence.

Curled into the leather chair across a coffee table from Lang, Vivi kicked off her heels, tucking her legs under her. Lang, on the other hand, barely sat on the edge of his seat, popping up occasionally to answer the door and get a report on what was going on upstairs, pacing with his hands deep in the pockets of his perfectly pressed khaki Dockers, his brow knit, his jaw clenched.

She never expected him to react so—so emotionally to her attack. Her own response was understandable, and easy to cover under the circumstances. But his? And the kiss?

What was that all about? The sexed-up lap dance was one thing, but that had to be the end of it. She couldn't... she wouldn't....

And neither would he. That would be against the rules, right?

"Right?"

She looked up from the phone at Lang's question, knowing her expression was blank and lost.

He gave her a sympathetic smile. "Can you repeat that for Ms. Angelino, Mr. Gagliardi? She's a little rattled."

"I am not," she shot back, sitting up. "I'm just trying to remember it all in detail."

A hard knock at the library door pulled away his attention and Special Agent Iverson stuck her head in, her blonde hair pulled in a hairstyle that made her angular features appear even more severe. "We have an ID on the vic," she said.

"Come on in," Lang said. "If there's an ID from finger-prints from the body, then I take it the guy has a record."

"He sure does," Special Agent Iverson said dryly, plac-ing a few computer printouts on the table between them. "His name is Sunisa—"

"Pakpao." Gagliardi said the last name in unison with Special Agent Iverson, bringing them all to a stunned silence until Tuttle's voice rose excitedly from the phone.

"Holy shit, we got him."

"No," Gagliardi said. "We got Pakpao. We don't have anything on Emmanuel."

Vivi and Lang shared a look, neither saying a word.

"Then I guess you know his rap sheet," Special Agent Iverson said, backing out. "I'm going back upstairs."

The minute she left, Vivi reached for the report but Lang snagged it first, reading out loud. "Wanted for federal indictment on charges of conspiracy to commit forced labor, falsifying social security records, accomplice to acts of human trafficking—"

"What?" Vivi shot forward like he'd yanked her on a chain. *Human trafficking?*

"Mr. Lang, it seems you've stumbled onto an active inves-tigation," Gagliardi said. "A major, high-priority investi-gation, possibly the highest in this office right now. Much, much more critical than the Red Carpet Killer, to be perfectly honest. Just not as sexy to the media, but very high profile. And, until this minute, I didn't relate the two, but now they seem to overlap."

Vivi jumped up to get closer to Lang and read the report next to him.

"Fill me in," he asked Gagliardi.

"Normally I'd do this privately, but Ms. Angelino may

be a witness in a federal investigation and may have to appear before a grand jury. That is, if we do this right."

Vivi's eyes widened as she looked at Lang. What the hell was going on? He held up a hand to stave off any questions and nodded to the phone. "Hear him out," he whispered.

"Sunisa Pakpao is, or *was*, the director of international relations for a company called RE Global Industries, owned and operated by multimillionaire Roman Emmanuel. Don't be fooled by the high-powered title—Pakpao is a henchman who follows Emmanuel's orders."

"What kind of business?" Lang asked.

"On paper? Temporary employment. In reality? They recruit cheap labor from third world countries, with a specialty in Laos, lure them with false promises of lucrative jobs, confiscate their passports, and threaten deportation if they don't take certain jobs, primarily as agricultural workers and child prostitutes."

Without thinking, Vivi put a hand on Lang's arm, steadying herself. "Oh my God," she whispered.

"It's slavery," Lang said, putting his hand over Vivi's. "Human trafficking."

He was so matter-of-fact, cold even. Of course, this was a crime the FBI dealt with all the time, but... Vivi swallowed, determined to think like Lang on this. Analytical. Unemotional. Focused. She had a client at stake here, not her own dark memories.

She stepped closer to the speaker phone. "What does Cara Ferrari have to do with"—*slavery*—"this?"

"Nothing that we know of," Gagliardi said. "However, she does have a connection to Roman Emmanuel, so it's entirely possible she knows more than she told us when we interviewed her a few months ago."

"You *interviewed* her about this?" Anger jolted Vivi. Why hadn't Cara mentioned that when they talked about the FBI? All she said was the FBI couldn't be trusted.

"She and her sister worked for the company years ago, when they both arrived in Los Angeles seeking acting jobs. Joellen Mugg took jobs as a temporary secretary, one of the legitimate businesses of RE Global. Cara, who was Karen Mugg then, actually got placed in the headquarter offices in Westwood, and worked directly for Emmanuel. They were romantically involved, and she was his mistress for at least a year. Then she started getting acting jobs, and she claims they split up and she doesn't speak to him, but they have been seen together."

"How did she explain that?" Lang asked.

"He's a very wealthy man and runs in the same circles in L.A. She could easily beg at the same party with him. She claims to know nothing in-depth of his business."

"Well, she knows something or at least has something he wants," Vivi said. "And that Pakpao guy wanted her to hand it over."

"Exactly," Gagliardi said. "Anything Miss Ferrari has on him could be helpful. So far we have nothing, just speculation."

"And one dead director of international relations who tried to kill Cara Ferrari," Lang said.

"And make it look like the Red Carpet Killer," Vivi added. "He said her winning the Oscar changed everything."

"Maybe he thinks he can get away with killing her now," Gagliardi suggested.

Vivi dropped back into the chair, the weight of this

news pressing. And the magnitude of the crime pressing harder. Human trafficking. Child prostitution. Her stomach roiled.

"How can we help?" she asked.

"We can find whatever it was he was looking for," Lang said. "I'll turn this place upside down and inside out."

"I think that's a start," Gagliardi said. "Evidence is what will bring him down in court. Anything to make a solid connection between his seemingly legitimate business and victims who've been forced into slave labor and the sex trade. He's elusive, and he's got people everywhere—many of them willing to kill for him. Emmanuel pays his people, if not his slaves, and he takes care of their families in Laos. Pakpao is—was—a perfect example."

"Have you interrogated Emmanuel?" Lang asked.

"Multiple times, and he was the subject of an undercover operation that went south. His business is a straight-up labor contracting firm that files taxes, and pays wages and benefits to real employees. The trafficking, which is where he's made millions, is completely hidden."

Vivi gnawed on her lower lip, thinking about her client. "If Cara has something on him from when she worked for him, why not turn it over to the authorities? Why hide it? Why help him?"

"Maybe she's involved."

Lang's words were like a punch. Could Vivi be working for someone who would knowingly sell a child into prostitution? A poor worker into slavery? "Then she can have her ten million dollars," Vivi said softly. "I'll nail her ass to the wall and clobber her with the damn Oscar."

"She has quite a bit to lose, no matter what her level

of involvement," Lang said. "I don't think even the great forgiving American public would let her off the hook for being involved in something like this, even if she was young and stupid at the time."

"Except now the world is going to think we got the Red Carpet Killer today."

"And maybe we want them to," Gagliardi said quickly. "We're still investigating the connection between the two murders and all we have is the hair. But we can string the media along and let them think we might have caught him and then what will be interesting is whether or not Ms. Ferrari chooses to come out of her self-imposed hiding."

Vivi and Lang looked at each other. Interesting indeed. "Maybe she's not hiding from a Red Carpet Killer," Vivi mused, "but from Roman Emmanuel, who can use this situation to his advantage by threatening to kill her and make it look like a serial killer if he doesn't get what he wants."

Lang nodded. "Maybe she's put herself in hiding and a body double here not because of an imaginary killer, but a very real one who, if he was creative enough, could make it look like she was simply victim number three."

"Maybe not imaginary," Gagliardi added. "We still have evidence to at least warrant protection and investigation."

"I understand that," Vivi said. "But this threat seems much more immediate and powerful."

"I happen to agree," Lang said.

"Ms. Angelino, I have a proposition for you." At the assistant director's statement, Vivi sat up straight.

"Whatever you need, sir."

"If Ms. Ferrari returns after learning that we've caught

the Red Carpet Killer, and maintains her side of your bargain, then this point will be moot. She's obviously only hiding from a serial killer whom she thinks we've caught. We'll add her to a suspicious persons list and we'll continue the investigation here in L.A., adding the new information to the mix."

"Okay." She held Lang's unwavering gaze.

"However," Gagliardi said, "if she chooses to remain where she is, and we understand that she hasn't disclosed her location to you, then we're right that she's hiding from Emmanuel. In that case, I'd like you to stay right where you are as her double. We can bring the FBI agents on site up to speed, but I will pull the necessary strings to get the Nantucket police out of there. I don't want anyone outside the FBI knowing Ms. Angelino is a decoy."

She met Colt's gaze, instinctively knowing he did not like this plan. Did she? It put her in the position of investigating her own client, but if Cara was guilty of any involvement in human trafficking and child prostitution, Vivi wanted to take her down. But, on the other hand, if she was innocent and needed help . . .

"You also want us to find this key, right?" Vivi asked. "The one Pakpao mentioned when he attacked me?"

"If at all possible."

"And if Roman Emmanuel or another one of his people show up," Lang said, "we'll bring him in."

"I would like that, Colt." Gagliardi's voice was rich with implication that Vivi had no problem understanding. This was another test for his new hire, and a good one. "You will remain the lead on this case. Ms. Angelino, you will do whatever Mr. Lang tells you to do. And Colt," Gagliardi added, his voice low and serious, "I don't need to tell you that this is an exceedingly crucial case to the Los Angeles office, specifically the Criminal Programs Division."

The division he would head if he got the promotion. Once again, his big promo, the one that would take him three thousand miles away, hung in the balance. Only now the stakes were even higher. And Vivi had an active role in their success.

So if they found this key, evidence, or even Emmanuel, she was essentially guaranteeing he'd be gone. Gone from her client roster, gone from her everyday life, gone from her schoolgirl-crush fantasies.

"You don't have to remind me, sir," Lang said. "I understand the importance."

"Report in regularly," Gagliardi said. "Thank you and good luck."

Lang lifted the phone from the table, ended the call, then leaned back on the desk behind him, one hip propped, one long leg holding him steady as he blew out a breath.

"So," Vivi said to break the silence. "Looks like we're back on the same team."

"And you get to stay in character, like you wanted. But something tells me you aren't going to get your fee."

"I don't give a shit about money when it comes to things like"—she closed her eyes—"this."

His eyes flickered, some admiration in the green-gold, some surprise, too. "You're in a lose-lose situation, Vivi. You nail her, you lose. She finds out you're working against her, even if she's innocent as snow, you lose."

"If I save one little girl from being"—*raped*—"I win."

He nodded, as if he understood. But of course he didn't. And he never would.

"And you've got a lot riding on this, too," she said quickly. "Your big promotion."

"Yeah, so you're even more motivated to succeed," he said jokingly. "So be a smart backup."

"Backup?"

"You heard the man: I'm in charge."

She just looked up at him, fighting a smile. "You always kiss your backup, Lang?"

For a millisecond he paled, then he just swallowed. "Once I did."

Really. "And how'd that work out for you?"

He leaned closer and for one crazy second she thought he was going to kiss her again. "It didn't."

"Why? She have an opinion you didn't like?"

"She didn't have anything I didn't like."

The words kicked her, but she managed zero response. "So what happened?"

He straightened slowly, looming over her, then he dropped his phone in his pocket and walked to the door.

"What happened, Lang?" She hated that she repeated the question, but hated not knowing even more. What had happened to this woman who didn't have anything at all he didn't like?

He turned as he opened the door. "She died."

"Oh." Something thudded in her chest. "How?"

"She took a risk she shouldn't have."

CHAPTER 7

Looks like they got him." Marissa walked into the kitchen, starkly pale and maybe even shaking, holding her cell phone as though it were some kind of proof of the statement.

A tingle of total disbelief radiated over Cara as she turned from the half-scrambled eggs on the stove.

"Got who?" Joellen asked for her.

"The Red Carpet Killer."

Cara dropped the spatula with a clunk on the pan. "What?"

"Vivi Angelino just called from Nantucket. A man broke into the house, accosted her in the bathroom, and the FBI escort shot him right as he was about to shoot Vivi. He's dead."

"Holy shit," Joellen said, slapping a hand over her mouth. "There really was a Red Carpet Killer?"

"Or a copycat," Marissa replied, her voice still taut.

"Who was he?" Cara asked.

"They're not releasing his name yet."

"So Vivi's talked to the police," Cara said, turning back to the eggs so her thoughts and expressions couldn't be read.

"She has," Marissa confirmed. "But you'll be happy to know she hasn't revealed her true identity to them. But she has been forced to tell the lead FBI agent on the case that she is a decoy."

Cara's pulse spiked. "What?"

"She swears that no one else will know, but she cut a deal with him. She said she knows him from previous cases and now that they've got the killer, it couldn't be avoided."

And she probably couldn't be held to the nondisclosure, either. Still, if Roman sent the killer and knows he failed, and thinks she's still alive and in Nantucket, he'd send someone else, or show up himself, and he'd do it quickly. Best to let Vivi stay there in her place.

"We need to issue a statement," Marissa said, dragging Cara back.

"Yes, we do," Cara said, her back still to Marissa, who hadn't yet earned the right to witness Cara's most personal moments.

"I'll get Leon on the phone and we'll draft something for your approval," Marissa said.

"Go," Joellen barked. "Do that. Now. I need to talk to Cara alone."

"You don't have to talk to me like—"

Cara held her hand out to halt the argument. "Marissa, please. Call Leon. You're absolutely right, we need to issue some kind of statement. But we have to talk to Vivi first and find out what she's told this FBI agent."

"Will you be heading to Nantucket to deliver the statement?" Marissa asked. "Or back to L.A.?"

Cara finally turned around in time to see Joellen put both her hands on Marissa's back and give her shoulders a squeeze, answering the question for her. "We're going to discuss this, Marissa, and when we've decided we'll let you know."

"I've already decided," Cara announced, surprising herself with the vehemence in her voice.

They both looked at her expectantly.

"Until there is proof that this man is truly the person who killed Adrienne and Isobel, I'm staying right where I am. Anything could still happen. If Miss Angelino can withstand the media pressure of this and continue to pretend to be me, then she deserves every penny I'm paying her and more. Marissa, let her know I said to carry on."

"But she told the FBI agent," Joellen whined. "You understand what that means, don't you?"

It meant the FBI didn't know where she was. "Our biggest concern is the media," Cara said coolly. "Go ahead, Marissa, get things started."

Marissa left and the Mugg sisters just stared at each other.

"It could have been one of his men," Joellen said. "It could have been *him*."

"We should be so lucky," Cara replied.

"He's not going to let this deter him."

"If I'm not there, he can't hurt me. He won't stop until he has what he wants, Jo." She folded the overcooked egg under the spatula. "Maybe I should go public."

Joellen choked. "Do you have any fucking idea what that would do to your career?"

Not to mention Joellen's free ride on the fame-and-fortune train. "I know what it would do, Jo."

"How do you think it would go over with your fans, Karen? That you were his right-hand girl, not to mention his mistress, completely aware of how boatloads of people were holed up and beaten, forced to live with no running water, drowning in their own excrement? How do you think it would fly on *E! News* that you stood beside him as he handpicked twelve-year-olds to be sex slaves, that you didn't turn your head when he tortured them until—"

"Stop it!" Cara screamed, grabbing the paring knife she'd used to slice tomatoes and holding it out toward Joellen. "Shut up!"

Joellen just crossed her arms and gave her a cocky look. "Just remember, Karen, I have nothing to lose."

The *bitch*. "You have a gravy train of money and coattails of fame to lose."

"You can't let the world know what you did, Cara."

She lowered the knife and closed her eyes. "If he gets indicted, I might have to. And hope I'm one of those Teflon celebrities."

"No one is that bulletproof, kiddo."

She scraped the overcooked eggs into the sink. "I should never attempt cooking."

"And I should never attempt sobriety." Jo stood in front of the selection of booze bottles in the cabinet she'd just opened. "Crap vodka, but it'll do the trick for a celebratory drink." She splashed a glassful and held it up. "This'll have to do."

"Cheers," Cara said dryly.

Joellen gulped, then slammed the glass down. "Maybe you should just give him what he wants, Cara, then he will keep you out of it when he's indicted. You know he's going to be indicted. You could just be the innocent in all this, nothing more than the—"

"I'm not saving his ass. I'm saving mine." Cara swallowed hard. "Just drink your vodka, Jo."

"Like I need an invitation to do that."

Uncle Nino had a name for people like Mercedes Graff. Several of them, actually. None very nice, Vivi thought with a smile she managed to hide. Mostly, Nino would probably just call the housekeeper *una tedesca*. A German. And, with Uncle Nino, the old-school Italian that he was, being *una tedesca* was not a compliment.

Mercedes perched on the edge of an uncomfortable beige sofa, her features as pinched and sharp as the decor of her simple quarters on the basement level. Cleaned within an inch of their lives, the rooms were not nearly as well appointed and luxurious as the rest of the house, lit by unnatural light without a single window anywhere. They were devoid of clutter, color, or personality, an eerie reflection of the chilly, humorless woman who lived in them.

The other agents had sequestered Mercedes after the shooting, and no one had yet asked her any questions to determine what, if anything, she knew about Sunisa Pakpao and how he'd gotten into the house.

Lang thought that bringing her up to speed, especially given the fact that she knew Vivi's real identity, was their first order of business. No surprise, he took the lead as they entered her subterranean apartment, telling her that for Cara Ferrari's safety, and the fact that they had nothing definitive on the killer other than a suspicious rap sheet, the FBI had opted to keep Vivi undercover as a decoy for the actress.

All the while, Mercedes stayed on the edge of her seat—literally—and listened.

"I fully understand and will abide by this decision," she said, her icy blue gaze on Lang.

"You don't have a choice, Ms. Graff," he said brusquely. "You will comply or you will be obstructing justice, requiring me to arrest you."

Her face paled a shade and her eyes registered something more like fear than surprise. "And take me somewhere?"

"That's the general course of action."

"This is my home."

"I understand that. But it's also a crime scene."

The light tap of dog feet on the stairs made her sit even straighter. "That dog is not allowed down here."

But Stella apparently didn't know that rule or was willing to break it just to get close to Lang, because she scampered in and sidled up to his leg. Lang absently rubbed her head, his attention on Mercedes. "As I was saying, ma'am, you need to answer my questions."

"The animal needs sedatives," Mercedes said, starting to stand. "Let me get her prescription."

"No," Lang said, shooting out a hand while Vivi got up to lead Stella out the door. "Ms. Graff, this is more important. Do you have any idea how the assailant entered the house?"

"None. Every door and window is locked and alarmed, and I change the code on a daily basis."

"What is it today?" he challenged.

She narrowed her eyes. "I've turned it off to accommodate the foot traffic."

"That's not what I asked."

"It's a combination of numbers and letters that only I know."

"And today it is..." he coaxed.

"615PTR."

"And yesterday it was?"

"504QVM. Please don't ask the day before."

"Because you've forgotten it?"

"I know every number back two years, Mr. Lang. I have a photographic memory. I don't want to bore you with nearly seven hundred numbers and letters and, beyond that, I can't imagine the reason behind this line of questioning." She crossed her hands on her lap. "What else do you want to know?"

"Does the name Sunisa Pakpao mean anything to you?" He spelled it to help her, but she registered no recognition. "Has he ever been here before?"

"No." She shook her head. "The name means absolutely nothing."

"Can you give me a list of people who visit this house on a regular basis? Specifically anyone who may have been here within the last two months?"

"If you want it printed out, please allow me to access my computer. Everyone is logged and photographed by the security cameras. Otherwise I'll repeat it from memory. I can assure you there is no Mr. Pakpao on the list."

Oh, yeah, definitely *una tedesca*. All precision, no passion.

"When did you turn off the alarm code today?"

"When Ms."—she indicated Vivi with one pointed finger—"when she arrived."

"I'd appreciate if you would just refer to her as you refer to Cara Ferrari," he instructed.

She barely nodded. "I turned the alarm off when I received the call that you'd arrived at the front gates."

"How long was it off?"

"A few seconds, until I knew the car had entered the garage. Then I escorted Ms."—she nodded toward Vivi—"*her* upstairs and returned to the kitchen. I spoke to you and then I escorted Agent Iverson down the pass-through to the guesthouse, when we heard gunshots."

"Why were you so anxious for Ms. Angelino to get in her room?"

"Because getting guests settled is what I do."

He waited a beat, giving her a minute to elaborate, then, "You never went outside after you left her?"

"No."

"Not for one minute, in the driveway, on the patio, anywhere you—"

"I never went back outside, Mr. Lang. Of *that* you can have no doubt."

He and Vivi shared a quick look, both probably thinking the same thing. *Then what should we have doubt about?*

"How about the night before? The day before? Was there ever another point in time when the house alarm was turned off and someone might have gotten in?"

"Not to my knowledge, but I suggest you contact the security company. They log every time the alarm is armed and disabled. With the packs of photographers and media gathering around the property, I've been quite vigilant."

"Except for the few minutes after we arrived, when you were not vigilant."

She just stared at him.

"How many staff members does Ms. Ferrari employ at this house?" he asked.

"Just me."

"No landscapers? Pool service? Additional cleaning assistance? Handymen? Any service personnel, like plumbers or air-conditioning repair?"

"I have all of those individuals logged, Mr. Lang," she said. "But I run this household. I do all the cooking, cleaning, and general maintenance. Yes, there is a landscaper, but he hasn't been here in over a week, as we don't require any daily or weekly upkeep in the winter and spring months."

"How often are you gone, leaving the house unattended?"

"I am never gone and the house is never unattended."

Lang looked surprised. "Never?"

"Never."

"You don't go shopping, to the movies, to church?"

She leaned forward to make her point. "I do not leave this house, Mr. Lang. Ever."

"Why not?"

She just stared right back at him, stone silent.

"Is that your choice, Ms. Graff?"

"Of course," she said quickly. "I'm not...held against my will."

Vivi could see where he was going, and she didn't agree with the line of questioning, but before he could fire off the next question, his phone rang and he excused himself and took the call outside.

Thank God. Now Vivi could have some time to try this interview her way. Because Lang was getting nowhere.

She stepped away from the counter that separated

the kitchen from the living area, slowly approaching Mercedes.

"You must be shell-shocked," she said as she got close enough to connect but not to invade the obviously self-protective woman's personal space. "In the space of an hour, your beautiful home has been wrecked and invaded, turned inside out, and packed with strangers." Because, clearly, she felt it was her home. Enough that she never left. "And your boss's life has been threatened."

Mercedes lifted a bony shoulder. "When Ms. Ferrari is home, there is constant chaos. I'm no stranger to upheaval."

"Upheaval is one thing," Vivi agreed. "But having an intruder shot in the master bath is something else."

"It's all upheaval."

Vivi eased into the chair Lang had been in but sat back, curling her legs under her. "Hard to imagine how someone could get into this place with all the security and your supervision."

"Yes, it is."

She needed to try another tactic. "Let me ask you something, Mercedes." She got a quick look of surprise, probably for using the woman's given name, but Vivi powered on. "If you didn't know about the switch, how long would it have taken you to realize I'm not Cara?"

"Me? A second. Most people? Quite a bit longer."

"So you know her that well."

She almost smiled, or certainly the closest thing Vivi had seen so far. "I've known her since she was a child, so, yes, I know her well."

Vivi blinked at her, digesting this new information. "And now you work for her?"

"I don't call it work, miss." She finally stood, her knees creaking a little. "She's given me a place to live, right here on the island where I've spent every year of my life, and, as you can see, it's quite beautiful. I really don't think of my life as a job, but more of a reward for...for all I've done for her."

"I had no idea you were that close to her—and Joellen, too, I imagine."

She nearly bristled. "Yes, I practically raised them both."

She had? "What about their parents?"

The older woman drew in a slow breath, making her long, thin nostrils quiver. "Both dead, many years now. Mr. Mugg was in an accident on the bog, where he worked. Mrs. Mugg passed from cancer when the girls were in their teens."

Vivi's heart folded a little. She shared the same history: a father killed when she was young, a mother taken by cancer. "And you raised them?"

"There was no one else, and I already worked on the bog."

Vivi frowned. "What bog?"

"The cranberry bog the Muggs owned, right here on this property. It's abandoned now."

"They lived in this house?"

She almost laughed. "No, in the bog house at the edge of the property. Karen—er, Cara—built this when she became successful. I've lived here since the day it was completed."

"Always down here?" In a tomb?

She got up and walked to the kitchenette, rounding the counter to stand at the sink, staring at the wall where anywhere else there would be a window. "These are my quarters. I'm not a member of the family."

"How was it you practically raised them?"

She shook excess water from her hands then opened a crisp, clean dish towel to dry them. "Their mother worked as a secretary in town. I watched the girls when they came home from school from the time they were kindergarten age."

She smoothed the towel on the countertop, folding it with military precision. "Are you finished interviewing me, Ms. Angelino? I have a house full of people who are no doubt going to be hungry."

"I'm not interviewing you," Vivi denied. "I'm fascinated by the history. I knew Cara was born and raised in Nantucket, but didn't realize it was on this land, or on a cranberry bog."

"You're interviewing me. I'm not stupid."

Lang opened the door, cutting off the next question. "I need you to come with me," he said to Vivi. "And, Ms. Graff? One of my agents will be in here shortly to continue our interview."

"He or she can continue it upstairs," she said, brushing by Vivi and Lang to the door. "I'll be in the kitchen."

She marched up the stairs and left them staring at the open door.

Lang blew out a breath. "She's tight-lipped."

"Not at all."

"No? So what did you find out that I didn't?"

"Plenty. For one thing, she's known Cara since she was a child, and practically raised her."

He frowned. "That doesn't tell us how someone got into this house."

"Maybe not," she agreed. "But I usually find that when

you discover the personal angle behind relationships, you get answers to questions you never thought to ask."

"Still doesn't tell us where the security breach is."

"But it tells us a lot about the gatekeeper."

Lang put his hand on her back and guided her to the door. "I don't know about her history with Cara, but I thank God she's an organizational fanatic who keeps track of everyone who has ever entered the house."

"And an agoraphobic," Vivi added.

"Did she tell you that?"

Vivi gestured toward the tomblike rooms. "Does she have to? She never leaves the house, lives in a hole, and reeks of OCD."

He fought a smile. "So you're a profiler, too."

She merely shrugged, not sure if his look was teasing or admiration. "She has a lot of emotional ties with Cara. A lot of history and, in my investigative experience, that can really affect a case."

"Well, in my investigative experience, finding the security breach that allowed a killer to get in the house can really affect a case, too. So come with me while we do a search of the grounds."

It wasn't a suggestion, but then, with Lang, nothing was. "On one condition."

He choked softly. "Vivi, I don't do conditions. And are you forgetting who's in charge?"

As if that would be possible. "There's something on the property I want to see."

He hesitated, then moved forward. "What?"

"The abandoned cranberry farm where, according to Mercedes Graff, Cara spent a good chunk of her childhood, in a bog house."

"Because you think you'll figure something out if you see the environment and get in tune with the emotional connection Cara has to this land?" His voice was thick with sarcasm. Definitely teasing. Why would she even dream it was admiration?

"Nothing so deep, Lang. We're looking for places Cara might have hidden something and, since I'm pretty much unable to cruise the crime scene up in her bedroom, I'm just trying to think outside the box."

"I'll buy that. Let's go."

CHAPTER 8

I found a pair of shit kickers."

The voice, the phrase, even the verbal attitude was so "Vivi" that Colt got a little jolt when he looked up from the ignition of the ATV to see a woman who appeared to be nothing like her bounding into the garage.

Even with the long, fake hair pulled up in a ponytail and stuck through a baseball cap, shades covering the made-up eyes, and the rubber-bottomed suede boots she proudly extended for his examination, Vivi—as Cara— was drop-dead sexy. Why didn't she try a little harder to look like a woman? It suited her. It slayed him.

"Shit kickers?"

She placed the foot in question on the running board of a Honda Rancher, one of several in the garage, gracefully swinging her leg over and settling behind him on the four-wheeler's seat. "The only shoes in that woman's closet without a heel. Let's roll, Lang. I love riding these things." She gave her legs a squeeze, smashing the inside of her thighs against the outside of his. "In fact I love them so much, it's difficult to let you drive."

"You're not *letting* me do anything," he said, turning the key so the transmission rumbled right underneath them, feeling as powerful as the contact with her body. "However, I am *letting* you come along." Rolling out to the drive, he reached into his pocket and pulled out his cell phone, already programmed to a satellite image of the property, and handed it to her.

"You can navigate." He revved the engine and headed to the back of the property, where he already knew he could pick up the first trail in the woods behind the house.

"Whoa, look at this map," Vivi said. "This place is huge."

"I want to check the perimeter where the privacy wall gives way to brush and foliage and swamp land. We'll start at the northernmost trail and work down. Hang on."

Instantly, she wrapped her arms around his waist and held on tight as he followed a path into an opening in the woods. The brush was thick along the trail, but the dead pines made a smooth path and he went a little faster than necessary just for the pleasure of having her hang on to him.

Before long, she let go, steadying herself with one hand around his stomach, working the satellite map with the other.

"We should be coming to the end of this trail, and either the privacy wall or—"

"A swamp." He hit the brakes and eased up as they reached a wide area of wetlands. "You'd need a swamp buggy to get through that, and if anyone had been through here they would have left tracks in this mud. Pakpao didn't come through, but we're going to have to get this opening barricaded right away."

They went through the same process on two more trails, one ending in thick brush that hadn't been trespassed, the other closed in by part of the privacy wall. They headed west, deeper into the woods, the wheels of the ATV rolling over large rocks and splashing through early spring mud. On the roughest patches and tightest turns, Vivi held firmly to him, close enough that he could feel her heart beat against his back and her breath on his neck. Her hand rested low on his abdomen, perilously close to his crotch, an area humming with life and a little too much blood, blissfully unaware they were on a security search at the moment.

The engine vibrated between his legs, aggravating the tightness in his balls, the dryness in his throat, the temptation to stop and drag her into the most secluded grove of trees, and—

"The bog's that way, Lang." She let go and pointed to another path. "I can see it right here on your phone."

He had to stop thinking about sex with her, because she was obviously not feeling distracted by the same thoughts. Knowing Vivi, she was probably planning her ambush on his personal life. It was his own fault; he'd opened the door by mentioning what had happened to Jennifer. Part of him wanted to tell her. Not so she pitied him, and not so she understood why he needed to escape the memories that lurked in every corner of Boston.

But because Vivi ought to know that taking risks had deadly consequences.

"Oh, look at that." She squeezed tighter, her breasts plastered to his back, images of her curves hugged by a white lace bra wiping out the view that had her gasping against him. "It's the cranberry bog. So pretty."

He concentrated on the panorama, slowing the ATV as they ripped through some overgrown brush that blocked the path. For acres in all directions, the shallow, murky water glistened under the sun, reflecting the clouds and making the whole stretch a mirror image of the sky. Some bushes and dried-up cranberry vines shot up through the murk like nature's craggy fingers, and the still barren tree line that encircled the bog only added to the sense of death and abandonment.

On the far western banks, a small weathered-gray wooden structure stood out in stark contrast to the natural beauty.

"That must be the bog house where Cara grew up," Vivi said, giving his right arm a nudge toward the handle accelerator. "I want to see it."

He took the four-wheeler that way, rounding the path until they reached the house. Vivi was climbing off and jogging toward the house before he'd even shut off the engine.

"Wait a second," he called after her, his attention on her instead of the dwelling.

She paused long enough to check it out, then looked over her shoulder to wave him closer. "I wonder why she doesn't publicize these humble beginnings," she mused. "America loves a rags-to-riches story."

"Same reason she changed her name, probably. The quest for glamour." And this place couldn't be less glamorous. He reached her in three steps and she grabbed his hand to pull him into her adventure, eyes glistening like they did when Vivi was doing something she shouldn't do.

Why the hell did that turn him on so much? That trait

should be a blinding red flag: *Run, Colt, run.* And that
was the plan, if this whole assignment went right.

"Let's go in," she said.

"Sure. Let's B-and-E unsafe, unsecured property. Why
the hell not?"

She just laughed, letting go of him halfway around the
back to the door.

Sometimes her force couldn't be fought. Like on the
plane, in the closet—when would he give in to the constant ache to touch her next? Here, in this desolate, vacant
house, on an old pine floor, naked...wrestling...doing
exactly what they shouldn't be doing.

Anyone could come by. He hung back, inhaling the
pine and musk of the afternoon air, listening to the ran-
dom call of a bird. And Vivi.

Her soft cry from the back of the house made him
drop the sex thoughts and run, his right hand toward the
weapon in his holster. She stood at the back door, hands
on her hips.

"No lock picking necessary, big guy. The door's wide
open." She gave him a meaningful look. "Like someone
just left."

"Or is still inside." He stepped in front of her, drawing
his weapon. "Stay out here."

He moved stealthily into a darkened, mold-scented
kitchen, no sign of life unless he counted the spider crawling across a cracked and yellowed Formica counter.

Dusty and as abandoned as the bog it overlooked, the
house couldn't have been a thousand square feet. He
could see into a living area at the front of the house,
empty except for a blackened mantel around an ash-filled
fireplace. There was one other room off to the side and a

bathroom that, from the looks of the pipes sticking out of the wall, once doubled as a laundry room. That was it. There was no furniture, only chipped paint and a stained and threadbare carpet.

"No one's here," he said from the front room, peering out a cloudy pane of glass to the bog outside. The front door was closed and latched with a flimsy lock that a good shake could probably break.

He headed into the bedroom, toward a closet door. He opened it, ready to fire, but it was as empty as the rest of the house, except for a pile of old paint tarps on the floor.

"The back door must have just been left unlocked," he called to Vivi. But his instinct said otherwise. The house smelled like it had been sealed up, not like fresh air had been blowing through.

He turned and crossed the space into the kitchen, noting the faded paint marks on the living room walls, the outlines where pictures once hung. Dust in every corner, dead bugs, and filth.

"It's a wonder she doesn't just tear this place down," he said. "Can't be a good memory—Vivi?"

She didn't respond and the kitchen was empty.

"Vivi?" he called again, heading to the door, freezing at the sound of the ATV starting up. What the hell was she doing? "Vivi!" He jogged to the door just as the four-wheeler disappeared into the woods, before he could even glimpse her on it.

Son of a *bitch*. He stuffed his gun back in the holster and listened to the fading engine, his temper choking. What the fuck was wrong with that woman?

• • •

Vivi opened her mouth to scream as some insect flew right in. Spitting madly, she threw her hands out into the darkness.

What the hell happened? Had she fallen? She'd been standing outside the house on the rotten wood of the deck when Lang went in and the board under her feet just caved in.

Or had it? She'd stumbled, instantly falling down into someplace dark and cavernous, cold and hard, then the board—or was it a trapdoor?—had closed above her. Had she been pushed? It happened so fast.

Where the hell was she?

The ground underfoot was hard, like cement. The walls were the same, and closed in. A tunnel? A way into the drainage ditches? She knew next to nothing about cranberry bogs, except that they were lined with drain-pipes and some of them had underwater platforms for farmers to walk across when they harvested the fruit.

Was that what she had fallen into?

And—holy hell—did Lang know? She reached out to get her bearings, touching rough, rounded concrete. Something tickled her fingers and she snapped back her hand.

Shaking a little, she swiped at her face, not sure if it was her imagination, her fake hair, or—God, spiders! She brushed at her arms. More of them. With a grunt of disgust, she protected her mouth to avoid swallowing one, then from behind her hand she let out a scream that thudded into the walls through the enclosed space.

No answer.

"Lang!" She tried again, so loud it shredded her throat.

The ground rumbled a little and she could have sworn she heard the ATV engine.

Was he leaving? If he was, she'd kill him.

Something bumped above her head. She peered up, half expecting another spider on her face, seeing nothing but absolute blackness. How far down was she? It hadn't hurt to fall, so she couldn't have dropped very deep in the ground. Was it a hole? A well?

Gingerly she reached up a hand, feeling air. She called for help, but the plea was swallowed up by the cement around her. Could he even hear her down there? Did he have any clue where she was? Was he right above her on the rotten wooden deck?

Then why wouldn't he hear her?

She screamed again, the sound muffled by the cement.

She stuffed her hand into the skintight back pocket of Cara's jeans, fishing out her phone, praying for a—*No Signal.*

"Shit!" But at least it cast a light. She turned the screen to see her surroundings and instantly wished she hadn't. Spiders crawled all over the walls, and the opening above was a good four feet from her reach.

Still, she tried again, spurred by frustration and the light pressure of a tendril of panic that was slowly curling around her chest. "Lang, I'm down here!" The sound just wasn't carrying.

She breathed through her nose, trying to stay calm, smelling dirt and mildew, and the tangy hint of cranberry. The light showed some kind of hole leading out of the bottom, about two feet wide.

Was there any other option? Could she crawl up? Could she somehow creep up the way she came?

Thanking God and whatever stylist had recommended that Cara buy rubber-soled boots, she reached her arms out, the phone in her teeth so she could see the spiders, squishing those that skittered over her hands. She made it a foot and slid back down. *Damn* it.

But it wasn't the only way out.

Crouching down, she shone the light into the tunnel. A rat scurried away, running toward blackness on the other side. This was a drainage pipe, she decided, used for irrigation when the bog was running.

So it should lead somewhere. To a water source or into the bog. Oh, Lord, please don't let that be the only way out.

Another, braver, bolder rat scurried toward her, his eyes trapped in the light. Chills crawled up her skin, her stomach turning.

"Fuck you, swamp rat," she said. "I'm fifty times your size."

But not too big to crawl through that pipe.

She hated the thought the minute it landed in her head. Surely a drainage pipe led out somewhere, though. Unless it led to another hole like the one she was in, with another covered opening, and then—

Was she eventually going to run out of air?

She took another breath and screamed again. "Goddamn you, Lang! I'm down here!"

Why would he leave without even looking for her? Did he think she would take off without him?

Anger, frustration, and not a little bit of fear rushed through her, making her flatten her hands against the side walls, using her arms to push up again but, even as strong as she was, she couldn't shimmy all the way up there.

But that tunnel. Eesh.

She tried to go up again, made it a little farther this

time, braced her feet, and tried to reach the door above. Not a chance. Shaking, her legs gave way and she hit the ground hard, her knees buckling, one stabbed by a sharp stone.

A *stone!* Maybe she could throw it up and he'd hear it hit.

The rumble she'd heard earlier rolled through the ground. The ATV. He was back. "Lang!" She snagged the stone and pitched it up as hard as she could, crouching to the side as it clunked right back at her.

Something slammed, then more footsteps clunked above her. Whatever trap she'd fallen or been pushed into was probably invisible enough that he'd never think to look where he was walking. Without a clue as to where she was, he was no doubt heading off to look for her in the woods or in the swamp or somewhere in the hundreds of acres around them. He figured she'd ignored his command, broken his rules, and taken off for her own search of the woods.

She could just hear him making the wrong assumption that she was *being Vivi*.

She had to get out of this, just to prove that son of a bitch wrong. The thought gave her just enough nerve to crouch down in the tunnel one more time. What was a rat or two compared to being buried alive and not ever getting to tell Lang he was wrong?

Spewing dust and spiderwebs and probably a few more pesky insects from her mouth, she got on her knees, using one hand to hold her phone as a flashlight.

Then she took a deep breath and started crawling. In her head she chanted an old Italian prayer to St. Jude, the patron saint of lost causes. It rose up from her memory in the lost cadence of her mother's voice and guided her along.

CHAPTER 9

Colt called for another ATV and a search party immediately. Arms scraped by pines and vines, he rumbled around the bog, fury slowing giving way to fear with each passing minute.

What could have happened to her?

Gripping the handles, he maneuvered around a copse of trees, his eyes scanning the landscape. She couldn't have disappeared. Unwanted images flooded his mind. Vivi held hostage. Vivi hurt. Vivi dead.

He waited for the kick of déjà vu, the flash of seeing Jennifer's body on the road, the agony of feeling for a pulse that wasn't there.

But for the first time in five years, that memory didn't roll up like bile into his mouth. Grief didn't consume him. Something else did. A feeling like he *cared*.

Oh, Jesus, no, Colt. Don't go there. Not again. Never again.

He smashed his thumb against the accelerator like he

could crush the turmoil that thought caused, kicking the
vehicle into the next gear, spitting pine needles and dirt as
a possum darted in front of him, barely missing getting
flattened by Colt's ATV.

Was he out of his fucking mind? Falling for someone
again? And not just anyone. No, Vivi Angelino certainly
wasn't just anyone. She was too much like—

His phone vibrated and he slowed just enough to grab
it. "Yeah?"

"We found an ATV abandoned in a ditch."

Shit. *Shit.* "Where?"

"About a half mile west of the bog, just across the road
from the water. There's a small lighthouse on a rise. The
ATV was right under it."

"No sign of her?"

"None. Whoever was driving it left by boat. Or swam.
Or is out there on foot."

She wouldn't leave without telling him. She was reckless, but not stupid.

If anyone was stupid in this partnership, it was Colton
Cautious Lang, who ought to know better than to *care*.

He arrived at the ditch in a matter of minutes, just in
time to see a crew moving the ATV up through the soft
peat of the outskirts of a bog, at a point where Nantucket
jutted about forty feet into the Atlantic Ocean. A road
separated the property from the water, and a single weathered dock extended past the shallows, which were dotted
with a small, abandoned lighthouse.

His gaze drifted to the water. It was relatively calm and
virtually empty except for fishing boats in the distance.

He'd never heard a motorboat, had he? Who could
have taken Vivi and where the hell was she?

He went through the motions of examining the ATV, organizing the search, and arranging to have the Coast Guard search the waters. After more fruitless searching, he ended up back at the house, his whole body aching.

Someone took her. Maybe Roman Emmanuel—maybe some lunatic who thought he'd snatched Cara Ferrari.

That was the only explanation that made any sense, and he wanted to shoot himself every time the words hammered through his head and kicked his heart.

Someone took Vivi.

He entered the kitchen, where Mercedes Graff sat at the long table in conversation with a man, who instantly stood.

"ASAC Lang?" he asked. "I'm Special Agent John Broder with IA. Can I talk to you?"

Jesus Christ, Internal Affairs, *now*?

"I have two minutes," he said gruffly, striding to the industrial-size fridge. "I need water." And Vivi. God almighty, he needed Vivi.

"The Sub-Zero's been emptied out," Mercedes said, pushing her chair back. "I'll get you some from storage."

"No." Colt shot up his hand. "Finish your conversation with Special Agent Broder. I'll get it myself."

He needed a quiet moment to collect his emotions before he faced IA.

"Water's in the pantry around the corner," she said.

He headed there, yanking open the door to a dark walk-in storage pantry. He hit the lights and closed the door behind him, leaning against it for a second, waiting for the hurricane of anger and worry and frustration to pass.

Someone took Vivi.

The impact of it was like a suffocating squeeze on his throat, cutting off his air. Or maybe that was a fucking lump forming because just the thought of losing her—damn it! He lifted his fist and slammed it into the wall next to him, wobbling the canned goods on the shelves.

What if she was—

The wall vibrated again, just as violently as when he'd punched it. For a second he didn't move, staring at the rocking bouillon.

Then he heard the thud—from the other side of the wall, making all the canned goods shudder again. This time the wall actually *inched out*. A can of corn toppled and clunked to the ground.

"What the hell?" he muttered under his breath, not wanting to alert whoever lay on the other side of that wall to his presence.

Slowly, he reached for his weapon, drawing it, unconsciously bracing his legs to fire.

The wall creaked and opened farther, pushed by someone on the other side. He raised his weapon, waiting for the intruder.

Hinges squawked. Very slowly, the secret, hidden door opened, someone panting breathlessly as he pushed. Someone...

Vivi.

For a second, neither of them spoke, too stunned at the sight of each other. Her hair was bedraggled, her face filthy, her clothes torn. He just stared, blinking, not able to believe what he saw.

"Vivi," he croaked, that lump in his throat practically choking him.

She fought for a breath as she stepped into the pantry. "I found the security breach."

She hadn't been expecting him, and she sure as hell hadn't been expecting *this*. Shock, a little horror, anger, for sure. But when Lang grabbed Vivi's shoulders and yanked her into his chest, the move stole what little breath she had left.

"Jesus, Vivi, I thought you were dead." He pressed his mouth to her hair and squeezed her harder.

"I thought I was, too," she admitted, pulling away enough to see his face, dying to tell him what she'd discovered, but he cupped her chin with a solid grip.

"Dead," he repeated as though he'd been holding the word in for a while.

"Hey, Cautious, have a little faith in—"

His mouth descended before she could finish the sentence. It was a harsh kiss this time, fueled by rage she could practically taste. This wasn't affection, attraction, or relief. This was just…raw, and the sensation almost knocked her right back down to the tunnel she'd just crawled through.

Her lips burned and her heart galloped and her whole body wanted more. She fought that urge, instead flattening her palms on his chest, half to push him away, half for the thrill of feeling his heart in perfect, wild syncopation with hers.

"You need to see what I found," she said breathlessly.

"What happened to you? Where did you go? Why the hell did you leave me?" he demanded, gripping her face, his expression so pained it was impossible to tell who exactly he was furious with: her or himself.

"I didn't leave you!" She managed to wiggle out of his fingers. "I was on the porch deck when I fell or was pushed into some kind of secret opening to the tunnel. I was right under your damn feet, Lang. Didn't you hear me screaming?"

He shook his head. "You think you were pushed?"

She dug into her memory, trying to capture the moment again. "It just all happened so fast I really don't know, and it's killing me. I was standing on the deck, the board under me kind of wobbled, then, wham. I was down. That tunnel must be completely soundproofed if you couldn't hear me screaming. But more importantly, the bog house and this one are connected. You can get from there to here without ever stepping foot outside. Although"—she brushed some filth from her face and tried to bury the memory of just how many creepy-crawly living things she'd encountered as she powered through the drainage tunnel—"it ain't a stroll through the park."

"Not now. The whole damn force is looking for you. For Cara," he added, pulling her from the door. "Everyone needs to know you're safe."

"No, wait. We don't want anyone to know about this breach. More importantly, if someone pushed me, Pakpao wasn't working alone. Someone could still be on this island right now."

"Or got off by boat. We found the ATV near a dock at the western edge of the property, by the water."

"Don't stop that search, then. If someone pushed me, they might still be in the area. We could catch them."

He considered that, and nodded. "Show me, fast."

"Follow me." Behind the door was a small landing, then steps that led down to the tunnel. "My phone's just about dead. You have yours?"

He reached into his pocket and pulled out a tiny halogen flashlight. "Yes, but I also have this."

"Remind me never to make fun of former Boy Scouts again." She guided him down the stairs. "There's another door down here—I saw it. But I couldn't get it open, so I just kept going until I found the kitchen."

He peered down the narrow tunnel. "This is a heck of a way to avoid cameras."

"Plus I'm pretty sure Cara Ferrari doesn't brave spiders and rats to avoid the glare of the spotlight."

He slowed his step. "You braved spiders and rats?"

The tiniest note of admiration in his voice almost buckled her. "Don't sound surprised. I'm tough."

"No kidding." He put his hand on her back as though to guide her, but it felt far more like protection—and affection. *Nah.* He was just relieved he didn't have a dead backup on his hands. L.A. wouldn't like that.

"We can easily go through this part of the tunnel, although you'll have to crouch down a little—it's barely five feet high. But at the other side, where it connects to the bog house, it's no more than a drainage pipe, which yours truly traversed just to come back and torment you."

"You shouldn't have left my side."

She stopped, letting her jaw drop. He was going to make this *her* fault? "*You* told me to wait outside."

"Don't you carry a weapon?"

"Don't worry, I'm never leaving home without it again. Come on." She led him deeper into the tunnel. "But I want to know where that other door leads."

"I really thought you took off on the ATV," he said, sounding like that was about the closest thing to forgiving her without actually saying it.

"I know you did, and the need to set you straight was the only thing that kept me going down there with the hungry rats."

He gave her a gentle hug, bent over to fit under the tunnel's low ceiling, making them eye to eye. The light, even pointed downward, cast a shadow on his face. She reached up, half wanting to reassure him she was fine, half just wanting to touch him. His skin was rough, his jaw set.

"Are those whiskers, Lang? You *were* worried. You put off the afternoon shave."

His lips tipped with a smile she could tell he didn't want to give in to. "I was more pissed than worried."

"Yeah, I can tell."

"I was."

Pissed enough to kiss the holy hell out of her—for the second time today. "I'm starting to think you like me now that I look all glamorous. Wouldn't that be just like a man?"

"I hate to break it to you, but you don't look anything near glamorous right now. Where are we going?"

"C'mon." She marched forward, brushing an imaginary spider from her face. "You know, after being involved with the building of a skate park, I can appreciate what a marvelous engineering feat this is."

"Like a residential version of the Big Dig," he agreed. "Why would someone go to this much trouble just to have a secret way into the house?"

"I don't know, but I really want to know where this door leads." She stopped at an alcove with a simple wooden door.

"This is probably how Pakpao got in and out, or he came through the drainage pipes like you did."

Vivi froze, grabbing his arms. "Oh my God, Lang. Roman's alley!"

"What?"

"Pakpao said..." She squeezed her eyes closed, trying to remember his exact words. "Roman's alleys. That's how he got in. This tunnel must be Roman's alley. Maybe this is what he needs the key for. To get into this room!"

Lang pushed at the door with his shoulder as Vivi started feeling along the walls for another way to open the door. In a few seconds she found it, a small latch on the wooden jamb.

Working in unison, Lang pushed as Vivi pulled the latch until the lock clicked, and the door opened.

"Looks like we don't need a key," she said. The opening led to a small, dark area, then deeper into...a closet.

"We're back in the house," he said. "You're right. The tunnel is an underground passage from one part of the house to another."

They inched farther past two rows of clothes and shoes. On closer inspection, she knew. "This is Mercedes's basement apartment," she whispered.

He nudged the hinge of folding slatted-wood doors and peeked through the tiny opening. "Yep."

The sound of footsteps made them both back up, but not before Lang quickly replaced the door in its original position. Through the slats they could hear her the soft beeps of a cell phone being dialed.

"Now she's missing," Mercedes said softly. "I need to know what to do about that."

Who was she talking to? Vivi looked up at Lang, who gave her a tiny head shake, neither one of them moving during a long pause.

"She's doing exactly what she's supposed to do and that's what we want, isn't it? It's certainly what the FBI wants her to do. Don't you wonder why?"

Who would wonder why? Mercedes moved away a few steps, and Vivi held her breath, praying the woman didn't leave her room so they could continue to listen. If she was talking to Cara, maybe she'd reveal the star's location. If she wasn't talking to Cara, then Vivi wanted to know who was on the other end of that phone.

"I doubt that." The wry words were followed by a laugh, a sound so out of character for the stiff housekeeper that Vivi blinked in surprise. Lang's eyes widened with the same response. "I promise you no one is going to find that key."

They heard the phone snap shut and both of them eased back, Vivi's heart kicking up at the possibility that Mercedes would suddenly yearn for a change of clothes. But the woman left the room, her low, sensible heels clapping on hardwood, the sound of her apartment door slamming a few seconds later.

"Let's go," Vivi said, moving forward instead of back.

"What are you doing?" Lang asked in a harsh whisper.

"That woman knows where the key is, I'm going—"

"Exactly! Don't show your cards yet."

Annoyingly, he was right. "So what do we do?"

"We don't let on that we know about any of this," he said. "I'll handle the FBI, call off the search, and say you made your way back up through the grounds. In the meantime, I'm putting an agent on her twenty-four/seven."

"She won't tell an agent anything," Vivi said as they tiptoed out the secret closet door, back into the tunnel. "Maybe I can get a little closer to her."

"Doubtful. She'll know what you're up to."

"We need someone she can relate to, someone she doesn't know is digging for information. Someone she'd never expect—" Vivi stopped dead, a slow smile forming. "I have the perfect Guardian Angelino for the job. When he's done, that *una tedesca* won't know what hit her."

"You are not bringing Uncle Nino into this. Just forget it."

"Then what do we do with this newfound discovery?"

"Knowledge is power. We use this little tidbit to our advantage."

It was hardly a little tidbit. "But, Lang, Nino would totally infiltrate her kitchen and find out every—"

"No!" He slowed his step, maybe as surprised by his vehemence as she was. "No," he repeated, softer this time. "Not after today. Thinking that something happened to you damn near killed me."

It had?

Even in the dim light she saw him close his eyes, like he wanted to take back what he'd just said, but couldn't.

A foreign, thrilling sensation wended through her, pleasurable enough to make her drop the Uncle Nino argument. Lang *cared* about her. She knew it.

And as he'd just said, knowledge was power. That must be true because *this* little tidbit made her feel . . . powerful.

CHAPTER 10

Even with a hallway and a few walls separating them, Colt could hear her whimper in the quiet of the house at midnight. A throaty, plaintive whine that he instantly identified as a plea for his company.

How could he ignore that?

Pulling on sleep pants to cover his nakedness, he slipped out the door, stepped into the hall, and listened. The pitch grew a little higher, a little more desperate. Damn, she wanted him.

When he got to the guest room where Vivi was sleeping, he tapped once, and the whining stopped.

And then Stella let out a full-fledged bark, and Vivi whisked open the door. "She's pathetic."

"Why didn't you just bring her to me?" He easily one-handed the dog up to his chest, getting a torrent of face licks in response. "All women should be so grateful to be saved," he said dryly.

"You didn't save me today, Lang, or I might..." She

didn't finish, but gave in to a smile and nodded to invite him in, her gaze flicking over his bare chest. His eyes did the same, over Vivi's thin tank top and men's baggy boxer shorts with happy faces on them.

He'd be smiling if his face was down there, too.

Damn, he knew what he should do, knew exactly what the procedure was for this situation: Ignore the invitation, say good night, take the whiny pup, and leave.

He walked right in.

"What are you doing?" he asked, seeing the laptop open on the bed, the screen casting the only light in the suite she'd chosen on the east wing's first floor since Cara's room remained a crime scene.

"E-mail, research." She reached to pet the dog's head, but Stella ducked and Vivi's fingers brushed his bare skin. She jerked back like she'd been burned. "I tried to sleep but she was relentless in her desire for you."

The way she said it sent a kick low in his stomach, the subtle implication drawing him in as she walked toward the bed, giving him the back view of two giant happy faces on each of her cheeks.

As helpless as the dog in his arms, he followed. "What're you researching?"

She gave him a funny look, pointed to the walls, then her ears.

"You have nothing to worry about," he assured her. "While we were out today, every inch of this house was inspected for bugs. Cara lied about monitoring you, except for the old lady, of course."

"All right. I'm researching human trafficking." She curled onto the bed with a laptop, which, unfortunately, cast a soft light right on the damn-near-see-through fabric of her tank top, highlighting her breasts and creating a sexy shadow of cleavage. "Which is going to give me nightmares."

Where had he ever gotten it into his head that Vivi wasn't feminine?

Colt dropped onto the chair facing her, letting the dog curl quietly in his lap. "What are you learning?"

"It's a shockingly big business, the single most lucrative business *on earth*."

He nodded, sadly knowing these facts just from FBI cases he'd read or heard about. "Fastest-growing crime in the world," he confirmed.

"They make it look legal, which is the scary thing, and these people think they are part of some federal guest worker program. They get here and their visas are confiscated and they're put in these horrible houses and"—she gave in to a full-body shiver—"and the girls, Lang. It's just horrific. We have to get this guy."

"I've had a few cases, much smaller than this, of course, and the stuff I've seen would curl your hair. Listen, why don't you give it up for tonight?"

"Actually, I'm on to another subject, namely our housekeeper. Much less stomach turning, but still a little creepy." She gave him a funny look, as if she expected him not to like what she was about to say. "I had my cousin Chessie do some cyber digging on Mercedes Graff."

"Yeah? Good call." He'd put the same order into his office, but he knew from experience that twenty-something Francesca Rossi could outhack the FBI. Another reason he liked working with the Guardian Angelinos: He liked their results, if not always their approach. "What'd she find?"

Vivi leaned forward to tap the keyboard, her long hair falling over one shoulder.

"Damn, that reminds me, Vivi. We gotta cut that hair."

She looked up, surprised. "You don't like my pretty fake hair?"

"Doesn't matter if I do or not," he said. "I need to send a sample to the lab. Remember, the clue that got me here was a match of some chemical in human hair from a wig they found in vic number one's car and vic number two's house."

She flipped a strand of her hair. "This came from Cara, or at least her stylist."

"What if someone in her circle killed the first two and managed to get close to the third?"

She gave him a raised eyebrow of interest, then ran her fingers through the hair, tugging. "It doesn't pull out easy. I'll cut a few hairs for you."

"We need the top business, where it connects to your hair."

"'kay," she agreed, scrolling some more through the computer. "In a sec. Listen to this. Mercedes hasn't lived here her whole life, certainly not since Cara and Joellen were children. She showed up after they moved away with their mother, who died. Then they came back, barely teenagers, and lived with her. That's the first real record Chessie could find of her. But since then, she's never been on a plane, train, or owned her own automobile."

"Confirming your agoraphobic theory."

"Especially since she's seen four shrinks in the last ten years, two of whom are specialists in that very disease."

He choked a soft laugh. "Do I want to know how your little cousin found that out?"

"No, Mr. Do-Right, you do not." She grinned, sneaky and sweet at the same time. Enough to make his stomach tighten up. No, lower.

"Any family?"

"Nothing yet, but Chessie will send more when she gets it." With a sigh, she pushed the computer away and corralled her mane up, then stretched, folding her torso over her leg with amazing flexibility. "I'm wiped."

"How can you bend like that?"

"I used to be a ballet dancer."

He snorted. "Right."

She hid her face in the stretch. "Scoff all you want, Lang. It's true. I danced from the time I was three until..." Her voice faded. "I quit at sixteen."

"Why?"

She waved her hand, dismissing the question, then flattened her body over the other leg, denying him the chance to interpret her expression.

"Gave up the tutus for ill-fitting painter pants, huh?"

She looked up through her hair. "No one calls them painter pants anymore, Mr. Stuck-in-the-Seventies. And I'm aware you don't like my style."

"I didn't say that."

"Oh, please." She sat up a little. "I'm also aware that since I've grown long hair, started wearing makeup and high heels, you've been doing a helluva lot of kissing. Shame you'd be so shallow."

"Shallow?" Was he?

"Falling for all that girlie shit. Just like a man." She walked her hands over to her other foot, her back table-flat, her legs wide, like human origami. "I don't like it."

His brain short-circuited just imagining what she could do with that body. "You don't like what?"

She straightened to stare him down. "All those months we worked together and you never kissed me. You never even looked like you might kiss me. You never even thought about kissing me—"

"That's where you're wrong." So, so wrong.

Her next words got stuck, but so did her jaw in an open position.

"I just didn't kiss you because"—*I'd never stop*—"it was inappropriate."

She still didn't reply, just looked at him, the seconds dragging as the admission hung in the air.

"I figured the Guardian Angelinos must have a rule against kissing clients," he finally said.

"We're not real big on rules," she said with a wink. "In case you haven't noticed."

"I noticed." Just like he noticed his heart rate was inexplicably high. Well, not totally inexplicable. The laptop was still beaming light on her breasts. And now her nipples were hard.

And so was he.

For a long, long moment—too long—they just looked at each other. He knew what he wanted, but did she? He started to say her name, but she bolted off the bed in one effortless roll.

"I guess we should get that hair for you." She disappeared into the bathroom, leaving the door open.

He didn't follow. His arousal would be obvious as soon as she saw him, and... and if he got one inch closer he wouldn't stop himself from kissing her for a third time that day.

"How much do you want, Lang?"

I want it all.

The kisses, the touching, the loss of sanity for a few seconds. That's what he wanted with Vivi, wasn't it? Would she consider that?

Of course she'd consider it. This *was* Vivi. The same Vivi who, on a private plane, had climbed on him and sucked him senseless with what was, in retrospect, a pretty flimsy excuse for reckless behavior.

Maybe she wanted the same thing? Just an old-fashioned get-it-out-of-your-system screw.

"I actually need more than two hands here," she said.

He stood, adjusting his sleep pants around his erection, and drew in a deep breath that quivered his nostrils. "She needs my hands," he mouthed to Stella. And his hands needed her. "Stay, kid."

The dog dropped her head on the sofa. Now, if only the other woman in this room would be as compliant.

He found her leaning against the vanity, close to the mirror, struggling to hold up her hair and get a grip on an underneath layer. She was angled far enough that the waistband of her ridiculous boxers tugged down, almost to the shadow of her gorgeous ass.

Jesus. His hands itched. His throat tightened. His cock made a mockery of his love of control.

"It hurts," she complained.

Yes, it did. It hurt to be this close to her. "Just a few hairs, Vivi. It has to be taken out in such a way that we get the glue that holds it in." He took a few steps closer. One touch and he was dead, aching blood and balls winning the battle. One hand on her body and he wouldn't want to stop. He *should not do this.*

"Let me help you."

Placing his hands on her shoulders, he eased her away from the mirror, standing close enough to feel the heat of her. He twirled a lock of the long hair.

She met his gaze in the mirror, her dark eyes even blacker in the dim light. That wasn't night vision causing her pupils to expand, he knew. It was arousal, just like his. Perfectly natural, utterly powerful, completely mutual.

"I'm going to have to pull some. I don't want to pull your real hair and hurt you."

Her expression grew as serious as any he'd ever seen. "I don't want you to hurt me, Lang," she whispered.

He got the message. A warning, mixed with an invitation, right? He wasn't misreading that, was he? He drew her closer. "I won't hurt you." He slid his hand up the nape of her neck, causing a bloom of chills across her skin. Leaning her head forward, he separated some hair, easily finding the BB-sized knots on her scalp. Her short hair was well hidden underneath. "Ah, here's Vivi."

"The real one," she said.

"The one I really do like," he whispered.

Under his touch, she stiffened. "Don't, Lang."

He froze, too. "Don't what?"

"Tease me."

"I don't tease. You do."

She whipped around so fast he got the hairs without trying. "Ow! How dare you say that?"

Her vehemence surprised him. "What?

"I have never teased you. You can't count that lap dance because that was done for a reason, and if you remember correctly, I finished the job. I don't tease men."

"I meant tease as in your sense of humor."

"Really?" Her eyes just glinted in the dim light, and fell to his tented sleep pants. "Because I didn't *try* to make that happen."

"I know," he said. "That's the thing, honey. You never try, but it always happens."

He closed his hand over her wrist, and placed her palm on his chest, just to let her know how hard his heart was beating, and then to inch her fingers down to singe his skin. "This is not an unusual occurrence around you. Even with your baggy clothes and stick-up hair."

"Oh..." The word came out like a sigh as she splayed her fingers over his chest, her palm dry and warm and precious. Their gazes locked, their breaths already shorter, their pulses pounding.

"This is a surprise to you?" He angled his head just the slightest degree, the way it would fit perfectly on her mouth.

"Why didn't you say anything?"

He managed a wry laugh. "Over the conference table, in front of your brother? Did you want me to announce my woody during strategy sessions?"

"You got...hard."

He let go of her hand, sliding his hands around her waist to lift her in one easy move onto the counter. Bringing her face a little closer to his, easily slipping between her legs, his crotch inches from hers.

He burned to close the space completely. To let his hard-on free, to pull her into him. "How is it that a girl with so much confidence doesn't realize her own sex appeal?"

She still had one hand on his chest; the other clutched the edge of the marble as though she needed stability. "Because...I thought I wasn't your type."

He smiled and let his hands ride over her hips and settle on the smooth skin of her thighs. "Yeah, I thought so too. Then we had the meeting about the Berkower case."

Her eyes flashed in understanding. "The one that went so late into the night. When Zach had to leave and—"

"And you went to retrieve something from the top shelf in the storage room?"

"I thought you stayed in the conference room. You were watching me?"

"I thought you might fall." He thumbed her skin, his hands already sliding closer to the inside of her thighs. To the opening of those little boxers. To her. "I had to make sure you were safe."

She narrowed her eyes at him. "You had to see my ass when I climbed up that step stool."

"And this..." He skimmed up to her waist, inching the top out of the way. "When your T-shirt rode all the way up."

"Was I wearing a bra?"

"Didn't go far quite enough." He dragged his hand higher. "But you aren't now."

She sucked in a little breath when he grazed the underside of her breast with his thumb.

"Lang..."

"So I went home that night..." One more centimeter of skin—and she wasn't stopping him.

"And?"

He leaned closer to put his mouth over her ear, the same moment he thumbed her pebbled nipple. "I imagined us in the storage room." She shivered in response. Exactly what he wanted, exactly what he'd hoped for.

"Doing what?" she asked breathlessly.

"*It.* Up against the wall." He closed his hand over her breast, filling his palm and shooting more blood and fire into his groin.

"So did I." The admission was barely a whisper.

It was all he needed to hear. He pulled her hips against his and covered her mouth with the kiss that had been gnawing at his imagination for months.

Full on, openmouthed, hot, wet, and demanding. And Vivi gave it right back to him, wrapping her arms and legs around him, letting his cock smash against the very place it had to be—right between her legs.

Perfect. *Perfect.* No hesitation, just surrender. She inhaled the kiss in one gasp of joy. She shuddered—no... she giggled. And again.

"You're laughing?" he murmured into the kiss, his hands already wild in finding new places to touch. The dip in her lower back, the side of her breast, her leg, her stomach—oh, Lord, the sweet, soft, sexy inside of her thigh.

"I'm happy."

He slowed his kisses and stilled his hands. Happy. Not exactly what he was going for. Hot, hungry, and ready to go horizontal, but, okay. She was happy.

"Because," she continued, her hand on his head to guide his mouth to a surprisingly responsive spot near her collarbone. "This crush is mutual."

He stopped kissing completely, lifting his head. "Crush?"

"What do you call it, Lang?"

Usually, sex. Sometimes something a little grittier. Like...fucking. But not a..."Crush?"

"Yes," she said, her head dropping back, her eyes glittering. "That feeling of excitement before you come to the office, when I'm all shaky and nervous? When we're together, I just...want...to touch you and know you. After I see you, I can't think of anything else for hours. Days, even." The admission tumbled out, peppered with self-conscious laughs and quick breaths.

He just stared at her.

"I fall asleep thinking about you, Lang. Wake up thinking about you. I...I..."

He still hadn't said a word. Because a crush was too much like an *emotion*.

"You don't," she said simply, realization dawning so hard and fast he could practically feel her skin freeze under his touch.

"I just told you," he said slowly, choosing every word carefully despite the blood drain from his brain that made thinking like hard labor at the moment. "You're the object of my fantasies."

She inched back, all that happiness gone. "Mine, too," she said quietly.

"Then what's wrong?" Because something was. Terribly wrong.

Endless seconds dragged by as she looked at him, a war raging inside, and he had no idea what side he was on or if he'd win in the end.

"Vivi?" he finally asked. "Are you still okay with this?"

She smiled, wistful and sad. "The thing is, Lang, I was never okay with it."

Instantly, he let her go.

CHAPTER 11

Of course she killed the deal. Wasn't that inevitable? Wasn't she just digging for an excuse to stop the luscious waves of lust he'd started in her body?

How could she possibly tell him that this was just about as far as she ever made it? Then he'd really call her a tease.

The word twisted her gut. The wounding, wicked word of an angry, violent boy. But not Lang, not any guy—just the one who ruined her.

Tease. It still made vomit rise in her throat.

"Vivi, why are you in here kissing me, if you're not okay with it?"

Fair question, asked in his old, humorless, golf-playing Lang voice.

"I...am...tempted," she admitted in a halting voice. "But I don't..." Now what could she tell him? Not the truth. Never the truth. No one knew that, except the bastard who did it to her. And he probably didn't even remember her name. "I really think it's a bad idea to have sex with a client." The words rushed out. "Even one I have a crush on."

He visibly slumped. "Is that all?"

No, that was *not* all. But it would have to do until Vivi could—no, Vivi could never again. "Especially since you aren't exactly reciprocating with the whole crush confession thing."

"I just didn't know what you called it," he said. "I just thought we were friends who...liked each other." He smiled and let his gaze drop to her body, warming her in spite of the fact that she suddenly felt very, very cold. "A lot."

"Friends with benes?" she asked. "Is that what you're looking for, Lang?"

He backed away, of course. Because that was what she was trying to get him to do, wasn't it? That was her goal: sabotage the sex, and stay safe. That was the Vivi Angelino signature move.

"Benes?" he said, sounding a little disgusted.

"Benefits," she explained.

"I get it. I was thinking more along the lines of... sex...without..." He just couldn't say it.

"Strings," she supplied.

He didn't argue, giving her the perfect excuse. Let him think that hurts. "Oh, sure, Lang. You're leaving for L.A. so we can just fuck like bunnies until you ship out to your big promo." She sounded bitter, which beat sounding pathetic and scared and victimized. "Fine."

"Sorry, Vivi. You didn't strike me as a woman who needed...paperwork."

Paperwork? Oh, that was good. She managed to look

insulted, although she was just relieved. He was handing her a perfect out. "No, I'm not really big on the whole screw-and-shoo gig. But thanks for the offer."

The sarcasm was hurting him, she could tell. Shaming him because he had come into this room acting like a perfectly normal man, and if only Vivi were a *normal woman*, she'd have gone along with it. Because Lang was her fantasy on steroids and she wanted him. *Bad.*

But some asshole had ruined her head forever.

And Colton Lang was paying for that right this moment. "Hey, listen." She managed to slide off the counter and, to his credit, he didn't give much of a fight. "We're cool."

He swallowed hard, stepping away completely. "I didn't mean to insult you, Vivi. I misread you."

"You didn't misread me, Lang. I've got major hots for you, and that's pretty hard to hide. I just…realized… that…" *I'm more psychologically damaged than the poor old bag who's scared to leave the house.* "You matter more than you should and with you going to Los Angeles, I'd just get all weepy and shit when you left."

He looked hard at her. "Why are you lying?"

Damn it. "Okay, I'm exaggerating. I wouldn't get weepy. I never cry."

"Never? Not once?"

"Once when my mother died," she said quickly. "And once when my dog got taken away a couple weeks later." And then that day she'd lain in some sterile clinic in Medford, all alone and so scared. She'd cried pretty hard that day. Cried until there were no tears left. "And the week I quit dancing," she said quietly. "I think I cried then."

Before he could stop her, she moved to the door and turned the knob. She had to get out of this room. "That dog sure is quiet when you tell her to be. Hey, Stella," she called, opening the door. "He's all yours—"

"What's the matter?" Lang was next to her in a heartbeat, peering into the empty room. The door was closed, but Stella was gone.

"She took the dog," he said, already marching to the door.

Vivi stuffed her feet into a pair of flip-flops and jogged after him. "Where are you going?"

"To get the dog back. I don't trust that bitch and her sedatives." He stopped at the door to his room and put up his hand for her to wait.

"You need a shirt to go get the dog?" Vivi asked.

"No, I need a gun to go get the dog."

A minute later, he came out, his Glock pointed down, gesturing for her to follow to the kitchen through the butler's pantry to the door that led down to Mercedes's basement apartment. It was locked.

As he lifted his hand to knock, they heard the bark, and a whimper.

Outside.

For a quick second, they both looked at each other, the same thought registering. If the dog was outside, then the agoraphobic who never set foot out of doors mustn't have her.

"I'll find Mercedes," Vivi offered. "You get the dog."

"No, you stay with me. I don't give a shit about the old lady—let's just get the dog."

But if Mercedes hadn't taken Stella outside, who had? One of the other agents? Was there a doggie door they didn't know about ? The kitchen was empty, and so was the fenced-in area where Mercedes usually let her out.

The whimpering came from the other side of that fence.

"She could have gotten under the fence," Vivi said. "I saw her digging at that spot earlier."

"Just stay with me," Lang said, opening the gate to the backyard.

She stayed close to him, peering around. They descended the few stone steps to a secluded pool area enclosed by thick poplar trees. A shroud of mist rose from the heated water.

The whimpering got louder.

"She's past those trees," Vivi said, pointing to the poplars. "There's nothing but brush back there."

"Stella!" Lang called, pulling out his cell phone to use as a flashlight.

They heard a scurrying through the brush, the sound of the dog running. "Here she comes," Vivi said, relieved. But no dog appeared.

"Stella!" he called again, walking toward the trees. "She's going that way. Stay here, Vivi. I'll go get her."

He disappeared through the trees and Vivi listened to him calling her, his voice getting a little distant as he moved deeper into the wooded property.

She rubbed her arms against the cold air, listening.

A bark from a completely different direction startled her, and she turned toward the sound. How had Stella gotten all the way over there? She took a few steps to the other end of the pool, frowning into the darkness, wishing like hell she'd been smart enough to bring her cell phone to use as a flashlight.

But, no, she had been too busy waging her inner sex wars to think about security.

Still humming from the encounter, tight and needy and so utterly dissatisfied with her choices and her issues and her brain-versus-body battle, she walked to the tree line and listened. A little doggie paw cracked a branch.

"Stella?" she called, glancing over her shoulder, half expecting to see Lang appear from the other side. Surely he realized she'd come over here now. "Stella! Come here, you little beast."

She wiggled through the trees toward the sound. "Stella. I know you hate me, but I'll hand you over to your true love."

The dog barked once, a good fifty feet away in the thick of the trees. Then she whimpered helplessly again, the sound of real pain.

"Stella?" Was she hurt? Vivi moved toward the sound, stones and sticks prodding the flimsy flip-flops, cold air and stiff branches brushing her nearly bare skin. She was dressed for sex in the bathroom, not dog searches in the woods.

The whimpering was louder now, and more than a little desperate. She pushed at pine needles and shook off a spiderweb—more of those bastards—and headed to the noise.

"Lang!" she hollered. "She's over here. I think she's—"

The gunshot shocked her into silence, so close she automatically threw herself to the ground. The next one made her roll as a bullet whizzed right by her head.

She dove for the cover of trees, scraping her arms and legs on pine needles, a scream of terror trapped in her throat. Her hands hit something soft just as the next bullet ricocheted off the trunk of a tree. This time she did shriek a little and so did the dog she'd landed on.

Grabbing Stella, Vivi started to get up to run, but froze at the sound of footsteps, hard, fast, and headed in her direction. Folding up to make as small a target as she could, she rolled deeper under the pine, earth and dirt chafing her face and filling her mouth, her whole body around the tiny dog.

Here it comes, she thought. The next shot.

I'm going to die. Out here, in the bogs of Nantucket, holding a dog, pretending to be someone else. She was going to die.

Damn. She should have never said no to Lang. Now she was going to—

The bullet hit the soft peat of the ground, so close she heard the thump. Inches away.

Cradling the dog in both arms, she scrambled forward, losing a flip-flop as she crawled army style under the lowest branches of pine, having no idea where she was going but away from the son of a bitch with a gun.

She stopped long enough to hear branches snap, footsteps hitting dirt. Away or toward her? She had no idea. She wanted to scream for Lang again, but that would give away her location.

Instead, she gripped the dog and dug her elbows and knees into the ground, creeping as fast as she could without crushing Stella, who was either too smart or too scared to bark.

Damn it, she wasn't going to die. She was going to live. And so was this stupid dog.

And the next time that man offered her his body, she'd take it instead of letting some memory ruin everything for her. The vow propelled her forward, just as another gunshot sent a bullet whizzing through the pine trees above her head.

Someone was running, snapping branches, breathing hard. Lang? Or the shooter?

She lifted her head to look. The pine trees blocked any chance of moonlight, so she might as well have been blind.

She made it five feet, then ten, rounded another tree and suddenly the earth fell away at her side, an unexpected hill that made her slide, slip, and roll like a log, losing her grip on the dog and holding in a shriek until she slammed against another tree.

"Vivi!" Lang was on her in the next second, full body coverage, flipping on his back, weapon aimed into the night.

"Someone shot at me," she said with a soft cry.

"Are you okay?"

"Yes, but someone's out here."

Stella leaped at both of them, and Vivi grabbed her, closing into a ball again, her hands automatically searching Stella for a wound.

"Listen!" Lang demanded in a harsh whisper.

They both stilled, stopping every sound, even their breathing, which was not easy considering that they were both winded.

"He's gone," she whispered. "I swear I heard him running away." Or *her* running away. Was Mercedes capable of that kind of attack?

More footsteps and voices broke the night. In seconds the other FBI agents were there, taking orders from Lang, fanning out, protecting her.

"Get her into the house," Lang ordered one of them, his hands on Vivi's shoulders as he passed her off to Agent Iverson. "And stay with her every second. We're going to find this bastard."

• • •

"Goddamn you, Jo." Cara stood over her sister and resisted the urge to pick up what was left of her last lemon-drop martini and pour it over her face. But even that wouldn't wake her. "I don't want to be alone tonight!"

Joellen didn't budge. She lay on the sofa, facedown, her mouth open just enough that drool would slide out any second.

Fuck. Cara had let Marissa go to spend the night with Bridget because Jo was getting looser and looser and God only knew what she'd say if Marissa pushed the wrong button.

But if she'd known her sister was going to pass out, she'd have kept Marissa here for company overnight.

Now she was all alone.

Huffing in disgust, she flounced away, and started what had become an obsessive nighttime routine, no matter who was here. Three times, she checked the windows and locks, reset the alarm, and made sure every drape and blind in the little house was pulled tight.

The ritual took five minutes, and gave her small comfort. If anyone came within twenty-five feet of the house, an alarm would blare, lights would flash, and all hell would break loose.

She could finally relax a little.

She paused in the bathroom door and surveyed the disaster that was Joellen in a too-small bathroom.

"What a pig." She started to pick up one of the makeup bags vomiting cosmetics and hair products, then threw it back down amidst the flat iron, blow dryer, hand mirror, a bra, underpants, and, of course, the ubiquitous empty martini glass.

The bathtub was clean, and that was all that mattered.

She just wanted to climb in, get burned by hot water, and figure out just how long she could play the game of cat-and-mouse with a man she'd once thought she loved. Back when she was young, foolish, and ambitious.

Now she was just ambitious.

And even if she used all those flaws as excuses, they wouldn't hold water with the public. Celebrities are constantly forgiven for their indiscretions, for needing rehab or having affairs, for picking up prostitutes or shoplifting.

But for selling little kids into slavery?

No excuse for her role in that crime, no matter how far behind her it was now, would fly. So she had to stay the course. There was only one thing to do when someone found out.

She swallowed hard. She'd keep Roman's secret if he kept hers—that was their delicate balance. But now the balance was upset, and the scales tipped in his favor.

She shed her clothes and barely glanced in the mirror, bending over to figure out the faucet, turning the hot water on full blast.

"Somewhere in this mess there has to be some bath gel." While the tub filled, she gingerly dug through the bottles, tubes, and makeup cases, knocking a few things to the tile floor in the process. Finally, she found some mimosa-scented bath gel.

Mimosa as in champagne and orange juice, not the flower, naturally.

"Even her soap is booze," Cara said as she poured and created a mountain of white bubbles.

She tested the water, which was fabulously hot, and slipped one foot in, nearly sliding on the slick surface.

She grabbed the towel rack, her body weight almost pulling it out of the wall as she righted herself.

"Jesus Christ, how about some traction on the tub, people?" Taking a second to get her balance and make sure she didn't fall on her ass, she dipped her body into the hot, bubbly water. When she lay down, her feet touched the tub at one end and she was still almost sitting up.

Not exactly the luxurious Jacuzzi she had in L.A. or in her Nantucket house.

Well, *Roman's* Nantucket house. He'd built it. He owned it. Just like he—

Everything went dark.

"Oh my God!" She popped her eyes open, the blackness and complete lack of sound like a blanket over the house. "Joellen! The fucking power went out! Jo!"

Unless . . . someone cut it.

Chills scrambled up her body as she sat straighter, slapping her hand over her mouth and cursing herself for being so stupid as to yell. A drunken Joellen wouldn't hear her, but someone else might. Someone who'd snipped wires and shut down the electricity and the alarm.

Maybe he'd kill Joellen, not her. In the dark, would he know if he had the right sister? Would he even know she was in the house? In this tub? Not if she stayed very still, very quiet.

She closed her eyes, trying to listen. Was that a creak? The wind? A door slowly opening? Her body started to tremble, cold despite the blistering water, scared right down to her bones.

Without the hum of a single electrical appliance, the house was unnaturally silent. She gritted her teeth to keep from making a sound. Was that a footstep? A hinge squeaking? The snap of a floorboard? Was someone breathing nearby?

She closed her eyes again to block everything but her hearing. Was that just the sound of her own terrified breaths? She couldn't tell anymore. Her heart walloped against her ribs, so loud it was like a bass drum in her head, her pulse so crazy she could feel her veins move as they thrummed blood and adrenaline.

A bitter taste rose in her throat but she managed a painful swallow. *That* was definitely a footstep. And another.

Oh, God. As silently as possible, she opened her mouth and breathed in, filling her lungs and letting the slippery surface slide her ass down the tub, dunking her head under.

Please don't find me. Please don't find me. Please don't—

Someone was screaming! Even through the water she could hear the high-pitched, endless wail. Joellen? Was Joellen being beaten and stabbed by someone who thought he was killing Cara Ferrari?

Her lungs started to burst, but she refused to rise. She didn't want to die. She'd rather hide like a coward and let her sister take the knife in her place.

The screaming wouldn't stop! It was one long shriek. Inhuman. Her chest ached with the need for air, her head light and spinning, her grasp on life almost gone.

She shot up to the surface and opened her mouth to suck in air and—

The lights were on. The whole house was lit again, and there was noise. So much noise! That must have been what she'd heard: the alarm wailing in a syncopated screech.

She pushed herself up, slipping on the porcelain and crying out as she fell back down, another sound breaking through her consciousness. A mechanical sound. A familiar buzz. A high-pitched hum.

The hair dryer was on!

Perched perilously at the edge of the vanity, right above the tub. She reached, but slipped again and saved herself from falling by grabbing the countertop, knocking over the empty martini glass and watching as it crashed to the floor. She jerked back from the flying shards, the move sending the hair dryer right over the edge.

For one time-suspended horrific second, she stared at the machine, tumbling in slow motion, clunking to the edge of the tub and sort of resting, its tipping point not yet decided. To the floor or—

Into the tub!

"Aaaahh!" She jumped over the side of the tub, grabbing the towel rack for help, ripping it out of the drywall, her kneecaps cracking on the hard tile floor, cut on broken glass.

"Karen!" Joellen stood in the doorway. "Oh my God!"

Behind Cara, the dryer bobbed in the water, sending blue and white arcs of electrical sparks into the air before the appliance shut off.

The alarm suddenly stopped, the only sound Cara's agonizing breaths.

"Holy crap, that thing could have killed you," Joellen said.

No shit. "Who set off the alarm?"

"Oh, I did, damn it. I wanted to go out for a smoke. Let me call the alarm company." She stumbled away.

"Who cut off all the electricity?" Cara demanded.

Joellen stuck her head back in. "I was asleep," she said. "I don't know what the fuck you're talking about."

Cara just stood there, naked, terrified, not even sure what had just happened.

Jo pointed to the water. "Can you believe how close you just came to continuing the Red Carpet Curse?"

Cara just shook her head, words impossible.

"Now that would have been ironic."

"You have no idea," Cara whispered.

CHAPTER 12

Mercedes didn't answer her door. Vivi pounded repeatedly and was just about ready to suggest Special Agent Iverson shoot the lock off when the door slowly opened and Mercedes appeared, wearing a housecoat, slippers, and a silver net over her hair. Still, she had the nerve to give Vivi a look of disgust and dismay, lingering on the happy-face boxers as if they offended her. She barely glanced at Special Agent Iverson standing behind Vivi.

"What?" she asked.

"You didn't hear the gunshots?" Vivi asked. *Or were you outside firing?*

Mercedes lifted her hands to show an orange earplug held in each. "I was sound asleep," she said.

"Is there a door to the outside anywhere in here?" Vivi demanded.

"No, there is not."

Vivi tilted her head. "Stop lying, Mercedes."

Under her rough complexion, she paled. "There is a way to another part of the house, but not outside."

Vivi managed not to look smug. "Would you please let us in so we can examine it? Someone is on the grounds, shooting—at me, I might add—and I need to see if an intruder could get in or out of this basement any other way."

"Come with me," she said, indicating the stairs. Vivi and the FBI agent followed, taken on a tour that Vivi had already experienced firsthand: through the pantry, down the stairs, to the closet, all through the tunnels.

Mercedes touched the wall and soft running lights guided them.

"Cara built this for me," she said quietly as they walked the same path Vivi and Lang had followed. "Because, in case you haven't noticed, I don't ever go outside." She turned to Vivi. "So I wasn't shooting at you. As for my condition, I can provide the medical records to prove it."

At the hitch in a voice that never neared vulnerable under normal circumstances, Vivi softened her expression. "But someone came in my room and took the dog."

"Mr. Lang?"

"He was with me," Vivi said, realizing what she had to reveal. "In the bathroom."

She felt Special Agent Iverson's eyes on her and a slow heat rise to her face. Mercedes, however, didn't seemed to think anything was odd about that.

"The dog knows her way around the house, and she probably left your room."

"And got outside?"

Mercedes shook her head. "She's wily, I told you.

Without sedatives, she burrows and digs. Probably found her way out and—"

"The dog didn't shoot me!" Vivi said, frustration rising as they reached the part of the tunnel where it became little more than a drainage ditch. "And do you know that hole right there connects with the bog house?"

Mercedes bit her lip. "It's unfinished. Cara was going to add to the tunnel so I could get down there."

"Why do you need to get down there?" Iverson asked.

Mercedes inhaled and exhaled slowly. "Because I would like to visit the house again. And the bog."

She certainly sounded genuine, but Vivi was still skeptical. They finished the tunnel tour and left Mercedes, returning to Vivi's room.

"I can't leave you," Agent Iverson said. "But I'll sit in the bedroom while you shower, if you like."

Of course, she was filthy. But could she go back into that bathroom? The scene where she and Lang had kissed and touched and talked?

And she'd turned him down, like the world's biggest idiot.

Instead, she grabbed a pair of jeans and gestured to the next room. Lang's room.

"I don't want to be in here," she said, not offering any more explanation. She didn't have to; Sarah Iverson was a smart agent and she had no doubt put two and two together and come up with . . . some rules being broken.

After her shower, Vivi grabbed a soft white undershirt from the open duffel bag in Lang's bathroom, inhaling whatever nice detergent he used before slipping it over her head. In the room, Agent Iverson was on her cell phone, but hung up when Vivi came out.

"They're giving up the search soon," she said. "They didn't find anyone. Mr. Lang will be up here shortly, if you want me to go back to your room with you."

"I'll stay here," Vivi said, curling up on the sofa next to Stella, who loped across the cushions and threw her head on Vivi's leg. "Oh, finally, you like me. Only took saving your life."

Across the room, in a club chair, Agent Iverson smiled. "So how well do you know Mr. Lang?" she asked.

Not as well as I'd like to. "We've worked together on a few projects." Vivi petted the dog, who at least had the dignity to stop growling at her now that her life had been saved. "How about you?"

"I've been in the Boston office for seven years."

So did that mean she knew him well? Vivi tried to decipher the woman's expression, but the seasoned agent gave no tells. "Have you worked a lot of cases with him?" Vivi asked.

"Some. I was in the same class with Jennifer."

Her stomach tightened at the way she said Jennifer. Like, of course, Vivi would know who that was. Lang's words were burned in her brain, about the backup who took a deadly risk.

She didn't have anything I didn't like.

"She was his partner, right?" Vivi ventured.

That earned a soft, maybe a little sarcastic, chuckle from the agent. "Define 'partner.' They hadn't gone public with their plans, but Jenn was just waiting for a transfer out of his department so they could announce their engagement—"

"Out!"

Both women flinched at the command, issued by Lang at the door.

Vivi was still processing *engagement*, but Agent Iverson jumped to the order and so did the dog, practically launching herself into Lang's arms like he'd saved her instead of Vivi.

The agent gathered her phone, weapon, and jacket. "You sure you're okay?" she asked Vivi.

She had been okay—before the engagement bomb was dropped. "Fine. Thanks again."

"Good night, Ms. Iverson," Lang said pointedly, waiting by the door until she left.

Then he closed it, flipped the lock, and placed his weapon on the dresser near the door. Wordlessly, he shook off a jacket that someone must have brought to him, still shirtless and in sleep pants underneath. His arms and chest were scraped from the branches; smudges of dirt clung to sweaty muscles.

Vivi tried not to stare and failed miserably. "So, anything?" she asked.

He kicked off his sneakers. "Got some bullets for ballistics, a few footprints which could be anyone or anything, but no shooter."

"I talked to Mercedes," she said, sitting up a little. "She claims she was asleep in her room."

"*Claims* being the operative word." His voice was tight with something that sounded like anger. Probably frustration, too, after a fruitless search.

"She took me to the tunnels, but didn't show me anything we didn't already know. She says Cara built them for her because she can't go outside. And she swears she didn't come in here and take the dog."

"Someone did." He still hadn't really looked at her, Vivi realized, although she'd been staring at him since he'd walked into the room. Lang crouched to give Stella an affectionate scratch and something beyond immature and jealous inside of Vivi wanted to scream "Hey, what about me!" but she didn't.

"I take it your gut says what mine does and this shooter has to do with Roman Emmanuel," she said instead. "Or do you think that was possibly some nutcase who kills Oscar winners?"

"Taking shots at you just doesn't seem to fit the MO of a so-called Red Carpet Killer."

She rubbed her arms. "I have to admit I feel pretty vulnerable here."

"Yeah, that's why we're going to Boston tomorrow." He finally looked at her.

"To get Uncle Nino?" she asked hopefully.

"I told you to forget that," he said, striding into the bathroom without closing the door. "It's not safe enough here for him. It's not safe enough for *you*."

She heard the water running in the sink.

"Are you making me leave for good?" When he didn't answer, she got up and walked to the bathroom, standing in the doorway to watch him stick his whole head under the faucet. "What about the evidence we've been asked to find, Lang?"

"We'll come back." He turned his head, soaping his face and neck. "I just want to get you out of here for a day while some other agents scour the property by light of day. We're missing something."

She didn't argue; she could use a break from this house. "Why don't you just take a shower?"

"Can't." He stood up and gave his head a shake that would have made Stella proud. "Unless you stand there and watch."

Fire licked through her belly. "That can be arranged."

He froze in the act of grabbing the towel, his gaze dropping over the T-shirt and jeans. "Why are you in here and not your room?"

"I just wanted to be close to you."

He still didn't dry his face, but just looked at her as droplets sluiced over cheeks that hadn't seen their usual razor in a long time. "Why?"

"I just wanted to be close to the man who saved my life."

"What do you mean by close?"

She wet her lips, ignored her thumping heart. "As close as we can get."

He stepped toward her, eyes burning green-gold in the dim light. "One brush with death and you change your mind?"

"I've had some time to think," she said slowly. "And I...I decided that maybe...you were right."

He studied her for a long minute, heat and sweat and something wildly intoxicating rolling off him. The scent of sex.

"I thought you were shot," he said gruffly. "For like the third time in two days, I fucking thought you were dead."

"I bet you were mad."

"Mad?" He slapped his hands on the doorjamb, his chest inches from her, his biceps tense like he could break the molding off the doorway if he wanted to. "Mad doesn't even begin to cover it. Why the hell don't you stay put when I tell you to stay put?"

"I heard the dog. Anyway, he could have shot me there, too."

"You could have been killed, Vivi."

"Tell me something I haven't figured out while I was trapped up here like Rapunzel with the girl guard while all the guys looked for the perp."

He grunted, animal like, pure frustration. "All the *guys* are FBI agents, armed and trained and willing to die for you."

She'd never win that one. "I saved your dog, didn't I?"

"She's not mine." He let his hands fall and land on her shoulders, plucking at the T-shirt. "But this is."

"I borrowed it."

"Take it off."

Her knees actually buckled at the order. "You want it back?"

"I want it off."

And, dear God, she wanted to take it off. Deep inside, an ache twisted. Lusty and low, superseding everything else.

She stared at him, taking a few steps backward into the room, but he didn't let go of her shoulders. "I've been thinking about you."

His eyes went smoky. "Good. Keep thinking about me." He walked her backward until she reached the bed. No smile on his face, no humor in his eyes. Dead serious, pure Lang. "Think about me while you take off my shirt."

She sat when her knees hit the bed, fingering the bottom of the T-shirt as she looked up at him. "I have to say something first. I have one...rule."

He lifted his brow. "You follow rules now?"

She had to feel...safe, or she couldn't do this. That was her only stipulation. She had to know she had an escape if her brain betrayed her body and freaked out. "If I say stop, you stop."

"Here's my rule." He pressed knees against the bed, holding hers between his as he eased her backward. "You shouldn't say *go* if you're gonna say *stop*."

Her gaze slipping to his sleep pants, the tent even bigger than it was before, the tip of his hard-on already straining the waistband. Her throat went dry. "If I did say stop, like if I *had* to..." she whispered. "I just want you to know it's not because I'm teasing you. It's just because... I changed my mind."

He braced himself over her, all muscle and man, hard and ready. Her whole body liquefied with want. She fell back on the bed, unable to fight the need to writhe against him and release the pressure that was building between her legs.

"If you change your mind, let me know. Until then, take my shirt off."

With shaky fingers, she lifted the cotton hem, watching his eyes move down to devour the sight. She revealed her stomach, her ribs, her breasts. His jaw loosened, his pupils darkened, his breath slowed to a ragged pull.

"All the way," he said.

She slipped it over her head, dragging the long, damp hair through, unintentionally making the extensions fan out next to her face. She held the undershirt up in one hand.

"Here's your shirt, Lang."

He took it and threw it across the room. "Now the jeans."

"Oh, God."

"What's the matter?" he asked, his eyes narrowing at her tone.

What was the matter? What could she tell him? That she'd never...No, if she told him to stop, he'd stop. But she also knew he'd demand to know what she'd refuse to tell.

"What is it, Vivi?"

"Ummm...I forgot to wear underpants."

That made one side of his mouth hitch up with sexy interest. "Yeah? Let me see."

She reached for the jeans snap, popped it, and unzipped, never taking her eyes from his.

But he looked down, inhaling slowly as she pushed the jeans down, slowly lifting her hips to help her reveal everything to him.

Everything.

"Christ, you're gorgeous." He barely breathed the words, and they obliterated every argument threatening to make an appearance in her head.

He dragged the jeans off her body and tossed them with the shirt.

Then she lay completely naked before him, barely able to take the next breath. Could he hear her heart clobbering her chest? Could he hear the blood rushing through her? Could he possibly know what this meant to her?

"So why'd you change your mind?" he asked, kneeling above her, burning every inch with his eyes, splaying his fingers over her body, like a maestro about to play.

"I haven't, yet."

"I mean about sex. A few hours ago you said you were morally opposed to friends with benefits. Now you're pretty friendly."

"The friend saved my life."

His hands came down and closed over her fists, which,

she only realized then, were clutching the comforter. "I don't need you to reward me."

"I'm not rewarding you."

His eyes grew smoky as he took another slow trip over every inch of her. "Then what are you doing?"

"Something I've wanted to do for a long time." Like sixteen years. "So please kiss me. Please."

"I will." He almost smiled, his eyes tapering. "I'm trying to decide where to start."

She closed her eyes. "Anywhere you want."

He lowered his head to her mouth, but skimmed away before they made contact, blowing soft air over her throat, collarbone, her cleavage. His tongue flicked over her breast, and she sucked in a breath, but he moved south, a kiss on her stomach, a brush of lips over the scar of her gunshot wound, navel, the scrape of his cheek right on her pelvic bone.

She let go of the comforter, moved her hands to his shoulders.

"Yeah," he said gruffly. "This is where I want to start."

Yes. Oh, God, yes. *This.*

He blew on her first, like he was warming her up, getting her ready. She bowed her back, whispered his name, and braced for impact.

His tongue was surprisingly cool against the heat of her flesh, but powerful and unrelenting. He sucked and licked, the sensation of his mouth against her making her groan with abandon.

Glorious.

Her body hummed under his mouth, rocking into his lips, a rhythm so natural and elemental she just surrendered to it.

He curled his tongue around her most sensitive spot before slipping in a little deeper. He held her thigh with one sure hand and manipulated her clit with the other.

Mother of God, was *this* what she'd been missing?

She cried his name softly, begged for more, squirmed and writhed and gasped for breaths of air that just weren't there.

Her orgasm flared under his lips. She transferred her grip from his shoulder to his head, hanging on for dear life as all the sensations coiled deep inside her, throbbing like the low rumble of thunder, building to a crescendo, racking her when she exploded in his mouth.

Endless, unstoppable, overwhelming...pleasure.

She cried out, her head back, her body helpless, her fantasies fulfilled and everything else—*everything*—wiped away by his competent, relentless tongue.

Grabbing his shoulders, she crunched her upper body to see him, sweat and sex rolling off her as the waves subsided and the aftershocks slowed. Until there was nothing left but a tingle between her thighs, a thumping of her chest, a few torn attempts at steady breathing.

He stayed between her legs for what seemed like forever, still kissing, still licking, still adoring her.

How did he know? How did he *know* that was exactly what she needed?

Finally, he crawled up her body, more kisses on the way, until he reached her face.

"I want a shower," he said, his voice tight.

She widened her eyes. "A cold one?"

"Wouldn't help. I just want to be clean for you. Because once I get inside you, I don't intend to get out of this bed again."

Her body still throbbed with the orgasm, and the heat of the words.

"Come with me, Vivi."

"I don't want to do it in the shower on . . . our first time."

"I promise, we're not going to do it in the shower. But I'm not leaving you alone. Sit on the counter and don't leave my sight." He kissed her and helped her up. "Come on. I've been climbing through the brush and mud. You deserve better than that."

Oh, God. Did he have to be so perfect? Couldn't he just be that guy who wanted to fuck and fly?

No. And he never would be. Not to her. "Okay."

Colt couldn't get in the shower fast enough and it had nothing, absolutely nothing, to do with the dirt on his body. That wasn't what stopped him from taking what he wanted so bad his dick was ready to explode and his balls were so high they smacked his teeth.

Everything had changed in the last two hours.

Able to see Vivi through the glass, he stepped into the vicious spray. He braced his hands on the wall and let the water wash over him; it was cold, but had very little effect on his libido.

So her brush with death made her want to have casual sex.

And her brush with death made *him* realize that there was nothing casual about it.

Because maybe it *was* better to have loved and lost, but it was really fucking stupid to do it twice.

"You never told me you were engaged."

He almost choked. So he had heard correctly when he'd walked into the room. Goddamn Iverson and her big mouth.

It was time Vivi knew the truth. "You never asked."

"It seems like something you'd tell a friend."

A friend with *benes* like he was about to get. "I was engaged," he said simply. "And I told you before, she was killed in the line of duty."

"What happened to you?"

He was grateful the watery glass obscured his face through the shower door. Just in case he couldn't hide the old pain well enough.

"I survived," he said simply. Even that dark, dark night when he'd played with a Glock too close to his own head. "It was five years ago. I've learned to cope."

"Where did it happen?"

"South Dorchester," he said, scrubbing so much harder than necessary with the bar of soap. "Drug bust." *On June 17, 2006. 2:54 a.m.* Not that he relived it every day or anything.

"Have you been with a woman since?"

He rinsed and swiped the glass to make sure she *did* see his look of incredulity. "In five years? Yeah." Hadn't felt anything, but he'd done the deed. Until tonight when he'd felt *something* and didn't want to. "Does it matter?" he asked.

"I'm just curious."

"I'm still human."

"So you've been with women, but they didn't matter?"

He popped the door open to remove every barrier. "Where are you going with this, Vivi?"

"I just want to know if it's difficult."

Something exploded in his head. "If what's difficult? To lose your fiancée? To hold the person you planned to spend the rest of your life with as she's bleeding out on the street? To know you might have saved her if you'd done something different?"

She paled, staring at him. "I meant...sex. With someone who didn't matter."

He closed his eyes, disgusted with himself for losing it. "You know what, Vivi? Maybe this is a bad idea."

Her jaw loosened a little. "Yeah," she said softly, reaching for a towel he thought she was going to hand to her but used to cover her naked body instead. "You're probably right."

She slipped off the counter and walked into the room, wrapping the towel around her.

"Vivi!" He twisted the faucets and shut off the water.

"Relax, Lang. No killers in the room."

Holy hell, how had this happened? It didn't matter how—it had. How could he go in that room and finish what they started, faking that it meant nothing to him? He heard her rustling in the bed, heard the sheets sigh. Or maybe that was her.

Because neither one of them was cut out for casual, commitment-free sex.

And neither one of them really wanted it.

But they really wanted each other, so where did that leave them? Where did that leave Colt, a man who'd sworn off commitments with any woman, not to mention reckless risk-takers who didn't always obey orders?

He dried quickly, brushed his teeth, picked up a razor, and put it back down again. Fuck it.

He turned out the light and walked into the darkened bedroom. There, Vivi Angelino was in his bed, ready, willing, and probably naked.

Against everything he thought he knew about himself, he dropped onto the sofa with the dog.

He waited, but she never asked him to join her. Because he would have. He would have silenced the voices in his head just to quell the aching in his body. But this was Vivi. And she never did what he expected.

Wasn't that part of what he—

Yeah. It was.

CHAPTER 13

On some level, it was a relief when Vivi and Lang boarded the private plane to Boston, with two other agents acting as "Cara's" bodyguards. She didn't want to be alone in that cabin with Lang, not after the sleepless night they'd spent ten feet apart.

You shouldn't sleep with someone you won't tell your secrets to, Vivi decided. No matter how badly you want to.

Which meant she could remain the world's oldest almost-but-for-one-horrific-incident virgin for a long time. Because no one would squeeze that secret out of her, not even Lang.

Who appeared to be hiding a few of his own.

They were supposed to fly into Logan, but changed the flight plan midair—the things the FBI could do— to avoid media, landing at Hanscom airfield outside of Boston.

As she stepped off the plane she inhaled deeply, the

suburban Boston air so different from the salty, swampy smells of Nantucket. Here the earliest hint of the spring thaw gave the air an earthy scent, clean and crisp. It smelled like grass and clouds and home.

"You know I grew up about ten minutes from here," she said as she and Lang walked toward a car that was waiting for them after saying good-bye to the two agents heading into the Boston office separately.

"Your family's still there, right? In Sudbury?"

"Well, my Aunt Fran and Uncle Jim still live in the house with my great-uncle Nino. All the seven kids have moved out."

"Really?" He gave her a sideways look.

Didn't he know all this? "Well, I'm not one of the Rossi kids, per se, obviously. But Zach and I arrived when we were ten, so it's our childhood home, post-Italy."

"I know that, Vivi. That's not what I was wondering about."

"What were you wondering about?"

He opened the passenger door of a nondescript black sedan, very much like the one he drove. As if it didn't scream Fed all over it. "I have an idea."

She got in and he closed her door without elaborating.

"What is it?" she demanded when he got behind the wheel and started the engine.

"I'm taking you home."

"What?"

"And don't call anyone and tell them," he said, reaching over to stop her from moving. "I don't want anyone to know where you are until you get there."

"No one but Nino is home," she assured him. "My aunt and uncle are down at their condo in Florida for the whole month of March, and you don't have to worry about Nino. He won't call the *Enquirer* and rat on me."

"Just a precaution," he said. "You'll stay there all day and I'll come back and get you this evening."

Now that she didn't like. "Where are you going?"

"Into town, maybe do some sniffing around on RE Global, check on my cases."

"Without me?"

"Yes." He held up a hand to stop the argument already bubbling up in her throat. "You need to stay in hiding, *Cara*."

She didn't like it, but knew better than to argue right then. And it was fine not to call Nino. He'd be thrilled to see her, as always, probably cooking something and wishing there were still all those mouths to feed.

Just the idea of seeing him, of being home, made her feel better. *Home* wasn't a brown brick apartment building in Brookline, though she'd lived on the fourth floor of that apartment right off Beacon Street for long enough to grow some substantive roots. Home was that cornflower blue Colonial tucked into rolling hills and surrounded by hundred-year-old oaks, perched over a pond big enough to be called "the lake" by the family that rowed and fished and skated on it with the neighbors.

Home was the Rossi family—where she and Zach had been wedged with just a little bit of force-fitting.

Although home also held some dark memories. The Taylors may have moved out sometime in the last ten years, but the ghosts remained. A road sign indicating the miles to the neighboring town of Concord caught her attention, and those ghosts made a quick mental reappearance.

It had happened the night they played Concord-Carlisle

High. Like it was yesterday, she could hear the echo of her cheerleading sneakers on varnished wood. The roar of the crowd when Kenny Taylor scored for Lincoln Sudbury High School. *Kenny Taylor, he's our man.... If he can't do it... nobody can.*

And he'd wanted to do it, all right. That night, a little drunk, a little mean, a little rough. The skirt, the panties, the thin arms of a dancer were no deterrent to him.

You asked for it in that cheer-skirt.

Her stomach turned.

"Nobody home, huh?"

She turned to him, blanking out, a million miles and sixteen years away. "What?"

"Unless your uncle Nino drives a brand-new red Mustang or—Jesus, is that purple thing a 'sixty-eight GTO?"

She let out a squeal, her hand on the door before he'd even pulled into the familiar drive. "The Mustang's Chessie's, but—oh my God—let me out of this car! Gabe's home!"

The second he stopped she practically flung herself out. She hadn't seen her cousin in nearly two years; his life in the very hidden world of black ops kept him underground even on the rare occasion when he was actually in the States.

Before she was halfway down the driveway, the bright red front door of the Colonial opened and Uncle Nino ambled out, his brows drawn over fierce dark eyes, his thinning gray hair uncombed, his body language looking like he would use those meat-hook hands of his to kill anyone who took a step farther.

"It's me, Nino! It's Vivi!" She half ran to him, and watched his wrinkled old face change from distrust to joy.

"Viviana! What the hell?"

She flipped at the hair. "Undercover. Movie star. Is Gabe here or did someone just bring his car out of storage?"

She gave him a cursory hug, but his return was much tighter, holding her back pretty effectively, considering he was eighty-something years old.

He opened his mouth to answer, then looked over her shoulder, scowling.

"You know Colton Lang, Uncle Nino. He's a client. He's—"

"Gabe won't like it."

"So he is here?" She wiggled out of his hands. "It's okay, Lang's with me." She looked over her shoulder at Lang. "You need Nino's clearance, but I'm going in." She pushed passed the older man and jogged through the door.

And there he was, glorious, gorgeous, and grinning like Wile E. Coyote.

"Oh my God!" She shrieked so loud it could have broken the chandelier, bringing Lang storming into the house behind her. But she was already being scooped and swooped around by a pair of beastly arms, her cheeks bussed by familiar scratchy whiskers.

"Gabriel Rossi, I love you!"

"Shhhh!" He gave her a squeeze, his amazing muscles almost cracking her back. "No one is supposed to know I'm here."

"Well, I brought an FBI agent along, so if that is a problem, you better let me know."

Out of her peripheral vision she saw Lang reholster his gun. Gabe saw it, too, his laser blue gaze slicing Nino. "You suck donkey balls as a bodyguard, old man." He took Vivi by the shoulders and inched her away, revealing his always impressive build barely contained in a white T-shirt. "Don't hire Nino for your company. He couldn't keep a fly off shit."

She just laughed. "But you're not available."

"I am now," he said. "And I'm better looking."

Nino snorted, but Vivi almost jumped out of her skin again. "You left the company? The one that—"

He put a hand over her mouth. "Hush, little cousin. I'm still living covert at the moment. And, buddy, please tell me that you are not a federal officer trying to locate me."

Lang eyed him harshly. "What are you wanted for?"

"Nothing," Vivi interjected. "This is my cousin Gabe Rossi, who prefers not to be recognized, remembered, photographed, or interrogated. So go easy on him. Gabe, this is Assistant Special Agent in Charge Colton Lang."

Gabe gave the look right back, only with a secret glimmer in his sky blue eyes. "FBI? Vivi, we gotta improve your taste in men." Then he grinned again. "Just kidding, dawg. Chessie mentioned you were a client."

"Chessie?"

"In here!" Chessie called from the kitchen. "Hard at work for the Guardian Angelinos."

Vivi sniffed. "Smells like you're hard at work on Nino's peppers and eggs." She looked up at Gabe. "Does Aunt Fran know you're home? You know they'd fly up in a heartbeat."

"Only Nino and Chessie," he said, adding his easy smile when he looked at his grandfather. "Don't sweat it, buddy. I can't hide from the family forever. It's only a matter of time till my gig is up and I have to go legit."

"What's going on?" Vivi asked.

"I do contract work for the CIA," he explained to Lang. "Some of those contracts are kind of drying up."

"Because the work that was being done was never supposed to be outsourced," Lang said. "I've read about it. Evidently the CIA's in some hot water for using some, shall we say, outside-the-envelope consultants."

Vivi gave an apologetic shrug. "It's a family curse."

"Hell yeah it is," Gabe said. "Shit's gotta get done. And some of the *federal agencies* aren't always willing to do what's gotta be done, if you catch my drift."

"I'm just so glad you're home," Vivi said, curling her arm through Gabe's.

"I'm not," Gabe said. "I'm in limbo. Nothing to do, not sure if there'll be work, not really in trouble—the higher-ups are—but I could be called in for interrogation."

"So why was Nino trying to keep us out?" Lang asked pointedly.

"I told him I don't want to see anybody until I get some word from on high. It's cool, man." Gabe guided Vivi toward the heart of the house, the oversize kitchen and family room, passing the staircase lined with dozens of family pictures on the way. "What the fuck is on your head, Viv?"

Behind her, she heard Nino mumble, "He swears too much, but he's a good kid."

Next to her, Gabe pulled her closer. "You work for this guy?"

"Sometimes he's a client."

"Didn't anyone ever tell you not to get your meat where you get your bread?"

She froze and pushed him away. "I'm not sleeping with him." Not technically. Not yet.

"Then why was he ready to kill me when you screamed you loved me?"

"Because Nino acted so weird and I..." She hesitated, her head filled with the tangy smell of Nino's caramelized onions and the dizzy sensation that Lang might actually be jealous. "Really?"

"Chessie told me a little about this job you're on—hope you don't mind. Sounds intriguing."

"You told him?" Vivi turned the corner to find Chessie behind two different laptops she had set on the long granite counter where Vivi had eaten so many breakfasts and watched Uncle Nino cook so many dinners.

"He tortured it out of me like the dangerous spook we all know he is." She bounded around to hug Vivi and check out her movie-star looks. "This is an interesting look for you, Vivi."

"You look smokin'," Gabe said. "You ought to try makeup and a hairbrush more often, V."

"Screw you," Vivi said, nudging Chessie aside so she could see what was on the computers. "What are you working on?"

"RE Global," she said.

Lang and Nino followed them into the kitchen, close enough to have heard the exchange. "You told her?" Lang asked her.

Chessie's eyes—the only ones in the family that matched Gabe's crystal blues—widened guiltily. "Sorry, Vivi."

"No need to apologize." Vivi warded off Lang's disapproval with a wave. "Look, the Guardian Angelinos aren't just my co-workers, they're family. Everyone here is utterly trustworthy and you know damn well Chessie's a hacker without equal. What'd you find, kiddo?"

"An address in Lowell," Chessie said.

"An address for what?" Lang asked, joining Vivi in front of one of the computers.

"I thought it was an office of RE Global," Chessie said, "but it looks like a private home. I found the address deep in the code of their Web site."

Vivi gave him a smug look. "That'd take the FBI a week to find. *If* they found it."

To his credit, he didn't argue. "Can you zoom in on Google Earth?"

"I tried," Chessie said, "but the location is one of those that only goes so far with satellite images."

"It's not far," Gabe said. "Let's go check it out. I'm dying to give the Goat a spin." He picked up the keys to his classic hot rod, shaking them.

Lang didn't nix the idea outright, but turned the computer for a closer inspection of the location just as Vivi's phone vibrated with a text.

"Unknown caller," she said, reading the message. Lang shifted closer to read over her shoulder. And torment her with his clean, had-to-be-Ralph-Lauren scent.

Where the hell did you go in the plane? Vivi read, her heart tripping. "Could this be from Cara? How would she know we took the plane?"

"We spies are everywhere," Gabe said.

"Well it's not Marissa's number," Vivi said, scrolling through her phone to check.

"Maybe the Bureau could trace it or triangulate it,"

Lang said. "Doubtful we could get much more than an idea of where the tower is. Nothing specific."

Gabe snorted in disdain. "Feds. What good are they?"

Chessie held out her hand. "Give me your SIM card, Vivi. I have some tricks." Chessie looked over Vivi's head to grin at Lang. "None of them are legal, so this would be a good time for you and Gabe to leave."

"Just get the information, no questions asked," Lang said.

Vivi beamed at him. "Welcome to the dark side, my friend."

"Yeah," Gabe said. "You'll like it over here. And I can get a location on that number, if you want. If it's Cara's phone, you'll have her."

"Do I want to know how?" Lang asked.

"Doubtful," Gabe said with a laugh.

Nino loaded plates with eggs, onions, and peppers, the aroma filling the air. "Don't wage the war over good versus evil on an empty stomach," Nino said, serving them all. *"Mangia."*

Gabe had his fork in the food before the plate hit the granite. "This is beast, Nino. And, hell, there's nothing that gives me an appetite like tempting Feds with our evil ways."

Vivi put a loving arm on Gabe's shoulder. "You're going to make the best Guardian Angelino, you know that? When can you start?"

"Don't tempt me, V."

"How close to the exact location could you get on that phone?" Lang asked him.

"How close do you want to get?" Gabe replied. "A lesser man with lousy connections, the county." He took a lusty bite of eggs and grinned while he chewed. "Me? I could get you the block, house number, and probably the color of her underwear."

Lang considered him thoughtfully, then nodded.

For some reason, that little break of the rules just folded Vivi's heart in half. She studied Lang from the side as he ate, a familiar ache in her heart. Everywhere, actually.

She wanted him so much. And last night, if she had just said the words, she could have had him. But she'd lain there silent, letting old demons keep her cold and alone. How long would she let Kenny Taylor win that war?

She pushed her plate away and gave Nino an apologetic look. "It's been a crazy week, so I'm not hungry." She needed to face these demons, now. "I'm just going to go out for some air."

"I'd come with you, but I'm busy breaking the law," Chessie said, her fingers tapping the keyboard.

"That's okay," Vivi replied. "I just want to see if… anything's changed out here."

"Doc Taylor moved out," Gabe called out, a tease in his voice.

Damn him. But, then, he wouldn't know. It was her fault, of course, for not telling anyone. But if she had, Ken Taylor would be a dead man. And while that wouldn't bother her very much, she'd hate to have to visit her brother in prison.

"Very funny," she said, not taking his bait.

"Like you don't remember the stud-muffin neighbor, Viv," Chessie added.

None of them knew. She couldn't fault them for what she'd never shared.

"Who's the stud-muffin neighbor?" Lang asked.

She opened the door and slammed it behind her, before she heard the rest. She crossed the patio quickly, hopped down the steps to the grass, and made a beeline for the water. The grass was winter brown and crunchy all the way down the hill to the small lake. This lawn had been the site of so many snowball fights, sledding marathons, touch football games, birthday parties—a lawn that separated this house from the next.

She slowed down as she reached the water's edge, rounding the few kayaks and the canoe they kept there, not used much anymore.

Taking a deep inhale of spring-thawed air, she let her gaze shift to the Taylors' old house next door. With the trees bare, she could see right to their basement door. Smell the bitter odor of beer and sweat. Hear Hootie & the Blowfish on the stereo. Feel the crushed-blue-velvet sofa where they'd always made out. Vivi and Kenny, the popular girl and the cool jock.

Only he wasn't cool. He was cold. Rough. Hard. Vicious. *You want this, V. You dressed for easy access, didn't you, baby?* She closed her eyes against the burn, the sound of her argument, the tearing, ripping, black ache between her legs.

"A doctor, huh?"

Vivi startled and gasped at the sound of Lang's voice, furious that she hadn't heard him. Digging deep, she found her composure. Just like she had when she'd stumbled home that night, telling no one, the guilt gutting her.

And later...after...

"Are you okay?" His tone changed, instantly concerned. Safe.

He was nothing like Ken Taylor, who'd gone off to

college, then med school in some Midwestern city, and never looked back. *Doctor* Kenneth Taylor, who apparently didn't have a problem living with guilt and shame.

"I'm fine," she said quickly, forcing lightness into her voice. "Are you thoroughly corrupted by this family now?"

"Not nearly enough," he said with a rueful smile, reaching out to graze her cheek with his knuckles. The gesture was somehow natural and shocking at the same time.

It felt right for Lang to touch her, but not here in the shadow of where she'd had so much stolen from her.

No, she'd *given* that power to a rapist. And with this man in front of her, she was ready to take it back. "Are we going back to Nantucket tonight?" she asked.

"Probably. Why?"

"I don't want to be away from you, Lang."

His eyes flickered. "I know you're scared, so—"

"No, I'm not." She covered his hand, pressing it against her cheek. "I was, but I'm not." They were talking about two different kinds of fear, she knew. "I want to be with you tonight."

His eyes narrowed and pinned her with heated intensity. "I won't leave you."

"I mean—"

"I know what you mean."

"And you won't…" She wet her lips, struggling for a word to describe how she'd lost him last night. She'd had him, and then—his own demon had gotten him. "Change your mind."

"I didn't change my mind," he said. "I just…" He struggled to swallow, looking past her, obviously searching for a change of subject. "So you were in love with the boy next door when you were a cheerleader. Color me astonished."

Bad choice of subject changes. "Screw Gabe for bringing up my past. And I was never in love. Not even close."

"But you *were* a cheerleader and, evidently, the neighbor boy *is* a doctor now."

"That's what we heard. I really haven't kept track of him." Just wished him dead most days. "And, yes, I did a little cheering before I found my way onto a skateboard. People change, Lang."

From the driveway, the raw, loud rumble of Gabe's ancient GTO ended the conversation for them.

"We're going to do a drive by that address Chessie found. Otherwise, Gabe will try to go by himself. He's as bad as you are."

"Oh, he's better," she laughed. "I'll stay here with Chessie and hack Cara's phone texts some more."

"You promise?"

She smiled. "I promise."

He leaned forward and kissed her on the head. "So one more question about the doctor?" he asked.

No, no questions. "What?"

"Why'd you break up?"

"Oh, nothing." She waved her hand, which, damn it all, shook a little at the lie. "Just—you know—teen angst."

"Was he the cause of the final teardrop?"

"Who knew you were such a sweet-talker, Lang?"

"Don't change the subject."

"Yes," she said simply. *Take that, St. Peter.*

"How did he hurt you?"

"He underestimated me." She turned to go back up the

hill but he caught up with her in a second, wrapping his arms around her from behind, putting his mouth to her ears.

"Then I won't make the same mistake."

"I hope not." He had no idea how much she meant that.

CHAPTER 14

The monster V-8 engine of Gabe's GTO roared over the roads that cut through the Boston suburbs. He chose to skip the busy interstates up to the industrial town of Lowell, winding instead around the quieter Route 27 with a sure handle on the curving roads. They rode in silence for a long time, not competing with the engine until Gabe gave him a slow look and Colt just *knew* what was coming next.

"So you like my cousin, huh?"

Bingo. "That took longer than I thought," Colt said. "I figured you'd be interrogating me before we got out of Sudbury."

Gabe shot him a grin that probably got the guy out of a lot of trouble and into a lot of beds. "Thought I'd let you get comfortable, Fedster. And you don't have to worry about me. Vivi's a big girl and if she wants to get down and dirty with you, have at it. As long as you don't hurt her, none of the Rossis will attack. Can't speak for the

Angelino side, though. Zach might cut your nuts off just for breathing in his sister's air space."

"Yeah, I know him pretty well."

"Does he know you're doing the nasty with Vivi?"

"We're not," Colt said simply. *At least not yet.* "And, for what it's worth, I don't think Vivi Angelino has a nasty bone in her body."

"You're probably right," Gabe agreed. "So you're not fooled by the skater-girl-with-the-nose-piercing shit?"

Colt shrugged. "That's just Vivi."

"Wasn't always," Gabe said.

"Yeah, you mentioned she used to be a cheerleader." Colt kind of smiled. "Hard to imagine."

"She used to be a lot of things," Gabe said. "A cheerleader, a dancer, popular. She even dated boys for a while."

Colt turned a little. "What do you mean?"

"Oh, I'm not saying she's into chicks or anything. I just mean, she doesn't really get funky as far as any of us know."

Ever? She sure seemed like she was about to *get funky* with him. *I want to be with you tonight.* Pretty straightforward invitation to sex if he'd ever heard one.

"Well, maybe she doesn't call you up in the morning after she's had a date." Or maybe Gabe was right; she did seem surprisingly inexperienced. Wonderful, amazing, and intoxicating, but inexperienced. "And then there is always the chance that Zach might kill me for even thinking about kissing her," he added. And God knows he'd been thinking about more than that.

"There is that." Gabe laughed. "Hey, we're coming up to Lowell. You have that address programmed in your phone?"

"I do." Colt directed him around some side streets, down a two-lane highway, past some warehouses and abandoned mills east of town along the Merrimack River. "Turn left at the next light, then take the third right."

The neighborhood disintegrated around them, the old structures that were probably built to house millworkers getting shabbier with each block. Windows missing. Cars on cement blocks. It reeked of poverty and crime, and probably a meth house around every corner.

"You armed?" Colt asked.

"Am I breathing?" Gabe replied.

He was good backup, Colt decided. This was not official FBI business, just a courtesy call. Whatever he found, he'd report it to the team investigating Roman Emmanuel and carry on with his end of the assignment. No one needed to know he'd taken an unauthorized government spy on the ride.

"This is the street," he told Gabe as they reached an intersection. "Turn right."

"I don't like this," Gabe said, peering down the street.

"It's certainly not Sudbury," Colt agreed.

The streets were deserted, but Colt had no doubt that eyes behind every window were on them.

"It's not the neighborhood that bothers me—it's the street." Gabe reached under his shirt and pulled out a top-of-the-line Walther. "It's a dead end. With woods. I don't like to get my balls in a sling."

The address was the last house on the street. They slowed in front of a two-story stucco dump that was lacking glass in one window, a hinge on the screen door, a step on the porch, and a coat of paint. A fence ran around one side; the other opened into acres of woods.

"You wanna go in?" Gabe asked.

"Maybe." Colt leaned down and looked out Gabe's window. "But I do want to know why this address would be buried in the code of RE Global, a temporary employment firm."

The front door opened and a girl stood there, Asian, thin, haunted. She wore little more than rags and a blank look.

"Baby hookers," Gabe said with disgust. "I hate motherfuckers who do that to little girls."

A woman stepped up behind her: mixed race, much older, almost as straggly, but way more used up. She put one hand on the girl's shoulder and gestured Gabe and Colt in with the other. "I have girls and boys," she called. "Twenty dollars."

Colt's gut turned.

Gabe looked at him. "You're the Fed. What do you want to do?"

"I'll get agents out here, but let's just check it out. If I can get any kind of connection to Emmanuel before we shut this down, the L.A. team will be grateful."

Gabe nodded. "Let me just turn the beast in the right direction in case we need to make a fast getaway." He accelerated forward so he could make a three-point turn in the road.

"Fifteen dollars!" she screamed, thinking they were leaving. "I find virgin for you!"

"Jesus," Colt mumbled.

"She's from Laos. I can tell by the accent," Gabe said. "Don't know if that helps your investigation."

"It might. You speak Lao?"

"Some." He turned the car around and shut it off. "I can say 'Shut your fucking piehole and tell me who you work for or you're gonna eat this gun' in ten different languages."

"That ought to come in handy."

They got out simultaneously, walking slowly toward the woman as she inched the girl closer. Son of a bitch—she couldn't be fourteen.

The lady's eyes narrowed to nothing as she checked them out. "You cops?"

"Nope." A Fed and a spook, but no cops. "You own this place?" Colt asked.

"This my daughter." If that was true, then she *should* eat Gabe's gun.

"How many kids you got?" Gabe asked.

She gave him a once-over, spending time on the guy's oversized pecs. "You want boy?"

"Not particularly."

"Two or three at once? You watch? Get a little rough, huh?" Her smile was sickening, and toothless. "That's okay, too. It'll cost you more."

Gabe said something in Lao, as slick and smooth as if he were in a bar in Vientiane.

The woman's eyes opened wide in shock. She screamed an unintelligible response, then looked at Colt. "I pay up, mister. I don't owe nothing. I pay that man two days ago."

"What was the man's name?" Colt asked.

"I don't fucking know his name," she said, then shoved the girl forward. "She give you blow job. Then go away."

Colt just closed his eyes in disgust and Gabe said something else, walking toward her.

"Yeah, yeah," she said, stepping to the side to let them in. "You count heads."

As Gabe strode by her into the house, Colt followed.

"Get 'em all down here," Colt ordered.

When the woman did nothing, Gabe got in her face and said something low and indiscernible in her native language. She screamed up the stairs, drops of spit flying from cracked lips.

Colt glanced at the little girl, whose almond eyes were filled with a mix of hate and hope. All he could do was shake his head, then she looked down in shame.

Shit, now she thought she wasn't good enough for him.

"Go," he said softly, giving her shoulder a gentle nudge. "Get the rest of the kids and bring them down."

She scurried away, the older woman hissing instructions at her. Whatever she said made Gabe spin around and fire a look at her, spewing out some more commands.

The woman started sputtering in a mix of English and Lao, waving her hands, but one word jumped out at Colt.

Pakpao.

"Sunisa Pakpao?" he asked.

The woman visibly paled. "I pay him. I swear I pay him when he brought last shipment. There was virgin on it! I give her to you if you leave me alone. I give her to you! Normally fifty dollars for virgin."

"When did the shipment come?" he asked.

"Few days ago. Right off boat. All from Ban Nape through Tonkin." From landlocked Laos through Vietnam, if Colt's geography was right. All the way around the damn world.

"Have virgin and four boys, too," she went on. "And more. Farm boys. They went to the western house. Plenty of good girls. Please." She started to cry. "No Pakpao. He hurt the girls until they screamed and bleed. Nobody will fuck girl with broken bones!"

More than ever, Colt was glad he'd shot the bastard.

But *how* was the scum-bucket bastard connected to Cara Ferrari?

Several more girls came down the stairs, and two young boys, all wearing the same vacant look.

"Where is Nirachee?" the woman screamed. "And PhanPhan?"

None of the kids answered. Some looked bored, others scared. All...ruined.

Gabe spoke softly to one of the boys in Lao. The child shrugged in response. The woman marched off, screaming for Nirachee, and the boy leaned close to Gabe and whispered something. They had a brief conversation that Colt couldn't hear or understand while he checked out the first floor. It was just this side of a rat's nest.

"Hey, Lang, listen to this." Gabe brought the boy forward, coaxing him with surprising gentleness. "Tell this man what you just told me, son."

He looked terrified.

"Come on," Gabe urged. "This little boy just arrived here on a boat. His English is good, though."

Colt nodded. "Is that so?"

"And before he came to this house, he said that Mr. Pakpao had them stop somewhere. An *island*."

Where was he going with this? "And?"

"Mr. Pakpao taught this boy a poem about the island. Tell him," Gabe said, an extraordinary amount of patience in his voice. "Tell him the island *poem*."

The child, maybe ten if he was a day, looked up at Colt. "There once was a man from Nantucket whose dick was so long he could suck it."

Nantucket. Jesus, they were bringing them through *Nantucket*?

"Isn't that funny?" Gabe asked, his look anything but.

A noise behind Colt made him turn to look at the street, just in time to see another boy fiddling near the trunk of the GTO.

"Hey, get away," Colt yelled.

The boy didn't move.

"If he so much as breathes on that car, there'll be hell to pay," Gabe said.

"I'll get him," Colt replied. "Maybe he knows more poetry." He hustled out toward the kid, who cowered on the other side of the car.

"Take me," the child said softly.

Colt just looked at him, not sure if it was an unwanted invitation for sex or a plea for escape. He couldn't take him out of here, but he'd have agents swarming this place in the next hour.

"Soon," Colt promised.

The boy just closed his eyes. He'd heard that before, no doubt.

"PhanPhan!" The woman bolted out of the house, screaming in another language at the kid, who crouched as soon she came near. "Where's Nirachee?"

He replied and she smacked him so hard he buckled to the ground. Gabe came tearing out as Colt drew his weapon and ordered her to stop.

She cut him with blazing eyes. "You cop! I know you cop! I already paid, damn it!"

A shot cracked from the upstairs window, ricocheting off the pavement. Colt and Gabe both dove for cover around the car, aiming their weapons up at the house.

"You hit this fucking car, dickhead, and you'll die an ugly death!" Gabe yelled.

A child's head came through the window, the shadow of a man behind him, a pistol at the kid's head. "Leave or he's dead!" the man yelled.

Son of a *bitch*.

"Get the fuck out of here or I blow this kid's head all over your pretty car!" the faceless shadow hollered, well protected by the boy.

The child didn't even flinch; his death was inevitable. Maybe it would be a relief.

"Your call," Gabe said without turning to Colt. "We can take them all, but the kid's gonna die."

"Let's go," Colt murmured. "I'll have this place raided by twenty agents in less than an hour."

"That might be long enough for these pricks to clear out," Gabe said, his words barely audible over the woman's screaming.

Kids would die if they tried to handle this themselves. At least that one in the window, and probably more. They were hostages, and so sadly expendable because the next shipment would be in anytime. Through *Nantucket*.

"We can be heroes, homeslice," Gabe said calmly. "But we'll have some baby blood on our hands."

"Five seconds, this kid is fucking dead, mister!"

Colt grabbed the driver's door without taking his gun down, slid in, and Gabe followed, turning on the car and peeling out with a deafening roar.

Before they hit the first intersection, Colt had his SAC on the line, reading off the location and knowing exactly how competent the agents were who would be out there, long before the local cops, who were probably on the take anyway.

"You want to stay and supervise the raid, dawg?" Gabe

asked. "Because I have to book. I cannot be seen and my ass will be burned grass if I get on any federal radar."

"It's fine." Colt didn't want to compromise Gabe, who'd helped so much. The agents would handle the job, and he had to get back to Nantucket. He had to find out where and how Emmanuel was using the place as a way station for slaves.

"I'm going take 495 if you don't mind breaking some speed laws," Gabe said.

"I don't mind."

"I figured." Gabe threw him a look. "You want to go get your girl. Unless you're planning to leave Faux Cara behind."

No, he wasn't. Because he wasn't going to spend one more minute without her. Oh, *man*. Where did that idea come from? "She'd kill me if I even thought about it."

Gabe lifted a brow. "Whipped already, are we?"

"Nah. Just..." How the hell could he describe how he felt?

"Just gone, it sounds to me." Gabe chuckled. "Dude, I'd fall for an easier chick than Vivi if I were you."

"She's not easy."

"No kidding. Complicated as hell, I'd say."

"And I didn't fall for her," he said, misery pressing down on him. He didn't? Then what else did you call the feeling of tumbling down a fifty-foot cliff onto a rocky landing?

In Colt's ear, Joe Gagliardi's phone was answered by an assistant, and in a moment he was on the phone with the man who would probably be his next boss. As he described the scene and gave him details, he could hear Gagliardi's approval and appreciation in every response.

"Get back to Nantucket, Colt, and figure this thing out," Gagliardi said, ending the call. "We need to tie this directly to Roman Emmanuel."

"Will do, sir."

"And great job," he added. "When you close this case, the L.A. job is yours."

"Thank you, sir." Exactly what he wanted—away from Boston and all his dark memories.

Except Vivi Angelino would be three thousand miles away. Why the hell that suddenly mattered, he had no clue.

Gabe swerved and passed a truck, sparing Colt a glance. "For a guy who, from the sound of this end of the conversation, is getting a juicy promo because of this, you kind of look like shit on a stick right now."

"Matches how I feel."

"I'da never guessed it," Gabe said with a soft whistle.

"Guessed what?"

"That Vivi'd get a straight shooter like you all knotted up and shit."

"I'm not knotted up *and shit*." Was he? Goddamn it, *was* he? He looked at Gabe as if he might have the answer. But Vivi's cousin just laughed and smashed the pedal until they hit three figures on the speedometer.

CHAPTER 15

Lang barely spoke to Vivi the entire flight back to Nantucket. He told her about the trip to Lowell in sparse detail, and she didn't have the stomach to ask for more. He briefed the agents on the plane for the duration of the short flight, and the rest of the time he was either on his phone or lost in thought.

The only substantive conversation they had was about Chessie's amazing hacking skills, and her discovery that the text Vivi had gotten came from a phone registered to Joellen Mugg. Vivi had responded with a vague text about why they'd gone to Boston, and hadn't heard anything else from anyone in Cara's crew.

What she didn't tell Lang was that Chessie also figured out a way to read all of Joellen's texts. There was nothing interesting to report in her messages, anyway. Not to mention that gaining access to those texts without some kind of warrant would probably curl his hair and earn Vivi a classic Lang lecture about rules and regs.

But after a few hours of the silent treatment, Vivi would have welcomed the lecture. Anything to connect with him.

Once they were at the Nantucket house, he was back on the phone and in discussions with his other agents about the official clearing of the crime scene in Cara's master bedroom.

Vivi was standing in her room, not quite sure what to do next, when Mercedes knocked at the open door.

"Would you like me to move your things upstairs? I imagine it would be easier to have access to Cara's clothes."

Did she want to stay in that gargantuan bedroom suite…alone? Would she be alone? Based on the way Lang was acting, probably. The reality of that tasted sour in her mouth, or maybe it was bittersweet. Lang was most likely not the best candidate for her first real sexual foray—even though she wanted him to be.

"I guess that would be easier," Vivi agreed. "Let me gather what I have here and take it up."

Mercedes helped her, stiff and silent, trudging up the stairs to the wide vestibule entryway that led to Cara's bedroom.

"This is really a gorgeous suite," Vivi said when they were near the top, to fill the uncomfortable silence. Her gaze moved to the oil painting on the wall, a huge canvas in a gaudy gold frame she'd barely noticed when they'd arrived. Now, however, there was something distinctly familiar about the landscape.

"That's the cranberry bog, isn't it?" Vivi asked.

"Yes," Mercedes said. "The view from the front of the house."

"It's beautifully done." Vivi paused in front of the painting, noticing the shadows of two children holding hands near the fog-laden bog, the entire work rich with haunting tones of violet and indigo. "Did Cara have it commissioned?"

Mercedes choked softly. "No."

Vivi turned at the strange tone in her voice. "Who painted it?"

"I did."

"Really?" She scrutinized the work again, then the woman responsible for it. They so did not match. "It's really"—*emotional*—"beautiful."

Mercedes's blue eyes turned cold. "In the eye of the beholder, I suppose."

Whatever the hell that meant. "Does Cara ever think about reviving the bog? Growing cranberries again? Fixing the house?"

Mercedes opened the door to the bedroom, ignoring the painting. "She did, once, but fortunately abandoned the idea."

"Fortunately?" Vivi followed her in, the old reporter instinct flashing with a noisy alert. "You said you'd like to go back there and visit, and that's why the tunnels connect, right? So why wouldn't you want to see the house and bog restored?"

"That'll never happen." She marched to the windows and started flipping plantation-style shutters closed, blocking out the early evening light.

Vivi put her bag down and sat on the armrest of a club chair, hoping to invite conversation. "Mercedes," she said gently. "Have you ever thought about...going outside again?"

The woman's shoulders tightened. "Please, I'd rather not discuss it." She moved to the next set of shutters.

"When was the last time you were down at the bog?"

"A long time ago."

"And Cara? When was the last time she was there?"

"I don't know. When she and Joellen had those architects and builders there, I guess."

"So she really has considered restoration?"

"Joellen put a stop to it before they got too far."

"Why? Doesn't Joellen want to see her childhood home beautiful and useful again? It would make a wonderful guesthouse, or just a place for parties—"

"Parties?" Her eyes widened in horror, then she instantly reined in the out-of-character response. "Some things and some places need to stay just as they are," she said sharply, a vein in her neck pulsing as she reached the last three windows. "Some people need to understand that." *Snap.* "Some people who think they own something." *Snap.* "Sometimes what's on a legal paper, what's signed, sealed, and in the bank, doesn't make it right." *Snap.*

Whoa. Hot-button hit. "So Cara, as the owner of the house, wanted to fix the bog house, but Joellen didn't? Is that what you're saying?"

She shut down, obviously realizing she'd said too much. "Do you need anything else?"

Information. Evidence. The truth. And a couple of hours in that bed with Lang. "No, thank you. I appreciate the help."

She was barely out the door and Vivi had her phone out to text Chessie.

Find out who owns this house and property.

Chessie wrote back in less than ten seconds. *Piece of cake.*

Smiling at her cousin's style, she went back into the hall and studied the picture painted by the most unlikely artist. Sure enough, the tiny initials MG were painted in the lower right corner. Mercedes Graff. Only something was off about the initials. They didn't blend, somehow, with the rest of the painting.

Kneeling down to get closer to the corner, she rubbed her hand over the letters, feeling the thick bumps of paint underneath. A lot of coats of paint. Like it had been painted over and over.

Maybe Mercedes hadn't really painted this. That made sense to Vivi; nothing about the woman appeared to be capable of this much feeling. Not *una tedesca* like her. Vivi's nails dented the thick coat of oil paint, and she glanced over her shoulder guiltily.

Certain she was alone, she prodded some more. The first layer of paint peeled away, revealing different letters, painted in black, definitely meant to be part of the original painting.

MM.

Not Mercedes Graff, then, unless she had a different name at one point. Vivi hastily mashed the flap of paint back over the letters, making it look almost the same. You'd have to look very closely to see that it had been tampered with.

She stood up and backed away, tsking softly when she realized she'd inadvertently tilted the painting. At least five feet wide and nearly as tall, framed in a heavy gilded wood, it wasn't going to be a cinch to straighten. But she'd have to or Mercedes would know instantly that it had been touched.

Gripping the side of the frame, she inched it up the wall, her hand sliding a little, her fingers gliding over a bump on the back of the frame.

That was weird, too. Something was taped to the frame.

Peering around and gingerly easing the frame away from the wall, she picked at the tape just as her cell phone vibrated with a text from Chessie. Ignoring the text, she flicked at the corner of the tape, which was pretty well glued and old. Finally, she managed to rip it off and a key fell to the floor with a clunk.

A key? A *key!* The key Pakpao had been willing to kill for?

She picked it up, turning it over a few times looking for any indication what the old silver key might fit. The phone text buzzed again, the words: *What do you think of that????* From Chessie.

She flipped back to the previous text.

U r gonna like this. 2 owners. Big house: Mercedes Mugg. Farming property: RE Global!!!!!

She stared at the words. The bog was owned by Roman Emmanuel? She almost screamed for Lang, pivoting to come face-to-face with Mercedes.

"What are you doing?" the woman demanded, her eyes stormy and threatening.

Mercedes Mugg. Holy shit. She was Cara and Joellen's *mother.*

Vivi met her direct gaze. "Just looking at your beautiful painting. Do you have any others you're hiding away, Mercedes?"

"No. That's the only one."

"Too bad," Vivi said calmly, the key tight in her palm, smashed against the phone. "I need to find Mr. Lang."

"He's just leaving the guesthouse and coming into the kitchen."

Vivi almost laughed. "You are so adept at knowing exactly where everyone is at any given moment."

She didn't even blink.

"You are a woman of many talents," Vivi added. "And many secrets."

She brushed by Mercedes, but the woman grabbed her arm with a vicious grip. "Give it to me."

"What?"

"I know you have it."

"I don't know what you're talking about."

Mercedes leaned in close enough that Vivi could practically count the tiny hairs on her chin. "What you have in your hand has nothing to do with—with what you want."

"What do you think I want?"

"That Red Carpet Killer."

"Maybe, maybe not," Vivi said, wresting her arm free. "But there's a lot more going on around here than that, isn't there?"

"Don't." She barely breathed the word. "Please don't do this to me."

Vivi searched her face. Why would a woman want to keep it a secret that she was the mother of a movie star? "What are you hiding, Mercedes?"

"Everything," she said softly, her voice cracking with raw emotion. Maybe she *was* capable of that kind of painting.

"What does this unlock?" Vivi held up the key, willing to fight to keep it if she had to, but wanting the answers this woman had.

"Nothing that will get you any closer to where you want to be."

"What does it unlock?"

"The fireplace."

Vivi frowned at her. "What fireplace?"

"In the bog house."

Vivi started to back away, so anxious to tell Lang she almost ran, but, one more time, Mercedes grabbed her arm. "Vivi," she said.

Vivi froze. "Yes?"

"Never mind." She let go. "Just, please, give me this chance. If you have a heart, you'll leave this be."

"I have a heart," she said softly. "But I also have a job to do." And right now, that meant unlocking whatever this key hid.

The scare of the night before had had a sobering effect on Cara. Unfortunately, it had just the opposite for her sister. By that afternoon, Marissa had left to run errands for them, Joellen was smashed again, and Cara watched the beach in the fading light by herself.

Was she by herself, though?

Or was one of Roman's henchmen right around the corner, waiting to set up a death that looked like an accident?

Or had that near electrocution by a hair dryer in the tub really been a freak accident? Some karmic retribution for her evil deeds?

She sucked in a deep breath at the thought of Roman, a man she had once depended on for everything. He'd used her right back, no doubt about it. But now they were in a different vicious cycle, and the only way to break it would be if Cara came clean.

Or one of them died. Not her, obviously.

She liked that plan, but it wasn't going to be easy. Murder never was.

Her fingers around the weathered wood of the railing, Cara lifted her face to the sea air and took a breath. She'd done the right thing once.

She'd also done some very *wrong* things.

The crash of the surf forced her eyes open, the sweet smell of salt pulling at her. She needed to feel the water on her feet, the sand in her toes. A quick glance over her shoulder confirmed that her sister was still in the shower, gearing up for round two of drinking. Cara made an impulsive decision, grabbing a creamy pashmina shawl from the back of a chair to wrap over her T-shirt and jeans.

The minute her bare feet hit the sand at the bottom of the stairs, she was happier. Liberated. Alive.

Face to the darkening sky, she spread her arms wide and let the cool breeze lift her hair. Joellen would come running out like a raving lunatic if she saw Cara like this, utterly open and unprotected.

But being trapped and scared—God, she didn't want to live like her mother. And yet, as long as Roman was alive, that was how she lived.

Climbing the first dune to the ocean, she almost laughed at the thrill of it. This section of beach was completely deserted, just a mile of rising sand and dune grass in either direction, and nothing but the ocean in front of her. The gunmetal gray water shimmered, the last of the sunset leaving a few peachy streaks on the froth of the surf.

She had to put her foot in that icy water. *Had* to smell the salt and feel the chill in her bones. One more glance over her shoulder revealed only the top half of the house, the dune blocking much of the view.

Joellen would have a cow when she got out of the shower. But Cara didn't care.

Certain it was desolate in every direction, she ran to the water, turning a full circle and almost tripping with joy. This was Nantucket Sound, she thought confidently. Joellen had tried to hide where they were, but Cara knew every grain of the wheat-colored sand on these islands, and this was Martha's Vineyard.

The first splash of surf was like ice water over her toes, instantly soaking the bottom of her jeans and pulling a childlike hoot from her throat. For a minute she just stood in the surf, letting the ebb of each wave create hollows around her feet, then gasping as the next wave of icy water rolled over her toes and up to her ankles.

Once again, she spread her arms like imaginary wings, tilted her head all the way back, and closed her eyes.

"Pretty."

She jumped at the man's voice like a live wire had prodded her skin, shooting around so fast she cracked her neck.

"You look like you're praying to the goddess of the ocean."

She stumbled backward, blood singing in her head at the sight of a big, scary, murderous-looking man. Icy blue eyes sliced her, his stance far more predatory than his tone, his shoulders double the size of hers.

"What do you want?" She backed away, a quick glance toward the dunes on one side, the ocean on the other. She'd never outrun this guy.

"Just walking the beach." He took a step toward her.

"Leave me alone." She danced to the left, choosing the

dunes over the water, unable to take her eyes off him. He looked deadly. That was the only word she could think of. A killer. This man had killed—and would again.

The laser-like look, the massive, lethal hands, the vein that throbbed on his neck, the slow rise and fall of his crushing chest, all confirmed that thought.

Deadly.

"Just leave me alone," she repeated, stumbling like a clumsy idiot in the sand when she tried and failed to make her feet move.

It was like he'd pinned her, and he hadn't even touched her.

Roman hired only the best to do his dirty work.

"Do you know me?" she asked, her voice as flimsy as her legwork.

"I'd like to." The hint of a smile only made him... deadlier. "But you don't seem to be inclined to talk."

She shook her head. "I'm not. Bye."

"Wait." He reached out a hand and she jumped away as if he'd offered a burning sparkler. "Let me give you my card. Maybe when you want to talk, you'll call me."

"Don't bother. I won't."

He reached back, into a pocket, the move lifting the bottom of his dark T-shirt.

And revealing a gun.

Holy God in heaven. She sucked in a breath and turned, breaking into a run, bracing her whole body for a bullet in the back.

The deafening crack of a gunshot exploded, and Cara threw herself onto the sand with a scream, waiting for the blinding pain that must take a second to register in the brain. Where was she shot? Where would it hurt?

"Get away from her!"

She looked up to see Marissa standing wide-legged at the top of the dunes, a pistol held in two hands. Terrified, Cara managed to look over her shoulder.

He held up both hands, away from his gun. "No harm meant, ma'am," he said to Marissa. "You can put your weapon away."

But she didn't, raising it instead, her hands remarkably steady. Where had Marissa learned to shoot like that? Cara ducked in anticipation of another shot, but Marissa just held him in her sights as he jogged forward.

He passed Cara; he didn't even slow, but slid her a look to the side. "If you ever need anything, Cara." He flipped a card at her and took off as fast as the bullet Marissa had just fired.

For a long minute, she just watched his body as it grew smaller, less threatening.

"Are you okay?" Marissa came running down the dunes, the gun now pointed at an angle in one hand, like a professional.

"I'm fine." Cara gave her an assuring gesture with both hands. "Thanks for that."

She looked less fierce close up, more like scared Marissa. "What did he say to you?" she asked. "Who the hell was he?"

Cara picked up the small white card from the sand, but Marissa's focus was on the runner, who was little more than a figure in the distance now.

"I don't know." Cara read the card. Ten digits, no name. "But he gave me his number."

"Was he trying to pick you up? Did he recognize you?"

Yes, he most certainly had. *If you ever need anything, Cara.*

If he worked for Roman, she was as good as dead. And if he was just a guy running the beach who discovered a movie star in hiding? Well, who could resist the chunk of change that information would get with the tabloids?

Either way, her secret was out. She looked at her assistant. "I don't know," she lied. "But we may not be as safe here as I thought. I may need to go back to Nantucket."

"Why?"

To deal with Roman once and for all. "To settle a score," she said vaguely.

CHAPTER 16

Let's go," Colt said, sliding his phone into his pocket after calling in this latest news to L.A. "I want to get down there before it's dark."

Behind him, Vivi jogged to keep up, even though she'd changed into her jeans and "shit kickers."

Digging-around-for-trouble shoes was what they should be called.

"Is that why you're running?" she asked. "Because it feels more like you want to keep as much distance as possible between us."

And that, too. "You're imagining things."

"Am I?"

He ignored the question, snatching the keys from the hook on the garage wall and climbing onto the ATV without waiting for her. But she hoisted herself right up, smashing her breasts and legs against him, wrapping a familiar arm around his gut. The gut that was screaming: Colton Lang, are you a fucking glutton for punishment?

"I thought you might fight me on this, or demand that half the Bureau accompany us to the bog house," she said as he turned on the engine and maneuvered them out.

"All the agents are at their posts, and this house has been thoroughly searched already. Anyway, you'd just bug me about it all night."

"All night?" she asked, plenty of implication in the question. "So you're not sending Special Agent Iverson to babysit me upstairs?"

"Upstairs?" he asked, glancing over his shoulder. "Why did you move?"

"Easier access to Cara's clothes. And it's more secure."

And private. So they could make all kinds of noise. He jammed his thumb on the accelerator and rolled over the brush and bramble, following the tracks they'd made the other day to the bog.

"You know, Lang, I like it when you don't fight me on things," she said, her mouth close to his ear so he could hear her over the engine. And feel her warm breath right down through his whole body. Jesus, he might not make it upstairs.

He might break into the bog house at nightfall.

"I only fight you when it's necessary." Or when it was going to wreck his head, heart, and life.

But he didn't know that for sure, right? If she was offering what it felt like she was offering, the best thing Colt could do was take it. One night, maybe two. A few memorable romps, some mind-numbing sex, and he'd get this out of his system and be on his way.

Wouldn't he?

"You're going to miss the turn," she said.

He wrenched the ATV to the right, turning into the path

between the pines to the bog house. Dusk was coming fast, the trees blocking the setting sun almost completely. He parked at the side of the house, able to see the back porch where the entrance to the drainage pipes had been thoroughly examined by the other agents and blocked off with yellow tape.

"They left the front door unlocked," he said. "Let's go in that way."

As they climbed the two steps to the tiny front porch, Vivi stopped and turned to look at the view. "This is exactly what that painting looks like," she said, a little awe in her voice. "If she really painted that, then the woman has talent. She has *heart*."

"She doesn't seem like she has enough heart to fill in a coloring book," Colt said, opening the door. "And for all we know, she could be sending us on a wild goose chase or worse."

"Worse?"

"The house'll blow up while we're in it."

Vivi froze with a gasp. "You think?"

"No, but keep the door open in case we have to run."

After he did a thorough check of the tiny house, they went directly to the fireplace and started looking. It had been searched by the agents, but not cleaned out, so they might have missed whatever this key fit. If the key fit anything in the fireplace.

He felt around the mantel, but Vivi stepped right into the hole and looked up to the chimney, coughing a little.

"Can you lift me?" she asked.

"Why?"

"Looks like there's something blocking the chimney, like a false wall. Maybe it locks. You'll need to hold me up while I check it out."

"I'll go up there," he said.

"Your shoulders won't fit, stud." She ducked out, a few soot marks on her cheeks. He brushed at one.

"You're dirty already."

"It's a fireplace. Dirt is expected."

"It's cute."

She narrowed her eyes at him. "You know, you haven't called me cute since I donned the Cara clothes."

"Only because I don't want to make you mad."

She grinned as they dragged the iron grate out of the way. "You live to make me mad."

He wanted to kiss her. Right then and there, halfway in a fireplace, with dirt on her face and trouble in her eyes. He wanted to kiss her so much it actually hurt.

"Kneel down," she said. "I'll get on your shoulders."

For a moment he didn't move. He just stared at her smudged, cute face. He adored that face. It made his heart do stupid things. It used to just make his dick go off the deep end, but now—it was more than that.

God*damn* it all.

She let out an exasperated sigh. "All right, Lang, just let me have it."

"Have what?" Because if she gave him the go-ahead, he would. Right now, right here, all night.

"I can tell you're about to fight me on this again. I can always tell when you have that look in your eyes. You're lining up an argument. What about this don't you like, exactly?"

Nothing. He liked nothing about this. "I just don't want anyone to get hurt."

She gave him a shove into the fireplace and onto his knees. "Then hold on to me and don't let me fall."

"All right." Someone was going to fall, though. And he had a feeling it was going to be him.

He cradled his hands and helped her climb up, her knees braced against his shoulders, one of her hands flattened against the chimney wall to stay steady. With the other, she reached up and started feeling around the metal panel that closed off the chimney.

"It doesn't move."

"Push harder—they usually release with some pressure."

She grunted, her weight pressing on him as she used all the force she had. "Nope. Let me see if I can find a—got it! Keyhole." She stabbed into her jeans pocket and produced the key, then stretched to unlock and release the panel.

"How are you going to get up there?"

"On your shoulders."

"That's what I thought you might say." He maneuvered her legs and she stepped up to his shoulders, her head popping through the hole.

"It's a way into the rafters," she said between coughs. "Disgusting, dark, abandoned and no doubt full of rat shit."

"We can get someone up there tomorrow."

"Like hell you can." She grabbed hold of something and her weight lightened on his shoulders. "This is what the Guardian Angelinos do, dude."

He laughed a little, his whole being warmed just by *her*. Her voice, her style, her reckless determination. He'd never met anyone like her. *Anyone*. This went past mourning for a woman he'd lost.

This was wanting a woman he might never have.

As she hoisted herself up, her weight disappeared from

his shoulders. But something else pressed so heavily on him, he could hardly breathe.

"Long rolls of paper," she announced, her voice muffled as she got deeper into the attic. "Looks like blueprints. Probably for the remodeling Joellen talked Cara out of because of nutcase mother. Just a wild guess."

Two tubes came tumbling down to his feet.

"There's something else up here. Hang on." Her feet disappeared from view as she went farther.

"Be careful," he said.

No answer.

"Vivi?"

Still no answer. "Vivi!"

"Relax, Lang." She stuck her head through the opening, her words nearly lost in the rush of relief in his head. "I found something."

"What?"

"A dead guy."

Vivi shined the light of her phone on the skeleton, yellow white, and perfect in his form. This dude had clearly been dead awhile. There was not a remnant of skin or hair, only some tattered rags that might have once been clothes.

"Get the hell down here!" Lang ordered, all kinds of panic in his voice.

"I'm coming, believe me." She scrambled to the edge, took one more look at Bones, then let her legs drop back into the lower half of the chimney. Her feet hit Lang's shoulders and he eased her down and they both crawled out of the fireplace into the air.

She was shaking a little when he grabbed her and pulled her closer. "You okay?"

"I'm fine, but…" Was Lang shaking, too? Something had him unnerved. "I saw the remains, not you."

"Let's go. We'll get CSI in here tomorrow morning. I have to call in—"

"No, wait." The words were out before she really thought about why. "Let's talk to Mercedes first."

"Oh, we'll talk to Mercedes. She practically led us here." He was already pulling her toward the open door, carrying the blueprints she'd found in one hand. "She knows way more than she's saying and I'm taking her in, whether it freaks her out to step into the open air or not."

Something unsettled inside her. Something about Mercedes.

If you have a heart, you'll leave this be.

"Why would she hide this?" Vivi said.

"Because she had something to do with it. Because he was murdered. Because her daughter—who she doesn't admit is her daughter—is a famous movie star who also, I might add just for color, has some connection to a guy at the helm of a human trafficking ring." He finally took a breath and got her out the door. "That could just be a dead Laotian farm worker up there. We'll talk to her in an official capacity. And then we'll put her ass in jail."

"Let me talk to her, Lang."

"You did your bit as the Guardian Angelino. I'll talk to her in an official, on-the-record FBI interview."

She didn't argue, choosing instead to climb onto the ATV and hold him as he took them through the darkening night light, back to the house.

She'd just come face-to-face with a dead body and yet what troubled her most was Mercedes. Was this what had turned her into an agoraphobic? Vivi had to find out, and she knew she could, if Lang didn't interfere.

They went to Mercedes's apartment together, without even stopping for water, which she desperately needed. The woman opened her door with a look of sadness, and as soon as she saw the soot and dirt on Vivi, her shoulders slumped in resignation.

"Who was he?" Vivi asked before Lang could even get in there in his damn official capacity.

Mercedes clasped her hands, wringing them, pain distorting her face. "A farm worker."

Behind her, she felt Lang tense. A Laotian farm worker, exactly as he'd predicted. But so far he'd stayed quiet, and Vivi took the lead.

"Did you kill him?" she asked.

Mercedes backed up, silently inviting them into her cold, drab, dungeon of a world.

"No." She swallowed hard. "Joellen did."

"Why?"

She brushed an imaginary hair from her face, glancing from Vivi to Lang. "Could I talk to you alone?" she asked Vivi.

"No," Lang said, his tone leaving no room for argument. "Just tell us what happened."

She shuddered a little and perched on the edge of her sofa. Vivi sat next to her, fighting the urge to reach out and calm the waves of dread and terror and pain rolling off her.

"Just tell us, Mercedes," she said softly. "Please."

Putting her hands to her mouth, she closed her eyes, obviously gathering scattered, wild thoughts. Her whole body trembled, all her cold control evaporating more with each passing second.

"I know you're their mother, Mercedes."

Her eyes flashed open for a second, then closed again. "I kept a shotgun for the possum and animals. Jo came home from school, and...shot him."

Vivi stifled a slight gasp. "Why?"

"Because he was..." She barely managed a breath. "He attacked me."

"Oh." Vivi let out the word and lost the battle not to take Mercedes's hand.

"I was alone in the house and he came in off the bog—it was out of season, just a few workers. He was looking for water and I got him some, even though I never liked to give the workers anything because—well, my husband was dead, and they could take advantage of me." She ran out of breath.

Vivi squeezed her hand, her own throat closing, her stomach tightening, her intuition warning her to brace for the worst.

"He raped me."

That was the worst. "I'm sorry," she whispered, vaguely aware that her voice cracked.

"Joellen walked in while he was..." She looked down at the ground.

"It's okay, you don't have to say."

"But I do," she whispered. "I have to say it because my girl killed him with that shotgun and she shouldn't be in trouble for that. But we had to hide him. And we had to leave because I was so scared and so...so..."

So ruined.

"We left. I took the girls and we left the bog and let the farm die out and then...I had to come back. It was the only place I could just hide."

"But did you sell it while you were gone?" Lang asked.

"No." She looked up at him. "I would never sell it."

"So you still own the property."

"I put it all in Cara and Joellen's name years ago. Lawyers handled it. But it's still in our family."

Vivi and Lang shared a look. Could Chessie's information be wrong? Why would Roman Emmanuel's name be on the deed for the bog house and farm?

Mercedes took a long, slow breath. "Are you going to make me...go somewhere? Because...I can't go outside."

"Not tonight," Vivi said gently, grateful that Lang didn't contradict her. "When did you stop going outside, Mercedes?"

"It happened little by little," she admitted. "Every day, after...that day...I could do less and less. Face less and less. I tried to get help, but the fears won out. When Cara became a star, she made it so I never had to go anywhere. I just do whatever my girls ask of me, because they made me safe."

"Why don't you tell anyone you're their mother?"

"If it ever comes out, I'm afraid the bad publicity could ruin Cara. Her career, her life, her ability to watch out for Jo." Mercedes tried to swallow. "Jo has her way of dealing with what she did."

Booze. Everybody compensated somehow. Vivi hid, too, in her own way. Hid from the pain and fear, letting them win.

Wasn't that what she'd done every time a man ever tried to get close to her?

She looked up at Lang, her heart filling. Every man except this one. He would be the one to break her out of her prison. She would not live like Mercedes, old and alone and without sunshine and air. Or sex and love. They were just as essential.

"It's okay," he said, holding up a hand as if he thought Vivi was about to launch into an argument. "She can stay. For tonight."

He'd misread her expression. He thought she was pleading for Mercedes. But she was pleading for herself.

"Thank you," she said to him, turning to the other woman. "Just rest now, Mercedes. Don't worry. There's no reason anyone in the world needs to know your secret. I promise."

For the first time since they'd met, Mercedes smiled, her blue eyes blurred with unshed tears. "Thank you."

Vivi reached out and hugged her stiff shoulders, and got a loose, light, partial embrace in response.

"Don't let him win," Vivi whispered into her ear.

And it was time she took that advice for herself.

CHAPTER 17

As they left the basement apartment, Vivi took Colt's hand, threading her slender fingers between his, her gaze full of gratitude, affection, and intimacy. Or maybe that was just a reflection of everything he felt for her that moment.

"I *really* like it when you don't fight me," she said. "Thanks for letting me take the lead with her, when I know that's not what you wanted to do."

"You were very...gentle." Masterful, in fact. Which only made him admire her more. "I don't know why it took me so long to see it."

"To see what?" she asked as they walked down the hall, toward the stairs.

"To see your tender side, your feminine side." All the things he craved in a woman and had been so certain Vivi lacked.

She laughed softly, tugging him up the stairs. "You ain't seen nothin' yet, baby."

He slowed his pace, then stopped with her two steps above him. She turned to meet him eye to eye.

"What happened to you in the last hour?" he asked.

Her smart-ass expression flickered away, and her whole face softened. "Other than finding a dead body and unearthing old secrets?"

"Yeah." Because something was suddenly different in her. "You came...alive. Is that just because you love the search so much? The investigation and interrogation and digging up the truth?"

She smiled. "I've always liked that stuff—that's why I do what I do. But, no, that's not what changed in the last hour."

"Then what did?"

She answered by putting her hands on his cheeks, bringing him closer until their lips nearly brushed. "You're right," she whispered. "I came alive. And you know what's going to happen now that I am well and truly *alive*?"

Of course he knew what was going to happen, like he knew he was going to take his next breath. And he was going to love every single minute and deal with the aftermath later. Hell, maybe there wouldn't *be* an aftermath.

"You're going to kiss me?" he asked.

She let their lips touch just enough to spark. "And then?"

"We're going up to your room?"

She opened her mouth, let their breath exchange. "And then?"

"We're taking a shower?"

She laughed into the kiss, flicked her tongue over his, added enough pressure to almost knock him backward off the stairs. "No dirty sex with you, ever."

He pulled her into him, wrapping his arms around her and returning the kiss with maximum force. Her hands slid from his face, down to his neck, clinging for life as their tongues entwined and teeth touched.

"Plenty of dirty sex," he said gruffly, his whole lower half hardening against her. "In the bathtub."

"The bathtub?" She leaned back to get a good look at him. "Is this my rule-following, golf-playing, old-school traditionalist Colton Cautious Lang?"

"Yes, Vivi Poison Angelino. That's who's about to make love to you and damn the torpedoes."

She giggled in his mouth. "*Damn the torpedoes?* Yes, this is definitely my Lang."

Her Lang. "Move it." He backed her up the stairs.

"We're going to do it in the bath?"

"In the bath." Two more steps. "On the floor." One more step. "In the closet. On the bed. Against the wall. Hanging from the damn chandelier, if we can." They reached the landing and he pushed her toward the door, his mouth on hers again. "Wherever the hell I can get inside you and stay there all night long."

"Oh, yeah." She practically melted in his arms, surrendering to the kiss and nearly tripping as he guided them into the room and locked the door behind him. "I love the way you roll, big bad Fed guy."

He had to laugh at that, grabbing at her shirt to pull it up. She raised her arms and he stripped it off, reaching around to unhook her bra.

A grunt came from deep in his chest at the sight of her creamy, womanly body, his hands covering her instantly. He wanted to touch everything, kiss every inch, own every cell in Vivi's body.

She gave it right back, electrified and hungry. They kissed and undressed, laughed, groaned, and gave each other assistance all the way to the bathroom, leaving a trail of T-shirt, shoes, jeans, underwear—the Glock he left on the dresser. The only thing he took was his wallet, for the condom he knew he had in it.

Fire shot through his body as he caressed her breasts, suckled her neck, and dragged her toward the bathroom. Moaning with appreciation, she fondled him with trembling hands, stroking the length of his hard-on, curling her fingers into his nest, cradling his sac, killing whatever shreds of self-control he hoped he might have.

"Turn the water on," she said as they reached a tub that could seat seven, the wall behind it still missing the mirror but everything else exactly as they'd first found it.

He flipped both knobs full force and they stood kissing while the water rushed through a wide-mouth faucet that made a waterfall down the back of the massive marble tub.

She broke their kiss, lifting her hands to his chest, examining her fingers and palms. "We are filthy," she said, stepping back to show her breasts blackened from the soot and ash on his hands.

"We need soap," he said.

"Right there." A wicker basket next to the tub was overloaded with high-end bottles of bath stuff, sponges, and brushes. "Pick one."

He grabbed two plastic bottles, one filled with aquamarine liquid, the other a golden amber. "Cucumber and aloe or warm vanilla sugar?" he asked, turning the labels toward her like two bottles of fine wine.

"Definitely vanilla."

"Good choice." He dropped the green bottle back in the basket, twisted the cap off the vanilla, and poured it over her chest.

"Ahh!" She jumped back, surprised and laughing, but he kept pouring, covering her with the honey-colored soap, letting it drip over her stomach, between her legs, down her thighs to the floor. "You are officially out of control, Assistant Special Agent in Charge of Soap."

"Shhh. You'll ruin my reputation." He tossed the half-empty bottle on the vanity and laid both hands on her breastbone and dragged them over her goo-covered flesh.

"Oh my God," she whispered at the sensation, dropping her head back and letting him caress her. He followed the trail of soap over her flesh, sliding his hand down her belly and right between her legs.

She almost buckled at the touch.

"In the bath," he ordered, helping her over the ledge.

It wasn't full yet, but they tumbled into the water, and he leaned her back on the sloping marble designed for just this kind of bathing. He braced himself over her body as clouds of bubbles erupted under the cascading water.

Her hair floated like seaweed as she inched down into the water, her skin slippery and sexy and so, so perfect against his.

"You look like a mermaid," he said, dragging his fingers through the locks, pushing them away from her body so he could see it before the bubbles covered his view. "No, an angel. A goddess. A water nymph."

"Pick a metaphor, Lang," she said with a laugh. "And kiss me before I drown."

He started to, then lifted his head, looking at her

again. His body was a lost cause right now, so why not just tell her what was on his mind and lose that, too? "I don't know the right comparison, but you're beautiful, you know that? I don't think I tell you that enough."

Her laugh faded to surprise, and a little wonder, her mouth in an O as she drew in a breath. "No," she said softly. "You really don't. Ever, actually."

"I should," he admitted, stroking hair from her face. "Because you are, Vivi. You are utterly beautiful."

"Oh, Lang." His name was just a sigh of pure astonishment.

"Don't be surprised," he said. "You are beautiful."

"I'm surprised that"—she glided soapy fingers over his cheeks, searching his eyes with her dark, intense gaze—"I just never imagined you'd be...the one."

The one? Was he the one for her? He tried to swallow, tamping down the disagreement that rose. She didn't like when he fought her on something, but...he did *not* want to be the one. For anyone.

"The one who'd pour soap over you and throw you in a tub? That one?" He tried for a joking voice, and almost succeeded.

She just smiled, like she knew he was attempting humor, making light of what really wasn't light at all.

So he kissed her again, stopping the conversation, putting his full concentration where it belonged: finally making love to this woman who constantly surprised and baffled and intrigued him. Her mouth tasted like vanilla and Vivi, a taste getting all too familiar and delicious.

The bubbles blanketed her now, so he used his hands to appreciate her body, moving them everywhere he could touch, making her close her eyes and rock under him.

Heat oozed through him, his erection swollen against her stomach, his legs trapping hers between his.

She reached between them and closed her hand over him, stroking slowly, every breath more of a struggle than the one before. He kneeled up to give her full access, reaching back to turn the water off.

The room went silent except for the softest splash of her hands as they moved up and down over his shaft, the sensation so perfect he just gripped the side of the tub and gave in to the pleasure that shot through him.

She studied his face, his body, then his erection in her hands as he grew bigger, harder, readier for her. She sat up, leaning forward to kiss the tip.

He automatically closed his hands over her head, guiding her mouth, letting out a soft grunt as she took him as far as she could. Agony and ecstasy exploded in his body, a squeeze of exquisite pleasure with a kick of painful need.

He almost lost it. "Vivi, wait."

Naturally, she ignored him, sucking harder like she'd never done this before and somehow didn't know that he'd explode in about three more strokes.

She doesn't get funky.

Gabe's words filled the bathroom's silence, making Lang's heart spike for a second. No, that was impossible. Unthinkable. A girl like Vivi surely—

She popped her head up and looked at him, something like pride and awe in her eyes. "Do you like that?"

"Are you crazy?"

"Right now I am."

He laughed a little and bent over to grab his condom from the wallet he'd left on the ledge. "You have to stop that now."

"Why?" She was actually ... innocent.

"Because it's time for"—he snapped the condom package—"this."

She nodded, half smiling, half ... trembling, then leaned back on the angled marble. "You put it on," she said.

"I want you to."

Her eyes expanded almost imperceptibly. "Me?" She looked like she wanted to argue, but she just shook her head.

"What's the matter, Vivi?"

"Nothing," she said quickly. "You're just ... you know, there's a lot of you."

He bit the condom wrapper and spit out the corner, opening it without taking his eyes off her. "I won't hurt you."

She wet her lips and nodded. "I know. That's why I picked you."

She *picked* him? Why did he not like the sound of that? He pulled out the rubber disk and held it out to her. "Please."

"Okay." She took the condom, flipping it once, placing it on him before quickly realizing it was upside down and wouldn't slide that way. She covered with a smile. "I'm a little nervous."

Really. "You've never been nervous in your life."

"There's a first time for everything, isn't there, Lang?" She gave him a meaningful look as she rolled the condom over him, taking her sweet time, hitting every nerve ending along the way.

A first time ...

He hissed in a breath when she reached the bottom,

fondling his balls, numbing his far-too-active brain. He didn't want to think about—that possibility. He couldn't. The aftermath would be too much.

Wordlessly, he laid her back and positioned himself over her, guiding her legs around his hips. She reached up to him, pulling him closer and as he came down, they held eye contact for one beat of his heart, two, then three.

"I'm ready for you," she whispered.

Holding himself with one hand, he let the tip slip into her, watched her shudder at the first inch. Tension rolled off her like the steam of the hot water.

"You sure?" he asked.

She nodded, biting her lower lip, reaching out to his hands. They locked fingers, both hands, looking at each other as he entered another inch. She was so tight, so hot, so damn sweet that he had to close his eyes to keep from ramming into her.

She squeezed his hands so hard the tendons cracked but her hips rose and fell, taking him in farther. "That's good. That's…" Pain tore her voice and he froze. "No, don't stop, Lang. Just…don't stop."

He inched in deeper into unbelievable tightness. He paused again, questions screaming in his brain, only slightly louder than the drumbeat of blood and need urging him in farther, the natural desire to plunge and push and bury himself inside her taking over every part of him.

She cupped his rear end, arched her back, and urged him deeper. "Please, Lang, please."

He let go and entered all the way, a soft curse falling from his lips at the bone-deep satisfaction that kicked his gut and his body and his brain into blissful silence.

"Oh!" She grabbed his arms and clutched, but there

was no way to stop. He let himself fall forward, splashing water and bubbles while they moved in and out, up and down, slowly at first, then a little faster.

"This is ... good."

Why did she sound so surprised?

"Oh, yes, this is so good," she whimpered in his ear, growing more emphatic with each thrust. "Oh my God, Lang, I had no idea. ..."

He closed his eyes and tried to chalk up the words to sexual bliss, holding her tightly, their heads well above the water that slapped and splattered and danced to their perfect rhythm.

Tiny, helpless mewing sounds from her throat coaxed him on, her greedy hands clinging to his backside and hips, clasping him with all her might, desperate for everything he could give her.

"Vivi," he moaned, release threatening low in his back and deep in his belly.

She let go of him, smacking her hands through the water like she just couldn't stand the pleasure, crying out again as he bowed his back and thrust every inch of himself into her.

"Come with me, Vivi," he urged. "Come when I do."

"I will." She flattened her hands on his chest, nails digging into him like she could barely hang on. "I will," she repeated, her eyes wild, her jaw slack. "I never dreamed it could be like this, Lang."

Jesus, was this her first time? The impact of the thought was enough to stun him into stopping.

Her eyes flashed open. "What's wrong?"

"You've never done this before, have you?"

The color on her face deepened, more blush than sexual

flush. "In a bathtub? No. Please don't stop, I'm so close." Her voice broke with frustration as she rode him, and he still didn't move.

"Anywhere," he said. "You've never done this anywhere."

"That's not true," she whispered. "But it has been awhile."

That helped a little. He didn't want her to be a virgin. Didn't want it to *mean that Goddamn much*. This was supposed to be—

"How long?" He *had* to know.

"Long," she said simply, her expression changing. "Please don't ruin this time with an interrogation, Lang. It's been a long time and I want you and you want me and please, please, *please* don't stop to talk."

He opened his mouth, then closed it again, lowering to taste her lips and suck her tongue into his mouth. Did it matter how long it had been? No. This was now. This was what he wanted. This was all he wanted.

He started to move again, getting rewarded with a soft sigh of relief and a matching roll of her hips.

"Come inside me, Lang," she urged. "I want to feel that. I have to feel that."

He didn't kiss her, didn't bury his face in her neck and hair and lose himself to the exquisite pleasure like he should have.

Instead, he just held her gaze, plunging in and out, watching each move change her face, letting every sensation roll through him until he had to release the pressure. Helpless and lost, he finally closed his eyes and let out a growl of release, coming hard to the music of her moans, the sound of his name, the gasps of her own orgasm against him.

His face against hers, water lapped over them, the sound of their hearts magnified through the whole tub. Neither one could breathe or talk or move any of their spent and exhausted muscles.

Nothing worked...but his brain.

And that was very busy trying to remind him that this was supposed to be sex without aftermath. But now he knew she'd *picked* him and it had been a *long* time and—

"Sixteen years," she whispered.

Very slowly, praying he'd misunderstood, he lifted his head to look at her. "What?"

"It's been sixteen years."

All he could do was let out a soft grunt of disbelief and close his eyes. Aftermath dead ahead.

CHAPTER 18

Vivi stayed in the tub until the water was cold, long after Lang had slowly lifted himself out, his green-gold gaze questioning and—yeah—a little bit mad. Maybe she should have told him sooner, but, really, what difference did it make?

Would it have stopped them? No. Would he have been any different? Any more tender? Kinder? More affectionate? How could he have been?

He was perfect.

And, damn, she was going to want more of him in a big fat hurry. Sex was more fun than a five-forty McTwist on the high ramp. This could be her new favorite thing. This could be—

Sheer hell when he was in L.A.

She pushed the thought away and listened to him move around the bedroom. He'd want to know why, of course, and she'd tell him—some. Not all. Never all.

She'd carry that around like poor old Mercedes, only

she was smart enough not to let the past imprison her. Just not free enough to give that knowledge to anyone.

Then she heard the door open and close, and silence.

Oh. No. He'd left her.

A low, deep pulse of disappointment and disbelief drummed in her belly as she climbed out of the tub, her legs shaky, her most tender parts...more tender than usual.

How could he just leave her like that? Not even want to talk about it?

The same way he's going to get on a plane and fly off to be an SAC in Los Angeles, that's how. With Lang-like ease.

"Great," she mumbled, opening a linen closet—walk-in, naturally—looking for a towel but spying a fluffy butter yellow bathrobe. Stuffing her arms in and tying the belt with a hard snap, she sighed audibly.

Just her luck. She'd finally found a man she could trust, who she wanted to get close to and who made her feel good right down to her toes...and he was leaving.

Why did he have to leave?

It had nothing to do with ambition, she suspected, and everything to do with escaping. He'd never gotten over the woman he'd lost—a blind person could see that when he talked about Jennifer.

"Nice work, Vivi," she chided herself. "You can really pick 'em, girlie."

Not only was he running away from the ghost of a woman he still loved, he didn't *want* to fall for another one. Resistance rolled off him in waves.

This was all just sex for him, so no wonder he'd left afterward. Colton Lang didn't want her and her sixteen years of emotional baggage. He wanted to get laid and get out.

Fine. So did she. Again. So where the hell had he gone, anyway?

She marched to the door and flung it open just as he reached the top of the stairs, a tray in his hands, Stella at his heels.

"I need food," he said simply. "And I figured you did, too."

God, she hated when she underestimated people. "Thanks." She opened the door wider to let him through, and Stella trotted in with her awkward little hitch, not so much as a sniff of Vivi on her way. "That dog hates me."

"She just likes me a lot," he said, putting the tray on a table between two chairs in a bay window.

"So do I."

He turned around and gave her a questioning look.

"I just want to make that clear," she said quickly. "I like you a lot, Lang. Enough to break a self-imposed celibacy. But not enough to...try and talk you out of your plans. So you can just relax about that. I'm not out to nail you to the wall and keep you in Boston."

He simply stared at her, expressionless.

"Though I wouldn't mind nailing you to the bed and keeping you in it all night," she said with a forced laugh.

He didn't laugh back. "You should have told me."

"The subject really didn't come up." She crossed the room, shifting her attention to the cold chicken and potato salad he'd brought for them, taking one of the two bottles of cold water. "Let's not talk about it yet, okay? Can we just eat?"

She twisted open the bottle and took a sip.

"Will you tell me why?"

The water caught in her throat. *Some, Vivi, not all. No confessions to a man who's leaving you anyway.*

"I had an abortion." She took one of the seats, falling into it casually, like she hadn't just shared something she'd never told—anyone.

"Oh," he said, still standing, looking down at her. "That's..."

She shrugged, digging for nonchalance she really didn't feel. "I know what it is, Lang. Shocking. Disappointing. Disgusting. I've been through the range of emotions. Still visit them occasionally—even now, all these years later."

He sat down slowly, scrutinizing her while she brusquely took the food and plates off the tray, giving them each silverware and napkins. If she acted like she didn't really care, maybe he'd believe it.

"I bet that was a very difficult decision to make," he finally said, his voice flat. Of course he'd hate that she'd made that choice. "Especially for a girl like you."

It had been a different girl, a different Vivi. "I was scared," she said, absently wrapping the robe tighter, then reaching for another drink of water. "I was sixteen and scared to death of hurting the family that adopted me. I thought I might be deported for...being stupid."

And he told me I asked for it.

"You did?"

"I was *scared*," she repeated. "So I took the chicken-shit way out of a problem I just didn't know how to handle. And I never told anyone. Not even Zach."

"Or the guy would be dead."

"As a doornail, as you would say." Her heart was hitting double time for no good reason. What difference did it make if Lang didn't approve? It was legal. She had a choice. She'd been raped by her boyfriend—who would believe that?

"Was it the boy next door?"

The old-fashioned phrase made Kenny Taylor sound so... innocent. That riled, but she just nodded, her thumbnail stabbing the moist label of the water bottle.

"Is that why you quit ballet and cheerleading?"

That was exactly why. Not because of the abortion. But because she couldn't stand to be in her own skin for one more day. Couldn't stand to be the cheerleader who kicked so high the basketball players saw her crotch. Couldn't stand to be the dancer who wore skimpy outfits and *asked* for it. Couldn't stand to be a woman completely vulnerable to a man.

"Yes," she said, absolutely loathing that he'd figured all that out *and* that it made her eyes sting. "That's why." Why she got five piercings in her ears and one in her nose. And why she gave up crying, chopped off her hair, grabbed a skateboard, and tried to be tough and... less female.

He reached his hand over the table, closing it around hers and the water bottle. "I understand why you've waited, then."

No, he really didn't. But he thought he did, and that was good enough for her.

"I just wish I had known," he added.

"Would it have stopped you?"

"No... maybe... yes. What I mean is that it would have been"—he looked helpless to find a word—"more."

"More what?" she asked. "Meaningful? Important? Life changing?"

"All of the above."

She just smiled. "It was to me."

He just paled and looked down at the food, silent.

In other words, sex with her wasn't any of those things to him.

"Your phone is buzzing," he said, angling his head toward the floor, where a line of discarded clothes spilled from the door to the bathroom. "Do you want to get it?"

"It's a text." She pushed away from the table to retrieve the phone and read the message from Chessie. *Vivi, call me stat! Urgent news.*

"Something's up," she said, already dialing. "From Chessie. Maybe she got something from Joellen's texts."

He looked up from the table. "You're reading them? You're illegally tapping her phone?"

"Just her texts," she said, cringing a little as Chessie's phone rang in her ear. "Chessie knew how and after we got the message and figured out it was—"

"Vivi, she's coming back to Nantucket," Chessie said as she answered the call. "Tomorrow afternoon."

"Let me put you on speaker so ASAC Lang is in on *everything.*" She put the phone on the table between them. "All right, Chess. What's going on?"

"Joellen is exchanging texts with someone about Cara coming to Nantucket tomorrow. I haven't figured out who yet."

"What does she say?" Vivi asked.

"The first text said 'CF ready to talk. Will bring her to NanT tomorrow aft.' I figured CF was Cara Ferrari and NanT was Nantucket, so, naturally, I followed this thread closely."

"Naturally," Lang said dryly, putting down a chicken leg after taking a bite, then wiping his hands on a napkin.

"And in less than a minute, she got a response from someone—someone who is blocking their number and is wicked untraceable—who said, 'That takes balls. Bring her.'"

"Okay, so she's coming here." Vivi sat back down, defeated. "We can't exactly look for evidence of her involvement with Emmanuel's trafficking ring if she's here."

"*You* can't," Lang said. "The FBI has every reason to be here protecting the real Cara Ferrari, so we can. In fact, it would be easier to interrogate her if she were right under my nose."

An unfamiliar thread of jealousy twined through Vivi. She didn't want Cara Ferrari under his anything. And she wasn't ready to leave him yet.

"Anyway, there was a little more to the exchange," Chessie added. "Joellen said they'd be arriving in the late afternoon on the ferry."

"From Cape Cod or the Vineyard?" Vivi asked.

"Not sure. But there was a response."

"Yeah?"

"This person wrote back, and I quote: 'Take care of her. Do the job I pay you to do.'"

Vivi and Lang looked at each other, considering all the possibilities.

"Mercedes?" he suggested.

"Roman?" she countered.

He lifted his eyebrows. "Doubtful, but interesting theory. This person said 'bring' her, indicating that he or she is already in Nantucket. So my money's on your friend in the basement."

"You think Mercedes pays Joellen to babysit her thirty-three-year-old sister who can afford the best bodyguards in the world?"

He shrugged. "Maybe she doesn't protect her; maybe she has another job. Just keeping her out of trouble or off the sauce."

"Joellen's the one on the *sauce*," Vivi said. "And, just for the record, Lang—"

"I know, nobody says 'sauce' anymore"—he grinned—" 'cept me."

She rolled her eyes and shifted her attention back to the phone. "Thanks, Chessie. If it weren't for you, I'd have no idea she was going to show up."

"Probably the way she wants it," Chessie said.

"Yep. The decoy body double is always the last to know."

"Not when you break the law and illegally tap people's phones," Lang said.

Vivi laughed. "We're just doing things the Angelino way."

"Speaking of which," Lang said. "Any word from Gabe? Did he have any luck finding a location on Cara?"

"I haven't heard anything," Chessie said. "But if I do, I'll let you know."

"Good work, Chessie. We'll be in touch." Vivi disconnected the call and leaned back with a sigh. "Guess the party's almost over for me."

Lang gave her a dark look, and a very sexy half smile. "We have a few more hours, Poison. And you have a lot of catching up to do."

The irony of that hit her hard. "Sixteen years of waiting for you, Lang, and I end up with a few hours to get my fill."

His sexy smile faltered, but his gaze never did. "Then you better make the most of them."

CHAPTER 19

Colt woke to an empty bed. At first he opened his eyes and stared at the indent on the pillow next to him, a single strand of black hair left behind. In the recesses of his sleep-starved brain he remembered that he was waiting for a report on that hair but didn't have anything yet.

The hint of sweet vanilla still lingered in the bed and the place where Vivi's body had been tucked so close to his was still warm enough for him to know she'd just gotten up, probably to go to the bathroom.

He didn't hear water running, or any movement at all, so he forced himself up on his elbows, blinking into the dawn-dim room to see Vivi cross-legged on the floor, wearing those happy face boxers and a tissue-thin tank top, architect's blueprints spread out in front of her.

Sensing his eyes on her, she looked up and smiled. "Morning."

And all manner of stupid stuff happened in his chest. Heart rate up, breathing tight, a band of pain he used to think was mourning but now knew was something else completely. Emotional *paralysis*.

"Hey," he said, his voice still gruff from sleep. "What are you doing?"

"Looking at the plans we found in the skeleton attic. All tunnels."

"Connecting the two houses?"

"Not really. These go all the way down to the water."

He sat up, more interested. "Which would be a helluva way to move traffic," he said.

"Human traffic," she agreed. "But I was in those drainage ditches and there's nothing like this down there. These even show a connection right where I was under that porch. And another on the other side of the bog in an old harvesting building that isn't even there anymore. Nothing on these blueprints was ever built."

"That would be too easy for us." He pushed the covers back, naked underneath, a morning erection threatening despite making love twice in the night. "I have two agents combing this island, but it's sizable and so much of it is inaccessible by foot or vehicle. My guess is they're moving people like cargo right off the ships in the main harbor."

She made a disgusted face. "How can they do that? And all the way from Laos? Why not move them in trucks across the country? Wouldn't that be easier than—what, going through the Panama Canal?"

"One would think," he agreed. "But a place like this? All tourists and art galleries? It's kind of brilliant, actually, when you think about it. Completely off the federal radar."

"Especially if you move them under your own house."

She leaned back, surveying him lustily. "What's on your docket for today, Assistant Special Agent in Charge Lang?"

"Give the woman three orgasms and she finally gets the title right."

"Four if you count that thing you did with the palm of your—where did you *learn* that, anyway?"

He chuckled softly. "Not in Quantico. If you come back to bed I'll teach you."

"Yeah, good skill to have when you're gone." Her smile wavered, and faded.

Neither of them spoke for a minute, the intimacy of the night before still heavy in the air, the inevitability that they might have just had their one and only night together just as intense between them.

Jesus. He never dreamed he'd *want* to stay in Boston. Would she ever—consider…living in L.A.? "I guess there's no chance you'd…" *Colt, are you nuts?* "Come back to bed."

She shook her head and pushed herself up briskly, brushing her legs like she was brushing the invitation off her. "Too much to do today."

"Get ready for the arrival of the star?"

"I'd like to go to the bank."

"Excuse me?"

She grabbed one of the blueprints, letting it roll back into a tube shape, then firing it at him, javelin style. "Read the back. If we can get that paperwork out of the bank before Cara gets back, you'll at least have real proof that a tie between her and Roman still exists. Part of this property is co-owned by RE Global and Cara Ferrari Enterprises. According to that, the Bank of America in Nantucket holds the title."

He unrolled the paper and read the words confirming that while she disappeared into the closet. "How do you plan to get that, Vivi? It would take at least two days to get a court order for a warrant and…" His voice trailed off. She didn't know the meaning of *court orders* and *warrants*.

She stepped out of the closet holding two dresses on hangers. One yellower and shorter and smaller than the other. "Which do you think Cara would wear to the bank? Mustard or sunflower?"

"You're going to walk into the Bank of America dressed as Cara Ferrari and demand to see the deeds to this property."

She raised the one on the right. "I think sunflower. So bright and optimistic, unlike some people I know."

"Vivi." He shot off the bed and strode into the closet just in time to see her strip the boxers down, her backside facing him, her front displayed in a three-way mirror.

His poor, mindless dick couldn't care less that they were arguing.

"You have a better idea, Lang?" She flipped the top off, standing stark naked and glorious.

"Yeah." He pointed to the chaise longue next to her. "Let's do it in front of the mirror."

She just smiled and shook her head. "Nice idea, but I want to get to the bank as it opens. Chessie is getting me—"

He held up a hand to stop her. "I don't want to know. As it is, my ass is going to be fired for breaking every law ever created to protect the rights of civilians."

"What about those girls sold as sex slaves?" She spun around, her eyes blistering with emotion. "Who's protecting their rights? If Cara Ferrari is aiding and abetting—even unknowingly—that man or *anyone* to take children and sell them on the open market and offer them up as prostitutes and cheap farm workers—"She shook her head, frustration stealing the rest of the words. "I'm going to do what I can to help stop it before she gets here. I think getting our hands on that deed—before she has any idea that the FBI has all this on her already and destroys it—is more important than going through the proper channels to get into that bank."

He just looked at her, a tsunami of déjà vu threatening to knock him over.

"What?" she demanded. "You don't agree? You think—"

"No," he brushed off the argument. "You just reminded me of someone for a minute."

"Of who? Jennifer?" The word stabbed him like a real javelin this time.

"Yes."

"Well, it's about time you admit she's in this room between us. Because it's getting awfully crowded here."

He narrowed his eyes at her. "I haven't mentioned her once. I haven't even thought about her. Not a single time last night, Vivi. I was...lost in you."

A soft breath escaped her lips as she held the yellow dress in front of her body, as if she were suddenly aware of how vulnerable and naked she was. "But you're not over her."

"Actually, I am." And just saying that felt good. "What I'm not over is...is the potential to go through it again. But, frankly, that balls-to-the-wall approach to every situation is exactly what got her killed."

She nodded, as if she understood. "I'm not going to get killed at the bank."

"Probably not," he agreed. "But I'll go as your body-guard anyway. And all you can do is take pictures of the stuff. You are not going to commit a federal crime and remove those papers from the bank. You got that?"

"I got it."

"Any other rules you want to break before I hit the shower?"

She nodded, and he just prayed it had to do with that chaise and those three-way mirrors.

"I don't want you to report the dead body."

His jaw just dropped. "What?"

"What's it going to change now, Lang? Mercedes was raped, she's emotionally wrecked, all this will do is bring it to light and force her to relive the whole situation over and over again. And, oh my God, with Cara's celebrity status, can you imagine the tabloids? Her secret mother, a bog worker shot by her sister, a body in the attic? Why? It happened years ago."

He just swallowed, already knowing where this was going.

"I'll talk to her," she said quickly when he didn't respond. "I'll get all the details and then we'll figure out how to report the death, if we have to, but keep it off the radar."

"Vivi—"

"In fact, when Cara comes here, I'll talk to her. And Joellen. I'll tell them we know and there has to be a report and if they work with us, maybe the police or the FBI could keep it quiet."

"Why?" he asked. "Why are you protecting any of

them? Mercedes has been a bitch to you. I still think she let the dog out so someone, if not her, could try and kill you."

"I just feel bad for her, Lang." She took a few steps closer to him. "If she were just another woman, then, okay. But the media, think about it. It will be awful for her. They'll want her on TV, and the press will hound her, they'll do reenactments...." Her voice broke and for one second he could have sworn he saw tears in her eyes. But Vivi didn't cry; she'd already told him that.

Still, the heartfelt plea hit home. "After you talk to her and Cara, I'll decide."

"Thanks, Lang." She reached up and kissed his cheek. "Now if we hurry, we can get home in time to use that chaise longue."

She winked and brushed by him on the way to the bathroom, leaving him unsure what just hit him. Hurricane Vivi. Category Five.

"The coast, as they say, is clear."

"As *you* say," Vivi corrected, climbing out of the blanket that covered her while they escaped the peering eyes of the paparazzi. The crowds near the gate had thinned considerably, but there were still some hangers-on, someone hoping for *another* Red Carpet Killer to somehow break the seal the FBI had put around the house and attack.

But the authorities had not yet released Sunisa Pakpao's name. Lang told her the FBI contacts had Roman Emmanuel traveling in Europe, and they'd successfully kept the shooting on the property the other night out of the media. Interest in Cara had waned a little, as the media waited for an ID on her assailant. No doubt with the real Cara under their nose, they'd release that name and close in tighter on whatever connection she had with Emmanuel.

Cara was not going to be a happy camper.

Vivi was probably not going to make a million dollars, nor would the Guardian Angelinos be the superstar of the security world with anyone but the FBI.

And her favorite client at the Boston Bureau would be long gone.

"It's my dad," Lang said.

Still situating herself in the subsize yellow outfit, Vivi frowned at him from the back, meeting his gaze in the rearview mirror. "What's your dad?"

"My dad uses all those dated phrases I love and you hate."

"I don't actually hate them," she admitted. "They're part of your charm."

He smiled. "He used expressions like cockamamie and malarkey and the coast is clear because he's an old 1950s TV aficionado. Loved *The Honeymooners* when he was a kid, then shows like *Green Acres* and every John Wayne movie ever made. He loved old Westerns like *Gunsmoke* and *Bonanza*. He quoted them, and that's where the language comes from."

"How old is he?" she asked, stealing a peek to make sure no reporters or photographers had followed.

"Mid-sixties."

"That's all?" she said. "You said he was getting on, and needed assistance."

"Well, he will be in a few years."

In other words, Dad was just another excuse for going

to L.A. She was going to have to accept this, no matter how much her heart—and various other parts of her body—didn't want to.

Maybe he'd come back and visit, and they could have no-strings sex. Which she already knew would make her nothing but miserable and leave her wanting more. No, thanks.

He parked in the lot at Bank of America, a few streets from the center of town, climbing out and opening her door in the back. "You have Cara's ID?"

"In here." She tapped an oversize handbag and pulled large sunglasses from the side pocket. "Marissa made me take it in case I got pulled over or something."

"Or something."

"Think I should bring the blueprints?" she asked, lifting the tubes they'd found in the bog house attic.

"Leave them for now. If we need them, I'll come back and get them." He put a light hand on her back, scanning the parking lot, which was deserted but for an older couple making their way to their car.

Inside, they attracted the attention of all four tellers, two customers, and one woman in a back glassed-in office, who jumped up the minute they walked in. Around fifty, dressed in banker's blues, the woman grinned broadly and waved a pink slip of paper.

"Cara, I just got your message. I was picking up the phone to return your call."

Vivi barely covered a shocked reaction. Cara had called her?

"But that's moot now, isn't it?" The woman continued toward her. "It's so lovely to see you again."

"And you," Vivi said coolly, channeling everything

she'd picked up from Cara while out in L.A. "And this is Assistant Special Agent in Charge Colton Lang. My personal protection."

The woman gave Lang a quick smile, then beamed back to Vivi. "And let me be one of the first locals to congratulate you on the Oscar, Cara. You've brought so much pride to Nantucket."

"Thank you. I've also brought us a lot of media, I'm afraid." She worked to keep her voice in the lower register that made her sound more like Cara as they walked back to her office, gratefully snagging a name on the door. "So I'm hoping we can get this over with as quickly as possible. Diana."

"Of course." Diana waved them to seats. "I've already pulled up your paperwork and can take you back to the conference room to sign the paperwork to release the documents."

Lang looked out the glass partition, watching every person in the bank while Diana grabbed a file on her desk and clicked a few keys on her computer.

"Now your message said you needed to see—"

"The property deeds," Vivi said quickly.

Diana nodded. "Yes, and as my assistant mentioned when you called, you don't need a key for those, they're not in a safe deposit box."

Cara had called and arranged this same thing? And even more stunning...was a safe deposit box key the one Pakpao was looking for? One they didn't need, after all?

"So it would have been fine to send someone else like your message said you wanted to," Diana continued.

"I decided I could sneak out without causing a scene. So far, so good."

"Be fast, though," Lang said. "I already see people on cell phones. The word that you're here will be out soon."

"Let's go to the conference room, then," Diana said.

"I'll wait here," Lang said, still locked on the bank lobby. "Assuming you won't be far."

"Just in the next room," Diana assured him.

Diana led her to a small meeting room. A table in the center was covered with a number of legal-size file folders. Vivi knew she couldn't take any of the paperwork; Lang would kill her for that breach. Anyway, if they were illegally obtained any information they revealed would be useless in court.

"Could I have a few minutes alone, Diana?"

The woman raised her eyebrows. "How will you know which files? You have several here. And your bodyguard said you were in a hurry."

"I want to be alone," she replied, putting just enough diva in the voice to be convincing.

"Of course," Diana said, backing out. "Just come out when you're done."

The minute she was alone, Vivi took off her sunglasses and started flipping through files, looking for the name Roman Emmanuel on anything. On the fourth file she hit pay dirt. Without taking the time to read a word, she used her cell phone to snap pictures of every page. At least they'd have something, especially since Cara was planning to come in here later and clean out.

Why?

She couldn't take the time to figure that out now. She and Lang could talk about it later. She got fifteen pictures and closed up everything. Just as she turned to get her purse, the door burst open, and Lang reached in and grabbed her. "Let's go! Now!"

"Is the media here?" she asked as he yanked her into the hall and hustled her forward.

"Worse. Move it. Stay on this side of me and don't stop at that woman's office."

"Why?"

"Later. Now move it—out the door!"

As they passed the glass wall of Diana's office, Vivi caught a glimpse of a tall, bearded man speaking in a raised voice. They hadn't made it five steps into the lobby when Diana called out.

"Cara! Ms. Ferrari! You can't leave!"

"Yes, we can," Lang ground out, pushing her to the door, just shy of a run.

"Stop!" A man commanded, but Lang ignored him. Still moving, Vivi glanced over her shoulder and met the gaze of the bearded man, aware that customers were staring, cell phones already out to snap pictures and take videos that would be on YouTube in an hour.

Lang covered her just as the man bolted out and ran in front of them, as tall as Lang, but not as broad.

"Back off," Lang said, one hand up, one reaching for a gun.

"You're not Cara," the man said, glowering down at her.

"Out of the way!" Lang ordered, in full bodyguard mode.

The man spared one quick glance at Lang, then returned his focus to Vivi. "Who the fuck are you?"

Vivi reached for the sunglasses, only to realize she'd left them in the conference room. "Mr. Lang, please, I'd like to leave," she said sharply.

Lang drew his gun, to a collective gasp and one loud scream from the onlookers. "I'm not at all afraid to blow your face off, buddy. That's what she pays me to do. Get the fuck out of our way."

"But she's—"

Lang had the guy on the ground in one move, just as an armed bank guard launched on to the scene. "I said, leave her *alone*."

The man squirmed, raising one hand to point at Vivi. "That is not Cara Ferrari, damn it!"

Vivi took a step back, copped an indifferent look, cursing the fact that she'd run out without the sunglasses.

"That's enough," Vivi said coolly. "The bank guard has the situation under control. Please. I want to leave."

Lang got up slowly, his gun still pointed at the guy, and then he motioned to the guard. "He's all yours."

"That is *not* Cara Ferrari!" The man hollered again. "She's an impostor!"

Lang hustled Vivi away while the guard positioned himself over the man. "Sir, we need you to stand up slowly."

He didn't move, still pointing at Cara, turning to the side to direct his comments to Diana Montgomery. "I hope to God you didn't let her in to see any private documents, Diana! That girl right there is not fucking Cara Ferrari and I can prove it! She's some kind of look-alike, but it's not her!"

"Go!" Lang gave Vivi a good push toward the door and she thrust it open.

"Ms. Ferrari, wait!" Diana called back. "Please, we need to address this situation! This man is—"

"Nuts!" Vivi called over her shoulder, just as the glass

door closed behind them. Together, they bolted to the Expedition.

She didn't stumble, no mean feat on heels and cracked asphalt, and almost kept up with him. His gun still drawn, Lang used it to point to the passenger side.

"Get in—it's open!"

She'd barely shut the door behind her when he threw himself into the driver's seat, jammed the key in the ignition, and peeled out.

"Holy shit," she muttered. "Who *was* that guy?"

"Roman Emmanuel."

She jerked like she'd been shot. "*What?* Why didn't you just arrest him?"

"For what? He's not a fugitive; he's a person of interest in an open FBI investigation. We were the ones breaking the law in there, in case you forgot." He took a breath and turned another corner, staying within the speed limit, watching the rearview mirror carefully. "So what did you find?"

"His name all over the deeds. I took pictures. Are you sure it was him?"

"I've seen his picture in the files."

She thought about that, holding on while he wended through the streets of Nantucket and her head swam with possibilities, returning to the thought she had last night.

"I told you that's who Cara is coming to talk to," she said. "Remember, the text said Cara's ready to talk and the response was do what I pay you to do."

Lang looked at her. "Then Emmanuel pays Joellen." He circled around the side street, giving them another view of the bank.

They arrived just in time to see Roman Emmanuel walking out, files in hand.

"And now he knows he doesn't need a *key* to get them," she said. "His name is on the files, so he can walk right out with them. Damn, I could have had that in my hand."

Lang didn't respond, watching the target as he walked toward town, pulled out a phone, read a text, and paused long enough to write a response. A few seconds later, Vivi's phone beeped with a call from Chessie.

"Yeah?"

"Joellen's texting again," she said. "Want to hear?"

Vivi looked at the man who'd just sent a text three hundred feet from them. A bastard who sold humans into slavery and ruined children. "Oh, yes, Chessie, tell me about Joellen's *texts*."

Lang turned to her, obviously drawing the same conclusion: Joellen was texting Roman Emmanuel. Vivi put the phone on speaker and held it between them.

"Joellen wrote, 'We are on our way. It's now or never.'"

"And what was the response?" Vivi asked.

"Didn't get one yet. Oh, wait, just in. Got it. The reply is, 'I got what I needed. Meeting Pakpao's replacement. Finish her off and I'll meet you at LH.'"

LH? What the hell was that? "Now what?" Vivi asked.

"As my dad would say, let's head him off at the pass."

"And *then* what?" *Please, Lang, please break some rules.*

"Then let's kick ass and take names."

She reached over and took his hand, squeezing his fingers like everything about him squeezed her heart. "Oh, Lang, I…I…" *Love you.* "I think that's a damn fine idea."

CHAPTER 20

Left hand? Last home? Little—"

"Lighthouse," Colt said as he rounded the corner, well behind Roman Emmanuel, who remained on foot. "I bet he's going to the Brant Point Lighthouse."

"That's what LH is!" Vivi exclaimed, peering through the windshield. "But the ferry docks way down here in the thick of town, on Broad Street."

"Our best bet is to follow him as well as we can." Which wasn't going to be easy considering the warren of narrow one-way streets that made up the heart of Nantucket's only real town. "This place is built for pedestrians, not SUVs."

Traffic moved at a crawl, if at all. Emmanuel kept a good pace, striding down the sidewalk without glancing into the dozens of elite art galleries, precious boutiques, and inviting sidewalk cafés along the way.

"Wherever he goes, if he talks to anyone, I want to hear him. Tape him if I can."

He shot her a look. "The man hasn't committed a crime."

"Sex slavery?"

"He hasn't been arrested or indicted. We're looking for evidence, legally obtained, then we'll get him."

"And how do you plan to get that without getting close enough to hear what he says or see what he does?"

He finally got through the next intersection, only for Emmanuel to turn the corner a block away. "Shit," he mumbled.

"We'd do better on foot," she said.

"Or you on *that*." Colt gestured to a skateboarder who cruised up behind them, leaving the idling cars in his dust.

"Oh." Vivi let out a sigh of pure envy. "Nice Plan B board, dude."

Colt barely looked at the rider as he mentally navigated the route. "Emmanuel could be meeting Pakpao's replacement anywhere around here, and I don't want to lose him. I haven't heard a ferry whistle yet, so my guess is the next ferry is coming around the lighthouse, but still has to round that horn and slide into the dock. He has time to meet someone."

"If I had that skateboard I could follow him."

"Like he wouldn't recognize you as the impostor in the bank."

She blew out a breath as he hit the brakes with a frustrated tap. Vivi looked at the store next to them. "Three minutes, Lang. Give me three minutes."

"To do what?" Or did he not want to know?

"Shop."

Shop? He turned to stare at her, but she was already

gathering up the bag and had her hand on the door handle. "I'm going into"—she dipped to see the name of the store—"Rags to Riches, only I'm doing just the opposite."

"You've got to change more than your clothes to fool him," he said, instantly getting her idea and not hating it.

"Trust me, I will. Do you have about three hundred dollars, maybe three fifty?"

"Yeah." He reached for his wallet, but she put her hand on his arm to stop him. "I don't need it. I have money. But when you pass that kid on the Plan B, offer it to him for the board. If I know anything about skaters, he'll take cash. Circle the block, get a read on Emmanuel, and pick me up in three minutes."

She opened the door and put one foot out before turning to him. "Thanks for not arguing with me on this."

Before he could do exactly that, she jumped out, slammed the door, and bolted for the entrance of Rags to Riches. He pushed through traffic to catch up with the skater, rolled down his window, made the offer, and had to lose thirty seconds negotiating but got the board and a "Totally dope, dude," as a thank-you.

Then Colt turned right on the street where Emmanuel had gone and scanned the packs of pedestrians, spotting him on the next block. Still walking, still carrying the bank files.

Colt rounded the corner and in about three minutes, he pulled back up to Rags to Riches as Vivi darted out the door, a bag in hand, and jumped into the backseat.

"Do we still have him?"

"Dead ahead. And the board cost me four."

"Thief," she said. "He could get two boards for that much, with titanium wheels."

"Is that why he called me a dope?"

Vivi just chuckled and yanked out the clothes. "I got the first two items of clothing I could find, but I think they're clothes Cara wouldn't be caught dead in. I also found out the next ferry docks in twenty minutes from Martha's Vineyard. And signed three autographs—ha! They totally believed I was Cara."

"And you think you can get by Emmanuel?"

"I don't want to get *by* him. I want to get close to him." She yanked the yellow thing over her head and grinned at him in the rearview, stripping down to a tiny black bra. "Quit staring, Lang, and follow the target."

"I can do both," he said. "Did you get a hat?"

"Better." She slithered into a short jeans skirt, then pulled a skimpy black T-shirt over her head. "But I am going to have to do this barefoot, because I didn't have time to get shoes."

Emmanuel was three blocks ahead now, still in sight, but disappearing fast. Then he paused at a café with tables on the sidewalk, taking a call. "What's better than a hat?"

"I got these in exchange for an autograph for the owner's niece, Becky." She pulled out a pair of orange-handled scissors.

"Seriously?"

"Don't tell me—I'm under arrest for forgery."

"You're going to cut those things?"

She held a chunk of hair to the side and poised the scissors close to her head. "Hell yeah, I am. If he sees this hair, I'm busted. Anyway, my client's coming home and, trust me, I'm not getting a million dollars for killing myself trying to tie her to a human trafficking ring."

"Don't," he said quietly, turning around to make his point.

"Don't cut my hair? I didn't think you were so into this fake long hair—"

"Don't kill yourself." He gave her his harshest look, the one that underscored most orders and got a resounding affirmative from everyone who'd ever worked for him.

Everyone but Vivi. She just grinned and snipped, the first strand of black hair fluttering to the floor. "Careful, stud. You're starting to like me."

He was way past starting. Hell, he was getting past *like*. "Just don't get too close."

"Then how can I hear what he's saying?" Snip, snip, snip, like a barber, as hair rained down everywhere.

"Just observe, Vivi. Don't try and talk to the guy. Just observe."

She rolled her eyes and brushed her hand over some funky-looking spikes, more chewed than cut.

"You want some help with that?"

"That bad, huh?" She laughed. "I'm good. Drive."

Traffic moved another two feet, then stopped for pedestrians to cross. Three blocks away, Emmanuel pulled out a seat at the café, still on the phone. When Colt looked at Vivi in the rearview mirror, she was transformed. Sawed-off hair, skater-girl clothes, fire in her eyes.

"It's you again," he said, unable to fight the smile. Jesus, he adored her.

"I'm telling you, Lang, don't look at me that way. There are six thousand better versions of this out in L.A.

They'll all be dying to strip you out of your golf shirts and khakis."

But he didn't want six thousand better versions. He wanted *her*.

"I need sunglasses. Have any?"

"No."

"What kind of bodyguard doesn't have sunglasses? Did you not see the movie? Kevin Costner?" She leaned to the right and looked in the rearview mirror. "Damn. I still look like her, don't I?" She pointed her fingers to her face. "Come on, look at me objectively."

"I can't," he admitted.

"Why not?"

"I'm not objective about you anymore." His voice came out huskier than he meant it to, probably because there was a vise around his chest.

"Some time to figure that out."

"I know." He turned around, confident that Emmanuel wasn't moving and neither was the traffic. "Lose the lip gloss."

She met him halfway, slipping her hand behind his neck and pulling her face to hers. "Do your job, Lang."

He kissed her, hard and long enough to transfer the sticky color to his mouth. Nothing could stop him from adding his tongue, tasting her, pulling her closer. When he broke the kiss, her eyes were closed. "And you need to get rid of the lashes, too."

Keeping her lids lowered, she grabbed the corner of one false lash and ripped it off, then the other.

"Ouch," she murmured, flicking the spidery things toward him, then rubbing the remaining makeup to a smudge.

He studied her. "Something's still not right," he said.

She made a face, crinkling her nose in frustration.

"That's it," he said, tapping the side of her nose. "Your nose thing. Diamond. Stud. Thing."

"Good call." Reaching for her bag, she dug into the secret inside pocket, pulled out a red silk pouch she'd gotten in Chinatown, and poured the diamond chip into her hand. "You're my stud, Lang. This is my nose pierce."

He cringed when she stabbed it in and snapped the back on. "I've always wondered if it hurt to get that."

She shrugged a little, then ran another quick hand through her chopped-up hair. "Ahhh. I love my own skin."

So do I.

He covered the jolt of that thought by ruffling her hair, which was as rough as grass and bumpy from the little extension knots close to her scalp. "You look best in your own skin, Vivi." He let his hand fall, grazing her cheek with his knuckles.

He saw her swallow and fight a response. "I just need to look completely ordinary."

"There is nothing ordinary about you, but you don't look remotely like the woman he just saw in the bank, I promise. Are you armed?"

She patted the little skirt and skimpy top. "A weapon hanging off my hip might bring a little too much unwanted attention. But I have this." She grabbed the board from the passenger seat. "And this." Slid out her cell phone. "And this." She tapped her temple.

"Use all three and I've got your back. What's your plan?"

"*Plan.* That's funny, Lang." She pointed to the funky letters on the board that spelled out Plan B. "Here's my plan."

She dropped the board and kicked it to the uncobble-stoned sidewalk, then leaned back for her parting shot. "Just think, Lang, we bring this guy's operation down and you'll be king of the FBI. They'll be begging for you to come be the Special Head Honcho in Charge of Ass Kicking in L.A."

"Yeah," he said softly, watching her roll off like a little Ninja.

Except right now, L.A. seemed way, way too far away.

With every bump, nausea threatened. In fact, there was no way Cara could make it across this Sound without puking.

She rested her head against the cool glass of the ferry window, her gaze locked on the squatty lighthouse at the edge of Nantucket in the distance. That did little to quell the roll in her stomach.

She didn't want to do this, really. But it was the only way out. Sometimes the little people had to suffer so the great ones could have their day.

Even for a great one, she felt very alone.

No Joellen to annoy her, no stylist or publicity person or assistant or second-skin hanger-on to breathe down her neck. No media. No man. No agent, manager, stalkers, or gawkers. She was taking this challenge on her own.

Well disguised for the moment, she bounced along on the ferry boat like a prisoner on her way to the gallows, certain of her decision. This really was the only way to get out of this horrible predicament. And if she handled it right, all the media about the Red Carpet Killer would just disappear—and so would Roman Emmanuel. Into the bottom of Nantucket Harbor.

And he would be the Red Carpet Killer who tried to kill her but she vanquished. Sure, there would be an investigation, but the authorities would believe her. Who would think Cara Ferrari would lie? And she'd have all that evidence to back up the truth.

She'd kill the Red Carpet Killer herself—and become a national legend. If everything went according to her plan, by this time next year she'd be starring in a new film, all her misdeeds a thing of the past.

With a little luck and distraction, *all* of the misdeeds would be forgiven, forgotten—or dead.

Nausea rolled through her again. She tried to use the lighthouse as a focal point to cure the queasiness, but that didn't work as well as it usually did. Instead she looked around the ferry, into the nearly empty rows of seats, her mind whirring, barely noticing a man in a black leather jacket cruising down the other aisle. As he passed she caught a glimpse of him, then they both looked away.

Oh, God. His eyes were so blue. Not the blue of the water around her, but the icy cold blue of…the man on the beach.

He disappeared into the back and Cara gripped the armrest as the white heat of fear threatened to consume her.

Had he followed her onto this ferry?

She turned to look back, but the bulkhead that housed the bathrooms blocked her view of the back deck. There was a stairwell to the lower level, and he might have gone down.

Was he the person who'd broken into the house and tried to make her death look like an accidental electrocution? That blue-eyed man from the beach? He could ruin everything! And what would he do here? Lure her to the deck, throw her body over—

He came back up the aisle, brushing by her but not looking. He smelled like the woods and danger, the jacket expensive and loose, but big enough to reveal that he was mercilessly strong.

He sat down a few rows ahead, in the middle section. She could see his right hand resting on faded jeans, a strong hand. A hand designed to close over someone's throat and squeeze the last breath out of it. A hand designed to reach into that jacket pocket and produce a pistol.

If she didn't move, he couldn't just take her out right here in her seat, could he? There were at least a half-dozen people around.

Plus, the *real* Red Carpet Killer would make it look like an accident.

A flash of her body tumbling into some kind of knife-sharp propeller at the back of the ferry burned in her brain. To erase it, she searched for the little lighthouse and estimated how much longer until they reached Nantucket.

There, she would end this. She'd meet Roman, as planned. They'd go to the lighthouse, he'd take her out to the landing, and she'd kill him.

She let her mind play the scene like a movie, refusing to think about Blue Eyes.

It had to be the same man from the beach. She'd never forget those mesmerizing, gas-flame-blue eyes. Or was this her imagination on steroids again?

Then she thought of a way to find out. She opened her bag and slipped her hand into the side pocket, pulling out the white card he had flipped to her on the beach.

Taking her phone, she carefully dialed the number. Then hit Send.

In her ear, the phone rang. He didn't move. Another ring. He moved—was he reaching in his pocket left handed? Her heart slamming, she refused to hang up. She had to know. She *had* to.

On the fourth ring, he stood very deliberately, his back to her. She saw his left elbow bend, into the jacket pocket.

A gun?

Slowly, he turned, steel blue eyes locking on her, narrowing, pulling something out.

She jumped as the deafening blast of the ferry horn screamed over the Sound, the very moment the man revealed his phone. He thumbed a button and the ringing in her ear stopped.

Then he smiled like Satan himself, revealing white, wolflike teeth.

A stalker. A fan. One of Roman's killers. It didn't matter. Her stomach clenched in fear and sickness. Shaking, she looped her bag over her arm and shot up, practically running for the bathroom. She'd stay there the rest of the trip if she had to. She wouldn't get off the ferry then. She'd just take it back to the Vineyard and come up with another idea.

Dragging open the heavy bathroom door, she threw herself inside, then leaned on the cold steel of the door. A woman was in one of the stalls, so Cara just dropped back and closed her eyes.

On the other side of the stall door, she heard the clicking of someone pressing phone buttons. Her gaze dropped down to the shoes, gorgeous Coach sneakers. They looked exactly like hers, even had the little black smudge—

Holy shit, they *were* hers.

Soundlessly, she opened the next stall door and slipped in, stepped up on the toilet, and looked over the top.

Marissa Hunter was sitting on the toilet, texting.

Closing her mouth to keep from gasping, Cara squinted at the phone screen, catching some words.

Meeting Pakpao's replacement.

This time she couldn't hide the gasp, and Marissa jerked up with one of her own.

Marissa. In a stall. Talking about…*Sunisa Pakpao?* The floor rolled under her and she had to grab the top of the stall to keep from falling, losing her footing anyway and stumbling to the floor.

"Cara!"

"Marissa."

This couldn't be happening. It couldn't. The toilet flushed. The sound of her career, her life, the people she once trusted. And yet she couldn't move. She had surprise on her side and she used it, stepping into the bathroom to face her assistant.

Marissa opened the stall door, blinked once, and at least had the decency to blush. "What are you doing here, Cara?" she asked.

"No, that's my question." *And why are you texting Roman Emmanuel?*

"I couldn't let you come alone." She dropped her phone in a bag and stepped out. "I was worried about you, Cara. Even with this disguise." She waved at the cap and sunglasses that covered makeup-free eyes and the baggy clothes. "Someone is bound to recognize you. And, really, you can't forget that there could be a killer out there."

There was. About twenty feet away. But the real threat was right in front of her. "Who were you talking to?"

"My agency. The employment agency that you used to find me."

Pakpao had the made-up title of director of something at RE Global, but Cara hadn't used them to hire Marissa Hunter. "Why? Are you looking for a new position?"

"I'm…yes, Cara. I am. I'm sick of your sister's snide comments regardless of what a good job I do for you." She walked to the sink and turned on the water.

Why was she lying? "Marissa, you were texting Roman Emmanuel, weren't you?"

"He owns the employment agency." She started to wash her hands. "The old agency was bought by one called RE Global."

It was possible. It was actually remotely possible. Maybe Roman had bought some little employment agency to gain more access to Cara. "Why would you talk to the owner?"

"Because my employment with you is very high level, and important to him."

The lying bitch. "What did you tell him?"

"That I'm leaving because…of Joellen. I don't like her. I'm not going to let her ruin my life."

A bolt of anger rocked her so hard she almost raised her hand and slapped the woman. "What does he pay you to do?"

"Nothing, Cara. They got a commission when you hired me."

She removed her hands from the sink, shook them, and reached for a paper towel.

"Does he pay you to spy on me?"

She didn't answer, calmly drying her hands, then reaching in her purse again.

"Does he?"

Still no answer. Nausea threatened one more time, enough to make Cara close her eyes, and when she opened them Marissa's horribly homely face stared expressionless, a small pistol in her hand.

Cara pressed into the door, vaguely aware that danger lurked on the other side. Which was worse? One of Roman's pawns ready to kill for him or a stranger who may or may not be a copycat killer?

She leveled her most imperious look at Marissa. "Put that away."

"Yes, he pays me to spy on you. He paid me to get on this ferry so he doesn't have to see you when you land. He pays me for a lot of things, Cara. I help him run that business. And we need to get rid of you. Frankly, that's been my job all along, but when the possibility of you winning an Oscar made it easier to get away with, well…"

Cara put her hand on the door, giving Marissa her haughtiest look. "You don't have the nerve to kill me," she said, delivering the line like a camera was right in her face. "You think you do because Roman makes you think you can do anything."

The color in her cheeks deepened, confirming that Cara had hit the mark.

"Trust me, I fucked the man plenty," Cara continued, an idea forming. Maybe she could make Marissa realize that Roman was using her, make Marissa hate him and turn on him. Maybe she could make Marissa kill him when they got to Nantucket! Perfect.

"He has a way of making you feel like you're the only woman in the world, doesn't he?"

Marissa took a slow, steadying breath, her nostrils fluttering.

"Did he tell you how he'd take care of you? And your family?"

A vein in her throat pulsed, but Marissa didn't answer. She didn't have to.

"I know what Roman Emmanuel can do for a woman who needs help," she said softly, remembering how she and her sister had returned to the bog house and found a "squatter" at the bog—and that man turned out to be generous, caring, so wonderful she'd turned half the property over to him. "I know how he makes you feel in bed, too. Like a sex queen."

"I don't have sex with him," she said. Maybe she didn't, Cara thought. Maybe she was too ugly even for Roman's indiscriminate dick. Then she had some other weakness.

"You want to be a movie star, rich, famous, what?"

Marissa looked disgusted. "Hardly."

Family. It must be family. "He's helping you with something, isn't he? What is it, Marissa? A sick parent? A dying kid? Roman feeds off the desperation of others."

"My sister...is in a hospital."

"Oh, of course." Confident she was safe now, Cara leaned forward and gave a knowing smile. "Sisters are his specialty, you know. Mine's a murderer, our mother is a recluse, and I needed help for them, so he took care of it. Small price to pay for peace of mind, isn't it? I gave him land, you give him...what? Information on me?"

"Yes."

Cara frowned, thinking about the events of the past few days. "Then why send someone to kill my decoy?" she asked. "Didn't you tell Roman it wasn't me?"

"There was a slight miscommunication."

Just as she'd thought: an amateur. "Did you try to put the hair dryer in the tub, too?" She didn't respond. She didn't have to. She was a try-hard, uncreative Red Carpet Killer. Roman had really lowered his standards.

"Put the gun down, Marissa. I need your help."

She didn't lower the weapon. "To do what?"

"Kill Roman Emmanuel."

"No." The bellow of the ferry horn burst through the loudspeakers, making Cara jump, and Marissa pull the trigger.

The sound of the shot covered by the horn, Cara stumbled backward, even though the actual impact seemed eerily soft in her sleeve. Then searing, hot, vicious pain shot through her arm.

The world spun, taking her with it. "Marissa…" Cara's voice sounded distant already.

Just as she started to slump, Marissa grabbed her under her arms.

"You're making a mistake," Cara said.

"I know. I missed." She yanked Cara toward the stall. "He'll hate that."

Cara started to fight, but Marissa put the gun to her temple and forced her into the stall, kicking the toilet seat down and throwing Cara onto it. Then she stepped back and aimed.

"No—" Cara tried to lunge, but Marissa stepped back, looking up at the loudspeaker.

"Come on!"

Once again, the ferry whistle wailed long and loud, and Marissa fired. Cara opened her mouth to scream, but nothing came out, the bullet hitting her in the shoulder this time.

As the blood and hope drained out of her, Cara's head fell back. Marissa positioned her against the toilet tank, lifting her feet off the ground. Vaguely, Cara knew what she was doing. Hide the victim in the stall, to be found... sometime. Later today, tomorrow?

And Marissa? Maybe she'd meet Roman at the dock. Get on the same ferry back to the Vineyard. He'd find her, figure out how to make it look like suicide. That's what he'd do.

From under shuttered eyes, she watched Marissa lock the door, then crawl underneath the stall and disappear.

The door opened and closed, the whistle wailed again, and blood oozed from Cara's wounds.

She tried to move, tried to open her mouth, tried to do anything, but she was just lifeless. Except for the bile that rose in her throat, and this time she couldn't fight he nausea. Her body's instinct won and she dropped her head and vomited.

In the distance, she heard the door open. *Please, please, help me.*

"Ew, gross, Mom. Someone's puking in there. I'll wait till we get off."

And the door closed.

So this was it. Cara Ferrari, Oscar-winning actress. A victim of betrayal, not a Red Carpet—the headlines formed in her mind's eye, swimming around, gurgling.

No, that was the sound of her blood pouring out of her body.

"Cara." A man's voice. Dark. Low. Distant. She opened her eyes to see booted feet, faded jeans.

Blue Eyes was on the other side of the stall.

Not exactly the help she was hoping for.

His hands gripped the bottom of the door, his head appeared, he pulled himself in, no doubt determined to finish the job Marissa was too lame to do right.

"You're too late," she rasped, then the set went black.

CHAPTER 21

Vivi cruised the street, negotiating a two-foot strip of concrete that ran alongside the cobblestones. The freedom from that ridiculous hair was so delicious she almost laughed, but the chilly sea air on her skin and the importance of her mission wiped away any humor.

She balanced and weaved with skill and ease, as at home on a skateboard as she once had been holding a ballet barre. For her, this was just a different kind of dancing.

She spotted Emmanuel and decided to go for the ultimate test. She'd cruise right by, slowly enough that he'd at least have to glance at her. He'd notice her crazy hair, maybe the nose piercing if he looked closely, and, based on the looks she was getting from most of the men she passed, he'd check out the miniskirt. But if there was so much as a spark of recognition or even surprise, she'd take off and come up with another plan.

She gave the Plan B board a rueful glance and kicked harder.

Whe̶n she was about twenty feet from the sidewalk table where Emmanuel sat sipping coffee, a stocky black man approached his table and sat down. Instantly, they were deep in conversation.

Pakpao's replacement. She had to get something incriminating.

She got a little closer, hoping he wouldn't even notice her if he was talking. She tapped her foot on the ground, slowing the board as Emmanuel placed the file folder from the bank on the table. A handoff? Then what should she do? Follow the new guy or the target? In her hand, her cell vibrated just as she reached the tables.

Emmanuel didn't even notice her; his attention was riveted on the other man. She paused two tables away from them and read her text.

How close can you get? Listen and record conv.

She smiled and thumbed back. *Illegal wiretapping. I like it.*

The table next to them needed to be bussed, but another was empty and not so far away that she couldn't inch to the right and hear them. She slipped into the seat, her back to Emmanuel, the other man to her left, the dirty table between them.

She was close enough to pick up snippets when no cars were driving by. She cocked her head to the side and pretended to dial her phone, but hit the voice-memo-recording feature instead.

And then had a brilliant idea. She pretended to talk on the phone in rusty but still passable Italian.

"Pronto! Che bello sentirti! Come va?" If, by any chance, either one spoke Italian, all she'd said was hello and how are you.

At the foreign words, both men casually glanced over, but she looked straight ahead and smiled, pretending to be a tourist on the phone. Her Italian was pretty limited and she could dig for better conversation ideas, but she didn't want to think.

She wanted to hear. And record. And have them think the only person who could hear them didn't speak English. Staying quiet, as though she were entranced in her own conversation, she repositioned herself, ostensibly to get the board out of the open, but really just getting closer, the wind cooperating by sending words her way.

"I can do it," the man said. "But it's a risk."

"Life's a risk, Mr. Sutton," Emmanuel shot back. "The payout is better that way."

The payout for what?

But the second ferry whistle blew, just loud enough to obliterate the next exchange.

Casually, she crossed her legs, resting her bare foot on the Alien Workshop sticker on the top of the board. Mr. Sutton threw a funny glance at her bare foot, then inched closer to Emmanuel and lowered his voice, denying her the chance to pick up a word. She used the excuse to say a few words in Italian then listen for Emmanuel's answer.

"Can I get you something?"

The appearance of a waitress startled Vivi and she almost answered in English. Just as the first word started to tumble out, she shook her head and gave the blank stare of a foreigner. "Espresso?" she asked, hoping the cross-over word would be all she needed.

"One shot or two?"

She lifted a shoulder, offered a smile. *"Niente inglese."* No English. *"Solo un espresso."*

The waitress nodded. "I'll get you a single, then."

Vivi smiled just as Emmanuel opened the file, the very same one she'd been taking pictures of in the bank. What was in there but legal deeds?

"Scusami," she apologized into the phone, then plucked the Italian for "What were you saying" out of a long-dormant memory bank. *"Cosa stavi dicendo?"*

From deep inside the file he brought out a folded piece of paper. One she hadn't seen and hadn't photographed. He opened it, and she stole a glance.

A blueprint, much smaller than the one she'd been looking at that morning. Maybe a reduced copy.

"Here's where you drop them off, and here's where they get picked up."

"Underground?" The other man asked, making Emmanuel motion for him to lower his voice.

What was underground? The sex-slave transfer station?

She switched the phone to her other ear and did a half turn so she could see Emmanuel out of the corner of her eye.

God, she had to get a picture of this. Of both of them. She rubbed her thumb along the inside of her BlackBerry, imagining the keyboard. There was no way to find the camera icon without looking at it.

No, she'd just continue to record and go for the money quotes.

"The next shipment will be here in less than an hour," Emmanuel said.

"From Laos?"

Emmanuel nodded. "Almost all girls, I'm afraid."

Her stomach roiled. That was the money quote, sickening as it was.

"Boys are worth more," Sutton commiserated, and Vivi just closed her eyes and counted. She would get this bastard. She would do whatever it took and she would kill herself trying, but if she saved one little girl or one little boy from—

"I want forty percent," Sutton said.

Her phone vibrated again and she could almost feel Lang's frustration with each unanswered text, but she couldn't stop the taping to respond.

"Fuck off," Emmanuel said. "This is my business. You're the—"

The waitress brought espresso. *"Grazie."* She sipped some and repositioned again, even closer still.

"You don't have a lot of options around here," Sutton said. "And now I know where you're doing business, bro."

Vivi leaned one inch closer, but stopped when some sixth sense told her Emmanuel was aware of her move. She quickly laughed and asked nobody to come to dinner. Then listened while she sipped espresso and ignored Lang's relentless vibrations.

"Can you get them out of here tonight? Delivered to Boston, then trucked down to New York? I got two boys, two men who're strong, and a dozen girls, but one of them's got a broken leg."

"Then you got eleven, because a gimp doesn't make any money."

Vivi bit her lip to keep from jumping out of her seat.

The ferry horn belched out another long howl, blocking out Emmanuel's answer, except that he ended it with "... 'cause I gotta go now."

To meet Joellen on the ferry that was rounding the lighthouse? Meet her at the lighthouse?

"Okay," Sutton said. "Thirty-five percent. Give me that map." He pushed out of his seat.

"Do it. Meet me at"—the howl of the next ferry horn cut off his words, three long honks that wrecked the other guy's response, too. Damn it.

With a heartfelt *arrivederci*, she shifted her phone below the table and texted Lang.

They're parting. RE going to ferry, I think. Mr. Sutton is going to meet next shipment!! Who should I follow?

Her gut said she should stay with Emmanuel, who didn't recognize her. Lang would get backup and follow the other guy. Unless he went all rule-book on her and said *Get back to the car.*

His answer came in seconds. *Follow Emmanuel. I'll get backup and go after Sutton and the shipment.*

Perfect. *Okay,* she texted back, the sound of her keypad drowned by the ferry horn again, well past the lighthouse and nearing the huge Broad Street dock. She glanced over her shoulder to see Emmanuel take out his cell to answer a call.

"What?" he asked curtly, rising and throwing some cash on the table. Now this would get tricky. She couldn't look like she was following, but she had to.

Just as he passed her, he said, "You're breaking up, Marissa. What did you say?"

Marissa? Marissa Hunter, Cara's assistant?

She must have reacted, damn it, because he shot her a look. It might have only been a second or two, but time dragged like she was under the spotlight for ten endless minutes. Attempting cool, she returned his look, defiant and disinterested, then picked up her espresso cup and sipped, scrolling through her phone messages like she was totally used to strangers staring at her crazy hair and nose diamond. She was.

Lang's text flashed. *Don't lose him, but don't get too close. Can't back you up!*

Damn straight she wouldn't lose him.

Emmanuel switched the phone to his other ear. "She's dead?"

A siren scream broke through the city, followed instantly by another, cutting out most other sounds and pulling his attention completely away from Vivi.

Did he say *she's dead*?

He started down Broad Street toward the dock, and Vivi reached for her handbag, which was—in the SUV. Shit! She had no money. Not a dime. And her target was now ten feet away.

And three ambulances wailed to get through the traffic on Broad, heading straight for the dock.

She's dead.

Cara? Vivi had to know. And she either had to stiff the waitress or steal Emmanuel's cash. The last thing she wanted was his attention.

She lost five seconds and fifteen more feet making the decision. Emmanuel started to cross the street, to the heavier crowds just as the ferry whistle sounded four short horns, announcing arrival. As one of the ambulances neared the dock, the crowd parted like a curtain opening, everyone gawking and many following.

She jumped up, snagged the board, and headed off, already across the street when the waitress screamed, "Hey! Lady! We don't steal coffee in this country!"

A few people looked, including Emmanuel, but Vivi worked not to meet his gaze. His attention on the phone, he continued to walk, passing the Steamship Authority building at the entrance of the dock, just as a second ambulance powered through to the vast cement landing area.

He paused long enough for Vivi to catch up with him, three feet behind him, stopping as he did. In the chaos of ambulances and sirens, she had to get much closer to hear him.

Don't lose him, but don't get too close.

Sorry, Lang. She got less than a foot behind him.

"How do you know that, Marissa?" He could turn at any minute. Any second. One semirevolution to his right or left and she'd be busted. But right now he was being recorded.

Just one more sentence. One more, and she'd back off. He took a step farther. She did the same. He switched the phone to the other ear. She lifted hers closer, recording.

"Well, the ambulances give me the impression she might still be alive."

Instinct made her suck in a breath through her nose just as he spun around and nailed her. Wordlessly, he flipped off his phone and narrowed his eyes at her. "Give it to me."

She took a step back.

"Give me your phone or you're dead."

Another step. Just as he charged, she threw down her board and his foot landed on it, throwing him off balance. She turned and ran, getting about twenty feet before coming face to face with her waitress waving a bill.

"Pay me, you little bitch. Can you understand that much English?"

"Please," Vivi begged. "This is a federal case."

"Damn right it is. Give me my fucking money!"

Two hands landed on her shoulders. "She's with me," Emmanuel said. "I left enough to cover her coffee, miss. Thank you, and I'm sorry for the inconvenience."

The waitress sniffed, inching away, looking at both of them. "Fine."

The pressure on her shoulders increased. She tried to wrench out of his touch, but he was too strong.

"Cara Ferrari's been shot!" someone screamed.

"They're bringing her off on a stretcher!"

A hum and buzz and a few shouts went through the crowd as it teemed forward like a mob. Vivi stumbled with Emmanuel clutching her with one hand, a gun slammed into her back.

"I don't know who the hell you are, lady, but you're coming with me."

The rough cement scraped her bare feet as he pushed her forward, surging with the crowd. Police vehicles followed the ambulances in, sirens blaring, lights flashing, officers unaware that someone right in that crowd was being held hostage.

"To the boats," he ground out in her ear.

The ferry finally docked at the end of the fifty-foot-wide platform, which was lined with smaller pleasure craft tied up along one side. He pushed her forward, to the outside edge of a crowd that was being corralled by cops already practicing crowd control.

"There she is!"

Several men ran to drop down a wide metal disembarkment ramp, locking it into place. Dozens of cell phones were hoisted overhead, pictures snapping like an orchestra of shutters. A woman screamed "Cara!" as paramedics appeared at the top of the ramp flanking a stretcher.

Vivi strained to see the stretcher, shoved deeper into the crowd by the man behind her. She scanned for an escape, but she couldn't risk it. He somehow managed to push her toward the front, where two EMTs on either side rolled the stretcher and a third followed with an IV on wheels. Uniformed cops surrounded them.

Two other men approached, flashing badges, talking to the uniformed cops that held back the crowd.

Emmanuel pushed closer, so determined that for a minute Vivi thought he might claim to know the victim.

"Her injuries are superficial, not fatal," one of the paramedics said to the plainclothes detectives. "But it's still a double gunshot trauma. Make it fast."

"Not fatal?" Emmanuel said behind her, obviously not happy with that news. He lurched Vivi forward and she tried to catch the eye of a cop, but no doubt she just looked like another frantic person in the crowd.

A fan, not the head of Cara Ferrari's current security detail.

They were close enough to see Cara's face as the stretcher rolled by, her eyes fluttering when one of the EMTs took her oxygen mask off and the detective leaned over her.

"He . . . saved . . . me," Cara said.

"Do you know who shot you?" the detective asked.

"The . . . angel . . . blue eyes . . . saved . . . me."

"An angel saved her!" The words rose up from at least ten people who were also within hearing distance, causing enough of an uproar that Vivi couldn't possibly hear what else Cara said. "A blue-eyed angel!"

"Move it!" Emmanuel shoved Vivi to the right as the

crowd surged in the opposite direction, moving toward the ambulances.

He urged her forward, the gun poking her ribs through the thin cotton top as she stumbled with him, against the crowd, her feet stepped on ten times as they threaded a pack of crazed onlookers who all wanted to go with Cara, not toward the water.

He thrust her toward the boats, to a sizable motor cruiser docked about ten feet away.

"Get in," he ordered, staying so close to her he could keep the gun hidden between them. On an ordinary day he'd never get away with this. But in this crowd, with all eyes on the movie star—not her decoy—he easily forced Vivi to do what he wanted.

She stepped off the dock onto the deck, the tight skirt restricting her movement as she scanned the crowds on the docks, considering one good, long scream before they took off. He shoved her toward the door leading to the cabin and she stumbled forward.

"Open it!" he demanded.

If she went down there, she was stuck. She scanned the crowds waiting to get off the ferry boat, but everyone was being held back by the cops.

"They're going to catch her," she said, trying to buy time. "No one can get off that boat without being interrogated."

"They're looking for some blue-eyed angel who saved her." He sounded disgusted and jabbed her with the gun. "Give me your phone. Now."

She handed it to him and he flipped it into the water. Idiot. If he'd read the messages, he'd know the FBI was following his man Sutton.

Just that thought gave Vivi a boost. Maybe Emmanuel was taking her to the same place. Or maybe she was going where the phone just went.

"Open the latch," he ordered.

She took one more look up at the ferry, to the two decks lined with passengers cramming to witness the scene on the docks. Her gaze moved to where one man stood away from the crowd. Even this far away, she could see the shadows of his face, his build, but not his deep blue eyes.

Oh, not an angel. An *Angelino*.

Gabe. He had followed Cara, and saved her life. But did he know who shot her?

And, more importantly, did he know that Vivi was being kidnapped right under his nose?

But his gaze was directed to the dock, not the man getting on his boat with a woman.

With shaky fingers, she slid the bolt and opened the hatch to a small cabin below. Emmanuel gave her a push and right before she went down, she looked up at the ferry again.

But Gabe was gone.

And Lang was chasing down the next shipment of slaves.

And Vivi? God only knew where she was headed. Possibly the bottom of Nantucket Sound.

CHAPTER 22

Colt had Special Agent Iverson on the phone and organizing an extraction team by the time his target got into a blue compact and started the engine. Colt waited at a stoplight and gave Sutton a friendly signal to pull out in front of him, making following him a breeze.

He stayed on a main road, easy to follow, heading south until he maneuvered onto Hummock Pond Road, leading southwest to Cara's house.

Lang wasn't at all surprised when Sutton chose that road and gunned his little Accord onto the open road. Colt called the location in to Iverson. Reinforcements were standing by.

Could the "shipment" be taken right to Cara's house? He pictured the geography of the bog, the surrounding brush, all the way out to a small perimeter road—and the lighthouse.

So Emmanuel didn't mean the Brant Point Lighthouse, but the small private one with a dock on Cara's property. The one looking right out over the water where any ship could come in, dock in broad daylight, and transfer its human cargo to other boats for distribution.

He called in to his agents and instructed them to stay hidden but surround the lighthouse and watch for incoming boats. Still, at the point where Sutton would have to get on foot or on an ATV to navigate the bog property, Lang would either lose him or be seen. Maybe the best thing to do was get up to the house, get on his own ATV, and beat Sutton there.

Head him off at the pass, so to speak.

He thought of Vivi, and something twisted in his gut. Why hadn't she called or texted? He hit her number on his phone and went right into voice mail.

Could he spare an agent to go look for her?

He cut across the road to the gates, laying on the horn and signaling for the small pack of media to get out of the way. Barreling through, he got up to the house and on the last ATV without seeing anyone else, practically crashing through the doors, into the brush, and down the path he knew led to the bog house and the lighthouse beyond.

Iverson called with a report that a medium-size trawler had been spotted off the coast, coming up from the south toward their location. One agent was stationed in the lighthouse. Five more surrounded the dock, all hidden from sight. The Coast Guard was on alert.

Still no word from Vivi.

Colt parked the ATV far enough away to get close to the dock and lighthouse without being seen. He took cover next to Special Agent Iverson and her backup, able to see the trawler in the distance.

"Ready?" he asked.

She nodded. "News from town. Cara Ferrari's been shot."

He stared at her. "What?"

"Someone tried to drill her in the bathroom of the Martha's Vineyard ferry. She was saved by a good samaritan of some sort—no perp yet."

The perp was Joellen, taking orders via text from Roman.

Was that why he hadn't heard from Vivi yet?

The engine of a second boat, a motor cruiser, broke through his thoughts and the seaside sounds. It was coming in from the north, taking them all by surprise.

Someone from a northern position texted an alert to the team. "Lone driver on a thirty-foot cabin cruiser coming toward the dock." Emmanuel? Or Joellen, who said she'd meet him at the lighthouse?

After she took care of Cara, like she was paid to do.

So Vivi had been right with her first theory, after all. He couldn't wait to tell her. But now his entire focus was on that trawler and the human cargo it carried.

The trawler was about a hundred yards from the dock, giving them a great view of the beat-up piece of crap that looked like it should have sunk in the Gulf of Tonkin instead of making its way across the Pacific Ocean and through the fucking Panama Canal carrying children for the slave trade. This was a huge bust.

Bringing this bastard in would close down a major human trafficking op, save hundreds of lives—and seal the deal for him as an SAC in L.A.

For a million reasons, he couldn't have cared less about the L.A. job right then. No, for *one* reason. The motor cruiser flew along at top speed, its big nose high in the air, the inboards screaming, headed right for the dock.

Even from the distance Colt could make out Roman Emmanuel at the wheel. *We got him.*

Emmanuel brought his cruiser into the dock a few minutes before the trawler, which lugged along at a much slower speed. Just then, an ATV broke through the brush, coming across the road, right past the ditch where they'd found the other ATV abandoned.

Steering it was the man Colt had been following in town, confirming that his hunch had been right. Was this Sutton the person who'd knocked Vivi into that tunnel? Was there an underground passageway from here to another transfer point?

They were about to find out, and Roman Emmanuel was about to go down.

Colt's heart hammered at a steady rate, a little faster than usual, but not as fast as it had at, say, three o'clock this morning, when he'd been making love to Vivi. This was a different adrenaline rush, a different high. He'd miss this feeling when he was sitting behind the SAC's desk in L.A.

And he'd really miss the three a.m. sex with Vivi.

Sutton turned off the ATV at the edge of the dock, completely unaware of the eyes of the FBI on him. Emmanuel docked the boat and stayed on it; they spoke, but from where he hid Colt couldn't make out the words.

A silent, palpable sense of anticipation rolled through the trees and bushes, and through the seven agents, all ready to move in as the trawler finally docked. When the trawler door opened, one man, older, probably Laotian or Vietnamese, stepped out and spoke to Emmanuel when remained on the cabin cruiser. A minute later, the "cargo" filed out from belowdecks of the trawler.

Skinny, ragged, none more than fifteen years old, eleven girls, two boys, and then two young men, barely twenty years old. Not one of them looked like they'd eaten in days, and all were shackled by the arms.

The captain of the boat shoved the two young men onto the dock first; they seemed to have lost any fight they might have had—along with most of their muscle tone. Then came the haunted, empty girls, who moved like they were going to the gallows.

Considering their fate, that might have been preferable. They walked single file past Emmanuel's boat as he eyed them like the meat they were to him.

"He should be shot," Iverson whispered next to him.

"Our job is just bring him in. Justice will take care of his punishment," Colt said softly even though he agreed with her.

The line traveled up the dock, toward the lighthouse, a stark contrast of human abuse against a picturesque background.

"If Emmanuel doesn't get off that boat, I'm going after him," Colt said. "You two back me up."

When the children reached the lighthouse with the driver, Colt held up one hand. Ten seconds and they moved.

One, two, three...

Just then, another girl appeared on the deck of the trawler, crawling forward, dragging a broken leg. Sutton reached over the side of the boat and hoisted her up. Shit, they could shoot her if Colt pounced too soon.

Sutton threw her into Emmanuel's boat and she hit the fiberglass with a thud.

Seven, eight.

He had to take that chance.

Nine. Ten.

"Do not move! FBI!" He charged forward before they could react. Instantly the agents appeared out of the bushes. Some of the kids cried out, and Sutton threw himself on the dock with a shout as Colt ran, his gun trained on Emmanuel.

"Do not move!" he repeated, still running down the dock.

But Emmanuel grabbed the girl on the deck, yanking her by the arm, eliciting a scream of terror.

"Then she's dead," he countered, holding a gun to the girl's head. "My freedom for her life."

"Your freedom is history," Colt said, aware that two agents ran behind him to restrain and cuff Sutton. "Drop your weapon."

They stared at each other.

"I will kill her."

"Then I will kill you," Colt replied calmly. "Let her go."

Next to him, Special Agent Iverson aimed her weapon at him as well. "Or I will. Let her go."

"Fuck," he mumbled, closing his finger over the trigger. "You want her to die? I will fucking kill this girl if you don't let me go."

Colt sensed Iverson looking at him. He couldn't sacrifice one more child for this bastard.

"Hand her over and get out of the boat, Mr. Emmanuel."

Emmanuel raised his elbow and jabbed the gun harder just as the hatch door cracked and popped open, shattered off its hinges.

"Let her go!" An ax blade came crashing out of the

hatch opening, landing square on Emmanuel's shoulder. "Let her go, you goddamn son of a bitch!"

Colt jumped backward at the sight of Vivi, fire and hate and fury in her eyes, a deadly weapon in her hands.

Emmanuel fell with the blow, losing hold of his hostage. Colt leaped into the boat to restrain Emmanuel and Vivi dropped the ax and fell, covering the screaming girl with her own body.

Iverson cuffed Emmanuel while two more agents jumped on board for backup.

In the middle of the chaos, Vivi cradled the girl, soothing her, calming her, wiping her tears.

Vivi looked up at Colt, her own eyes moist, her skin pale.

"What are you doing here?" Colt dropped to his knees next to her.

"He took me," she said simply. "I found a fire ax and used it on the hinges."

He couldn't speak, rage rocking right through him. If Emmanuel wasn't already in custody he'd kill him for touching Vivi.

"It's okay," she said. But he wasn't sure if she was talking to him or the girl. "Shhh. Honey, no one's ever going to hurt you again. No one. I promise."

Vivi looked up at him and a single tear trailed down her cheek. The girl who said she never cried.

Vivi stepped out of the hospital room to find Lang leaning against the wall in the hallway, arms crossed. His gaze lit up when she opened the door. The same thing happened to her insides at the sight of him.

"How is she?" he asked, pushing off the wall.

"Asleep." Vivi had to fight the urge to fall into his embrace, but he didn't offer one. "Her leg's been broken in three places and there's a bad infection, but they've got her on an IV. God, I don't even know her name."

"It's Souvanna," he said. "She's from a Laotian village on the Vietnamese border. They're all from the same tiny village."

Souvanna. Damn, she loved her already. "What about Emmanuel?" she asked.

"He's in custody. Want to go see Cara? She's one floor up."

Vivi hesitated. "I don't know. Do I? Have you interviewed her?"

"Yes, and her story is pretty solid, actually. She says Marissa worked for Emmanuel and shot her because she was on her way to Nantucket to turn over evidence she's been holding about him."

"I heard him talking to her, not Joellen."

"We sent agents to her and confirmed that she was using Joellen's phone, and it was Marissa who was in contact with Emmanuel. Marissa's in custody, too, taken on the ferry when we interviewed Cara."

"So what is Cara guilty of?"

"Other than bad judgment? Maybe some conspiracy charges that will probably get dropped. Evidently, when they moved away for a while, Roman Emmanuel, who was a regular visitor to Nantucket, handpicked the abandoned place as an East Coast transition point for his business, for all the reasons we thought. It was relatively deserted, and the last place the authorities would look."

"How did Cara get involved?"

"Romantically," he said. "She met Emmanuel when

they returned, and started a long-term affair with him. Then she and Joellen moved to Los Angeles to pursue acting careers. Joellen worked for him, and so did Cara for a while, then she broke into show business and made it big. And here's the most interesting tidbit of all." He paused in the hall to let his words sink in. "Joellen Mugg, then an RE employee, once worked for Adrienne Dwight and Isobel DeSoto."

She blinked at him. "She knew them?"

"Had access to them. And probably a motive."

"Lang, seriously? You think she's the Red Carpet Killer?"

"We think it's worth pursuing. And so's she. We're searching Martha's Vineyard now."

"Does Cara know?"

"We haven't told her yet. She's kind of out of it, despite the fact that her wounds aren't that serious. Could have been, though. Gabe took a bullet out of her before they docked even though he wasn't supposed to be following her."

She smiled. "Never underestimate a Guardian Angelino. You've been busy while I stayed with . . . Souvanna." The name just made the little girl dig deeper into Vivi's heart. "Did you find out how Emmanuel's name got all over those deeds?"

"Yes." He guided her to elevator doors. "While they were involved, she signed over half the property to him. She knew what kind of business he was in, and they had each other in a blackmail deadlock. When Marissa, who was Emmanuel's spy, learned that Cara was going to break it, she was following his orders to kill her."

"Dear God, she *is* a lousy judge of character. It's a wonder she had the brains to hire me."

His hand hovered over the elevator buttons. "Up to see her and tell her that, or down to go home?" he asked.

She should see Cara. But all she wanted to do was fall into Lang's arms and stay there forever. She leaned against him a little, just at the thought of how good it would feel. "I'd prefer to go back to her house. Can we just do that?"

"I'll take you there."

His voice was kind of tight and distant, and he didn't get the cue. Or didn't take it.

"What about you?" she asked.

"Me?" He hit the Down button with a little too much force. "I'm off."

"More interviews? Paperwork? Meeting with the team? Find Joellen?"

"Los Angeles."

Her heart plummeted. "Today? Tonight?" She wasn't ready for that. Not yet.

"In a few hours." The elevator doors opened and there were reporters in there, snooping around.

Not one of them recognized Vivi, who'd been under their nose for days pretending to be Cara.

They rode down in silence, and drove back to the house in a car with two other agents, who talked about the case, about Cara, and about what a coup it was for everyone to bring in one of the largest human traffickers on the planet.

It was a coup. Everyone won. The Guardian Angelinos came through and did the right thing for Cara. ASAC Lang was a hero, and now he would get his just rewards. Souvanna would be safe.

And Vivi would have . . . fantasies.

At the house, she climbed the stairs without enthusiasm, slipping into the master suite. Behind closed doors, she let out a long, slow, pained breath.

How could he just *leave*?

"Hey." The tap on the door made her startle, but Lang's voice made her smile. "Can I come in?"

She flung open the door and stared at him. "Don't leave me." Damn, the words were out before she could even think to stop them.

He stood stone still; only his eyes moved, searching her face. "I have to," he finally said.

"Why?" She pulled him into the room, committed now. "Why can't you stay here? There must be promotions in the Boston office. Move your dad here if you're worried about him. There's always an answer, there's..." Her voice trailed off as she watched his expression harden.

"I have to leave."

She ignored the punch to her stomach. "*Why?* Is it because you're not over...Jennifer?"

"It was," he said. "I won't lie, that's what started it. But now if I stay..." He didn't finish, just pushed by her, heading toward the closet. "I left some clothes in here and I need to get moving."

"You need to move *on*," she said, an ache wrapping around her. She hugged her arms and followed him, her heart kicking, her body shaking with how much this mattered. How much *he* mattered.

He was in the closet, retrieving clothes she'd stripped off him the night before.

"Do you hear me, Lang?"

"I hear you." He stood up, a shirt in his hand. "I do need to move on."

"But not out of town," she cried softly. "You can't run away from imagining her around every corner or remembering.... You have to get over that and on with life, Lang."

"I have," he insisted. "Really, I have. It's just that—"

"That what? You're scared of this? You're scared of *me*."

He crouched to grab a pair of khaki pants that were draped over the chaise in front of the three-way mirror. Khaki Dockers she hated on every other man but loved on him. *Loved*. Why wasn't *she* scared of that?

"I've just been dead inside for so long," he said, shaking them out and smoothing them to a Lang-like crease as crisp as the one he was putting into her heart.

She circled the chaise, got in front of the mirror to face him. "I don't know what that means... for me," she said. "Dead inside when? Past? Present? Future?"

"Until now."

She waited for him to say more, but he just looked at her, the Hollywood chaise between them. And a whole country. Not to mention his ex-fiancée. Could she get past all these obstacles and make him understand?

"And you're right," he said on a disgusted sigh. "I'm scared to death of you."

"Why? Because I'm like her? A little daring? A little reckless? Able to hatchet my way out of a jam and give the asshole what-for, as you would say?"

"That doesn't scare me," he said. "What scares me is how much I... could..." His voice trailed into silence.

"You could what?" *Care? Love you? Say it, damn you.*

"Get hurt again. If something happened to you..." He swiped his hand through his hair, barely tousling the short locks. "I just... I couldn't go through it again."

That's what was holding him back? "I'm not going to get killed, Lang. And even if I did, haven't you heard it's better to have loved and lost than—"

"No." He put a hand over her mouth. "No, it's not."

Silenced, she just stared at him, stepping back, away from his touch. "So you'll walk away—three thousand fucking miles away—to protect yourself from the possibility of pain?" She let her voice rise in disbelief. "How is that living, Lang?"

"It's not," he said. "It's just existing."

She gave the chaise a shove with her knee. "Well, have fun with that, pal." Goddamn it, her voice cracked. She had to get out of there. "I'll miss you."

He was over the chaise in a flash, seizing her by the shoulders before she took two steps. "Don't."

"*Don't?* Don't what? Don't *cry* for you, Lang. I don't—"

He pushed her toward the mirror, his jaw set, his grip tight, frustration rolling off him like heat waves. "I know, I know, you don't cry. You don't follow rules. You don't take orders. You don't let me control you. You don't... care." He bruised her mouth with a kiss.

"That's where you're wrong." She shoved him back but he didn't budge, merely pressing her against the cold glass. "What do you think I'm trying to tell you? Last night wasn't just sex to me. But it was for you. Just an escape from your... bad memories." She spat the word and got jammed harder into the mirror in response.

Her own black memories washed over her. No. *No, don't do this to me, Lang.*

"You're not an escape."

"Shut up." She tried to break free, but he trapped her

with his body, his legs, his mighty arms. "I'm a pastime, a distraction, a fun fantasy *fuck*. Didn't I prove that in the bathtub last night? That's all I am. I asked for that, didn't I?"

"Stop it, Vivi." He braced her with his leg. "What do you want me to say? I *love* you?"

Yes. Yes, I do. The realization pressed her as hard as his body. Each breath strangled her, her throat so choked with pain she couldn't breathe, her pulse galloping, her eyes...stinging. Oh, God in heaven, she was going to *cry*.

"How hard would that be?" she demanded. "Because I—"

He silenced her with a kiss she didn't want but couldn't escape. Fierce, furious, bubbling with words he couldn't say and emotions he either didn't want or couldn't handle. His tongue ravaged her, sucking hers into his mouth, his torso smashed against her, his hands bracketing her against the mirror, his erection...growing harder.

I love you. The words screamed in her brain, no whisper, no echo, no mild suggestion. They reverberated through her being, certain and real and right. *I love you, Colton.*

She kissed the words into his mouth, flames of need licking up her thighs with the same vehemence of his tongue, his hands finding the most vulnerable places, his knees spreading hers apart. She wanted this. She wanted it even though she knew it was meaningless.

I love you. She gasped too hard to speak, her breath stolen when he yanked the little skirt up over her hips.

A wave of a dark memory threatened—*a cheerleading skirt, another desperate male*—but she let lust crush the mental flashes, returning his kisses, fumbling with his belt.

He ripped at his fly, practically tearing the zipper out of the fabric, wrenching the pants open to release his swollen erection.

He jammed her against the mirror, her backside smashed against the glass. His hands under her arms, he slid her up the mirror. She wrapped her legs around him, the skirt bunched at her waist. He held her steady and used his hard-on to push her sliver of panties to the side.

The move made her dizzy. Crazy. Feral with need, but wild with shock. This was how he was going to say it? *This?*

He rammed into her, no tenderness this time, no worry for her pain.

But there was little pain, just burning, hot, helpless need. She took every bit of him inside her, squeezing him with her walls, clinging to him.

Her head dropped, biting the litany of love into his shoulder.

I love you. I love you.

Her climax seized her, nothing slow and sweet, but lightning fast, relentless, a quake that twisted her body and shattered her. She came like a thunderclap, like nothing she'd ever known before, like it was the first time—and the last.

He followed in three mighty strokes, his face distorted, his grip relentless, his body out of control as he drove into her. Head back, eyes closed, he growled like a beast as he managed to drag his length out of her and spurt helplessly as she watched.

Like he couldn't believe it himself, he looked up at her, astonishment and horror in his face as he slowly lowered her quivering body back to the floor with a surprising amount of tenderness. Somehow, he managed to find the next breath, and release her death grip on his arms.

"Lang." She mouthed his name, blinking against— moisture. A hot tear singed her cheek for the second time that day.

"I made you cry." He didn't sound proud, just shook his head.

"No, no you didn't. He did. *He* did."

He inched back. "Who did?"

"*Doctor* Ken Taylor."

"Who?"

She lifted her finger to touch the tear, salt already trickling into her mouth. "The boy who raped me when I was sixteen."

Breath whooshed out of him. "What?" He barely mouthed the word. "You were—oh, my God, Vivi. I'm sorry. I'm so sorry." He gripped her shoulders, then let go suddenly as if he might break her. "I got carried away. I got crazy. I wanted you to...just one more time...I..."

He released her completely, backing away.

"No," she said, fighting for calm in her wild swirl of emotions. "This isn't about you. You didn't—"

"I did. Just then, I—"

"No," she insisted. "If I wanted you to stop, you would have. I know that."

"I would have. I would never hurt you. I would never..." He blew out another disgusted breath. "Not physically, and not intentionally."

"I know." She flattened her sweaty palms on the mirror behind her for stability and looked into his eyes. "And that is only one of the reasons why I love you," she said simply.

"I don't know what to say," he whispered. "I...I can't." Pain wrecked his face. "I want to, Vivi, but I...can't."

"That's a shame," she said softly, the agony she expected lifting from her heart. "Because I can. Now, I can love and be loved. And that, Colton, is the real gift you gave me. After all these years, I finally want to love and be loved. By you. And you deserve love. You really do."

"I..." He reached his hand as though he wanted to touch her, but he was already too far away. Already one foot out the door. Already escaping pain he might never feel. "I want to but..."

He swiped two hands through his hair, his eyes wet with tears.

"If you want to..." she said. "Then you can."

"I can't." He zipped his pants, took a step away. "I want to, but I can't."

And then he walked out, leaving his clothes still in a pile on the chaise and Vivi still propped against the mirror.

She closed her eyes and didn't move until she heard him leave and close the door with a resounding click. She let her body glide down the glass and sigh onto the floor.

Reaching to the chaise, she took his golf shirt and brought it to her face.

Then she finally, *finally*, cried.

CHAPTER 23

Vivi stayed in the shower until the water ran cold. Until the icy spray washed away any remnant of salty tears.

No more crying, now.

When she turned off the faucet, she grabbed a towel, dried her face, and took a slow, head-clearing inhale. She had a job to do, a business to run, an adopted family that gave her all the love and support she'd ever need.

And she was going to take care of Souvanna. Escort her back to Laos, if that was what she wanted. Give her money. Show her love. Maybe she'd adopt her.

Buoyed by the idea, she headed downstairs, not surprised to find all evidence of Lang packed and gone. Even the kitchen was empty, the whole house unnaturally quiet now that the FBI agents had left.

The free world knew Cara Ferrari was in the hospital, so the chance of a Red Carpet Killer attacking was slim to none. Especially since Joellen had been moved up to Suspect Number One.

Only Stella remained, lying flat out on the tile floor, her expression utterly forlorn.

"I feel your pain, Stell," Vivi said as she stepped over the little dog to head into the kitchen. She paused, crouching down to scratch Stella's head. "Golf Guy has left the building."

Stella heaved a sigh and turned away.

Something was different. The sliding door to the patio was open—that's what it was. The shades, usually drawn so that most sunlight was absent, were pushed back and the sliders were fully open.

"Mercedes?" Vivi called, stepping out.

She stood stick straight in the sunshine, staring ahead. "It's warm for March," Mercedes said, without turning.

"Yes, it is." Vivi took a few tentative steps forward, not wanting to break the spell but unable to stay back. "Are you all right?"

Mercedes nodded, then lifted her face toward the sun and closed her eyes. "I wanted to try."

"That's good," Vivi said encouragingly. "That's a good step, Mercedes."

She finally looked at Vivi, her eyes as bloodshot from crying as Vivi's must have been a few hours ago. "They're looking for Jo, aren't they?"

Vivi swallowed. "Do you know where she is, Mercedes?"

Closing her mouth to a tight line, she turned back to the sun. "She's a good girl."

Really. "Then we need to find that out. The FBI needs to talk to her and find out—"*If she could possibly be the Red Carpet Killer.* "Things," she finished lamely.

"She didn't do it." Mercedes crossed her arms. "She

did one really bad thing and you already know what that was."

"Not so bad, in my opinion."

Mercedes almost smiled. "You understand, then."

"I was raped," Vivi said simply, kind of amazed at how liberating the statement was. She might not be ready to tell her family, but if it helped Mercedes, then she wanted to share. "I know how it feels."

"Will you protect her, then?" Mercedes asked. "The way you protected Cara? And me?"

"I don't know how well I protected Cara, but I still don't see any reason to drag you into this. And if the FBI wants to investigate the death of a farm worker—"

"That's not what I mean." She turned and walked back into the kitchen, and Vivi followed, curious when Mercedes picked up a file folder and held it out to Vivi.

Vivi took the folder, frowning as she opened it.

She scanned the words, her chest tightening at the picture of the dead movie star Adrienne Dwight. The first victim of the Red Carpet Killer. Under that, a clear plastic envelope, papers stashed inside. Receipts, lists, notes, computer printouts.

She untied the string on the back and opened the envelope, pulling out a piece of paper with swirling writing at the top, Middle Eastern symbols. Curious, Vivi examined it more closely, her gaze dropping to the bottom of the page.

Bhanjee Hair: Human, Artificial, Wigs Natural and Dyed. Indian wigs. "She bought the wigs?"

Mercedes glanced at the page. "Actually, I ordered those for Cara to have here."

But Joellen used them. Setting the paper down, she

pulled out the next. MapQuest directions printed off the Internet, two locations in the Hollywood Hills, a yellow highlighter used to color in the roads. Mulholland Drive was circled and one location marked with an X. The road where Adrienne Dwight's life had ended.

Next was a simple parchment invitation. Dinner at the home of Angus Gaites. She recognized the famous director's name, but another one on the page jumped out at her.

To honor Isobel DeSoto's Oscar Winning Performance.

The other victim of the Red Carpet Killer. Isobel died after attending a party given by a director in her honor.

A dance of chills worked its way up Vivi's spine, landing at the base of her brain, where her investigator's cells had just woken up to go to work.

"Where did you get these?" she asked.

"I found them in Joellen's room."

She looked up and met Mercedes's painful gaze. "You realize what this means?"

"I don't believe it. She's not capable of . . . that."

But maybe she was. "Mercedes, do you have any idea where she is?"

Her lip quivered. "No, I really don't. But . . . " She blinked away moisture in her eyes.—"She instructed me to let the dog out that night when you were shot."

"She called and told you that?"

"She texted."

"But Marissa's been using Joellen's phone."

A light of hope sparked in the other woman's eyes. "Maybe Marissa was the person who did this."

Vivi looked at the papers again, flipping through them.

"Where were these? In a desk or what?" It was all so...
neat. Too neat. Too incriminating.

"Under her bed."

"Was anything else there? Any other evidence?"

"No, but you're welcome to look."

The cell phone Vivi had stashed in her back
pocket vibrated. As she pulled it out, she cursed herself for hoping it was Lang. But the name that lit the
screen dashed that hope and replaced it with genuine
curiosity.

"Cara?" she asked tentatively.

"Vivi, I need you." The actress's distinct voice sounded
strained and stretched. "You have to meet me at the airport, now."

"You left the hospital?"

"Let's just say I got out. I had to, and you'll understand when I see you. But you have to meet me at the
lot near the private-plane tarmac, right now. Where are
you?"

"At your house. But, Cara, are you driving?" She had
two bullet wounds, for crying out loud. Neither serious,
but surely she shouldn't be up and about yet.

"I'm fine. Just meet me at the airport."

Vivi looked down at the papers in her hands. "Have
you heard from Joellen?"

"Not a word. Bridget covered for me at the hospital,
but they'll find her soon, so we have to hurry. I have to get
out of here before the press or... anyone else figures it out.
Meet me at the airport, now. I need a decoy."

"I'm out of my disguise, Cara."

She puffed out a frustrated sigh, the sound of Cara not
getting her way. "Get a wig in my closet, wear my clothes,

and meet me. Vivi, I need your help and you *are* still working for me, right? I'm still paying you an astronomical sum of money, right?"

"Yes."

"So you're still responsible for my safety."

No argument. "I'll be there."

"Okay—and, Vivi, please, please bring Stella. I can't go another minute without her."

"Will do." When she hung up, she gathered the incriminating evidence. "I'm keeping this," she told Mercedes. "I have to show Cara. Maybe she can convince Joellen to come to her. So we can help her," she added.

Mercedes just closed her eyes.

"She wants me in costume," Vivi said. "Can you help me?"

Mercedes followed her back upstairs, getting clothes while Vivi put on a wig and a fast pass of makeup. When they finished, Mercedes gave her that same look she had when Vivi had first walked in.

"You really do look like her," she said.

"But you don't," Vivi replied. "Or, more accurately, Cara doesn't look like you. Joellen has your coloring."

Mercedes's cheeks deepened. "Cara isn't my biological daughter."

"Oh, really? She was adopted?"

"I never really adopted her. Her father...my husband...just brought her home as a baby, and announced she was his. I raised her as mine, but we don't share blood."

Vivi searched the woman's face. "You've been through a lot in your lifetime."

She lifted a brow. "And I have a lot more to go

through," she said. "But you must know something about those papers we found."

"What is it?"

"Joellen isn't capable of that."

But Vivi thought differently. "That's what we need to find out," she said, gathering her stuff and heading back downstairs.

In the kitchen, she paused to scoop up the dog, who growled low when Vivi slipped her hands under her warm belly. "Come on, pooch. We're going to see your favorite person. Your *other* favorite person."

"Oh, and Vivi." Mercedes was on her heels in the utility room.

Vivi turned. "Yes?"

"I just want you to know that..." She took a shuddering breath.—"I think that FBI agent loves you very much."

The statement, so not what she was expecting, made Vivi inch back. "Yeah? Well, he hasn't figured that out yet."

"But you have."

Vivi smiled. "I have," she agreed.

"I bet that feels good for you." Mercedes's rare smile was empathetic. One only another survivor would understand.

"Like stepping into the sunshine," Vivi said, extending her free arm to give Mercedes a quick hug. "Go wait for news. On the patio."

Despite the exchange, Vivi climbed into an SUV in the garage more aware of the low throbbing pain in the back of her head.

The ache she felt when something was really, really wrong.

• • •

Colt paced through the tiny Nantucket air terminal after getting his ticket, threw his bag on a chair, and fell into the one next to it, his gaze drawn to the distant row of private planes out the eastern-facing window. Plenty of props and a few jets, but way at the end, one sleek Gulfstream G650, big enough for a private strip show in the back.

She'd been raped.

Anger, hatred, all vile and black and real, roiled through him. And he didn't even know who to hit with all this hate. Some boy rapist who wrecked a beautiful, sweet, innocent girl, or himself, who took her against the wall because he couldn't *say* what he didn't *understand*.

And she loved him. Deep down, he already knew that. And what had he done with that love? Abused it. Thrown it away. Ran like the chickenshit dickhead moron pig he was.

Really, there weren't enough bad words to describe him.

He forced himself to look away from the tail of that plane, refusing to remember how much better getting to Nantucket had been than leaving. And what had he said to her after she'd made a brilliant and brave move to keep him quiet that day?

You could have been raped.

He grunted softly, self-loathing infiltrating every cell in his body, just as his phone rang. Gagliardi. A welcome distraction.

"Lang here." He even thought of himself as *Lang* now.

"You're not in the air yet?" Gagliardi asked, hope in his voice.

"Thirty minutes. What's up?"

"Because we just had a break in the Red Carpet Killer case."

Colt sat up straighter. "What is it?"

"One of the hairs found in the bathroom matches the other two, purchased at a manufacturer in India called Bhanjee."

His heart kicked up. "Found at the site or taken from Vivi Angelino's extensions? I thought you said they weren't a match."

"Vivi's extensions didn't match. This is a whole new hair, picked up by our forensics people in the Nantucket house after Pakpao was shot. We've got an agent interviewing the owner of the wig company now and he's acquired a list of U.S. customers. Guess who's on it?"

"Joellen Mugg?"

"Uh, no. Mercedes Graff, Cara's housekeeper."

"Well, she's not a suspect; she doesn't leave the house."

"Are you sure?"

Actually, he wasn't—just that he'd never seen her leave. But if that was correct, then Vivi was in that house with her, unprotected and uninformed. "I'm going back, then. So I'll be delayed."

"Send someone else. We need you here."

Not a chance. "No, I'm going myself."

"Mr. Lang, we need you in Los Angeles. There's a press briefing on the Emmanuel case and it's a perfect opportunity to introduce the man who cracked the human trafficking ring as the new Criminal Programs SAC for the L.A. office. Sorry, but PR duties are a large part of the job."

Not when he had it they wouldn't be. "I'll do my best to be there, but I'm not making any promises." He grabbed his bag and headed across the terminal.

"You have to—"

"No, Joe. I don't. If this…" His voice trailed off as an image caught his eye way out on the tarmac. A woman hauling ass across the wide-open space, long black hair flying. "I have to check on Vivi," he said simply, squinting at the woman in the distance.

It looked exactly like… Vivi as Cara. Or maybe Cara herself. She hustled toward the Gulfstream G650, all purpose and speed.

Was that Vivi or Cara? Just like the first time he'd seen that woman get on that plane, he wasn't entirely sure. He forced himself to listen to the man calling the shots in his life right now.

"Mr. Lang, get to L.A. No one's going to kill Cara Ferrari today."

The woman stopped, turned, waved to someone back in the parking area that lined that end of the airfield, then ran up the stairs into the plane, and seconds later, *another* woman with long black hair ran across the tarmac. Carrying a dog.

Now *that* was Vivi. In a wig, for sure, but he recognized that body even from this far away.

"I'm not going to L.A.," he said vaguely as Vivi set the dog on the ground, running toward the plane, the dog at her heels, its funny little lopsided gait confirming that was definitely Stella. What the *hell* was going on?

"Excuse me?"

"I changed my mind, Mr. Gagliardi. I'm needed here."

"You get to L.A.," Gagliardi said, as if Lang hadn't even spoken. "And tell the agent you put on this there is one more thing that's interesting to note."

"What is it?" he asked, barely listening as he watched Vivi, back in disguise, cross the tarmac.

"It's about the dog prints."

That pulled him back into the conversation. "What dog prints?"

"There were dog prints in the dirt on Mulholland where Adrienne Dwight's car went over the cliff. They perfectly match a set of paw prints taken just outside the Nantucket house."

Something dark and cold twisted in Lang. Stella's prints? "Cara has a dog. A dachshund. Pretty common breed." *I'm looking at it.*

"Not a common print, though. Front left paw turns out at a strange angle. It's clear in the print from Mulholland, and the one at the house."

Why would Joellen have Cara's dog at these crime scenes? Unless—his blood turned icy as the realization hit him. The ugly, impossible realization of who killed Adrienne Dwight and Isobel DeSoto.

He dropped the bag and started toward the emergency exit. "I won't be coming to Los Angeles today."

"Unacceptable, Mr. Lang."

He slammed the bar and shoved the emergency door open, setting off an alarm that drowned out his words. "Or ever."

"Sir! Sir!"

"You can't go there!"

His right hand shot up with a badge. "FBI! I'm going out there."

"What the hell is going on?" Gagliardi demanded in his ear.

But he stashed the phone and ran on gut and fire. Because if he had to shoot the damn engine out, he was not going to let that plane take off with Vivi on it.

• • •

"Oh my God, I'm so glad to see you." Cara stepped out of the back cabin, her hand on her shoulder as Vivi boarded. "And look who's here!" Cara's voice rose to falsetto as Stella bounded up the stairs behind Vivi and launched into Cara's one good arm. "My baby!"

Vivi looked around the main cabin, peering into the back. "Are you all alone?"

"Yes, which is why I need you. I want the media to follow you while I do some other stuff." She finally put the dog down and leveled a midnight gaze at Vivi, her face in full makeup.

"You don't even look tired, let alone recently shot."

"I'm in pain," Cara said. "But I'm a professional. And the show must go on."

"What show?"

She didn't answer, sizing Vivi up instead. "I could get used to this," she said. "Having two of me would really help improve my life. Would you like a permanent position?"

Well, look at that. Cara Ferrari was handing her a job that was probably based *in Los Angeles*. "No, thanks," she said, giving it less than a nanosecond of thought. "But this is really important, Cara. I have to talk to you about Joellen."

"What about her?"

Vivi drew her bag closer and reached into it for the envelope. "I think what I'm about to tell you might shock you."

Cara blinked, her jaw loosening so her lips could form a perfect O. "I don't think I like the sound of this. Come on, in the back. The pilots listen and that room is soundproof."

"Fast," Vivi said, following Cara into the back.

Nice to know the scene of the Great Lap Dance was soundproofed after all that worrying about being heard. She buried the memory and dropped her bag on the floor to open the envelope. "Mercedes found this in Joellen's room in your Nantucket house."

"What is it?" Cara closed the door tightly, her brows drawn in worry and concern.

Vivi took a breath. "Cara, is it possible, even remotely possible, that your sister is the Red Carpet Killer?"

"What?" She packed ten different kinds of shock and outrage into the one syllable, grabbing at the papers Vivi held, taking them with her to sit in the side-by-side passenger seats.

Where she'd stripped for Lang a few days and heartbreaks ago.

Get focused, Viviana. That was then. This is a million-dollar client. And you are about to break the biggest case imaginable.

Cara picked up an oversize tote bag that was in one of the chairs and dropped it on the ground, falling into the seat, flipping through the papers. "Oh, my God. That's the very spot on Mulholland where Adrienne's car went over the cliff. And, come here, look at this, Vivi."

"I've seen it all," Vivi said, not moving. "I have to find her. I have to get her into the FBI for questioning. Are you sure you have no idea where she is? Where the house in Martha's Vineyard is located?"

Cara just shook her head, still looking at the papers. "This is unbelievable, Vivi." She beamed at her. "I think you've found the killer, I really do. Please sit here for a minute while I take this in."

What the hell was these to *take in*? Vivi's head felt like it was exploding at the base of her neck now, patience and time evaporating with each passing second.

"Sit here," Cara ordered, in a voice she might use for her dog.

"The FBI has some solid leads on some artificial hairs found at both crime scenes," Vivi said, a sharp edge of impatience in her voice. "I need to deal with this now."

"I've heard. Did they tie those hairs to Joellen?"

"Well, according to those papers—"

"Please sit down, Vivi." It was no longer a suggestion, and Vivi knew if she didn't follow the instruction she'd get no help from Cara. Irritation scampered up her spine, but Vivi took the window seat, still holding her phone.

"Who knows about this evidence?" Cara asked. "Have you told your FBI agent yet?"

He wasn't *her* FBI agent. "Mercedes just gave these to me."

"Mercedes found them?" She considered that. "I guess that's okay."

"Okay?"

"We have to do something about this," Cara said softly, bending over. Stella trotted closer at the cue, but Cara didn't pick her up. Instead she dug through a designer bag open in the aisle next to her.

Vivi chose her words carefully, itching to jump and run but knowing she couldn't. "I know you need me, Cara. And I know you want the luxury of a second body to be where you can't, but getting Joellen into the FBI for questioning is far, far more—"

Cara jumped up, the papers fluttering all around as she pointed a gun directly at Vivi. "No, it isn't."

Vivi just blinked in shock. "What the hell are you doing?"

"Saying good-bye to my decoy, who is flying to Boston as me." Her last words were drowned by the whine of the engines starting up.

"Seriously?" Vivi asked with a choke. "You're going to threaten to shoot me if I don't go? You can't force someone to work for you, Cara. I don't want to do this but, sorry, you leave me no choice." She pushed up, staring at the gun without fear. "And you can leave the drama on the movie set. Tell the pilots to—"

"Sit!" She lifted the gun, her hand remarkably steady as the plane lurched back. "I'm a good shot and you'll be dead before we hit the runway. And the cabin, as I may have mentioned, is one hundred percent soundproof. Put your seat belt on."

"Cara—"

"*On.*" Gone was the innocence, the interest in what she'd found. It was replaced by the deadly calm expression of a woman who would kill.

If Vivi put the belt on, she couldn't jump her and get the hell off this plane.

But if she didn't, something told her Cara was completely capable of firing that gun.

She pulled the belt over her hips, purposely holding Cara's gaze. As she did, she secretly pressed a button on her phone and hit Send. It was somebody's speed dial, but she had no idea who.

"Throw the phone," Cara said, using her head to indicate the other side of the cabin. "Now. One, two…"

She pitched the phone and it landed softly on the bed. "Why are you doing this?" Vivi asked.

"Because you're a hell of an investigator. And that was my biggest fear when you walked into my trailer in L.A. But also my greatest opportunity. That's why I called you here. I certainly didn't expect you, or Mercedes, to find this." She gestured to the fallen papers. "The FBI should have. Weren't they searching that house?"

Why was she behaving like this? "Cara, are you trying to protect Joellen? Because if she killed those actresses—"

"Protect her?" She snorted softly. "I'm trying to frame her. But the plan wasn't for that to happen quite yet. I still need the publicity of the Red Carpet Killer, now more than ever since my name will be associated with that pig and his vile business."

"Why would you frame her for murder?"

She just angled her head and gave a wry smile. "Better her than the real killer, kiddo. And they're finding hairs and God knows what else now that the FBI is on the job. It's only a matter of time until they zero in on...me."

Cara was the Red Carpet Killer? Vivi just stared at her, speechless.

"You don't have to be so surprised, Vivi. This is Hollywood. Only the strong survive. And, Christ, I hated Adrienne for beating me out of that award. I was pissed." She spat the word, venom in the hiss.

"You weren't even nominated," Vivi said, vaguely aware of the plane easing back to the tarmac, turning slowly as it taxied toward a runway.

Please, God, let it be a busy day at the Nantucket Airport.

Wasn't Lang taking off about now? Would his plane delay them long enough to get out of this? She had to get off. Or reach the pilots. She risked a glance to the call button, too far away for her to make a dive.

"I read for that role," Cara said. "It should have been mine. And since Joellen had worked for her for a while, it was easy enough to find out Adrienne's schedule, her driving route."

"You're the last person I would have imagined," Vivi said honestly. "So much for my investigative skills."

"But you honed in on Joellen, and that was what I wanted. She's the perfect fall guy for this. The poor, drunk, overlooked sister. But you'll have to die in her last act of stupidity: killing the decoy."

"Someone else will investigate this, Cara." Her gaze dropped to the gun, steady in Cara's hand. By the time she got the seat belt off she'd be dead. "You'll never get away with this."

"Oh no? I've gotten away with a couple other murders," she said. "I'm not worried about the investigation. They'll never focus on me if my *decoy* is accidentally the victim of the Red Carpet Killer. They'll hone right in on Joellen, who isn't even my sister after all."

Vivi swallowed in a desert-dry mouth, sweat prickling under her arms. Cara wasn't lying...about anything. "Why did you kill Isobel DeSoto, then? Did you plan to be a serial killer?"

"She had the part in *Now, Voyager* and I wanted it. I knew it was my breakout role. So I helped her take a few pills, okay? If you put this to someone's head—"She glanced at the gun. "They do stuff."

Still holding the gun, Cara reached into her bag again and pulled out a roll of bandage adhesive tape. "Taking this from that hospital was pure genius."

"What are you going to do?"

"Timing, they say, is everything." She stepped closer. "If I time this right, you'll go down in the Nantucket Sound, so it'll be a watery crime scene, giving me weeks and weeks to produce more evidence that will nail Joellen's ass once and for all."

Her blood ran ice-cold as Cara used the gun to push Vivi's arm onto the rest. What was she planning?

Cara bit the tape and kept the gun on Vivi, the seatbelt latch far enough from Vivi's fingers that if she even made an attempt to get it, she'd be dead. One strip of tape smashed over Vivi's arm, securing it.

Then Cara held the pistol, a sleek little Kahr K9, to Vivi's temple. "I'm going to do the other one. If you move, I pull the trigger."

Vivi just closed her eyes, her pulse pounding against the barrel of the gun. She'd get out of this, but not by doing something risky. The tape zipped over her arms, then Cara stripped off more and really secured her.

The phone on the bed beeped with a call and Cara glanced at it, then backed up, grabbing it to read the screen. "Lang," she said. "The FBI guy?"

Vivi just stared, fighting the tape with every ounce of strength, doing exactly nothing to tear it. She'd speed-dialed *Lang*. Help was so close…and so far away.

Maybe Cara would answer and Vivi could scream.

Cara threw the phone on the bed, peeking out the window to see where they were. Vivi didn't dare look away from her as she waited for the slightest opportunity to do something.

But what? Kick a shoe at her? Scream in a sound-proofed cabin?

With Vivi secure, Cara set down the gun and returned to her designer bag of tricks, this time pulling out a small black device with red and blue wires wrapped around it.

"Roman Emmanuel was good for a few things," she said softly. "Sex and creative ways to kill people. I will say that everything I've done, I learned from him." She held the device up. "Like making a bomb."

She set the bomb on the end table, pressing a button on it then turning the device toward Vivi so she could see a small digital readout of 10:00. "Ten minutes ought to be perfect. And we are done here, Miss Stella. Victim number three of the Red Carpet Killer. You've seen them all, pooch."

Like she was packing up from a business meeting, she picked up the papers, stuffed them in her bag, snapped her fingers at the dog, and they both walked to the door.

"Thank you for all your hard work, Vivi. If it's any consolation, I'll see that your company gets full remuneration and they can start a scholarship in your name or something." She flashed a Hollywood smile. "I'll mention it in my next acceptance speech." As she pulled the door open, she yelled, "I need the stairs opened, stat!" and disappeared into the cabin, closing the door before Vivi had a chance to open her mouth.

Vivi jerked her hands but they were thoroughly fastened to the armrests. Writhing, she caught a movement out of her peripheral vision. A man, running toward the plane, hundreds of feet away. But not so far that she didn't recognize that body, that build, that savior of hers.

"Lang!" she screamed as loud as she could, more out of joy than hope as she watched him running like a damn fool down the tarmac. To profess his love or save her ass? Right now, she didn't care.

She just couldn't let Cara escape and this plane take off.

But from the window across the cabin, she could see Cara bolting down the stairs in a run. Lang would see her and go after her while the plane took off. How could she get his attention?

The stairs lifted, and in seconds the engines screamed back to life.

No! She had to get this tape off. She lowered her head, trying to bite the edge of the tape, but her teeth barely nipped it. She had to bend deeper, lower. Just like she did to get those damn boots off when she stripped in this very same seat.

With a grunt she doubled over again and locked her teeth on the tape, ripping. Something cracked—

The porcelain that the dentist had applied to make her slightly chipped tooth match Cara's flawless one. She bit again, a fiery pain where bared enamel scraped tape, sending a flare into her head, but she ignored it.

She had to rip a hand free. Had to get to that bomb. Had to get off this plane.

But her teeth couldn't get a grip and the engines whined with increased speed. As the jet turned a little, she caught a glimpse of Lang, his step slowed, his attention shifted, his body turning in the direction Cara had run.

"Lang!" She screamed at the sealed up window, banging her head against it. Even from this distance, she could see him take his phone out. Calling for backup. Doing things in order. Certainly not running after a private jet about to take off. That would be a stupid, foolhardy risk he'd never take.

She bit the tape and yanked as hard as she could, her grunts of frustration and misery drowned out by the roar of the jet engines that were about to take off for the last time.

CHAPTER 24

Hold it!" Colt yelled, but his words were drowned out by the whine of the mighty Rolls-Royce engines of the G650.

Even if she heard him, the woman who'd just gotten off the plane kept running toward an opening in the chain-link fence. Was it Cara or Vivi? From this distance, it was impossible to tell.

"Stop right there! FBI!"

She broke into a full sprint, stumbling a little as she held on to the dog. The plane rolled backward again, the engines revving once more to taxi to the runway. His phone rang incessantly, and he stole a look at the screen.

Gagliardi again. He grabbed it and barked, "Not now."

"Yes, now! Urgent break in the Red Carpet case. Cara Ferrari is—"

The Red Carpet Killer. He didn't even have to hear the words.

"I *know*. And I'm two hundred yards from her in a full-out run." Or was he chasing after Vivi?

"Roman Emmanuel's been talking and that woman knows how to use explosives. Get her! That's an order!"

But his gut screamed a different order. *Explosives.* If Vivi was on that plane, a victim could be set up to be killed—making Cara the last possible suspect if she made it look like someone had targeted *her* and killed the body double instead.

Lang smashed the End button without responding, his attention split between the rolling jet and the running woman. She slowed a little and dropped the dog on the ground, then bolted faster. The dog rushed to keep up, its crooked gait slowing it down.

No doubt about who that woman was, then. Stella wouldn't run after Vivi.

But he would. He would *not* let that plane take off.

He tore across the tarmac as the jet started to pick up speed. The roar of the engines deafened him, but the plane was still on a slow taxi out of the parking area. Once he reached the tail, then what? Flag the pilots? Shoot?

He *was* going to have to climb the landing gear. Or at least grab the back of the wing when it turned on to the runway. He ran right by the opening to the parking area where Cara Ferrari disappeared.

Let her go. Vivi was on that plane, probably thinking she was doing some favor for her client, unknowingly flying to her death.

Twenty feet, ten. Heat rolled off the engines, the roar vibrating right through to his bones. Even if he got to the cockpit they wouldn't see him. Just behind the left wing, the mighty wheel topped off at eye level, spitting gravel at him, making a mockery of his chances of stopping the plane.

Unless he could grab hold of the landing-gear door, which was thin enough for him to grip as the plane slowed to turn. He'd have to time it just right, swing up to the wing, and get Vivi's attention, and she could get the pilots to stop. He'd never get their attention from this angle.

Blinded by sweat, his legs burning from the run, he reached the back of the plane, then scrambled to the left wing just as the engines changed pitch to a lower octave and the wheels slowed a bit.

He could do this. He could get that door and hoist up. He had one try. There was only going to be a split second when the plane lurched to make the turn. That would be his chance.

Five feet, two feet. He reached out, his hands aimed at the metal flap beside the tire.

Now. He closed his hands over the hot steel with a loud grunt.

It burned, but not enough to let go. With another growl of determination, he swung one leg up and hooked his shoe over the wing, then pulled himself up, every muscle in his body invested in the act, the wind over the wing doing everything to throw him back.

He landed on the wing with a thud, grabbing hold of the metal window frame of the very last round window that lined the side of the jet. His only hope was that she'd taken the aft cabin.

Their cabin. She was probably as far away from that place as possible.

Holding on, he smashed his face against the glass, relief rolling through him at the sight of Vivi in one of the passenger seats, strapped in, her head bowed. No, her head bent over like—

She was dead.

"Noooo!" He banged on the window and her head shot up, sending another surge of white-hot relief through him.

He couldn't hear her, but her scream was instantly comprehended.

Help me!

She writhed around trapped by her seat belt—and tied to the armrests. Jesus, she was *taped* to the armrests. And the pilots either didn't hear or didn't care. And couldn't see him on the wing.

The engines screamed louder, the power sucking him toward the beasts. He clasped the rounded edges of the windows. Smashing his face against the glass, he tried to assess her situation and read her lips. But then he wished he could read something other than what they said.

Bomb! Bomb! Bomb!

He peered up toward the cockpit, the aerodynamic lines of the brand-new jet denying any view of the pilots. Unless they were on a suicide mission, they'd want to get the hell off this plane.

The engines revved again and the plane started taxiing toward the runway. He had one choice, one chance.

The only way to hang on was with his right hand, the wind and speed plastering him to the fuselage. Using his left hand, he reached for his weapon and managed to draw it out, grateful he'd racked during his run across the tarmac.

Hanging off this plane was risky, and shooting the cockpit could be stupid. But he had no choice.

Lifting the gun into the merciless wind, he tried to

aim, his goal to graze the cockpit window, breaking it, forcing them to stop. He had one shot before they accelerated and he was thrown behind the jet. One shot.

He risked a glance into the cabin, his gaze meeting Vivi's, locked for one split second. Easy to read her lips. *Fire the gun, Lang!*

The jet engines roared and he shot. The bullet glanced off the side of the cockpit, cracking the glass. He stumbled onto the wing, his fingers frantically trying to hold on to the metal, a bolt, a seam. Anything.

The sound changed. The speed changed. The damn jet was slowing down. And he was falling off the wing.

He lifted his head just enough to get one more look at Vivi, long enough to see the hope and horror in her eyes.

"I love you!" he hollered as his fingers let go and he went flying down to the unforgiving concrete.

Vivi let out a howl of pain that ripped through her whole being, filling the cabin with her shriek as the engines quieted in a shocking instant. He couldn't have survived that fall.

Lang must have shot the cockpit window, forcing them to stop. Which was risky and brilliant and she loved him—and he loved her. Agony jolted her as she struggled fruitlessly with the binding tape, checking the clock that read two minutes and ten seconds now.

Outside the cabin, she could hear footsteps, a man shouting, the door opening, the stairs clunking down.

Couldn't they hear her? Or were they too concerned with the guy who'd shot at the window? The guy who was probably dead on the runway right now.

The door to her cabin jerked but didn't open, a fist pounding.

"Ma'am? Are you okay?"

"There's a bomb in here!" Her voice was almost gone from screaming. She stole a glance to the digital readout.

Had they even heard her?

"We're trying to get you out." Far too calm for them to know what she'd just said.

A blast made her scream as the lock exploded. A booted foot kicked the door open and Lang charged in, Glock blazing, clothes torn, face bloodied.

Alive. *Alive.*

"Bomb! Next to the bed!" she screamed.

He got her first, ripping off the tape and pushing her out of the seat. "Go. Get off the plane! Run!"

She did, scrambling across the cabin and herding the stunned pilots with her. "Go," she ordered. "We have less than two minutes."

Vivi stumbled at the bottom, turning around to look up at Lang, who was carrying the device.

"Go farther!" he yelled. "That way! There's no time to defuse it!"

They all ran away from the plane—all except Lang, who jogged down the steps and tore in the direction of the empty, open field. Twenty feet from them, he hoisted the bomb overhead and threw it like a football, flinging it another forty feet away. He started to run away, but just as the device hit the ground, a tiny brown creature launched out of the parking lot and started running toward Lang.

Stella! Lang froze, watching the dog bound gracelessly across the grass toward him. Five seconds later, Cara shot out from behind some shrubbery and screamed for her dog, running after her. Stella was twenty feet ahead of her on a dead run toward Lang, toward the bomb.

Vivi sucked in a breath and slammed her hand over her mouth just as Stella leaped over the bomb, but Lang was five feet away.

Cara hollered one more time, but Lang scooped up the dog, pivoted, and sprinted away. But Cara never stopped. Crazed, screaming, her hair flying, she kept running. Just as she reached the center of the field, the ground exploded in a ten-foot-high ball of orange flames and black smoke.

Vivi's eyes burned as Lang fell into her outstretched arms. He dropped Stella and reached for Vivi, pulling her into his chest with an embrace that could last her a lifetime.

"I knew you'd come back for me," she whispered into his kiss.

He lifted his head and looked into her eyes. "Or die trying."

Cara's house just seemed to swell with new arrivals, first the FBI agents, then the FAA staff, and of course the police. Eventually, Cara's friends and entourage showed up and they let in some select media. By evening, Mercedes was overwhelmed trying to keep up, so Vivi started a batch of Uncle Nino's cacciatore to help feed the crowd and keep her hands busy while she waited for Lang to get back.

They'd found Joellen in Martha's Vineyard and brought her to Nantucket. He was still interviewing her and working through the details with the FAA. After Vivi's brief exchange with him at the airport, and the certainty that she'd seen him mouth the words "I love you" right before he fell off the plane, she was tense with anticipation for his arrival.

"There are some people asking to see you out front," Mercedes said as she entered the kitchen carrying a tray with empty coffee mugs and water bottles. She set it down with a clatter and sniffed the cacciatore. "That has so much garlic in it," she said.

Vivi rested her wooden spoon in the pot, turning to the kitchen entrance. Lang? Because he was the only "people" she wanted to see right now.

"Of course there's garlic in it," she shot back. "It's cacciatore, tailor made for comfort and a crowd."

Around the corner came the one man who could make the comforting recipe better than she could. "Nino!"

Her old great-uncle ambled into the kitchen, followed by Chessie, who offered a little wave, and then Zach, who, despite his patched eye and scarred face, always looked beautiful to her. A wash of family love poured over Vivi as she rushed to greet them, holding each extra long, especially her brother.

Nino inhaled, wafting the scent toward his nose. "You didn't use enough garlic."

She just laughed and slid an arm around Zach and Chessie, making the introductions to Mercedes, who eyed Nino like he was the enemy in her kitchen when he instantly picked up the spoon and went to work on the cacciatore.

"I am so happy to see you," Vivi said, putting her head on Zach's strong and supportive shoulder. "Did Gabe send you?"

"He's with us," he said. "Talking to Colt Lang outside."

"Lang's here?"

No surprise, her brother gave her a sharp look at the instant reaction. "I hear you two are pretty chummy."

Chummy? That word reeked of Lang. She tried for a shrug, aware of her brother's ruthless scrutiny. "Whatever that means."

"You know what it means, Viviana," he said, tightening his grip. "Is it true?"

"We're friends."

Chessie leaned into the conversation. "Is that why he's checking on the whereabouts of your old boyfriends?"

Vivi frowned. "What?"

"He called me for a 'research' favor." Chessie used air quotes around one of her favorite words. "Mr. By-the-Book FBI Agent asked me to use my hacking skills to track down none other than Dr. Kenneth Taylor, formerly of Sudbury, currently of St. Louis, Missouri."

"He did?" For a second Vivi couldn't breathe.

"Must be pretty serious if he's trying to dig up dirt on your exes, Viv," Chessie said.

"Did you find any dirt?"

Chessie lifted her eyebrows. "Dude's in prison, Vivi. Beat his freaking wife with a hammer and almost killed her."

Vivi's jaw dropped. "No way."

"I always hated that prick," Zach said.

"What did you tell Lang?" she asked Chessie.

"I e-mailed him a full report. He was most interested in when the guy comes up for parole. Does he really think some kid you dated in high school is his competition?"

"I don't know what he thinks," Vivi said honestly, a strange sense of relief and an even stranger sensation of *love* filling her. "But he's been full of surprises this week."

"Yeah, like cracking one of the FBI's biggest cases," Zach said. "He's the golden boy, now. Colt can write his ticket."

"His ticket's to L.A.," Vivi said, working to keep her voice completely casual. "So we better parlay all this success into a new contact at the Bureau if we want to keep them as a Guardian Angelinos client."

Zach pulled her closer. "You going to California, Vivi?"

"As if, Zach. What would even make you say a thing like that?"

He and Chessie shared a look, saying nothing.

"What?" Vivi asked. "What is it?"

"Just something Mr. Lang said," Chessie replied. "Something…weird."

"What did he say?"

"I said…"

Vivi jumped at the voice in her ear, the man's body behind her, the sure, solid hands around her waist.

"That Vivi Angelino and I are a helluva good team."

She dipped her head to hide the full-body shiver at the feel of him. "We're total opposites, Lang."

"Opposites attract," he said, then inhaled deeply. "Good Lord, that smells good."

"I made Uncle Nino's cacciatore," Vivi said. "Guaranteed to fix what ails you."

"Then I better bathe in it."

She turned to look at him, sucking in a soft breath at the violet contusion on one side of his face and how his jaw was red and scabbed and badly in need of a shave.

Before she could reach to comfort him, he eased her out from under her brother's arm. "Come with me."

As if she could possibly say no. With a quick look at Zach, who let her go with just a little reluctance, Vivi let Lang lead her away, around the corner to the storage closet.

"Are we going into the tunnels?" she asked as he opened the door, ready to dive back into work mode even if it was pretty much the last thing on earth she wanted to do right then.

"No." He eased her into the dark room, then closed the door behind him. "I just want to be alone with you."

Instantly he pulled her close and tight, wrapping his arms around her and putting his bruised cheek against her head.

Weak-kneed and loose-limbed, she let herself lean into the warmth of his body and the strength of his muscles, still seeing him fighting the wind on the wing, mouthing his last words—

I love you.

Finally she looked up at him. "Been a tough day," she said, trying to laugh.

"It's been a good day," he replied, humorless. "A stellar day. An unforgettable, remarkable, magnificent day."

She stroked his swollen cheekbone. "If you like to bring in killers, stop bombings, and save lives."

"Actually, I do." He kissed her forehead. "But I like when somebody kicks sense into my thick skull, too."

"Did I do that?"

He closed his eyes and pulled her back into him. "I wish," he whispered into her ear. "That I could take all the pain away, Vivi. The stuff from before, and the truckload I added to it."

"Lang—"

"Shhh." He kissed her hair, her forehead, then her mouth, gently. "I can't—"

"I know what you can't do, Lang."

"I can't change the past," he continued. "But I can do something about the future. Your future."

She just looked at him, her eyes adjusted to the dim light but not the unfamiliar sting of tears. Again. "Is that why you were checking on the whereabouts of Ken Taylor?"

"He's in prison."

"I heard."

"Where he'll stay no matter how many times he comes up for parole. A very small act on my part, but something I can do for you."

It didn't seem small to her. "Thank you. I don't know what that does for my future, but it does make me feel slightly better about the past."

"That's not what I'm doing for your future."

She just looked at him. "What do you mean?"

"Vivi, please forgive me for today."

"Forgive you? For risking your life on the airfield? You pretty much cleaned your slate for a while. We're good, Lang."

"No, Vivi, we're not."

"We're not?"

"We're great." He squeezed her closer. "We're great together. We're opposites, we're complements, we're... meant for each other."

Her mouth opened, useless again except for gaping in disbelief.

"Tears of joy and speechless with happiness. Now this is a good look for you."

She laughed, but it made a tear roll. "What are you saying, Lang?

"I'm not going to Los Angeles."

Not going to Los Angeles. God, those words sounded good. Too good. And they made no sense. "Today, you mean."

"Ever. The job is more management than law enforcement. It's all PR and paperwork. It's too much procedure and not enough... Vivi."

"You love procedure." Tendrils of joy and hope and happiness curled around her heart, but she forced them to stay loose and still.

"I love Vivi more."

She bit her lip, fighting tears again. He *loved* her. "So you're not taking the job?"

"I'm not taking the job," he confirmed, stroking her hair, trying to smooth it down. "Because there's no way you're moving to Los Angeles when this business of yours is about to explode." He eased her even closer, one hand sure and tight on her neck, the other sliding around her waist. "And there's no way I'm spending any more of my life in the dark when Vivi Angelino is around to light it up."

That did it. Her heart collapsed with love. "That's quite a risk you're willing to take, Lang."

"I live for risk." He grinned. "And I want to live for you. With you." Closer, he put his mouth against her ear. "Inside you. Every night. I love you, Viviana Poison Angelino."

She closed her eyes and leaned against his chest, listening to his heart... the heart she owned. Taking a deep breath, her whole body filled with contentment. "I love the smell of cacciatore."

"Yeah. It smells like happiness."

She beamed at him. "Yes, it does. I can cook it, you know. Uncle Nino says it'll cure a heartache."

"I don't have a heartache." He kissed her forehead and let his lips rest there like they'd found a home. "I have you."

Something scratched at the door, then barked. He pulled back and gave her a sheepish smile. "Oh... and we have a dog."

EPILOGUE

The receiving line was endless, especially in heels that pinched her feet and a strapless dress that required constant adjustment. But Vivi's smile was genuine as the guests made their way past a long row of cousins and finally reached the maid of honor and best man.

"The next motherfucker in this line better bring booze," Gabe whispered to her as some old friends moved on to kiss their congratulations to the newlyweds.

Vivi laughed and glanced over to see if Zach had heard the comment. But he was too busy beaming at Samantha, just pronounced the next Mrs. Angelino, the vows spoken, the rings exchanged.

The original Mrs. Angelino would have been pleased with her son's choice of a home for her wedding ring, a gift she'd left Zach in a letter addressed to "his intended." Had there been a similar letter for Vivi? She hadn't asked Uncle Nino, who'd given Zach's letter to Samantha. But there was the other half of her mother's ring set: the engagement ring Rossella Angelino had worn. Where was that?

"I'm the next motherfucker and you can have my wine."

Vivi turned at the low voice, letting out another laugh at the sight of their second—or was it third?—cousin, John Christiano. She gave him a warm hug, getting an arm full of muscles and a kiss on each cheek, family-style. "I haven't seen you in a long time, Johnny."

"Hey, Vivi." He backed up and gave Gabe a shameless grin. "So they finally sprung you from spookville, eh?"

Gabe shook his distant cousin's hand and exchanged manly back pats. "I'm done with government work," Gabe confirmed. "Nice to see you, JC."

"You're done? Excellent. You have to come down to New York and meet my boss. We could put you to work in a heartbeat."

Speaking of heartbeats, Vivi's doubled. "Oh, no you don't," she said quickly. "He's already gainfully employed."

"I've heard you're killin' it, Vivi. Good job." Johnny beamed with admiration.

"We're doing okay," she said.

Gabe fake-choked at Vivi's modesty. "We're kicking ass and taking names," he said, warming her heart with the corporate *we*. "The Guardian Angelinos are bicoastal, multifaceted, and run by"—he indicated Zach and Vivi—"the geniuses of the family tree."

"My boss is a genius," Johnny said.

"She wasn't smart enough to hire me," Zach interjected, leaning into the conversation. "A fact we file under unanswered prayers."

Johnny shook Zach's hand, his blinding smile even brighter. "Congratulations, *paisano*. Hope you're as happy with Sam as I am with Sage. I met her on a case, just like you, Zach."

Vivi grinned knowingly. "It happens."

"Not to me it won't," Gabe said under his breath.

Johnny just nodded, with a "Yeah, right" kind of dare in his bedroom brown eyes. "Anyway, while I have the top Guardian Angelinos together, Vivi, I actually was asked by my boss to deliver a message."

Vivi lifted a brow. What did Lucy Sharpe have to say now that she'd pronounced Zach not good enough to work for her? If she wanted him now, Vivi would howl with laughter.

"She's impressed with what you've done in such a short time," Johnny said. "She might be in the mood for an acquisition."

She snorted instead. "Fat chance."

"We have very deep pockets," Johnny assured her.

"I bet you do. You're overpriced and overrated," Vivi said, the sting of Zach's rebuff still burning. Zach had been wounded inside and out, and he'd sought a job with Lucy Sharpe's elite security firm. His injury had kept the owner from even letting him fire a gun at her precious range, the rejection giving birth to Vivi's vision for the Guardian Angelinos.

"We're not interested," Zach said simply. "But give Lucy my regards and tell her if she's ever in Boston, she should visit the family."

Johnny nodded. "I will. And, seriously, man. Congratulations. You'll love being married."

"I already do."

From behind, warm fingers tugged on the back of Vivi's dress, inching it higher.

"This thing isn't going to last the night." A kiss pressed against her bare shoulder, brushing away the hair that she'd started to grow longer. "Not that I have a problem with that."

Lang's touch still gave her chills.

"Dance with me, gorgeous."

She sighed at the endearment, and the way he'd made her believe it. "Johnny, you do any undercover work in that operation?"

"All the time. What do you need?"

"A stand-in maid of honor." She stepped back into Lang's arms. "I want to dance with my boyfriend."

Before she had to do a round of introductions, Lang led her straight to the dance floor. Instantly they melded as one, as always.

"Who was that?" Lang asked. "I sense some animosity."

"Distant cousin. No animosity, just professional jousting. He works for a competitor." She smiled up at him, any threat to her stable world forgotten. "Are you having fun at a big Italian wedding?"

"I am." He curled his fingers into hers, his arm securely around her waist to dance old-school style. "The maid of honor is very . . . cute."

"Cute, huh? Talk like that and you're sure to get lucky and go home with her tonight."

"I'm not that kind of guy," he said. "I like to follow the rules."

She rolled her eyes, and let him turn her sweetly, the heels not bothering her when she was on air.

"In fact, I was just talking to your uncle Nino about that."

"You were?" She glanced over to find Nino, who had left his spot in the rapidly disintegrating receiving line to join the men she'd just left. Marc was there, too, with Devyn, whom he'd married in a much smaller, family-only ceremony just last month when she could no longer hide her pregnancy and didn't want to. Her oldest cousin, JP, loomed behind them all.

They all turned to look at her at the very same moment after Nino said something. And they all looked...funny. Especially Zach. Hadn't he gotten used to the idea of her with Lang yet?

"What were you talking about with Nino?" she asked.

"Oh, he had something to give me. A letter. From your mother."

Her knees buckled a little. So there was a letter from her mother. Zach's fiancée had gotten one. And now—

Her heart galloping, she looked up at Lang. "What did it say?"

"Beats me—it was in Italian."

"Then why did he give it to you?"

"He likes to do things the proper way, too," Lang continued. "And, of course, so do I."

He turned her again, and now she could see some of the females of her clan clustering around the bride. Her cousins Chessie and Nicki wore the same strapless peach dress she had on, and there was Aunt Fran—all looking at her. Samantha, her closest friend and former neighbor, had tears in her eyes.

Well, it was her wedding day and she had waited an awful damn long time for Zach to get his act together.

Still, the look on Sam's face—on all of their faces—had that little thump in the back of her neck warning her of impending...something. She glanced around the room. *Everyone* was looking at them.

"Lang," she whispered, a slow heat crawling up under her silky dress. "We're out here alone."

"So we are." He didn't take his eyes off her. "Guess the dancing hasn't officially started. See what a rebel I am?"

She laughed, totally self-conscious. "Why is everyone looking at us?"

"Because I told them to."

She almost stumbled. "Why?"

"Because I wanted to be sure every single person you know and love witnesses what I'm about to do."

Her arms and legs grew numb and light as he let go of her hand and reached into his jacket pocket, pulling out a diamond ring.

She stopped dancing. Not any diamond ring. Her mother's diamond ring. She wanted to look at Nino, at Zach, at the whole damn wedding, but she couldn't take her gaze from the man she loved as he lowered himself to one knee.

Everything just blurred.

"Viviana Belladonna Angelino. I love you with all my heart and all my soul, and can only hope that you can love me the same way for the rest of our lives. Will you do me the honor of being my wife?"

She laughed a little and cried a little and shook a lot, aware that everything—laughter, voices, music, dishes, time itself—hung in suspended silence. The world held its breath for her answer.

"Do I have to golf?"

"Never."

She smiled. "Then, yes, Colton Gregory Lang, I would love to be your wife."

He slipped the ring on her finger, where it fit perfectly and reminded her so much of her mother that a tiny whimper caught in her throat. But the applause and hollers and clinking glasses drowned everything out as he rose, lifted her, and whirled her around with a kiss.

"That was so *traditional*," she whispered through her tears.

"Of course it was." He winked and wiped her cheek. "That's how I roll."

She laughed and looked over at her brother, who raised his champagne glass in a toast. On his hand, the other half of their mother's wedding ring set glinted in the candlelight.

Two halves of a set, finally where they belonged.

The killer she can't escape . . .

The heartbreak she can't forget . . .

The one man who can stop

them both . . .

———————

Please turn this page

for an excerpt from

EDGE OF SIGHT

CHAPTER 1

I understand you got into that little law school across the river."

Samantha Fairchild scooped up the cocktails from the service bar, sending a smile to the man who'd been subtly checking her out from behind rimless glasses. "Our trusty bartender's been bragging about me again."

Behind the bar, Wendy waved a martini shaker like a sparkler, her eyes twinkling. "Just a little, Sam. You're our only Harvard-bound server."

Sam nodded to the light-haired gentleman, not really wanting to start a conversation when Paupiette's dining room was wall-to-wall with a Saturday night crowd. Anyway, he wasn't her type. Too pale, too blond, too . . . safe.

"Nothing to be ashamed of, a Harvard law degree," the man said. "I've got one myself."

"Really? What did you do with it?"

The smile widened. "Print money, like you will."

Spoken like a typical Harvard law grad. "I'm not

that interested in the money. I have another plan for the future." One she doubted a guy dripping in Armani and Rolex would appreciate. Unless he was a defense attorney. She eyed him just as two hands landed on her shoulders from behind.

"I seated Joshua Sterling and company in your section." Keegan Kennedy's soft voice had a rumble of warning in it, probably because she was flirting with lawyers in the bar when her tables were full. "I'll expect a kickback."

"That sounds fair." She shrugged out of his grip, balancing the cocktail tray.

"I bet he's a generous tipper, Sam," the lawyer said as he placed two twenties on the bar and flicked his wrist for the bartender to keep the change. "You'll need it for the Con Law texts alone."

She gave him a wistful smile, not too encouraging, but not a complete shutdown, either. "Thanks..."

"Larry," he supplied. "Maybe I'll stop in before you start classes with some first-year pointers."

"Great, Larry." She forced a more encouraging smile. He looked like a nice guy. Dull as dry toast, but then he probably wouldn't kick her in the heart with an...army boot. "You do that."

She turned to peer into the main dining area, catching a glimpse of a party of six being led by the maître d's second-in-command.

Joshua Sterling's signature silver hair, prematurely gray and preternaturally attractive, glistened under the halogen droplights, hung to highlight the haute cuisine but casting a perfect halo over this particular patron.

It wasn't just his tipping that interested Sam. The last time Boston's favorite columnist had dined here, they'd gotten into a lively debate about the Innocence Mission, and he ended up writing a whole article in the *Globe* about the nonprofit. The Boston office where Sam volunteered had received a huge influx of cash because of that story.

"Good work, Keegan." Sam offered a grateful smile to the maître d', who had vacillated between pain in the ass and godsend since he'd started a few months ago. "Count on ten percent."

He laid a wine list on her cocktail tray, threatening the delicate balance of the top-heavy martini glasses. "He tips on wine, so talk him into something from the vault. Make my cut fifteen percent and I promise you we will not run out of the tartare. It's Sterling's favorite."

She grinned. "Deal, you little Irish weasel."

After delivering the cocktails to another table, she headed toward the newly seated party, nodding to a patron who signaled for a check while she paused to top off the Cakebread chardonnay for the lovers in the corner, all the while assessing just who Joshua Sterling was entertaining tonight.

Next to him was his beautiful wife, a stunning young socialite named Devyn with sharp-edged cheekbones and waves of golden hair down to trainer-toned shoulders. Two other couples completed a glossy party of six, one of the women finishing an animated story as they settled into their seats, delivering a punch line with a finger pointed at Joshua and eliciting a hoot of laughter from the rest. Except for Devyn, who leaned back expressionless while a menu was placed in front of her.

Joshua put a light hand on his wife's back, waving casually to someone across the dining room. He whispered to her; then he beamed at Sam as she approached the table.

"Hello, Samantha." Of course he remembered her. That was his gift, his charm. "All ready to tackle *Hahvahd*?" He drew out the word, giving it an exaggerated Boston accent.

"Classes start in two months," she said, handing over the wine list, open to the priciest selection. "So, I'm ready, but nervous."

"From what you told me about that volunteer work of yours, I think you've got more legal background and experience than half that first-year class. You'll kick butt over there." He added a smile to his laser-blue gaze, one that had been getting more and more television airtime as a talking head for liberal issues on the cable news shows.

No one doubted that Joshua Sterling could hit the big time down in New York.

"I hope you're right," she said, stepping aside for the junior maître d' to snap a black napkin on Devyn Sterling's dark trousers. "Otherwise I'm going to give it all up and go back into advertising."

"Don't doubt yourself," Joshua warned with a sharp look. "You've got too much upstairs to push computers and burgers. You need to save innocent victims of the screwed-up system."

She gave him a tight smile of gratitude, wishing she were that certain of her talents. Of course, doling out bullshit was another gift of his. "What's the occasion?" she asked, wanting to get the conversation off her and onto a nice big drink order.

Joshua waved toward the brunette who'd been telling the story. "We're celebrating Meredith's birthday."

"Happy birthday." Sam nodded to her. "We have two bottles of the '94 Tattinger left."

"Nice call for champagne," he said, "but I think this is a wine crowd. You like Bordeaux, right, Meredith?"

The woman leaned forward on one elbow, a slow smile forming as she looked at him. "Something complex and elegant."

Sam waited a beat, as the woman's gaze stayed fixed on her host. Devyn shifted in her seat, and Sam could practically taste the tension crackling in the air.

"Let me get the sommelier," Sam suggested quickly. "I bet he has the perfect Bordeaux."

"I know he does." Joshua handed Sam the wine list back without even looking at it. "Tell Rene we'd like two bottles of the 1982 Chateau Haut-Brion."

"Excellent selection." Was it ever. "While I get that, can we offer you sparkling water or bottled?"

They made their choices, which Sam whispered to a busboy before darting down the narrow passage from the dining area to the kitchen, her shoes bouncing on the rubber floor as she left the gentle conversation and music of the dining room for the clatter and sizzle of the kitchen.

"Where's Rene?" she asked, a smell of buttery garlic and seared meat rolling over her.

"I'm right here." The door to the cellars flipped open as the beefy sommelier hustled toward her, carrying far too many bottles. Two more servers came in right behind him with similar armloads.

"Rene, I need two bottles of '82 Haut-Brion, stat."

"After I help with the upstairs party," he shot back.

"Then give me the key and a general idea where I can find the '82s."

"You're not getting the '82s, sister." The faux French accent he used with customers was absent as he deftly set bottles on the prep deck. "One slip of the hand and you just cost us both a month's pay."

"Come on, Rene. I can get two bottles of wine, for crying out loud."

"You can wait like everyone else, Sam." He started handing bottles to one of the other servers, who gave her a smug look of victory.

The doors from the dining area swung open, and Sam squinted down the hallway, just in time to get a glimpse of Joshua strolling across the room, reaching out to greet a gorgeous former model and her date sitting at the deuce near the bar. So he wasn't in a huge rush for his wine. She glanced at the plates on the stainless steel pass, calculating exactly how much time she had to get this wine poured before her four orders for the old Brahmins on ten came up.

Not much. She wanted the Haut-Brion delivered first or she'd lose her whole rhythm.

One more of the waitstaff came up from the cellar, several bottles in hand. "This is the last of it, Rene. I just have to go back down and lock up." ·

"I'll lock it," Sam said, snatching the keys.

"No." Rene sliced her with a glare. "I'll get them, Sam. Five minutes is all."

"Come on, Rene."

The door from the dining room flung open and Keegan marched through. "Sterling wants his wine," he announced, his gaze hard on Rene.

"Then you get it," Rene said. "Not Sam."

But Sam was already on her way. "Thanks, Keegan," she said quietly as she passed. "You know I'll slather you with payola tonight." As she opened the door, she called back to Rene, "The Bordeaux are in the back nests, the Haut-Brion on the lower half, right?"

"Sam, if you fuck this up—"

"I will dust the bottles! You can watch the video tomorrow," she added with a laugh. As if that prehistoric camera was ever used.

"I will!" Rene shouted. "I just put a new tape in."

She hustled down the poorly lit stairs, brushing by one of the sous-chefs carrying a sack of flour from the dry storage pantry. Farther underground, the temperature dropped, a chill emanating from the stone walls as she reached the heavy door of the wine vault.

A breeze blew the strands of hair that had escaped her ponytail, making her pause and look down the dark hallway. Was the alley exit open again? The busboys were always out there smoking, but they sure as shit better not be taking lung therapy when Paupiette's was this packed.

Tarragon and rosemary wafted from dry storage, but the tangy scents disappeared the moment she cranked the brass handle of the wine vault, the hinges snapping and squeaking as she entered. In this dim and dusty room, it just smelled of earth and musk.

She flipped on the overhead, but the single bare bulb did little to illuminate the long, narrow vault or the racks that jutted out to form a five-foot-high maze. She navigated her way to the back, her rubber soles soundless on the stone floor. Dust tickled her sinuses and the fifty-eight-degree air finished the job. She didn't even fight the urge to sneeze, managing to pull out a tissue in time to catch the noisy release.

Behind the back row, she tucked into the corner where the most expensive wines were kept and started blowing and brushing the bottles, almost instantly finding the distinctive gold and white label of Haut-Brion.

Sliding the bottle out, she dusted it clean, and read the year 2000. In racks stocked chronologically, that made her a good eighteen years from where she wanted to be. She coughed softly, more dust catching in her throat. Crouching lower, she eased out another, 1985.

Getting closer. On her haunches, her fingers closed over a bottle just as the door opened, the sound of the brass knob echoing through the vault. She started to stand but a man's hushed voice stopped her.

"I'm in."

Freezing, she worked to place the voice, but couldn't. It was low, gruff, masculine.

"Now."

There was something urgent in the tone. Something that stilled her.

She waited for a footstep; if he was another server, he'd walk to a stack to find his bottle of wine. If it was Rene, he'd call her name, knowing she was down there, and anyone else...

No one else should be down here.

Her pulse kicked a little as she waited for the next sound, unease prickling up her spine.

Nothing moved. No one breathed.

Praying her knees wouldn't creak and give her away, she rose an inch, wanting to get high enough to see over the stack. As she did, the knob cracked again, and this time the squeak of the hinges dragged out as though the door were being opened very slowly. She rose a little higher to peek over the top rack of bottles.

A man stood flattened against the wall, his hand to his

chest, inside a jacket, his head turned to face the door. In the shadows, she could hardly make out his profile, taking in his black shirt, the way his dark hair blended into the wall behind him. Not a server. No one she'd ever seen before.

He stood perfectly still as the door opened wider, and Sam tore her gaze from the stranger to the new arrival. The overhead bulb caught a glimmer of silver hair, instantly recognizable. What the hell was Josh—

The move was so fast, Sam barely saw the man's hand flip from the jacket. She might have gasped at the sight of a freakishly long pistol, but the *whoomf* of sound covered her breath, the blast muffled like a fist into a pillow.

Joshua's face contorted, then froze in shock. He folded to the floor, disappearing from her sight.

The instinct for self-preservation pushed Sam down behind the rack, her head suddenly light, her thoughts so electrified that she couldn't pull a coherent one to the forefront. Only that image of Joshua Sterling getting a bullet in his head.

She closed her eyes but the mental snapshot didn't disappear. It seared her lids, branded her brain.

Something scraped the floor and her whole being tensed. She squeezed the bottle in her right hand, finding balance on the balls of her feet, ready to pounce on whoever came around the corner.

She could blind him with the bottle. Crash it on his head. Buy time and help.

But no one came around the rack. Instead, she heard the sound of metal on metal, a click, and a low grunt from the front of the vault. What the hell?

Still primed to fight for her life, she stood again, just

high enough to see the man up on a crate, deftly removing the video camera.

The security camera that was *aimed directly at the back stacks.*

She ducked again, but it was too late. She heard him working the screws in the wall, trying to memorize his profile. A bump in a patrician nose. A high forehead. Pockmarks in a grouping low on his cheek.

Dust danced under and up her nose, tickling, tormenting, teasing a sneeze. Oh, please, *no.*

She held her breath as the camera cracked off the wall, and the man's feet hit the floor. In one more second, the door squeaked, slammed shut, and he was gone.

Could Joshua still be alive? She had to help him. She waited exactly five strangling heartbeats before sliding around the stacks and running up the middle aisle.

Lifeless blue eyes stared back at her, his face colorless as a stream of deep red blood oozed from a single hole in his temple. The bottle slipped out of her hands, the explosion of glass barely registering as she stared at the dead man.

God, no. God, *no.* Not again.

She dropped to her hands and knees with a whimper of disbelief, fighting the urge to reach out and touch the man who just minutes ago laughed with friends, explained a joke to his wife, ordered rare, expensive Bordeaux.

This couldn't be happening. It *couldn't* be.

The blood pooled by his cheek, mixing with the wine. The smell roiled her stomach, gagging her as bile rose in her throat and broken glass sliced her knees and palms.

For the second time in her life, she'd seen one man take another's life. Only this time, her face was caught on tape.

The legacy that haunts her . . .

The mystery she must solve . . .

The man who threatens to

reveal her secrets . . .

———————

Please turn this page

for an excerpt from

SHIVER OF FEAR

CHAPTER 1

The halogen headlights sliced through the downpour like laser beams, turning the rain eerily white and illuminating each sudden turn in the nick of time. With every near miss on the twisty roads of the North Carolina woods, Devyn Sterling cursed the rental car company for not offering GPS, damned the weather for delaying her flight until this late at night, and wished to God that she had a clue which street was Oak Ridge Drive.

And threw in one more vile curse for the impulsive nature that landed her in this situation.

Arriving on the doorstep of her birth mother to shatter the woman's life should really be done under sunny skies. But Devyn couldn't wait another day. Or night. No matter the weather.

Squinting into the downpour, she tapped the brakes

at a cross street, slowing to a crawl to seize the millisecond of clarity between windshield wipes to read the street sign, aided by a sudden bolt of lightning.

Yes. Oak Ridge. Thank God.

Thunder rolled just a second or two later, but Devyn powered on, inching down the residential street, peering at the houses, set far apart on acre-sized lots, most of them dark for the night. As she reached the end of a cul-de-sac and neared the address she'd memorized, Devyn drew in a nervous breath, practicing what she would say when Dr. Sharon Greenberg opened the door.

No matter how many times she rehearsed, the words came out wrong. Especially because Devyn doubted she could get through the whole story before she got the door slammed in her face.

Still, she needed a game plan for this encounter.

Her icy New England upbringing told her to be brutally blunt. Just knock on the door, open her mouth, and say, *I'm the daughter you gave up in a secret adoption thirty years ago.*

But deep inside, because her blood wasn't truly the chilly WASP of her Hewitt upbringing but some cocktail of hot Irish, she wanted to tell Dr. Greenberg the story with all the drama that had unfolded a few months earlier on the streets of Boston so the woman could fully appreciate the reason for Devyn's visit.

I hired an investigator, found out your identity—and that of my fugitive mobster father—and told my husband, who decided to betray me, only to get murdered by his mistress and a dirty cop who tried to frame Finn Mac-Cauley for the crime. Uh, can I have some shelter from this storm?

Without knowing much about Sharon Greenberg, it was hard to be sure if that tack would work any better than cool bluntness.

She slowed at the last home, the brick ranch house bathed in the headlights of her rental car. Snapping the lights off, Devyn turned into the empty driveway and stared at the house. Maybe she should go for the heartfelt approach.

I'm sorry, Dr. Greenberg. I know you don't want to meet me, and I really planned to respect that wish, but I told my husband your name and I don't know if he told anyone else before he was murdered. Just in case he did, I thought it only proper that I be the one to screw up your life....And while I'm here, can we talk about why you gave me up?

Don't go there, Devyn. Not at first. The woman had every right to give up a child fathered by a legendary street thug like Finn MacCauley. She didn't even have to *have* a baby.

Still, Devyn thought as she looked at the darkened house, maybe...maybe they would talk about it. But first, Sharon had a right to know that her secret was no longer buried. And Devyn had a right to know who gave birth to her.

Another flash of lightning illuminated the night, followed almost immediately by a quick explosion of thunder. Chills feathered Devyn's skin despite the warm blasts from the dashboard. The storm was close.

As her eyes adjusted and the rain washed the windshield, she studied the large picture window in the front, nine panes of glass, the blinds behind them closed tight. Water sluiced out the gutters, noisily splattering mud below.

Proper New England upbringing pinched at her conscience. A lady would call before arriving.

Okay, she could do that. Devyn picked up her cell phone and pressed the speed dial she'd foolishly programmed in while delayed at Logan. Back when she was still waging an internal debate, considering abandoning the plan and driving home. But rationale won over reason, and she'd stayed at the airport, gotten on the late plane, and...here she was.

If she hit Send, maybe she'd wake Sharon, and then when Devyn knocked on the door, it wouldn't be such a shock. The older woman would have a minute or two to prepare. That seemed fair.

Devyn watched the words appear on the tiny screen: *Calling Dr. Sharon Greenberg.*

Oh, God.

The fourth ring cut off halfway and clicked into voice mail. Devyn pressed the phone to her ear, blocking out the rain beating on the car so she could listen and absorb the sound of her birth mother's voice for the first time.

"Hey, it's Shar. I'm not able to take your call, but do what needs to be done and I'll get back to you. Leave a message, try my office, text me, send a smoke signal. Peace out."

Devyn stabbed End and slipped the phone back into her purse, staring ahead at the shadows around the house, her heart matching the rhythm of the rain. Fast. Hard. Loud.

Was she going to turn back now? Away from a woman who invited callers to send a smoke signal? Obviously Sharon had a sense of humor. But did that mean she had a heart?

What she had, Devyn thought, was a right to know that somewhere, someone might know her darkest secret. That information could be damning to her career...or worse.

So, really Devyn was doing her a favor.

Holding tight to the justification that had gotten her this far, she scooped up her bag and opened the car door, soaked before she could jog up the three stone steps to the covered front porch. There, she intrepidly opened the screen door and rapped hard on the front door.

Fifteen endless seconds passed; then she knocked again. Emboldened, disappointed, and frustrated, she pounded with the side of her fist, an unwanted lump forming in her throat.

"You have to be home," she murmured, her hand sliding down to the large brass handle. A blinding burst of lightning tore a gasp from her throat, making her squeeze the latch in fear and hold tight as the thunder cracked the night air.

And the door opened.

Devyn jerked her hand away the moment she realized *she'd* unlatched the unlocked door. The next blindingly close bolt of lightning pushed her inside, survival instinct trumping everything else.

"Dr. Greenberg?" she called, still knocking on the open door. "Are you here, Dr. Greenberg?"

This was so not how she wanted this meeting to unfold.

Pitch-black inside, the cloying scent of candle wax and potpourri fought with the muskiness of a closed-up house.

"Dr. Greenberg, are you home?"

Obviously not. And Devyn, with the blood of a man who once topped the FBI's Most Wanted list cascading through her veins, took another step into a house where she hadn't been invited. Her adopted mother would keel over in disgrace. But right now, her adopted mother didn't matter. Her *real* mother did.

Two months had passed since Devyn's husband had been murdered. Two months she'd waited for the investigation to close and the police to clear her to leave the Boston area. Two months she'd struggled with a question no one had ever asked and only Joshua Sterling could answer: Had he taken the name of Devyn's birth mother to the grave? Two months was too much time not to have this conversation and deliver the potentially bad news to Dr. Greenberg.

And have the perfect excuse to meet.

All she had to say was, *Your secret is no longer safe.*

In fact, under the circumstances, a simple note could do the job. Not as satisfying as face-to-face, but maybe this was what was meant to be.

She called out again, blinking to get night vision, able to make out an entry table in the shadows where brown sticks surrounded by curled, dried leaves poked out of a vase.

Either Sharon had been gone awhile, or she really didn't care about living things.

And, really, wasn't that what Devyn had traveled to North Carolina to discover?

Somewhere to the left, an antique clock ticked. The soft hum of the refrigerator buzzed from a kitchen around the corner. Rain thumped on the shingles, but there were no other sounds.

On her right, through French doors, Devyn could see the green light of a printer and the shape of a large desk stacked with papers and files. The office was the place to write and leave a note...or find a clue as to what made Dr. Sharon Greenberg tick.

With a shiver of apprehension and a stab of guilt, she pushed open the door and walked to the desk, flipping on a tiny halogen lamp to scan the mess. There were little hills of papers, files, articles, medical journals, a leaning tower of DVDs, and a half dozen candles melted into various sizes and shapes.

For a moment, she just drank in the first impression. Mom was a slob, she thought with a slight twist of a smile. An untidy, disorganized, hardworking scientist who... had sex with mobsters?

Curiosity burned, along with something else Devyn couldn't identify. Something that felt like hunger. A burn to...bond.

Let it go, Devyn.

She lifted some papers, eyeing the magazines, the arcane terminology, seeking clues to who this woman was. The investigator she'd paid dearly for bits of information said Dr. Greenberg was divorced, childless, and working as a researcher at the University of North Carolina teaching hospital.

The tabs on a stack of file folders confirmed her life as a scientist. Retrovirology. Immunology. Serology. Pathology. Belfast.

Belfast?

The word was scratched in pencil, light enough that it looked like it had already been erased. Devyn tugged the file, something pulling at her as the manila folder slid out from under the others.

Belfast. The city conjured up twenty-year-old newscasts of bombings, violence, deaths, Irish mobs, and...

Irish mobs.

Slowly, she opened the folder, her pulse kicking up after it had finally slowed. Inside, there were several pages of notes, some drawings, an e-mail. And on a "Recycle for Life" notepad were the words *US Air Arrives 2:45 pm Belfast w/ layover Heathrow 8/29. Rtn open.*

August twenty-ninth was almost two weeks ago. She glanced at the papers in the file, obscure scientific drawings, several printouts of e-mails, a magazine article with the name *Liam Baird* underlined. She lifted it to read the story, but her gaze was pulled to a grainy photograph in the file behind the article. Taken from a distance, the image was of a girl on a bike, a backpack on her shoulders, her hair in a pony—

"Oh my God." The words stuck in her throat as she stared at the photo. She knew that bike, that street, that girl.

It was her.

Which meant Sharon knew her identity. She knew enough about Devyn to have a picture of her!

Trembling, she flipped the picture over and stared at the small handwriting.

Finn 617-555-6253

Finn? Finn MacCauley with a Boston phone number?

Lightning flashed blindingly bright with a simultaneous, deafening crack of thunder. The desk light went black, and thunder rolled with such intensity that the hardwood floor vibrated under Devyn's feet.

Had the house been hit? She stood there, the file still in one hand, as the thunder stopped, followed by the soft digital sound of her cell phone. Grabbing her phone, she read the caller ID.

Dr. Sharon Greenberg.

"Oh my God." Sharon was calling her?

She took a moment to breathe and think, too paralyzed to answer. Sharon must have just redialed, curious as to who had called her a few minutes ago.

But she has my picture in a file on her desk.

With unsteady fingers, she tapped the green button and put the phone to her ear. "Hello?"

Nothing. Silence. But someone was there; she could tell.

"Dr. Greenberg?" She pulled the phone away, checked the name again to be sure she hadn't imagined it. "Hello?"

No response. The house was silent around her, all electrical buzzing dead from the power outage. Devyn stood in the pitch blackness, holding the lifeline to her birth mother... which was just as silent. She'd lost the call.

With a soft cry of frustration, she hit Redial. From down the hall, a digital ring cut through the silence.

Sharon was in the house? The call that just came in was made... from this house?

Slowly, like someone was guiding her with puppet strings, she walked around the desk, through the darkness, her arm automatically slipping through the shoulder bag she'd set on top of one of the piles.

The phone stopped midring, and there was a soft click in her ear.

Someone had picked up the phone. Someone in this house.

"Dr. Greenberg?" she said it loudly, not to the phone but toward the hall. "Are you there?"

Silence.

Icy panic prickled over her skin, sending the hairs on the back of her neck straight up. She wasn't alone.

Fumbling through the dark, she found her way back to the entry hall. There, she stood still, listening, then turned back to call out to Sharon one last time, just as a hand clamped over her mouth and yanked her back into a solid man's chest.

"What are you doing here?" The man growled the words, adding so much pressure that her neck cracked.

White terror flashed behind her eyes, a scream trapped in her throat.

"What?" he demanded, lifting his hand enough for her to breathe and speak.

"Looking...for...Shar—"

"Why?"

"I...I wanted to..." She tried to think of a reasonable answer. "Leave her something."

"What?"

Whoever this guy was—a husband, a boyfriend, or a guard dog—he probably knew where Sharon was. She had to be calm and come up with a plausible story.

"I'm her student," she said in a controlled voice. "She needed me to give her some papers. In person."

He tightened his grip, pressing so hard across her chest she could feel her heart beat into his forearm.

"Who sent you?" he ground out.

"Nobody sent me. I'm a student—"

"A student who broke in?" He lifted his left hand, palming the side of her head while a beefy arm pinned her. Slowly, he pushed her head to the side until her neck muscles strained and tendons snapped. Pain ricocheted down her arm and terror shot up her spine.

"Who sent you?"

"I came on my own. It's personal." Miraculously, her voice didn't crack like her neck. "I have to talk to her."

He pushed her toward the door, which she just realized was open. Had she left it that way? Had he followed her in? Or had he been waiting?

She dug her feet into the mat, refusing to be pushed into the screen and out into the rain. "I have to talk to her," she said again, trying to squirm around to see his face, but he wouldn't allow it.

Had he hurt Sharon? Was her body lying bloody in the back of the house?

"When you find her, give her a message." A shove sent her flying against the screen door, popping it open. She twisted just enough to see a glimpse of his face, older than she expected, light eyes, grim mouth.

He whipped her around and braced her again. "If she comes back here without getting her job done, she's dead."

Devyn squirmed, finally getting her brain to work enough to try fruitlessly to jerk out of his grip. "What job?"

"She knows what job. She steps into this house a failure, she'll leave in a box. We're watching and we're waiting."

He shoved her outside, still holding her so tight she couldn't turn to see him. One more push and she was out from under the overhang, drenched, as the screen door was slammed shut behind her.

She spun around to get a look at him, just as an ear-splitting sound sent her jumping backward, staring in disbelief at the hole in the screen.

He'd backed into the shadows of the house and shot at her! Instantly, she pivoted toward the driveway, slipping on the concrete. Using the banister to right herself, she sailed down the stairs, taking another look over her shoulder.

Fear vibrated through her, her heart hammering as if it would explode out of her chest. The rush of blood and rain drowned out the little cries that escaped her lips as she stabbed in her bag for the car keys.

Had she left them in the house?

Panic almost knocked her over, just as the keys scraped her knuckles. She whipped them out and promptly dropped them in a puddle.

"Shit!" Falling to her knees, photos and papers she'd taken from Sharon's file fluttered to the ground. The picture? Everything was soaked before it hit the pavement.

One more shot exploded out into the night.

Abandoning the papers except what she could scoop in one shaky grab, she snatched the keys and dragged open the car door, scrambling inside and tossing the remains of the file and her purse across the console. She found the ignition, turned on the car, and jerked it into reverse. With her full weight on the accelerator, she launched backward out of the driveway.

She stole one last glance at the picture window, the reflection of her headlights illuminating the blinds. They parted briefly as her attacker watched her leave. A man who would kill Sharon Greenberg if she returned... *without getting her job done.* What kind of job was that? Research for UNC? In Belfast?

She managed a quick look at the papers she'd thrown on the passenger seat; the picture was still there.

A picture of Devyn taken seventeen years ago. *Why would Sharon have that?*

A hundred answers clobbered her brain, all dizzying in their possibilities. But only one electrified her. Her birth mother had been keeping track of her.

Her birth mother *cared.*

Was that possible?

She had to know. The burn intensified until she could taste the metallic, bitter flavor of need in her mouth. She had to know why Sharon had that picture. And she had to warn Sharon that her home was under surveillance and that she was in danger.

But how?

Trembling, she followed the darkened street back to the curvy Carolina roads. Finding Dr. Sharon Greenberg had just gone from an impulse to a mission. *Belfast.*

Fortunately, she'd brought her passport.

THE DISH

Where authors give you the inside scoop!

♥ ♥ ♥ ♥ ♥ ♥ ♥ ♥ ♥ ♥ ♥ ♥ ♥ ♥ ♥

From the desk of Margaret Mallory

Dear Reader,

I was a late bloomer.

There, I've said it. That single fact defined my adolescence.

When I entered high school at thirteen-going-on-fourteen, I looked like a sixth grader. Was it the braces? The glasses? The flat chest? The short stature? Red hair and freckles did not lend sophistication to this deadly combination. I have a vivid memory of one of my mother's friends looking at me that summer before high school and blurting out, "What a funny-looking kid."

To my *enormous* relief, I entered tenth grade with breasts, contact lenses, and no braces. Boys looked at me differently, girls quit ridiculing me, and adults ceased to speak to me as if I were eleven. And older guys—who had utterly failed to notice my "inner beauty" before—appeared out of nowhere

Although it took my self-esteem years to recover, suffering is never wasted on a writer. With THE GUARDIAN, I wanted to write a story with a heroine who goes through this awkward stage—along with several dangerous adventures—and eventually comes out the other side as a confident, mature woman who feels loved and valued for her beauty inside and out.

Of course, I had to give Sìleas, my ugly-duckling heroine, a hero to die for. Ian MacDonald is the handsome young Highlander she has adored since she could walk.

Sìleas is an awkward, funny-looking thirteen-year-old when Ian rescues her from her latest round of trouble. Ian is not exactly pleased when, as a result of his good deed, he is forced to wed her. Although Sìleas lives in the Scottish Highlands in the year 1513, I know exactly how she felt when she overheard Ian shouting at his father, "Have ye taken a good look at her, da?"

When Ian returns years later, Sìleas is so beautiful she knocks his socks off. Not surprisingly, Ian finds that he is now willing to consummate the marriage. But as Sìleas's self-confidence grows, she knows she deserves a man who loves and respects her.

Our handsome hero has his hands full trying to win his bride while also saving his clan. Eventually, Ian realizes he wants Sìleas's heart as much as he wants her in his bed. I admit that I found it most gratifying to make this handsome Highland warrior suffer until he proves himself worthy of Sìleas. But I had faith in Ian. He always did have a hero's heart.

I hope you enjoy Ian and Sìleas's love story. THE GUARDIAN is the first book in my Return of the Highlanders series about four warriors who return home from fighting in France to find their clan in danger. Each brave warrior must do his part to save the clan in the troubled times ahead—and to win the Highland lass who captures his heart.

Happy Reading!

Margaret Mallory

www.margaretmallory.com

♥ ♥ ♥ ♥ ♥ ♥ ♥ ♥ ♥ ♥ ♥ ♥ ♥ ♥ ♥ ♥

From the desk of Roxanne St. Claire

Dear Reader,

Character notes? Character notes! Where did I put my character notes for Vivi Angelino? Oh, that's right. I never had any. She wrote herself.

I have never subscribed to the theory that "a character tells their own story," despite the number of times I've heard writers discuss that phenomenon. Sure, certain characters are vivid in the writer's head and have personality traits that, for whatever reason, make them standouts on the page. They're fun people to write, but letting them take over the book? Come on! Who is the boss here? Whose fingertips are on the keyboard? Whose imagination is at work? A good author should be able to control their character.

And then along came Viviana Angelino. From the first book in the Guardian Angelinos series, Vivi was not only vivid and three-dimensional to me, she seemed to liven up every scene. (Make that "take over" every scene.) When I could finally give her free rein as the heroine of FACE OF DANGER, I did what any writer would do. I buckled up and hung on for the ride. There were daily surprises with Vivi, including her backstory, which she revealed to me as slowly and carefully as she does to the reader, and the hero.

The interesting thing about Vivi is that she is one of those people—or appears to be on the surface—who knows exactly who she is and doesn't give a flying saucer what other people think. I think we all kind of envy that bone-deep confidence. I know I do! She scoots around Boston on a skateboard (and, yes, this is possible, because this is precisely how my stepson transports himself from home to work in downtown Boston), wears her hair short and spiky, and has a tiny diamond in her nose...not because she's making a statement, but because she likes it. She's a woman, but she's not particularly feminine and she has little regard for fashion, makeup, and the "girlier" things in life. I wanted to know why.

About five years ago, long before I "met" Vivi, I read an article about a woman who looked so much like Demi Moore that she worked as a "celebrity lookalike" at trade shows and special events. Of course, the suspense writer in me instantly asked the "what if" question that is at the heart of every book. What if that look-alike was truly mistaken for the actress by someone with nefarious intentions? What if the look-alike was brave enough to take the job to *intentionally* attract and trap that threatening person?

I held on to that thread of a story, waiting for the right character. I wanted a heroine who is so comfortable in her own skin that assuming someone else's identity would be a little excruciating. Kind of like kicking off sneakers and sliding into stilettos—fun until you try to walk, and near impossible when you have to run for your life. When Vivi Angelino showed up on the scene, I knew I had my girl.

No surprise, Vivi told this story her way. Of course, she chafed at the hair extensions and false eyelashes, but that was only on the surface. Wearing another woman's identity forced this character to understand HERSELF better and to do that, she had to face her past. More importantly, to find the love she so richly deserves, she had to shed the skin she clung to so steadfastly, and discover why she was uncomfortable with the feminine things in life. When she did, well, like everything about Vivi, she surprised me.

She pulled it off though, and now she's FBI Agent Colton Lang's problem. I hope he can control her better than I could.

Enjoy!

Roxanne St. Claire

www.roxannestclaire.com

♥ ♥ ♥ ♥ ♥ ♥ ♥ ♥ ♥ ♥ ♥ ♥ ♥ ♥

From the desk of Isobel Carr

Dear Reader,

Do you ever wonder what happens to all the mistresses who are given up by noble heroes so they can have their monogamous happily-ever-after with their virginal brides? Or how all those "spares" get on after they've been made redundant when their elder brother produces an heir? I most certainly do!

In fact, I've always been intrigued by people who take charge, go out on a limb, and make lemonade when the universe keeps handing them lemons. So it comes as little surprise that my series—The League of Second Sons—is about younger sons of the nobility, the untraditional women they fall in love with, and what it takes for two people who aren't going to inherit everything to make a life for themselves.

The League of Second Sons is a secret club for younger sons who've banded together to help one another seize whatever life offers them and make the most of it. These are the men who actually run England. They're elected to the House of Commons, they run their family estates, they're the traditional family sacrifice to the military (the Duke of Wellington and Lord Nelson were both younger sons). They work—in a gentlemanly manner—for what they've got and what they want. They're hungry, in a way that an eldest son, destined for fortune and title, never can be.

Leonidas Vaughn, the hero of the first book, RIPE FOR PLEASURE, is just such a younger son. His father may be a duke, but he's not going to inherit much beyond the small estate his grandfather bequeathed him.

My heroine, Viola Whedon, took a chance on young love that worked out very badly indeed. Since then, she's been level-headed and practical. A rough life in the workhouse or a posh life as a mistress was an easy decision, and keeping her heart out of it was never a problem...until now. Brash seduction at the hands of a handsome man who promises to put her desires first sweeps her off her feet and off her guard.

I hope you'll enjoy letting Leo show you what it means to be RIPE FOR PLEASURE.

Isobel Carr

www.isobelcarr.com

♥ ♥ ♥ ♥ ♥ ♥ ♥ ♥ ♥ ♥ ♥ ♥ ♥ ♥ ♥ ♥ ♥

From the desk of Katie Lane

Dear Reader,

When I was little I used to love watching *The Andy Griffith Show* reruns. I loved everything about Mayberry—from Floyd's barbershop where all the town gossip took place to the tree-lined lake where Andy took his son fishing. I would daydream for hours about living in Mayberry, eating Aunt Bee's home cooking, tagging after Barney to listen to his latest harebrained scheme, or just hanging out with Opie. And even though my life remained in a larger city, these daydreams stuck with me over the years. So much so that I ended up snagging a redheaded, freckled-faced Opie of my own...with one tiny difference.

My Opie came from Texas.

Welcome to Bramble! Mayberry on Texas peyote.

You won't find Andy, Barney, or Aunt Bee in town. But you will find a sheriff who enjoys grand theft auto, a matchmaking mayor, a hairdresser whose "ex's" fill half of Texas, and a bunch of meddling townsfolk. And let's not forget the pretty impostor, the smoking hot cowboy, the feisty actress, and the very naughty bad boy.

So I hope you'll stop by because the folks of Bramble, Texas are just itchin' to show y'all a knee-slappin' good time. GOING COWBOY CRAZY, my first romance set in Bramble, is out now.

Much Love and Laughter,

Katie Lane

www.katielanebooks.com